Contents

THE LAST ALEURIAN

CITY OF MERCHANTS

DREW R. STOWELL

EMPEROR BOOKS

City of Merchants

Copyright © 2025 by Drew Stowell

All rights reserved.

Published by Emperor Books

Bellerose Village, NY

ISBN

Digital 978-1-63777-723-7

Print 978-1-63777-724-4

This book is dedicated to my grandfather. You've always been there for me and are a constant inspiration. Thank you so much for everything you've done.
I love you, Papa.

"Greed is the driving factor behind Human ambition. It is only a matter of time before they realize such actions will be their downfall."

- Æferth Solaris, Fourteenth King of Aleuria

See detailed map

VALTION SILMA CITY STATE ALLIANCE

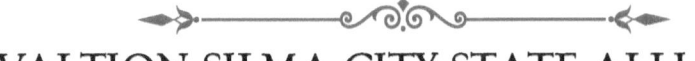

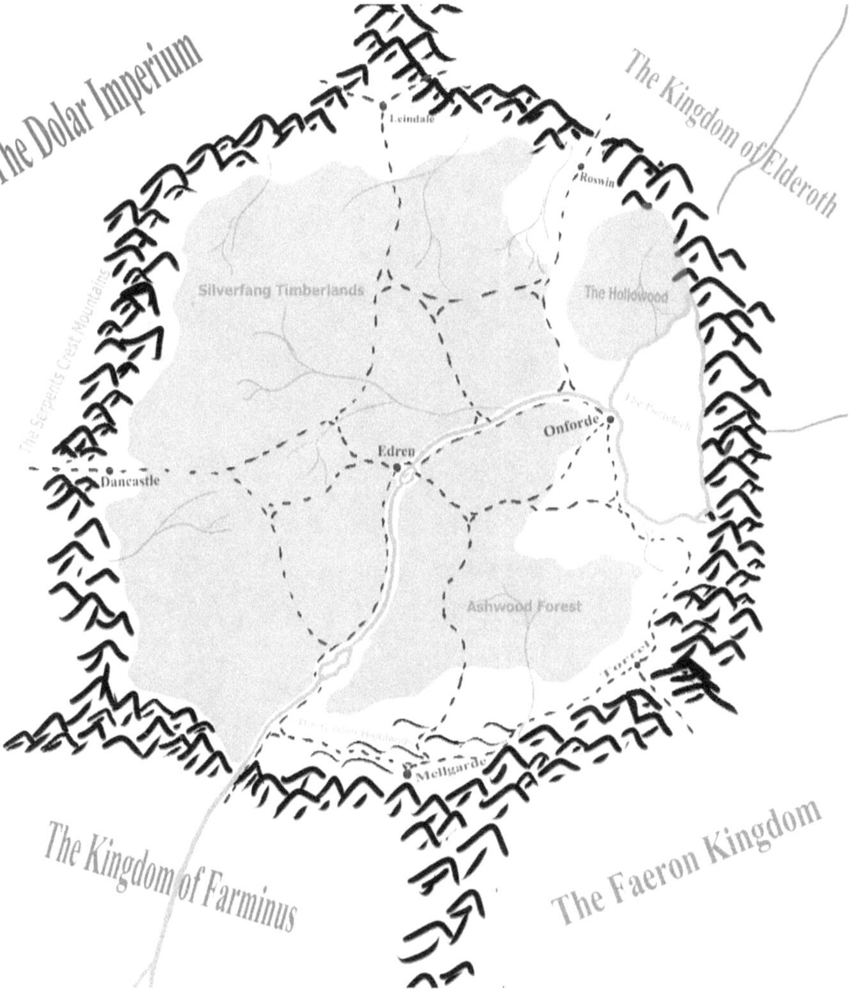

The Dolar Imperium
The Kingdom of Elderoth
Leindale
Roswin
The Serpents Crest Mountains
Silverfang Timberlands
The Hollowood
Onforde
Edren
Dancastle
Ashwood Forest
Torrel
Mellgarde
The Kingdom of Farminus
The Faeron Kingdom

PROLOGUE

In the northern part of Edren was a rundown building, an old warehouse, not far from the Tungsten River that flowed through the center of the city. The warehouse was used to store goods before they were sent down the river, so the building came with a large yard next to it.

Anyone walking past the old warehouse would be able to hear the sound of hammers from within. Burly men were seen carrying all kinds of construction supplies in and out of the freshly crafted doors.

For those who lived in the area, this was an unusual sight. The decently sized warehouse had been abandoned for many years, yet now it was full of life. Even stranger, the yard contained large stacks of logs, much more than were needed to repair the old structure.

"Mr. Elric!" One of the men yelled toward the top of the building, "we're all done with the sign."

A head popped over the edge of the roof. The man had short, dirty blonde hair and sapphire-blue eyes. Unlike the other men who had quite a large mass of muscle, Elric had a much more toned physique. He wore a short-sleeved blue shirt that revealed two steel bands wrapped around his toned biceps.

"Awesome," Elric shouted back with an accent not found in this part of the world, "I'll be right down."

Elric turned back to the two others on the roof, each one hard at work replacing the roof like Elric had been just a moment ago.

"Can you guys finish up here?" he asked.

The two men looked up and one of them responded, "No problem, boss. Compared to felling trees, this is easy as pie."

The other man nodded in agreement.

Elric smiled, "Sweet, thanks."

He climbed down the ladder set up for roof access and made his way to the front of the building.

There were two men with a bucket of paint to the side and a large sign propped against one of the walls.

"It looks great, guys," Elric said as he saw it.

"No need to flatter us, Mr. Elric," the man who had called up earlier responded.

"I'm not lying, Carl. I like it," Elric responded reassuringly.

Carl didn't seem to know how to respond and just stood there awkwardly.

Anyway, Elric continued, let's get it up there, yeah?

The other two nodded and grabbed the rope hanging from the roof. Two of these ropes had been attached to the sign and fed through pulleys on the roof.

Elric gripped the other rope and said, "Ready?"

With a nod, they began to pull on the rope.

To anyone watching, the scene would have been amusing. Two large men were pulling a rope from one end while a skinny man pulled on the other. The funny part, however, was that the smaller man seemed to have to slow down for the other two as the three of them hoisted the sign into the air.

As soon as the sign was in position, two men who were on standby rushed forward with ladders. They quickly climbed up to where Elric and the others were holding the sign in place and began to nail it into place.

After a few minutes, the lines went slack, and the sign was firmly in place.

Elric took a few steps back and smiled with pride, "It does look good, doesn't it?"

The sign's carved border depicted a serpent eating its own tail with a large black area in the middle. There, in big white letters, were the words, "The Ouroboros Initiative."

Carl nodded, "Now that it's up there, I see what you were saying."

Just then, the sound of laughter and the pattering of tiny feet could be heard as a small group of children came running around the corner of the building, and one of them ran head-first into Elric.

The collective group of children gasped as the one who had run into Elric looked like he was about to cry.

"Are you okay?" Elric asked as he knelt in front of the child.

The kid looked scared of Elric and simply nodded.

Then, another figure came around the corner.

"Oh, dear," they said, "I've told you, children, many times to watch where you're going."

The figure was a tall woman with long blonde hair. She seemed to be in her mid to late twenties, but most people wouldn't even try to guess her age once they saw the pointed ears.

"It's all right, Erdwyn. I'm not mad," Elric told her.

She shook her head, "You should be, Mr. Elric. The kids could run into something and get seriously hurt!"

"It's okay, Mommy." A kid came from behind her. "We're young, so we heal fast!"

He flexed one of his arms as he said it with a wide, toothy grin.

Erdwyn sighed, "I can't believe you're the one lecturing me, Aeif."

Despite how she sounded, she also had a smile on her face. These two were Erdwyn and Aeif Lux. The first time Elric saw Erdwyn, she had been a complete mess. Aeif had been kidnapped, and she had fallen into deep despair.

Though the first time Elric saw Aeif, he had been attached to a bunch of strange machines and was about to be killed by a mad scientist, so he wasn't sure who had it worse.

After that whole thing, Elric decided not to visit them. It wasn't because he didn't care what happened to Aeif; he just didn't know how to handle a mother's gratitude.

However, Erdwyn had other plans. She had tracked Elric down and thanked him profusely. Elric didn't know what to do and just stood there awkwardly until she said she would do anything to repay him.

He had The Ouroboros Initiative in the works for a while and decided to offer her a job. Now, she helped him run the Initiative and looked after the place when he wasn't there. She also brought Aeif with her to work every day.

They had already started helping people, and the kids were their children. Erdwyn looked after them while their parents went to find work, and today they had gone on a little excursion to the river.

"So," Elric stood back up, "what do you think of the sign?"

Erdwyn looked up at it and said, "It's beautiful."

Elric looked at Carl, "There you go."

Just as Carl opened his mouth to say something, another voice cut in.

"Excuse me!"

Elric turned to the voice and spotted a woman in uniform. She wore well-made leather boots and a steel chest plate. On her back was a large pack that seemed to be filled with supplies, and a kettle helm graced her head.

"Good day. Is there something we can help you with?" Elric asked with a hint of confusion. It was not often that a runner for the city guard would stop to chat with someone.

"Yes. I have something to deliver." Her eyes scanned him, "You wouldn't happen to be Elric, would you?"

"That would be me."

The runner nodded, "Yep, you match the description."

She pulled the pack off her back and retrieved a small letter from within, holding it out to Elric. "The Esteemed Lord Samuel Aulcrest of Edren wishes to express his gratitude and wishes for you to join him for dinner."

Somewhere in the Central Sea ~

The sound of crashing waves were accompanied by the rhythmic rocking of a lone ship out at sea. It was a ship unlike any other. Its hull had no visible difference from the pieces of lumber used to make it. The sails were made from a fibrous plant, not unlike the leaves of a giant tree.

Leaning against the railing on the deck of this curious ship was a woman so beautiful that even the stars dimmed in her presence. Her shimmering golden hair fell to her hips, and elongated ears poked out from the sides of her head.

She wore comfortable travel attire, high boots, and loose-fitting clothes, all dyed in shades of green and various earth tones. Across her back was an intricately carved longbow, a quiver at her waist, and a pair of slightly curved short swords that were sheathed at the small of her back.

She let out a deep sigh as her cerulean eyes stared out across the rolling sea.

"Princess, I know you do not wish to do this, but this is a directive from the king, and it would be prudent to at least *act* as though you are honored."

The person who spoke was an older woman with mostly gray hair and pointed ears, much like the princess's. She wore the elegant attire of a lady-in-waiting.

"I apologize for giving you the wrong impression," the princess turned and smiled at her lady-in-waiting, "I am filled with joy to once again venture out into the world."

Her expression turned to one of sadness.

It has been many, many years since I left the palace, and while I am grateful to have the opportunity to finally leave that cursed place, the princess continued, I know the world will not be as I remember it.

The princess looked out upon the waves once again, "My father used to be a kind man, a great ruler, and an even greater father. I sometimes wish we could return to those days."

"The world has changed much, Your Highness," the lady-in-waiting replied gently, "and your father, the king of our people, changed to meet it."

The princess knew what she was referring to. The Aleurian civil war had drastically changed world politics, adding immense stress to her father. Trying to fill in the gaps left by the Aleurians, dealing with upstart factions trying to fill the void, and negotiating with Guldar was hard work. However, the final nail in the coffin was The Midnight Massacre. The loss of so many of their people changed the king for good.

"I wonder what they would make of this..." the princess mumbled as she continued to stare out to sea, the salty air reminiscent of a time long past.

CHAPTER 1

The Request

The sun had nearly set for the day, yet the streets of the Inner District were still bustling with life. People went around lighting the lamps that lined the streets, and some shops were just opening.

Before arriving, I had gotten my clothes cleaned and my boots polished. I also wasn't carrying any weapons or wearing my armor. As such, people paid me no mind as I journeyed toward my destination.

However, something was on my mind as I walked. Ever since I received the letter from the lord of the city, I had been filled with a sense of dread and anxiety.

The contents of the letter weren't the source of these feelings, it was the fact that I didn't know why I was being summoned. The runner had said that the lord wanted to express his gratitude, but I had already been paid by the Association. As far as I knew, it was unusual for the lord of a city to personally thank every mercenary who helped solve a crisis, but perhaps things had changed in the millennia I'd been gone.

Though I did think of one thing it could have been. Recruitment.

It had been several days since I told Reginald and Myrril my true identity. My name is Elric Wolfram Tors, and I'm an Aleurian, a race of people that went extinct over a millennium ago.

Reginald's face was priceless when he finally realized I was telling the truth, while Myrril was stuck deep in thought. After that, they said that they needed to process everything I told them and left me at the park.

I haven't spoken to them since then, but I had the feeling that they would eventually make peace with the reality. That's why the last reason was so hard to even consider: that maybe Reginald had told his father.

It made sense, being the son of the lord, but I didn't get the feeling that Reginald would do such a thing. Outwardly, he seemed like the kind to rush into situations head-on, but he was actually a very level-headed individual. It was one of the reasons I trusted him enough to reveal myself.

Before I knew it, I had arrived in front of the gatehouse leading to the castle in the center of the Inner District, the generational home of the Lords of Edren. Funnily enough, it's also built atop the same hill as the Tomb of the Fallen.

The gate itself was nearly fifteen feet tall and consisted of a metal portcullis and a large set of wooden doors reinforced with bands of steel. Two tall towers flanked it on either side and were topped with conical steeples. Atop the towers were flags flying the ruling family's crest: a wolf carrying a broken blade in its mouth.

Above the wooden gate itself was a large painted carving of the Aulcrest coat of arms. A green shield surrounded by a ring of stone, a sun slowly cresting over a lone mountain stood within. Flanking the shield were a pair of wolves, one with a broken blade in its mouth, the other with a hammer.

At the base of the gate were six guards, each one more heavily armored than the ones that patrolled the city. They were each armed with halberds and short swords to accompany their full plate armor and bascinets.

One of the guards called out to me as I approached.

"Halt. State your name and business."

This guard wore the same as the others except for the red half-cape thrown over his shoulder, held with a silver clasp.

I responded in a confident tone despite my nervousness, "I am Elric Tors. I have an invitation from the esteemed lord of this city."

The decorated guard approached, "May I see this invitation?"

"Of course," I said as I produced the letter and handed it over.

The guard read over the letter for a moment before handing it back.

"We were informed of your arrival. Lord Aulcrest is waiting for you in the castle."

"Thank you," I replied and promptly tucked the letter into my pocket.

The man turned to one of his subordinates and made a gesture with his hand. The guard he gestured to saluted before pulling out a key and unlocking the small wicket gate off to the side of the main gate.

"One of the castle staff will lead the way," the decorated guard informed me.

"Got it," I nodded.

I walked forward, past the odd stares I felt coming from some of the guards, and made my way into the inner bailey.

Waiting for me on the other side of the gate was a well-dressed butler with graying hair.

"Welcome, the lord is waiting in the dining hall," he said with a bow before waving his arm down the road.

Beautiful gardens flanked either side of the road as it led to the entrance of the modest castle.

I was led through the front doors and through the entrance hall. We walked down a corridor lit with brass sconces and decorated with a red carpet and intermittent paintings or small tables. When we reached a set of double doors, the butler stopped and knocked.

"My lord, Elric Tors has arrived."

From within the room came a voice filled with dignity, "Enter."

The butler opened the door and stepped back. I could feel a bead of sweat roll down my forehead as I took a deep breath and entered the chamber.

In the center of the room was a large, finely carved table. Above it hung a well-made chandelier that came down from between the ceiling trusses. The rest of the room was decorated similarly to what I had seen on my brief trip through the castle.

There were four other people in the room.

Seated at the head of the table was a man who seemed to be in his late thirties with well-kept brown hair that had started to prematurely gray. He wore fine, but not overly garish, clothing and very little jewelry. His emerald eyes were trained on me as I entered the chamber, his hand resting on his short beard for a moment.

On his right was a beautiful woman with a kind face and emerald eyes. Her dark hair was intertwined with blue ribbons in a simple coiffure, and her light blue dress was at the peak of beauty while at the same time lacking a flashy design. She wore a simple, but beautiful necklace, but otherwise was sparsely bejewelled.

On his left was a man in his late teens wearing functionally nice clothing. He had short brown hair and green eyes. His toned body was normally hidden by armor, but tonight it was peeking through his clothing. His name was Reginald Aulcrest, someone I was well acquainted with.

The final person in the room was seated next to the woman I assumed was Lady Aulcrest, a timid-looking young woman with raven-black hair that stopped at her shoulders and teal robes. Her light blue eyes were locked on me, begging to be saved. This was Myrril Delahaye, another acquaintance of mine.

The man at the head of the table stood from his chair and spoke, "Welcome to my home, Elric."

I gave a deep bow, "I am honored to have been invited, my lord."

He waved his hand, "There is no need to bow on this occasion. Please take a seat."

I nodded and took a seat next to Reginald.

The man cleared his throat, "I believe introductions are in order. I am Lord Samuel J. Aulcrest of the city-state Edren. This is my wonderful wife, Elene Aulcrest."

He gestured to the woman seated next to him before continuing, "And of course, you already know my son Reginald and his friend Myrril."

After nodding towards them, Lord Aulcrest started again, "Now that we are all here and introductions have been completed, how about we eat?"

He clapped his hands and a door on the far end of the room opened, releasing a wonderful smell wafting in from the kitchen.

Servants carrying trays and platters appeared from beyond the door and began to place our meals in front of us. The first course was the appetizer, a dish of fresh fruit and cheese paired with red wine.

"Please allow me to extend my gratitude for saving my city," Lord Aulcrest said as we began to eat.

"There is no need for that, my lord," I said, "I simply have a grudge against the necromancer."

He smiled, "It's all the same. You saved this city, and for that, I am truly grateful."

I took a deep breath, but I couldn't let myself relax. So far, everything had been as it seemed, but I still had an uneasy feeling about the situation.

"Elric," Lady Aulcrest began, "I've heard about your service from my husband, but I'm interested to hear you tell it."

The look in her eyes was one of intrigue and hunger for a story. I felt it would be rude to deny her request, so I started from the beginning.

"Of course," my lady. "I suppose it started when I happened to stumble upon a crime scene..."

I explained what had happened in fair detail, though I left out everything that would have spoiled the dinner.

I went over how I had solved the crime for the investigators, Frank Duncan and Khris Lockemor, and was eventually found by them again and asked to help with a kidnapping.

During all of this, I could feel Reginald awkwardly glancing at me from time to time. His conflicted feelings about me were obvious.

By the time I started to explain how we followed the kidnappers into the sewers, the second course had arrived. It was a creamy soup made from some kind of root vegetable, and it was some of the best food I had eaten since arriving in Edren.

"Oh my! There were beasts in the sewers?" Lady Aulcrest exclaimed.

Reginald nodded and opened his mouth for the first time that night, "Yes, they were... unpleasant to say the least."

Lord Aulcrest seemed perturbed by my story, "I was briefed about your excursion into the sewers, but they failed to mention how easy it was to enter the unfinished section."

"Um... is that a problem?" I asked curiously. As far as I knew, the grate I had opened to enter the unfinished sewers had been similar to the other grates I had seen around the city.

"They were supposed to be secured, right dear?" Lady Aulcrest looked to her husband for confirmation.

He nodded, "Indeed. The project was started by my father, but the funding for it dried up by the time I took over. I had ordered every entrance into the unfinished section to be sealed to prevent them from being used by criminals. They were also a hazard for the children who liked to play in the streets."

"Father, do you believe it was..." Reginald started saying before remembering they were in mixed company.

"Hm," Lord Aulcrest seemed to think for a moment. "He would be the most likely suspect... Anyway, that's not something to speak about in front of guests. Please, continue."

I nodded and continued with the story. I went through the whole sewer ordeal and spoke about the mad scientist who had tried to kill Aeif Lux, causing Lady Aulcrest to gasp in horror.

As we came up on the meeting at the Association, the third course had arrived. It was comprised of a juicy venison steak and garlic potatoes. Once again, I found my taste buds overloaded with flavor.

We took a break from talking during this course and just enjoyed the food. Afterward, we had a salad course where I continued the story.

"Elric, that meeting was hectic. You should probably just summarize what Sean McCloud said," Reginald told me as I started talking about the meeting.

"You're right," I agreed.

After summarizing the contents of the meeting, I talked about our time with Lost Light and the finding of the Tomb of the Fallen.

"I still find it hard to believe the tomb was found so easily after all this time," Lord Aulcrest said.

I shrugged, "The entrance was already uncovered when we arrived, so we can't take credit for that."

We went over the tomb and what happened inside as we enjoyed fruit parfait. After dessert, we moved to a sitting room where I finished speaking about the battle in the tomb and my encounter with the Lich. Obviously, I didn't tell them about the fact that the lich was my uncle.

Amazing, Lady Aulcrest said, "I never imagined it would be such a thrilling story."

Lord Aulcrest nodded, "Indeed. It's much different from reading the reports."

"Yes, well. I couldn't have done it without the help of Myrril and your son," I said, nodding toward my two compatriots.

Reginald nodded back but Myrril was stiff as a tree in her chair.

"I see now why Louis has taken a liking to you," Lord Aulcrest mused.

"I'm glad you agree with me," a voice said out of nowhere.

My head snapped in the direction the voice came from, where I saw the door to the sitting room open.

The man who entered the room carried his lithe figure in a dignified way, similar to a foreign ambassador. He wore fine clothing, almost finer than the lord's, and his shoes were polished like mirrors. His blonde hair had a slight green tinge to it and fell just to his shoulders in an almost wave-like fashion that covered most of his slightly pointed ears.

As I saw him, a chill went up my spine. I didn't have a clue who he was, but my instincts were trying to tell me something.

Myrril's face went white as a sheet, and Reginald jumped from his seat, "Director!?"

"Ah, Louis. Perfect timing, as always," Lord Aulcrest said to the man.

The man bowed to the lord and lady, "Of course. I wouldn't want to waste your time."

Then, he turned toward me. It was then that I focused my

vision and was able to see a soft green aura emanating from him, similar to a half-elf.

An aura is a magical discharge caused by an overwhelming amount of Megin contained within someone's body. All living creatures have an aura, but only the elder races can see them, and the intensity of the aura is caused by the magical presence of the creature.

He squinted his eyes for a moment before speaking, "Greetings, Elric Tors. I am Director Louis Renard of the Association branch in Edren."

Tch, I knew it.

I had been ignoring letters from the Association ever since the incident at the Tomb of the Fallen. They wanted me to meet with the director for some reason or another, but I hadn't changed my mind about the Association, so I just tossed them.

The director ignored my glare and sat on the soft couch across from me. The sly look in his eyes was that of a child who had just gotten away with doing something he shouldn't have.

"So this whole thing was a ruse to get me to meet with the director, wasn't it?" I asked with a bit of vitriol.

"You put that together quite quickly," Lord Aulcrest smiled, "but you aren't entirely correct."

"Father!" Reginald shouted in mild distress.

Lord Aulcrest waved him off, "Calm down, Reginald. I wouldn't have had to resort to such efforts if young Elric here had just met with Louis on his own."

"Indeed," Director Renard added, "I've sent countless letters to Elric, but I received no response."

"You could have just gone to him," Reginald argued. "There was no reason to use your friendship with my father for such petty reasons."

Lady Aulcrest spoke up, "Reginald, you do not know what this is about. It would be best to sit back down and listen."

Her tone was motherly, but with quite a bit of force behind it.

"Mother..." Reginald whined.

"It's okay," I said. "We're already here so there's no point in making a fuss about it."

I dropped my casual and subservient tone and went full nobility. I couldn't quite match the force being projected by Lord Aulcrest and Director Renard, but I wasn't going to be a pushover either.

"Thank you for understanding," Director Renard nodded at me.

I narrowed my eyes and continued, "However, I am curious as to why you've gone through such trouble to meet with me. I am not a member of the Association, therefore, I am not subservient to your will."

I attempted to use my annoyance as a point in the tone I used, similar to how I had seen my father speak many times. The sound of an annoyed noble is enough to shake a man, or at least to make them think twice about what they are about to say.

Director Renard seemed to recoil a little bit as I spoke, a single bead of sweat rolled down the side of his face.

"Hah!" Lord Aulcrest clapped and the tension in the room lessened, "I like this kid. He's so much more than I had expected."

"Yes, but that just makes him all the more desirable," Director Renard replied.

My body tensed a little at the director's comment, but I managed to keep my cool. If I messed up here, it could have catastrophic consequences for not only me but the other two as well.

"No need to look so tense, Elric," Lord Aulcrest said. "We aren't here to recruit you into my service or whatever it is you think is going to happen."

Ding. Ding. That's exactly what I was thinking. It wasn't too odd to have a noble recruit strong mercenaries into their service, but it was something I didn't want to happen. If you have been recruited by a noble, you either have to accept or make an enemy out of them. Nobles tend to hate being refused and are known to make your life hell if you do.

"Then what is it that you've gone through all of this trouble for?" I asked, still keeping my guard up.

"It's quite simple. There is something that we need you to do," Director Renard said with regained composure.

Lord Aulcrest continued from there, "You see, we've been trying to track down where Lost Light came from. After inter-rogating those three followers of Kane Ovid that you captured, we were able to piece together some of their movements."

"So you want me to retrace their steps?" I asked curiously.

"That's part of it. The other part is to discover what damage they did on their way here and attempt to mitigate it if possible," Lord Aulcrest responded.

"Have you heard of the attempt on the life of the Merchant Elect of Onforde?" Director Renard asked.

I shook my head, "I have not. However, I assume that you believe Lost Light was involved?"

"We do. I'll give you and your companions a letter to give to the Merchant Elect that will explain the situation," Lord Aulcrest answered.

Reginald looked confused for a moment and looked like he wanted to say something, but I beat him to it.

"I assume by companions you mean Reginald and Myrril, yes?"

Lord Aulcrest nodded, "I do."

"I see. Then I have another question," I started, "Why us?"

"Well, you three have proven yourselves quite capable. We believe you can get the job done," Director Renard answered.

I felt like he was fibbing, so I kept pushing.

"That's not why," I shook my head. "If you just wanted capable people, you would have chosen someone like Friedrich."

"Look, I–" Director Renard started but was cut off by Lord Aulcrest.

"To tell you the truth, you three had the most contact with Lost Light, so it's only logical that you be the ones to follow their trail."

It made a lot of sense, but it still left me uneasy. However, I decided to accept this answer for now and continue with the conversation.

"That's fair," I said before giving it a moment of thought. This was a request from the lord of Edren so I had little ability to refuse at the moment. Also, it gave me a good excuse to leave the city for a while and see more of the world. If I ended up tracking down whoever was associated with Lost Light and the necromancer, then that's an even bigger win to me.

I nodded, "All right, I accept."

"That's marvelous!" Director Renard said with excitement, but I wasn't finished yet.

"On one condition," I continued, "I get to pick my own reward."

"What!?" Several people shouted as Lord Aulcrest sat silently thinking about what I said.

"Of all the foolish things to say!" Director Renard said in a huff.

"Elric, you can't just do that," Reginald scolded.

Myrril seemed to have yelled as well but then she went back to trying to hide in her seat.

Lady Aulcrest also seemed surprised, but the smile she tried to hide said more than words.

"Silence!" Lord Aulcrest's voice carried a weight that made everyone stop talking the moment the words left his mouth.

"I had planned to give you a reward for saving the city.... However, I believe I can grant your request should you fold that reward into this one," he said.

"My lord, you can't just–" Director Renard started.

"I have made my decision, Louis," Lord Aulcrest interrupted. "It would do you good to hold your tongue."

Director Renard seemed taken back by the sudden intensity directed toward him, but he obeyed Lord Aulcrest.

I smiled and held out my hand, "I accept your terms."

Lord Aulcrest grasped my hand in his own and shook it, "Then it's a deal."

After discussing the required materials for the mission, I quietly made my way toward the exit of the castle. As I was walking down a dimly lit hallway, I passed by a tall figure cloaked in black; a mask of pure obsidian covering its face.

I had to do a double-take to ensure my eyes weren't deceiving me, but it was nowhere in sight. The light of the twin moons illuminated the hallway, but the figure had simply disappeared, almost like it was never there in the first place.

I sensed no magical presence from the figure as it passed me, but I could just feel that it wasn't a trick of the light. The lack of Megin was always seen as impossible, so the idea that a being possessed none sent a chill up my spine. I had no idea who, or what, it was, but I knew for certain that it wasn't human.

CHAPTER 2

Setting Off

I lazily opened my eyes as rays of sunshine flowed through the window in my small room at The Hungry Boar. The sound of birds happily chirping sounded from outside as I moved to sit on the edge of the bed. I just couldn't stop thinking about the night before.

After I left the castle gate and entered the Inner District, I saw Myrril happily chatting away with Reginald. He had said that he would walk her home because of how pale she was, and I was glad to see her feeling better.

Yet, even that feeling was overwhelmed by the panic attack I had tried to hide from them. It wasn't from the meeting with Lord Aulcrest and Director Renard, though it brought with it plenty of anxiety... It was actually because of that person in the hall.

The way that they moved without making a sound, the lack of a magical presence, and the way they disappeared without a trace set off something instinctual within me. My body was telling me that it was simply wrong.

As I got to my feet and began to stretch, I could feel a bit of tension in my chest. It seems that some of my anxiety had stayed with me, and I knew why. Tomorrow was the day we would leave for Onforde.

I was both excited and scared about what this journey would entail, but it was a feeling common with travel. I knew it was nothing more than that, so I continued with my morning ritual before getting dressed and heading downstairs.

"Good morning, Elric," the owner of the inn, Fredrick, greeted me as I made it to the ground floor.

"Morning, Fredrick," I said back. "I actually needed to talk to you."

"Of course," he replied.

"I'm actually going to be leaving town for a while, and I'm not sure when I'll be back," I said.

Fredrick nodded, "I see. Well, you'll always be welcome here. When do you leave?"

"Tomorrow morning."

He smiled, "Well then, I wish you luck on your journey."

Thanks, Fredrick, I returned the smile.

After that, I headed into the tavern on the ground floor and ate a hearty breakfast before setting off for the day.

I couldn't help but think about the strange way that Edren is laid out as I made my way through the bustling streets. On a map, it seems to be a walled city next to three separate towns that decided to combine into one, leaving large areas of empty land in between. The residences of Edren refer to each "town" as a district based on its cardinal direction.

There are the Northern and Southern Districts, which sit on the western side of the Tungsten River, and the Eastern District on the opposite bank. For reference, the Inner District is closer to the Northern District than the Southern District, and the grand market is situated in a field between all three.

The currency exchange I went to a few weeks earlier was in the Northern District along with many warehouses and larger businesses that use the river for transportation. The Southern District had more residential and smaller businesses that had permanent buildings instead of the Bazaar-like construct of the market. As for the Eastern District, well, I hadn't actually visited it but I heard it housed a lot of farmers and fishermen as well as Edren's textile industry.

Oh, I almost forgot. There is a smaller cluster of buildings just outside the Inner District that doesn't have its own name, but that's where the Lux family lives.

Anyway, I walked down the packed dirt roads that ran through the three outer districts and approached the massive cluster of tents and stalls. The market sold just about anything you could think of, including some stalls from local businesses. It was the perfect place for me to gear up for the journey ahead.

As always, the market was packed. People went about their business almost shoulder to shoulder, and the noise level was unreal. People peddling their wares and the sound of haggling or small talk overwhelmed my ears every time I went there.

How can Humans tolerate such noise? I thought to myself before remembering our physical differences. Human and Aleurian hearing is very different, and I have to constantly remind myself of that, among other things.

I perused the stalls as I went, grabbing a few things I thought I would need. Then, I saw something that caught my eye.

"No way..." I muttered to myself as I moved to get a closer look.

One of the various stalls in the market had an array of different items on a table. A pudgy man behind the stall was calling out to everyone who would listen.

"Artifacts, get your genuine Aleurian Artifacts here!" he hawked.

As I approached the table, he called out to me, "You, sir! You are interested in these artifacts, yes?"

"I may be," I said as I looked at his wares.

It was a hodgepodge of different items. There was silverware, chunks of stone with bits of carvings on them, a few amulets in decent shape, and they were all fakes. Well, almost all of them.

"What's this one?" I pointed at an item near the back of the table.

"Hm? Oh, this one?" he picked it up. "This is a dagger found near some ruins on Alurlind, an Island once known as Aleuria! However, I'm not too sure if this is actually an Aleurian artifact or if it was made by someone else. It's just in such good condition, but..."

"But what?" I asked.

"Well, it doesn't have an edge," he said after a bit of hesitation.

"Can't you just sharpen it?"

He shook his head, his chins rustling around, "I've tried to have it sharpened, but nobody seems to be able to do it."

"May I have a look?"

"By all means," he handed me the dagger, still in a leather sheath.

I pulled the blade out, and my mind began to run on over-time. The blade was a dull grey with no edge, just as the merchant had said. Imprinted near the base of the blade was the image of a sun rising over a mountain.

The handle of the dagger was made of some type of antler and used its natural shape instead of being cut and molded. The pommel was emblazoned with the symbol of a wolf carrying a hammer in its mouth.

"I see," I returned the dagger to its sheath. "How much do you want for it?"

"Are you sure? It wouldn't be very useful in combat and with its origin in question..." the merchant started to say.

"I'm sure," I affirmed.

The merchant, after making sure I understood what I was buying, asked for twenty gold Sovereign, which I happily paid.

With the dagger strapped to my belt and the rest of my shopping complete, I headed into the Northern District.

The bustling atmosphere of the Northern District was the same as always. Carts rolled up and down the street carrying goods to and from the various warehouses along the district. People were hauling goods into some shops, and others were just going on a stroll.

Every time I wandered the city, I saw the joy on people's faces. While there were people less fortunate than others, Edren was a fairly happy city. It really put into perspective how well-managed it was.

The building I was looking for soon came into view. It was a two-story wooden structure with yellow walls and large white letters on the front that read The Hidden Grove Logging Company.

I walked through the doors without hesitation and entered the reception area.

The room was brightly lit by sunlight filtering through the windows at the front and a bronze chandelier that hung from the ceiling. The furniture that decorated the space had some wear, but they were all well-maintained. On the far end of the room was a large counter that served as the reception desk, which was currently unmanned.

I walked past the desk and pushed open the door behind it. I went up the staircase nearby and knocked on the large wooden door at the end of the hall.

"Come in," a voice replied from the inside.

Opening the door revealed a spacious office with bookcases lining one wall and filing cabinets lining the other. In the center of the room, sitting behind a large desk piled with documents, was the person I was looking for. He was an older gentleman with a kind-looking face and small spectacles that sat on the bridge of his nose.

"Ah, Elric," he said with a wide smile, "how has your

project been going? What did you call it, The Ouroboros Initiative?"

Mattias and I acted like we had known each other for years ever since I bought half of the company from him. When I first arrived here, the logging company was about to close down for good, but my money and... other skills managed to bring it back from the brink.

I returned the smile as I took a seat across from him, "It's going well. The new building should be done before winter sets in."

Mattias nodded, "Good, good. That old warehouse won't hold heat very well."

"Yeah," I agreed. "How has work been going?"

"Pretty good, actually. The first camp has been set up, and the others will come soon after," he replied.

"Hm. How about sales?"

Mattias shifted in his seat, "Not as much as we'd hoped. There isn't much demand for lumber in this area."

He must have seen my face because he quickly added, "I'm not saying there's none, but Edren isn't undergoing much expansion at the moment. Most of our orders are from areas downriver."

He turned a ledger around for me to see, and indeed, our sales weren't as high as we wanted, though one particular settlement is paying for regular deliveries in quite large quantities.

When I asked why they were ordering so much, Mattias explained.

"Riverbrook is a village that's seen a lot of rapid expansion over the years, and it's continuing to grow. I think the mayor finally realized that the town couldn't get much larger without attracting attention from bandits and Beasts."

"So they've started work on a defensive wall?" I asked.

He nodded, "They started work as soon as the ice thawed,

but they were met with constant delivery problems and increasing costs."

Ah, so that's why they are buying from us.

While Riverbrook was still within the area owned by Edren, it was closer to Onforde. I had wondered why they didn't just source the lumber from there, but Mattias' explanation filled in the blanks for me.

"I know the situation doesn't look good at the moment, but rest assured that we have everything in hand." He gave me another smile, "I've sent Amy to the Kingdom of Farminus to try and broker a trade deal."

The Kingdom of Farminus was an agricultural country to the southwest that comprised mostly plains and rolling hills. What little forests that did exist were protected by the country for being crucial sources of food and herbs. Farminus has been dealing with a lumber shortage among a constantly growing population, making it the perfect opportunity for us. Even when factoring in the transport costs, we still stand to make quite a sum of money.

"So that's why the front desk was empty," I mused.

"Yes," Mattias said, "we are currently in the process of getting a temp to fill the position, but it will still be a few more days. But enough about that, he continued. You came here for another reason, yes?"

"Oh!" I had almost forgotten. "Right, I needed to tell you I would be leaving for a while."

I explained the situation to Mattias, and he nodded in understanding.

"I wish you luck in your mission, Elric, and hopefully we'll have some more good news by the time you return

After saying our goodbyes, I headed toward a building not far from the logging company's offices. It was an old warehouse I had purchased and was now using to help people of elven descent find new lives in Edren. Of course, we helped anyone who needed it, but it was mostly intended for elves.

I only stopped by for a moment to inform Erdwyn Lux that I was leaving for a while, to which she chirped, "Don't worry, I'll have everything covered here while you're gone!"

I left her some money for expenses and said goodbye to the children before heading to the Inner District for my most crucial stop of the day.

As I approached the squat building, I could already hear a muffled clanging coming from the back.

Small clackers went off as I opened the door to the shop. Excellent-looking weapons and armor were displayed around the room, while less expensive options were stored in barrels off to the side. However, I wasn't here to browse, so I made my way to the counter in the back just as a figure appeared from around the corner.

He was a six-foot-tall man in his forties with arms like trees and a large bushy beard. A set of goggles sat upon his bald head as he looked at me with a smile, "Yo, Elric, what can I do ye for?"

"Hey, Fergus. I came to get my sword repaired. It's not too bad, but the blade received a slight warp," I said while placing my sheathed sword on the counter.

He picked up the sword, "All right, let me 'ave a look. Yer right, it's not bad," he said. "It probably wouldn't affect much, but it's better to get her fixed up before it becomes worse."

He plopped down next to an anvil behind the counter and started working on the blade. "I heard ye were involved in that commotion the other week."

"Yeah, it was... not the best," I replied.

"Aye, it sounded like quite a problem," Fergus started. "By the way, the edge on this blade is pretty short. What's up with that?"

"Oh, that's because that sword wasn't meant to be used long-term. It was more of a training blade, you could say," I happily answered. There was no reason to keep that part from him.

My sword was actually part of a set of three weapons I received from my father as a gift. The set consists of a longsword, rapier, and spear. None of them were made for the sort of situations I put them through, but I haven't even considered replacing them. Though that's mostly due to the fact that they're still in great condition.

"Hey, Fergus, how did you find out that I was involved in the Tomb?" I was curious as to why I was being talked about.

"Hm?" He looked up at me, "Everyone's talking about it. You didn't exactly enter the Tomb quietly, now did you?"

I cursed my former self for making such a grand statement to calm the crowd.

Fergus got up from his stool and inspected my sword once more, "There we go. That's much better." He returned it to its scabbard and placed it back on the counter.

"Thanks, Fergus," I grabbed my weapon and dropped a few coins on the counter.

"Not a problem, Elric. But before ye leave, I've got something for ya." He went through the door in the back and came back a moment later with a large sack. He set it on the counter with a loud thud.

"Wait," I said cautiously, "you finished the armor?"

Fergus smiled, "That I did."

I was astonished. The armor I ordered had been completed a week earlier than we had originally agreed on. I had come to terms with the fact that I wouldn't have new armor for the journey, so this was a joyous moment.

I opened the bag and pulled out a piece of armor. The silvery metal was connected with a layer of Direwolf hide underneath, giving it higher durability and much greater shock absorption.

"I can't believe my eyes! I said with astonishment. It's perfect."

Fergus smiled, "Glad ye like it. That special request of yers wasn't the easiest, but I managed to get somethin' good out of it."

He was referring to my request to use bloodstone, crystals of condensed Megin, as a binding agent for the metal. And indeed, I could feel a slight magical current running through the metal. Though it was a lot less than I had wanted, it was really good for someone who's never forged with magic before.

I couldn't help but smile, "Thank you so much, Fergus!"

"Happy I could be of assistance," he responded.

I pulled his payment out of my bag and added a few extra coins before dropping it on the counter and gathering my armor.

"I'm heading out of town for a while, so this is a bigger help than you realize," I said. "And I'll make sure to take good care of it."

"Is that right?" he asked. "Well then, I'll be here whenever ye return. Knowing yer track record, I'll have my work cut out for me," he said with a chuckle.

I smiled back, "Fingers crossed that I won't need new armor again."

We both let out a good laugh at that before saying our goodbyes. I hoisted the sack on my back and left Fergus's shop.

Just past noon, I made my way outside the city gates and into the Silverfang Timberland. My objective was simple: to break in my new armor.

You see, when you get a new set of armor, it's not very comfortable or easy to move in. The leather is stiff and not very malleable. You can vividly feel the straps and buckles, and sometimes you get pinched, perils of a new armor.

The more you use it, the more it conforms to your body, and the more your body gets used to it. Even if you get a set of armor that's exactly like your old one, it won't feel the same. I suppose it's similar to shoes in that aspect.

For example, the first time I wore my previous armor was in the Sewers. I had neglected to break it in, and as such, my body didn't move as I wanted it to. I had no desire to make that mistake again. Just thinking about it made my ribs ache.

So, I found a good spot not far from the city walls to don my armor. Once I had it on, I began to stretch and feel my range of motion.

"Not bad," I mused absentmindedly.

I could tell it was well-made and formed specifically for my body. This made it a little bit easier to use, but it still wasn't ready for combat.

To start with, I began by going through some simple exercises with my sword. I brought my blade forward and swept it up in an arc before turning the blade and quickly slashing diagonally down, then diagonally up, then straight down, and finishing with a stab.

It wasn't anything too special, but I could already feel some resistance to my movements. I went with simple motions for about thirty minutes before the summer heat really started to hit me.

Around this time of year, Humans tended to wear lighter clothing to combat the heat. Aleurians had different temperature tolerances than Humans, so it wasn't normally a problem for me, even with my longcoat.

However, add exercise and fur-lined metal armor to that, and even I couldn't help but feel uncomfortable.

I wasn't going to let it get in the way of my training, though. So, I took a swig from my water skin and ate a few of those berries that I had stashed away and continued.

The next morning, I got off my bed and blinked the sleep out of my eyes. The morning sun barely peeked through the window, telling me that it was still early. I yawned and began to stretch my body. The soreness from the training I did the day before had made my joints and muscles stiff.

Once my body felt a little lighter, I got dressed and began packing my things right away. I would be leaving for an unknown amount of time, and it was better to bring everything with me, as little as I had.

Downstairs, the wonderful fragrance of food wafted from the kitchen. I made my way into the tavern area and took a seat at the counter.

About fifteen minutes later, the barkeep appeared to take my order. Today's breakfast was fluffy eggs, fried jerky, and rich sausage. Since we would be traveling, I just had some water to drink.

I tipped the barkeep and shouldered my travel bag before making my way to the entrance. I didn't see Fredrick on my way, but I had said my goodbyes the day before, so I didn't feel too bad about it.

As I stepped outside, the chilly morning air felt nice on my face. I took a deep breath and headed for the eastern gate. This required me to cross a nearly eight-hundred-foot-long bridge that crossed the Tungsten River and into the Eastern District.

It was my first time there, but I didn't have the time to look around. I continued through the city until I arrived at my destination.

In front of the gates, just off to the side of the road, was a small cart being pulled by two horses. Another horse was hitched next to the cart, and two people sat in the back.

I instantly recognized them.

"Morning," I called out to Reginald and Myrril.

"Oh, hey," Reginald called back.

"Are you guys ready to go?" I asked as I approached the cart.

"Mhm," Myrril said with a small nod.

They were both wearing their normal gear. Reginald had his set of polished half plate, his Association Medal affixed to the left side of his chest plate, and at his waist was the short sword he had taken from Connor. His round shield seemed to be affixed to the pack on the third horse.

Myrril was much simpler. She wore a darker set of robes today over her usual trousers and shirt. Her Association Medal hung from a chain around her neck like a medallion, and in her hand was a staff affixed with a red Bloodstone at the top.

Reginald nodded as well, "We're good to go." He hopped off the cart. "The plan is to have you and Myrril on the cart, yeah?"

"That's right. I have some experience driving a cart, so we should be good," I said.

"Good," Reginald scratched the back of his head. "Neither of us has ever driven a cart before, so getting it here was a little rough."

I winced, "Sorry about that. If I had known, I would have met you guys at the castle."

Myrril shook her head, "I-it's okay. It was fun."

A smile grew across my face as I got into the driver's seat. "I'm glad to hear that."

Reginald climbed into the saddle of the lone horse and looked at us, "All right. You set the pace, Elric."

I nodded and gently urged the horses forward. The horses began to move, trotting down the road, until eventually pulling us through the open gates embedded in the wooden ramparts. Reginald followed us close behind until we made it outside the city, where he pulled up next to us.

As we slowly crossed the open ground, keeping to the road, I looked back at the city. I had grown attached to it in the last month, so leaving it was a little hard. However, I knew I would be back. If not for me, then for the promise I made to my uncle.

I turned back to focus on the road ahead. Wherever our journey may take us, I had the feeling I was intrinsically connected to Edren and its people.

CHAPTER 3

On the Road

The road split into two directions, but we had already decided on the route we would use. I directed the horses down the road to our left, one that followed the Tungsten River. It was the longer route to Onforde, but we are certain it was the route taken by Lost Light.

It didn't take long before the view of Edren behind us was obscured by trees. This was the Ashwood forest. It was a bit safer than the Silverfang Timberland due to the lack of dire-wolves, but I had heard rumors of other dangerous creatures lurking within.

About an hour into our trek, Reginald broke the silence.

"Okay. If we are going to be working together for the next two weeks, I feel like we need to address the elephant in the room," he said, a little exasperated.

"Hm? What's that?" I asked curiously.

"You!" He nearly shouted, "How the hell can you be an Aleurian!?"

Ah, that's what he's referring to...

I thought he had come to terms with that fact, but bringing it up explained how he had been acting around me.

"I-I want to know, t-too..." Myrril piped up.

I sighed, "Where do I even begin?"

"At the beginning, preferably," Reginald responded to my rhetorical question.

"Hm. Well, when a mommy Aleurian and a daddy Aleurian love each other very much..." I started with a playful grin.

"Wha–" Myrril gasped in surprise.

"Whoa, not that far back!" Reginald cried out, though I could see him trying to suppress a smile.

"Alright, alright..." I couldn't help but laugh a bit, but soon regained my focus. "Well, I suppose it started with the rumors of a civil war. I had just finished basic training a few months earlier and was stationed in my home city of Tors, on my father's request..."

I began to recall the events leading up to my death before reaching that subject. The rebels had made it into the heart of Aleuria and besieged Tors. We were outnumbered and outmatched, but we held on for as long as we could.

When they finally broke through the gates, we fought like beasts on the ground. It was my first time killing someone, but it was me or them. However, we were eventually overrun.

"Then, I woke up in Kyrtvale. I fought for my survival for two years before I made it out. It's funny, really, the beast at the exit was a pushover compared to the normal creatures I had to fight."

As I finished up my story, both Reginald and Myrril were looking dumbfounded.

"Excuse me, what? Kyrtvale? As in the underworld?" Reginald asked, completely shocked.

"Yeah," I responded, "I was pretty freaked out myself when I realized it."

"Do you even understand how insane that story is!?" Reginald shouted.

Myrril nodded, "I-it does sound pretty far-fetched, but... um..."

"Yeah, I feel the same," Reginald said with a sigh, "there's no way I would believe him if we hadn't already spent time together."

I couldn't help but chuckle.

"What are you laughing at?" Reginald asked.

"Oh, it's nothing. I was just thinking about how well you two understand each other." For a moment after I spoke, both of them were eerily quiet. I couldn't see them because my eyes were on the road, so I could only use my imagination.

"Ahem," Reginald cleared his throat, "so uh, what's the plan?"

I decided to hide my smile and humor the change in subject. "Well, there are three settlements down this road. Once we check up on all of them, we'll head for Onforde. In total, it should take around four days to get there."

"Um..." Myrril started, "I-I thought Onforde was only two days away..."

I nodded, "It is if we took the direct route. One of our objectives was to check the route Lost Light took, so we have to go the long way."

"Hm, but still, shouldn't it be only three days?" Reginald asked.

"No," I shook my head, "If we factor in the number of times we have to stop and the speed of the carriage, we're looking at four."

"Speaking of," Reginald started, "why *did* you get a carriage? We could have made do with two horses, and the journey would have been faster."

He was right. Using just horses would have cut down on the amount of time we needed to be on the road, but I had a few reasons for taking a cart. For one, it would make carrying items such as tents and cookware much simpler. It could also be used to haul feed for the horses, which was important in an area as heavily wooded as we were.

However, the main reason I got a cart was to blend in. If we looked like an armed escort for cargo, then it would be easy for people to miss us. Though that line of logic is assuming that we are being looked for, which I couldn't discount as a possibility.

"Ah, that makes sense," Reginald said after I finished my explanation.

Myrril looked up at me, "Y-you said that was the main reason. T-there were more?"

I was hoping she wasn't going to ask, as the other reason was kind of embarrassing, but I told them anyway.

"The second reason I got a cart was due to me, or more specifically, my weight. You see, the average weight of an Aleurian is higher than a Human, probably due to the denser muscle and bone structure. This, coupled with a lack of general variety of horses in Edren, meant that we were only able to get horses meant for general labor, such as pulling carts.

It was unfortunate, but Edren simply didn't have any horse breeds that I could ride in good conscience. It would have been extremely uncomfortable for the horse and could even harm it. So, I decided to just take the cart."

When I relayed this to my companions, I got a dual response of "Oh..." followed by some more awkward silence.

The first few hours of our journey were uneventful. We chatted a little bit more about various things to pass the time.

As we went down the road, we passed by a few lone travelers as well as a merchant caravan heading the way we came. We spoke with the head of the caravan for a moment about what to expect ahead before going on our way.

The nice merchant told us about rumors of a beast roaming the forest that seemed to attack at random. Apparently, it was surrounded by some sort of blue light, and you always knew it was near because the air smelled strange.

They didn't run into it, but they thought it best to give a heads-up anyway. That, along with the normal warning about bandits, was the entirety of our conversation.

"I don't think we have to worry too much about bandits, these roads are well-patrolled," Reginald said once we continued on our way.

I shrugged, "It's better to be safe than to be sorry."

After a moment of my companions trying to explain that my expression had been shortened to "Better safe than sorry," we went back to being vigilant in our watch of the surroundings.

Not long after midday, we arrived at a fork in the road. There was a small sign just off to the side that had a cluster of houses carved into it. I suppose since most people out there were unable to read, they used an image to convey directions.

We turned and headed down the side road.

A little way into the forest, it opened up into a wide clearing. A few dozen houses were clustered in the center of the clearing, with small fields on the outskirts. A few seemed to be dedicated to crops, but most of them held medicinal herbs.

A few people watched us as we passed, but their faces were filled with more curiosity than anything else.

We arrived at the town square within a few minutes. The center had a small podium where the head of the village would make announcements and where they collected taxes. There was even a pillory lying off to the side.

I spotted someone heading toward us, so I brought the carriage to a halt.

"Howdy, strangers!" the man said as he approached. "Fine weather we're having."

The man looked to be about middle age with hardened features and kind eyes. He wore light, earth-tone clothes, high boots, and a wide-brimmed hat made of some kind of leather.

"It is," I nodded in response. "It's the perfect weather for travel."

The man gave us a once-over, sending Myrril hiding behind my back.

"Say, are y'all the adventuring type?" the man asked.

I smiled, "Something like that."

"We're actually under the employ of Lord Aulcrest," Reginald added.

The man's eyes widened slightly, "Well, I'll be a ham on a Tuesday night! What brings you fine fellas to our neck of the woods?"

Reginald looked at me, his face asking what we should say.

"We're checking up on the settlements," I said. "Lord Aulcrest wants to make sure there aren't any unaddressed problems in the realm."

The man gave a soft smile, "Oh, that lord of ours. He's always so concerned with us common folk."

"Has anything strange happened around here recently? Anything befalling the village?" I asked the man.

He put a hand to his chin in thought, "Not much's happened around these parts lately. Though the elder might know more."

The man pointed to a large building on the edge of the square. "That's his house, right over yonder."

"Thank you for the help," I said to the man.

He tipped his hat at us, "My pleasure."

I nudged the horses forward and took the cart around the square, stopping just off the village elder's house. It looked just like all the other houses, a sturdy timber building with a wooden tiled roof, except it was much larger.

We disembarked from our rides and approached the front door. A few moments after we'd knocked, the door opened with a creak.

"Oh, hello, youngsters. How may I help you?" an old man asked from the doorway.

He seemed to be human in his sixties with gray hair and a slight hunch. In one hand was a cane carved from dark wood.

I took the lead, "Good afternoon, Elder. My name is Elric, this is Reginald and Myrril. We were sent by Lord Aulcrest of Edren to assess the needs of the villages along this road."

The elder smiled, "It's always so nice when he sends people to check up on us. Please, come in."

As the elder spoke, I realized something instantly. He had the same accent as Reginald and Myrril, not that of the man we had just met. I found this to be a little strange, but I tucked it in the back of my mind for later.

Directly through the door was a large hall with a table in the center. He motioned for us to sit. "Would any of you like some tea?" he asked.

"Yes, please," I responded.

The elder pulled a kettle out of the fireplace and poured its contents into four clay cups. He placed them on the table, and I got a whiff of an earthy, herbal smell.

"Please, help yourselves," the elder smiled.

I gave thanks and gave my cup a sip. It was quite bitter and had a strange aftertaste reminiscent of plant life. I didn't care for it, but my companions seemed to enjoy it.

The elder took a sip of his own tea before speaking, "So, is there anything specific you three wish to know?"

Reginald and I took the lead with the questions, asking various things about the state of the village and any strange happenings around it. The elder answered us to the best of his ability.

According to him, the village had everything it needed. The harvest was good, the roads were well-patrolled, and the beasts of the forest didn't roam too close.

When we asked him about Lost Light, he answered, "Hm, I

don't recall anyone like that in the village. Did they do something?"

It took us a moment to explain the situation, and the elder was aghast by the end of it.

"I cannot believe such people came so close to our humble village. If they had wanted to, they could have killed us all!"

It took a moment to calm him down before continuing with our questions.

He said that there was a rumor of a beast, or more likely an Abnormal, roaming the forest farther to the east. Though none of the villagers had seen it, they were still cautious of the forest for now.

We thanked the elder and made our way back to the main road.

"Well, that was some interesting information," Reginald mused as the horses clomped down the road out of the village.

Myrril nodded, "I-I want to know what that Abnormal i-is that they were talking about."

"By the way, I've heard a few folks talking about Abnormals. What are they?" I asked curiously.

They both gave me a look of disbelief before changing to an "Ohhh, right" face.

"Right, I forgot you aren't from here," Reginald started. "Abnormals are like Beasts, but far worse. They like to hunt for fun and leave their prey without eating it."

"T-they are unnatural creatures," Myrril added. "T-they are not from this world."

I nodded at their explanations, "I see. I think I understand now."

"Did your people have a different name for them?" Reginald asked.

"Yeah," I responded. "We called them Ondvaettr. In the common tongue, it would mean Evil Spirit."

"Huh. That's interesting," said Reginald.

Myrril nodded with a smile, "I-I want to hear all about your people."

I returned the smile, "I'd be happy to tell you all about them."

I regaled Myrril with tales from my people as we traversed the road, and before we knew it, the sun had begun to set. The road itself had started moving farther from the bank of the river, probably as a precaution against flooding, but it made a perfect area to set up camp. The trees were thinner than in the forest proper, but they still helped provide adequate cover from the elements.

"Hey, Myrril," I approached her after we had unhooked the horses from the cart, "if you want to know more about my people, you should read this."

I held out a large tome with a well-maintained leather cover.

"W-what's this?" Myrril asked, a little taken aback.

"It's called *The Rise and Fall of the Aleurian Empire*. I picked it up back in Edren, and I've already finished it. It's pretty accurate, considering the amount of time that passed before it was written."

"O-oh..." Myrril timidly reached for the book, "I-I would be happy to read it."

After that, we worked together to clear some of the brush so we could set up camp, all the while being cautious of the dry season and placing the fire pit accordingly.

"Hey, Elric, I was thinking of doing a little training after we're all set up," Reginald began to speak as we worked together to assemble the three tents we had brought.

"Funny, I was thinking the same thing," I replied. "Mind if I join you?"

He smiled, "Not at all. In fact, it's better to train with someone."

With that, we hoisted the last tent and stood back to take a look at our work.

I turned to Reginald, "I've still got to bring the water up, how about we meet at the cart?"

"Sounds good. I'm going to make sure the horses are taken care of."

With that, I made my way to the lazily moving river. As I began to fill up buckets, I noted that there was a small area of clear land on the banks that would be perfect for our needs.

I lugged the water buckets back to camp and set them down next to the empty fire pit. As I began to head toward the cart, I noticed Myrril was sitting on the ground, totally engrossed in the tome I had given her.

It made me somewhat happy, yet I was unable to give a genuine smile. For some reason, my emotions were still acting strangely.

I pushed the thoughts from my mind and met up with Reginald.

When I arrived, he was leaning up against the cart.

"Ready?" he asked.

"Yeah, one sec." I reached into the back of the cart and retrieved the broadsword I kept inside. "I found a good spot by the river."

"Lead the way."

It took but a moment to arrive at the banks of the river. There, I moved a little bit away from Reginald and tossed the sheathed broadsword at him.

His arm moved fast to snatch the sword from the air.

"What's this?" he asked.

"I picked it up from that Draugr that nearly got me," I explained as he drew the blade. Its strange diamond-shaped guard moved into the hilt and blade, giving the impression of a four-pointed star. The light of the setting sun reflected off the murky white gem resting in the center of the guard.

"Whoa," he muttered.

"This is a type of weapon known as a Blade of the Wind, though it's more commonly known by its nickname, Air Cutter." I continued, "Though I must confess this one is more stylized than any I've laid eyes on."

Reginald looked at the sword, then at me, before opening his mouth. "Why are you giving this to me?"

I shrugged, "You needed a replacement, and I just happened to have a spare broadsword lying around, your specialty."

He shook his head, "I... I can't accept this. This has to be a priceless relic!"

"A blacksmith once told me, 'A weapon's only desire is to fulfill its purpose for being created.' So please take it. It brings great dishonor to the weapon and its creator if it should be left to rot."

The man I had quoted was an old friend of my father and practically an uncle to me. In my time, he was known as the great blacksmith Durin Voefor. He taught me many things, and I took each lesson to heart.

Reginald looked somewhat conflicted for a moment before nodding, "All right. I shall take this blade and put it to good use."

"Good," I said, feeling swelling joy in my chest before it quieted down, "Now, before I teach you about why they call it Air Cutter, you should get used to the new weight."

Reginald nodded and took his stance.

I pulled my weapon from its scabbard and held it forward, closing my eyes. I searched deep inside of me for the energy that courses through my body like a second set of veins. As soon as I felt the flow of energy, I grasped onto it tightly.

At that moment, my eyes flew open, and I kicked off the river stone.

Ting!

My blade rested not but an inch from Reginald's neck as he stared at me in disbelief.

"That... that would have killed me," he stated, his eyes wide open.

"True," I responded, "but your reaction speed is impressive."

I motioned my eyes down at Reginald's weapon, held aloft with both of his hands firmly in the grip. At the moment that I sped toward him, he was able to move his blade to block, but had been about half a second too slow.

"Besides, I wasn't trying to kill you. My intention the whole time was to stop before I hit."

I pulled away from Reginald, and he gave a long breath of relief.

"So," I said, "I think I should start at half that speed this time."

Reginald shook his head and looked me in the eye, "No. This is good. If I take it easy, I'll never learn."

The unease in his eyes was overshadowed by determination.

This man is a true warrior, huh?

I took stock of my time with these two. Though it had not been the longest we'd known each other, I still felt a little attached. They felt.... nostalgic. Like they carried with them the spirit of my people.

I felt a small smile spread across my lips, "I like your gumption. Very well, prepare yourself."

Our training session went on until the sky was nearly completely dark, and the stars started to shine through. When we returned to camp, I removed the cooking utensils and ingredients from my pocket dimension and started to make a high-energy soup.

"Sorry, Myrril, we trained for a little bit too long," I apologized as I cooked.

She shook her head, "I-it's okay. I've had time to read."

I looked over at her, "That's good to hear. How far did you get?"

"Hm," she took a moment to think," i-it's talking about King Sigurd Solaris the Third at the moment."

"Wow. You got a good way in!" I was genuinely surprised at how fast she read. "Do you find it interesting?"

Myrril nodded, "I d-do... But it's a lot of information..." she mumbled a bit at the end, but I understood.

The book I gave her encompassed a detailed history of the Aleurian Empire fairly accurately. Where she was currently was one of my favorite stories.

It is said that Sigurd the Third was a generous and benevolent king who worried about the prosperity of his people. A plague had just swept through the land not but a few years earlier, and everyone was still wary because of it.

To help the people recover, and to prevent future outbreaks, the king sunk a countless amount of money into public works. He commissioned the construction of new roads, canals, and aqueducts. He had the entire kingdom rebuild its aged sewer system and implemented laws against throwing refuse on the road. He employed those from the slums into sustainable jobs in waste cleanup. He even constructed public bathhouses for the people to use, meaning the drinking water was cleaner and the people were healthier.

However, the biggest thing he is known for is how he paid for all of this. It is said that he emptied the royal vaults of all their treasures, and when that wasn't enough, he began to sell the furnishings and decorations from the palace.

His decisions were directly credited to the age of prosperity that lasted two thousand years. The people of the time were so grateful that they erected a bronze statue of him in the main square. The best part is that even though the city expanded, the square is still there with the statue in the center. The reason it has not been moved or torn down is because of an ancient law that states that anyone who destroys, removes, or otherwise defiles the statue shall be put to death. Apparently, even the royals were included, so nobody had the gall to do anything other than maintain it.

But it's not like I personally knew him. He lived around fifteen hundred years before I was born.

As Myrril and I were happily discussing the book, Reginald returned from washing up.

"Oh, wow, that smells good!" he exclaimed.

"Thanks. It's a basic soup we were taught in the army in case we got separated from our main camp. Though I had a hard time finding the ingredients in town." I laughed a bit. "Who would have thought that names can change over a thousand years?"

Myrril and Reginald both looked at me a bit confused, "Wait, you were in the army?" Reginald asked.

"Hm? Oh, I guess I never told you," I said after a moment of thought, "Yeah. I was a foot soldier assigned to the forge city, Tors. Though I had only been out of basic training for a few months when..."

They both seemed to pick up on what I meant when I trailed off.

"Th-that makes sense, I guess."

"Yeah," Reginald nodded, "you did seem fairly well trained while we were fighting those Husks."

"Ha," I chuckled, "my father trained me from a young age, just in case I took over his title."

"Huh? What do you mean by that?" Reginald asked.

"Right, you guys have a different inheritance law than us." I pulled out three bowls and began to fill them each with soup. It was just made from basic root vegetables, dried meat, and a smidge of salt, but it was better than starving on the battlefield.

I handed out their bowls and took a sip of mine. It was okay, but I once knew a camp cook who could make a kingly meal with less.

"Oh, wow, that's really good!" Reginald exclaimed.

Myrril nodded in agreement, her eyes wide.

"Really?" I asked in disbelief.

"Yeah. Normally, when we're out on a job, we eat dried meat and vegetables. It's risky making a fire while on a hunt," he explained.

"Ah, I guess that makes sense," I said, "Now where was I... Oh yeah, inheritance."

I took another sip before continuing.

"As I understand it, human nobility passes their title down to their oldest child, right?"

"That's the standard," Reginald confirmed, "but it's not always the case. Sometimes the eldest son is disowned or marries into another family, so the next sibling takes their place."

"I see. Well, it's not like that in Aleuria," I began to explain, "Our government, our nobility, and basically every public position is appointed based on merit. It wouldn't matter if your family had been a duke for thirteen generations; if you could not do your job, then the royal family would find someone who could."

They continued to look confused when Reginald asked, "Anybody?" in disbelief.

I nodded, "Yes. Any noble family could lose their titles and become commoners, and any commoner could gain a title. We did not recognize a caste system like yours where people cannot rise above their station."

"W-what about the k-king?" Myrril stammered.

"The royal family's position is the only secure one... well, other than the Children of Creation, but that's a whole other story." I paused for a moment to eat some more soup. "However, the royals do have a form of merit-based promotion. Any of the children of the king can become the new ruler through their actions instead of the order they were born. There have even been cases where the princes weren't fit to rule, and the new king was chosen from the extended family."

"Phew. That's crazy," Reginald leaned back and mused.

"Did you um... d-did you have to compete with anyone?"

"Yes, but not so much compete," I answered. "You see, I was content with letting my older brother take my father's title while I focused on the things that were important to me."

After a short pause, I said, "Besides, Reina, the youngest of us three, has no interest in becoming a count."

"C-count!?" they both yelped in surprise.

"Yeah," I replied, ignoring their surprise, "it was my grandfather who first received the title of count, uplifting us from the lower nobility through his military campaigns."

I finished off my bowl of soup and helped myself to some more as my companions sat wide-eyed, processing the info I had just dumped on them.

Maybe I shouldn't have said anything. I could have just brushed off their questions or lied...

I thought for a moment about how things could have played out differently before shrugging it off. What was done was done, and nothing can change that. It was best to just move on and work with what you have.

Besides, it wasn't a big deal anyway.

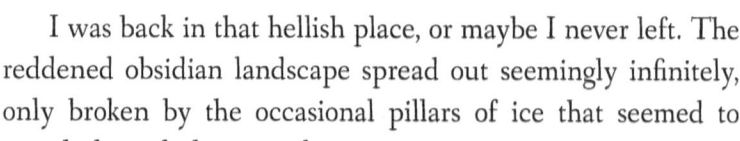

I was back in that hellish place, or maybe I never left. The reddened obsidian landscape spread out seemingly infinitely, only broken by the occasional pillars of ice that seemed to punch through the ground.

In the distance was a black obsidian mountain, one I once climbed to escape from this place. Or perhaps that was just a dream.

The wind of Kyrtvale blew past me, carrying blood-curdling screams and simultaneously burning and freezing my skin.

That's when I heard it, the sound that sends chills up my spine and sets off alarms in my head.

"REPENT."

Suddenly, my face was on the floor. Hands that seemed to appear from nowhere grabbed my ankles. The sharp obsidian ground tore at my flesh as I was dragged at incredible speed.

I tried to struggle, but the hands would not let go. I let out a scream, a cry for help, but it was lost in the expanse.

"REPENT!"

The sourceless voice commanded as the ground began to liquefy. Out of the inky darkness below me, more hands emerged and grabbed onto me, slowly dragging me down.

I got off one more scream before the dark liquid took me, and I sank beneath it.

In the darkness, faces began to appear. Hollow faces of those long since dead seemed to be drawn toward me. Low groans reached my ears, coming from each one of the faces. However, behind the groans was the faint sound of voices.

They seemed to call out, curse the Gods, or scream about their misfortune. The regrets of the dead resounded deep within them.

"REPENT!"

The voice resounded like thunder next to my ear before my eyes flew open and I shot up from my bed, breathing hard.

I quickly scanned my surroundings and took a deep breath. I was in my tent in the middle of the woods on the way to Onforde.

Just then, I heard footsteps rush up, and the entrance to my tent flew open. There, I locked eyes with Reginald.

"Hey," he looked around the tent, "you okay?"

Behind him, I saw a worried-looking Myrril who looked like she had just been awoken.

"...Yeah..." I responded, still a little shaken up, "I'm okay. It was just.... It was nothing."

"That scream didn't sound like nothing," Reginald swiveled his head outside the tent before peaking back in. "You sure you're all right?"

I nodded, trying to regain some composure, "Yeah, I'm sure. I looked at Myrril, Sorry for waking you."

She shook her head, "I-it's fine. I'm just glad y-you're okay."

I smiled weakly before looking back at Reginald, "Give me a few minutes and I'll take over watch. It's about time anyway."

"Alright, if you're sure," Reginald didn't seem entirely convinced, but he left the tent anyway.

I did hear the two of them whispering a moment later, but I was too distracted to make out anything they were saying.

I took another deep breath, got dressed, and buckled my weapon to my belt. Having it with me made me feel much better. When I had it with me, I felt solace in the fact that I could fight off whatever came my way.

CHAPTER 4

Riverbrook

In the morning, we made a quick breakfast, packed up camp, and returned to the road toward Onforde.

We made some light conversation, but I could tell my companions were a little apprehensive. It made sense considering what had happened last night, and though I was embarrassed about it and apologized profusely, it was hard to shake off a sense of unease from the group.

Putting that aside, the travel was quite nice. The area around the road was lightly wooded and still fairly close to the river, so the sounds of nature permeated the air. We also encountered a few travelers on the road as well, but it wasn't too busy.

As the sun rose higher and higher into the sky, the temperature skyrocketed with it. Soon, the heat became almost unbearable, prompting me to remove my coat and lay it across the back of the driver's seat.

"Holy crap!" Reginald shouted.

I snapped to attention and quickly surveyed the area, "What? What is it?" I asked with urgency.

"Sorry, sorry. I didn't see anything," he quickly stated, causing me to relax a bit. "I was just surprised at the size of your arms."

Confused, I looked at my own arms, but nothing about them had changed. They were toned but sleek, a testament to the harsh training I had endured over the years.

"What about them?" I asked.

"It's nothing," he replied, "It's just…"

Myrril jumped in to save Reginald in an unexpected role reversal, "Y-your coat is deceptive. It makes y-your arms look smaller than they are..."

"Ohhh, that makes sense," I said.

"Wh-what are those bands? Jewelry?" Myrril asked.

"Hm?" I thought for a moment before realizing she was pointing to the steel bands wrapped around the midsection of my biceps. "Oh, these? Well, I suppose that's not entirely incorrect."

I looked down at one of them. It was fairly plain except for the small ring of intricate scrawling running the entire side of the band in a continuous loop.

"These were used as a type of fashion," I explained, "but they could also be used to signify a promise. The ones I have are of the latter."

"What type of promise?" Reginald asked curiously.

I took a moment to think before responding, "It's a... well, it was an ancient tradition that warriors participated in for centuries, eons even. It had already gone out of style by the time I was born, but my father and grandfather both took part in the tradition, so I decided to do the same. As for the promise," I continued, grasping for the right words, "it's... about a warrior's training. The bands are removed at the end of a stage of training, which is often used as a badge of honor that signifies a person's combat strength."

"D-do they get in the way of combat?" Myrril asked.

I shrugged, "Yes and no. Their removal is meant to be symbolic of a warrior pushing past their limits. But, in reality, you get used to them."

Clip Clop Clip Clop

"Heads up. Looks like a patrol," Reginald called out.

I cast my gaze back to the front and spotted what Reginald had seen. It was a small patrol of five armored guards on horseback. They each wore a set of half-plate armor and carried cavalry-style sabers at their sides, along with a polearm. The column leader, with a decorative shoulder cape, took center while the four behind him fell into a two-wide line.

One of the men near the front had a large blue flag mounted on their spear, akin to a military standard bearer. The flag itself was divided into four parts much in a checker pattern.

On the top left square was the symbol of the Valtion-Silma Alliance, an eye-shaped oval with three mountain peaks within. Opposite it, in the bottom right corner, was a symbol I didn't recognize. It reminded me of a fish jumping from a stream. The other two opposing squares were left a starch white, giving the banner a checkered pattern.

I pulled our carriage as far to the side of the road as I could, allowing the patrol to continue without issue. However, they slowed as they approached.

"Good day, travelers!" the man in front of the column called out to us, stopping just to our left. "Might I have but a moment of your time?"

The man's tone was kind and well-meaning, and I detected nothing that would concern me, so I replied, "Of course, sir. How may we be of assistance?"

The man's head moved slightly, almost as though he wasn't expecting such a kind reply. He removed his helmet and allowed us to get a better look at his rugged face, bright eyes, and short blonde hair. He didn't seem to be older than forty.

"I am Captain Theobald of Riverbrook. We've been tasked with patrolling this road and checking on the village ahead. Since you've come from that direction, I was wondering if you've seen or heard anything during your travel."

I smiled at Captain Theobald, "We've had an uneventful journey from Edren, thanks to your hard work. Coincidentally, we had visited the village about a day's travel behind us and saw nothing amiss. The people were very happy, and the elder had no concerns."

Captain Theobald raised an eyebrow at my statement.

"You stopped by and spoke with the elder?"

"Our apologies," Reginald stepped in. "Allow us to introduce ourselves. I am Reginald Lee Aulcrest, and these are my companions, Elric Tors and Myrril Delahaye. We've been tasked by Lord Aulcrest of Edren to verify the status of settlements along this road and track the movements of a trio of individuals."

I couldn't help but be a bit surprised at the well-said statement from Reginald, and it seemed that Captain Theobald shared my sentiment.

The captain respectfully bowed his head toward Reginald before speaking once more, "I have not heard wind of any trio of miscreants in Riverbrook, though that is to be expected. The guard within the city has been bolstered within the last month or so, thanks to the Abnormal stalking the woods outside the city." He placed his helmet back upon his head. "Thank you for the information, and please be wary as you grow closer to the town. We have found the remains of many travelers unfortunate enough to cross paths with the creature."

He nudged the side of his horse and moved down the road the way we came with his column of soldiers in tow.

"Interesting," I mused, "so it would seem the creature that the villagers were so afraid of is real after all."

"Y-you didn't believe them? Myrril asked.

"It's not that I didn't believe them," I responded as I urged our horses to continue forward, "I simply believed they were afraid of something from folklore. Some kind of superstition based in reality, but not the entire truth."

"I know what you mean," Reginald said. "There are many

creatures that were thought to be real before they were proven wrong."

I nodded, "Someone may find strange scratches on trees, hear an unfamiliar sound in the night, or see a shape in the darkness. These experiences, while real, are what gave birth to folklore. It is a way to explain the unexplainable." I gave a sigh, "Though, in the end, people end up too afraid to venture into the forest and confirm their fears. If they did, they may just find it to be an ordinary animal."

It wasn't much longer before the town of Riverbrook came into view. The first thing I noticed was the massive construction project taking place on the outskirts of town.

We could see dozens of men working in a freshly cleared area of the forest, digging holes lined up along the border of the forest. Behind them were more men, hoisting timber upright and hammering them into place before moving on to the next one.

The variety of people working on it was no joke, either. Soldiers kept watch around the work and upon the parts of the rampart that had been constructed on the inside of the freshly built wall. We could see off-duty soldiers still wearing their uniforms working together with scores of people dressed in everyday attire. Some had the build of manual laborers, while others were clearly not used to this kind of work.

"Wow. Looks like everyone's pitching in to help. They must be desperate," Reginald observed.

"You would be, too, if an unknown creature was growing closer to your town by the day," I said in response.

Myrril piped up, "W-why don't they just kill it?"

"They've probably considered it, but it's just not realistic,"

Reginald replied. "This is actually their best option given the lack of information."

"Yeah. Most of the time, a simple wall is enough to discourage creatures from trying to enter. Though I am surprised that the town was able to get the funds together for a proper wall," I added.

"No kidding," Reginald chuckled, "I remember my father talking about how hard it was to get the funds for the rampart around Edren."

In general, defense structures were extremely expensive and took years to gather the funds for, not to mention the costs of the actual construction. Although the material of this wall is made of wood instead of the more expensive stone, it would still cost quite a penny to procure the material and manpower.

As we approached the partially constructed gatehouse, Myrril asked another question.

"W-why don't they just use the forest for material?"

"Good question," I responded, "Probably due to the size of the trees. If you look around, the timber that makes up the wall is fairly uniform in size, meaning that they all came from trees of similar size. Now look at the forest around us."

Myrril looked at the trees behind us and gave an "Oh."

"Yep. A lot of these are younger trees. They were probably replanted after various expansions of the town," I said.

"Not to mention that they don't know where the Abnormal is, so they probably don't want to venture too far into the woods," Reginald added.

"Either they save money by risking people's lives, or they potentially lose money but maintain minimal risk to the people," I mused. "This town's choice was one that not many rulers can make. I wonder what kind of man the lord of the town is..."

To say we had no issues entering the town is an understatement; there were no procedures of any kind. The only thing of note was a pair of guards flanking the gate who briefly glanced at us as we entered. I found it quite odd but attributed it to the state of emergency.

I wasn't the only one who noticed it; both Reginald and Myrril said something similar but supposed that the town was worried about leaving lines of travelers outside the walls. Speaking of the walls, they were spaced some distance from the edge of town, allowing expansion in the future.

The town itself could be described as quaint. Puffs of smoke lazily drifted from the chimneys of many of the two-story buildings that made up the town. As we grew closer to the center, the buildings, which had wonderful gardens, grew sparse, and the structures became more dense.

The center of town was a circular crossroads with a small fountain as a centerpiece. To the north was a road lined with shops of all kinds, leading to a large stone bridge that crossed the Tungsten River.

We often saw people going about their day, but the center of town was much busier, even with all the people working on the wall. It was here that we really got a feel for how tense the situation was. The air within the central square was heavy, and we could see the worry on people's faces.

Circling around the fountain was a road that led farther east and out of town. We, however, turned down the south road, which ended at a large wrought iron gate protecting a small but beautiful manor surrounded by lush gardens.

We parked the cart and horse on the side of the road and approached the gate. Slumped in a chair next to it was a single, exhausted guard staring off into the sky.

I cleared my throat, "We're here to see Lord Martin."

The guard lazily moved his head down to look at us, and

though his face was obscured by the helmet, I could tell he didn't want to deal with us.

"Is he expecting you?" the guard asked unenthusiastically.

"Um... no, but..." I began before the guard cut me off.

"Then go away."

The guard went back to staring up at the clouds.

We stood there shocked for a moment, and as soon as I began thinking of other options, the guard sighed and stood from his seat.

"I'm sorry, that was rude of me. We've been taking shifts helping out with the construction, and I just relieved the previous watch," he explained apologetically, "but I also can't just let anyone in to see Lord Martin."

"We understand," I said, "but we were sent by Lord Samuel Aulcrest of Edren to check in on the town."

"No way." The guard was surprised.

"Yes, so if you could see if the lord is available, we would be very grateful."

The guard nodded, "All right, I'll go and inform him. Please wait here."

The man went through the gate and disappeared inside the manor.

What felt like ten or so minutes later, he reappeared with a well-dressed man in tow. The middle-aged man wore excellently tailored clothing and jewelry that were impressive but not overbearing. As he drew closer, I noted his well-kept hair and mustache that had begun to gray, but strong and assertive eyes that were still filled with youth.

The guard promptly opened the gate, and we were welcomed with a smile by the man he brought.

"Welcome, visitors from Edren. I am Lord Martin of Riverbrook," he said with a small bow. "What brings a messenger of Lord Aulcrest this far east?"

There was a hint of anxiety and hope in his voice. Considering the situation that plagued the city, I could guess at what he was hoping to hear.

"Lord Martin," Reginald stepped forward, "it has been some time. How's the family?"

"Ah!" Lord Martin said with excitement, "Young Reginald! I did not expect to see you all the way out here. The family is doing well, thank you. My son recently started an apprenticeship with a local merchant, if you can believe it."

"Really? I never expected him to be able to stay still long enough for that sort of work! I always saw him as joining the city guard or the Association," Reginald said in surprise.

"You and me both," Lord Martin smiled, "but please, let us talk inside. I'm sure you are tired from your long journey."

He turned to the guard, "And you must be exhausted, as well. Please feel free to help yourself to some refreshments in the kitchen. I'll also see about getting some shade set up out here. It's much too hot to be sitting in the sun all day."

The guard bowed, relief filling his voice, "Thank you, milord."

Turning back to the rest of us, Lord Martin gestured for us to follow him into the manor, and we kindly obliged.

"Lord Martin," I started, "if I may say, it is quite unusual for the lord of a city to personally meet guests at the gate."

"Ah, yes. It is quite odd, isn't it?" he replied. "Well, you see, most of the manor staff is helping with the defensive preparations, so I'm a little understaffed at the moment."

Indeed, as we entered the manor and were led down a well-furnished hall, there was nary a sound emanating from within besides our own footfalls.

"However, I am quite happy to answer the door myself from time to time. It's nice to be able to take a break from all of my work to greet my guests."

He led us into a large sitting room where he gestured for us to take a seat, Please, make yourselves at home. I am eager to discuss many things with you.

Lord Martin sat in a comfortable-looking armchair, and the three of us sat on small couches.

In the room was a large mirror hanging over a cold fireplace, while sunlight streamed in from the large windows next to it. There were many brass fixtures that hold candles to light the room at night and a large bookshelf stood on the other side of the room.

I quickly noted the doorway we came in from as well as one behind me before returning my attention to Lord Martin.

"Now then, let's get down to business," Lord Martin rubbed his hands together in anticipation.

"Yes, let us," Reginald took the lead. "My friends, Elric and Myrril, and I have been sent by the Lord of Edren to follow the trail of a trio of criminals. They've already been apprehended, but we are here to see what other damage they may have caused."

"Oh..." Lord Martin's voice dropped.

"Were you hoping that we were here to inform you about aid from Edren?" Reginald asked.

Lord Martin took a breath, "Yes.... Yes, that is what I was hoping."

"I see. Well, if my father knows of your situation, I'm sure he will send what aid he can. However, as you have probably heard, Edren was recently the location of a necromancer attack, so I'm sure the forces are thin trying to clean up that mess."

"Lord Aulcrest is a kind lord and will always help if he is able, but it seems he has been having his own problems recently..." Lord Martin looked dejected.

"If I may ask," Reginald started, "we've heard some tale

about this creature you are trying to defend against, but we don't know the specifics. What is it?"

Lord Martin looked at us and seemed to ponder what he should say before responding.

"It... well, we don't know what it is. We don't even have much to go on."

He took a breath before continuing, "All we really know is that it leaves its victims in a terrible state, almost as if they had been burned from within."

I couldn't help but raise a brow at the statement. I was fascinated by what sort of creature could burn a man from the inside out.

"Oh, yes," Lord Martin continued, "we also do know what it smells like."

"Its smell?" Reginald asked.

"Yes, its smell," Lord Martin answered. "It is very strange and unique because when you smell it, you can also taste it in the air. It has an almost blood-like tinge to it and is somewhat acidic tasting. It feels almost like the air is tingling."

"That's unlike anything I've ever heard before," Reginald turned to me, "Elric?"

I shook my head, "I don't believe so. I would have to experience it firsthand to be certain, but for now, I'm gonna say no."

"How unfortunate," Lord Marin responded with a solemn tone. "Well, I'll get that information you requested, but it might take a while. I should have it by the morning."

"Sounds good," Reginald said, standing from his seat, and I suppose while we are here, we can help with the construction."

Lord Marin perked up at hearing this, "Really!? I would be forever grateful for any assistance you can offer. If we can finish this wall even one day earlier, the people will feel much safer and be able to return to some semblance of normalcy."

"Of course. We can't just sit around in a tavern all day, right, guys?" Reginald turned to us.

Myrril, who had been trying to make herself small, gave a little "Eep!" when the attention was directed toward her, but she managed to make a small nod.

"Yeah, I've gotten a lot of carpentry practice lately, and the road has made me restless," I replied.

Turning back to Lord Martin, Reginald spoke once more, "There you go. We'll head out there and do some work."

Lord Martin had such a deep look of relief that it made me believe he had been debating whether to ask us for help or not.

"Oh, thank you, thank you. You do not understand how helpful it will be to have your assistance," Lord Martin said, almost teary-eyed.

"Of course, Lord Martin. Just don't forget those records."

"Yes, Yes. I will not."

Reginald led us out of the room as Lord Martin slumped back into his seat, seeming like a weight had been taken off his shoulders.

As we made it outside, I couldn't help but ask what that was about.

"Oh, yes, well. You see, Riverbrook has never had its own fortifications before, so they don't have any experience constructing them. Lord Martin seemed to be looking to ask me to help because I was trained in the basics of battlefield construction," Reginald answered.

"That makes a lot of sense now," I said. "Do you want to take the eastern side while I take the western?"

"Yeah, that sounds good. But first, let's get rooms at an inn."

In agreement, we retrieved the cart and horses and rode down the road in search of a place to stay for the night.

CHAPTER 5

How Not to Befriend a Wild Animal

It didn't take us long to find an inn where we could board the horses and cart for the night, and for only a little more than The Hungry Boar charged back in Edren.

Like many of the buildings I had seen in the last few months, it had two floors with a gabled roof and an outward façade consisting of wooden beams embedded in some kind of plaster. The building was weathered, but it still had a bright feel to it that welcomed us with open arms.

We ate a quick lunch and set out to help with the construction of the wall. I went to the west, the direction we came from, while Reginald helped on the eastern side. Myrril said she would help with what she could but confessed that she wasn't the best at physical activity.

I set off to the western wall and quickly noticed three men standing around a drafting table next to the construction site. All three of them were well-built and around their thirties to forties. Two of them were noticeably dirtier than the other and seemed to be leading teams on-site. At the moment, most of the workers had taken a break for lunch.

"Hey, guys, how's it going?" I called out as I approached.

All three of them looked toward me, but the one who seemed to be in charge actually responded.

"Not too bad," he said. "You're new in town, aren't you?"

"Yeah, the name's Elric." I stuck my hand out. "Lord Martin said you could use some help."

The man in charge shook my hand, "I'm Ron, and these two are Todd and Howard."

Todd nodded at me while Howard looked like he had a question on his mind.

"Hey, Elric was it?" Howard started, "I don't want to be rude, but where do you hail from? I've never heard an accent like yours."

"Howard!" Ron snapped.

I put my hand up, "It's okay. I'm actually surprised I don't get it more often."

I turned to Howard, "I was born far out west, but I'm actually based out of Edren. How about all of you?"

"Oh, we're all Riverbrook born and bred. This is our home, and we're gonna make sure it stays safe," Ron said with a bit of passion.

"Aye, Ron here is the best carpenter in the town," Todd jumped in.

"Hey now, you and Howard aren't too bad either," Ron responded before all three of them started laughing at what I assumed was some kind of inside joke. It was nice to see laughter amidst the tense atmosphere.

"Phew," Ron wiped a tear from his eye,. "You said Lord Martin sent you, right? Well, good. We could use some more hands."

I nodded, "Yes, that's what he said. Also, if it is of some help, I've been trained in battlefield fortifications."

The three men went wide-eyed, and I could see some of the tension melt from their shoulders.

"Oh, thank the Gods!" Todd shouted to the heavens.

"Thank the Gods indeed," Ron let out a sigh of relief. "We may be decent carpenters, but we know nothing about defensive structures."

"Well, civilian and military carpentry have a lot of overlap,

I said. Just from what I've seen, you've done a good job. Mind if I take a closer look?"

"No, not at all," Ron said. "In fact, I'll come with you."

We took a walk through the current construction area first.

"The general rule is to have about a third of the length of the log set in the ground," I said as I stared into one of the dug holes. "Yeah, that looks about five feet deep. What do you pack these with?"

"We use the soil we excavated," Ron replied.

"A mixture of gravel and clay would be better, but the soil works for now."

"Gravel and clay?" Ron asked.

Yeah. It helps protect the wood from rot, especially this close to the river." I got to my feet, "But you're still looking at around a decade before any of these will have to be replaced."

He wrote a note in a small book, "I see. That would make sense."

"As for the wall itself, I took a closer look at how it was constructed. The ten-foot-tall wall was lashed together with rope and left little gaps between the logs. It's looking really good."

The wall so far had been made very well, but as I took a closer look at the inside, the inexperience started to show.

"Is something wrong?" Ron asked with trepidation.

"Well, kind of," I replied in a calm tone, "The wall in its current form is not more than a deterrent."

Ron looked shocked at my statement.

"See here? The wall is pretty flimsy against anything that *wants* to get in." I pushed the wall a bit, showing that it had some give. "Normally, we would put horizontal beams on the back of the wall and then we would install diagonal braces... You know what, let me just show you."

I walked over to a pile of logs that were awaiting installation and hefted one onto my shoulder. I could hear gasps from some of the workers taking a break nearby as I carried the fifteen-foot-long timber to the wall.

I gently laid the timber diagonally against the side of the wall, So it would kind of look like this with a section of the end buried in the ground. This way, the wall will protect you against not only beasts trying to break through, but it also offers good protection against people as well.

I turned my head to look back at Ron, whose eyes looked like they were about to burst from his head.

"Did you get that?" I asked.

He blinked a few times, "Uh... yeah, yeah. I got that."

Pen furiously scratched against paper as he jotted down notes and drew a small sketch.

After a moment, he looked up from his notes, "Um, how did you..."

"Magic," I simply responded.

"Ah, yeah. That makes sense."

During my time in Edren, I found that it was easier to say I used magic to do something than it was to come up with some other explanation. It also helped that people kept buying it.

"Oh, yeah, I forgot to mention. Since this is interior work, you can easily do it after you finish the main wall," I added.

"That would work best for us..." Ron trailed off in thought.

"Alright, shall we continue?"

The rest of the day went by fairly quickly. I helped create a diagram for how the gate should be built and gave a few pointers here and there. I also suggested expanding the clear-cut area to make sure the trees can't fall and break a hole in the wall.

Mind you, this wasn't the only thing I did. In fact, after I was done helping Ron, I went and assisted the workers pulling the logs into place. It was grueling work in the heat, but after I had seen what we accomplished, I felt a sense of pride and achievement.

At the end of the day, I shook hands with all the men I had worked with and bid them farewell. They were nice people, and I wouldn't have minded working with them again in the future.

Exhausted, I made my way back to the tavern attached to the inn and was greeted by a full house. Nearly every table was packed with patrons. At the far end of the tavern floor was a slightly raised platform with a few people loitering on it.

Off to the side, I spotted an equally exhausted-looking Reginald and Myrril seated at a round table next to a window.

I pulled a chair out and sat down faster than I probably should have, provoking some unpleasant-sounding creaks from beneath me.

"You guys look like you had a lot of fun," I teased my companions.

Reginald raised his head, "Yeah. They didn't need as much help planning as I thought, so I got dragged into placing logs."

"Same here." I turned to Myrril, "What about you?"

Myrril's head dropped onto the table with a *Thump*.

"So much walking," she groaned.

I had seen her appear from time to time, so I assumed that she was running all over the place. It must have been rough.

"Well, let's get something to eat. I'm sure we'll all feel better afterward."

I flagged down one of the tavern staff, and soon we had hot food in front of us. Not a moment after it was on the table,

Myrril started digging in like a ravenous wolf. Reginald and I exchanged looks of surprise.

Not too long after we started eating, the people on the raised platform organized themselves, and a pretty young woman took to the center.

Three people behind her started playing their respective instruments. A set of drums, a stringed instrument similar to a Pandura, and a flute were all present.

Then, she started to sing.

"Wow," Reginald muttered.

"Yeah, she's good," I said.

Myrril paused a moment and looked shocked, "I think that's Aileen Grace! She's a traveling minstrel. I-I heard her once from outside a tavern in Edren."

"Oh, yeah?" I replied offhandedly.

We took a few minutes to listen to her sing. Her voice carried with it a sort of comfort that seemed to ease the tension in my shoulders.

"So, we still have one more stop before Onforde, right?" Reginald asked between bites.

"That's right. There's one more village on the road, though this one isn't within Edren's territory, so they may not be as willing to talk," I responded.

"Oh, yeah, that could be a problem."

I shrugged, "Not much we can do about it in that case. They don't have to answer any questions from an envoy of another nation. Even if they're allied."

"Then after that, it's off to Onforde, where we get to investigate an attempted assassination. Yay," Reginald's voice was devoid of enthusiasm.

"Speaking of, do you guys think it's related to Lost Light?"

My question prompted Myrril to look up from her meal and tilt her head in thought.

70

"I'm not sure, but father seemed to imply that's what he thought."

"Yeah, I picked that up as well." I leaned back in my chair, "Though, that just means it's up to us to—"

That's when I heard something that sent chills down my spine. My attention snapped to the stage as I was unable to comprehend what I was hearing.

"What?" Reginald sat straight and alert, "What is it?"

"It's.... it's something I thought I would never hear again."

I couldn't help but stare at the stage as water welled in my eyes. The singer, Aileen Grace, had begun to sing a beautiful song about a woman who was waiting for her lover to return from sea, not knowing he was dead.

However, I was sure I was the only one able to appreciate it. The song was one heard all over the Aleurian Empire, and Aileen was singing it beautifully in the tongue of my homeland.

My heart was heavy as I wiped the tears that had begun to form and just listened. My very soul seemed enraptured as I felt a warmth within me. It was a warmth I had never experienced before, but the best I could describe it was that of someone far from home who saw a familiar face. It made my heart ache for home.

"Excuse me a moment, I'll be right back," I got up from my seat and moved toward the stage, not waiting for a response from my companions.

I pushed through the crowded tavern and made it to the front just before the song ended, but the feeling was still there.

The minstrel group seemed to be taking a break after that song, so I called out to them.

"That was beautiful."

The woman named Aileen turned back toward me and gave a gentle smile.

"Thank you for your kind words."

71

"If I may ask, where did you learn that piece?" My mind was filled with possibilities and the desire to know.

"Oh?" She looked troubled. "Nobody has asked that before. They normally want to know what language it is."

Aileen seemed to think for a moment, "Well, there's no harm in telling, I suppose. I learned it from an elderly woman whose family had passed it down for generations. Unfortunately, she is no longer with us, so I sing it in honor of her."

I nodded solemnly, my heart in a knot, I see. "Well, you sang it perfectly. If I didn't know any better, I would have thought you were a native speaker. Thank you for carrying on a piece of my people."

I reached into my pocket, pulled out my last Gold Solaire, and tossed it into the tip basket they had set out. Then I turned and walked back to the table, leaving Aileen with a somewhat confused expression.

"What was that about?" Reginald raised his brow.

"That song..." I hesitated, "It's from my homeland. She even sang it in the Aleurian tongue."

"Ah, I see," Reginald nodded, seeming to understand.

My heart was still heavy with thoughts of home, then the feeling dissipated almost instantly. It felt as if I had never had those feelings to begin with. The sudden ending was off-putting, but I had started getting used to it.

Skreeech!

Within a moment, another chair had been pulled up to the table.

"I was wondering who the idiot was that pushed past me, but I guess it makes sense being a friend of yours, Reginald." The woman who spoke had appeared from nowhere, yet she sat at the table as if she belonged.

She had short, curly red hair and blue eyes. She wore a comfortable shirt with a leather corset, pants, and boots. Two silver bells the size of walnuts hung from her silver-banded belt opposite a small dagger, and yet they did not ring when she moved.

Just next to the bells was a necklace tied around her belt, letting hang a medallion similar to Myrril's but depicting a set of spread wings, the symbol of a Svífa Væng.

"Leone!" Reginald happily shouted, "I wasn't expecting to see you until we made it to Onforde. What are you doing all the way out here?"

The woman, Leone, gave Reginald a toothy grin, "Nice to see you, too, Reggie."

Myrril choked a little and sputtered, "Reggie?" in quiet bewilderment.

Leone took a drink from her wooden tankard before continuing, "I was out here for a job. Helped protect some of the workers while they built the wall."

"Ah, yeah, that's just like you," Reginald replied.

"Anyway, are you going to introduce me to your friends?" Leone asked.

"Oh, right!" Reginald turned to Myrril and me, "This is Myrril Delahaye. I've been working with her for a while. She's a little shy, but she's a good person. And this is Elric Tors. We've only known each other for a little bit, but he's smart and reliable. I'm happy to call him my friend."

Then he gestured at Leone, "This is Leone Scarlette. She's a fellow mercenary whom I met a while back when she visited Edren."

Myrril let out a small "H-hello" before shrinking back.

"Well met, Leone." I gestured with my tankard and took a sip.

"So, you asked me a question, now it's my turn. What are

you guys doing here?" Leone asked Reginald. "I didn't think you'd ever leave Edren."

"Rude!" Reginald said in a huff. "Just because I like to stay around my hometown doesn't mean I'd never leave."

"Right," Leone smiled, glad that Reginald had taken the bait, "but why did you finally leave?"

I detected a hint of pure curiosity in her voice. Despite her teasing, it seemed that she had a genuine interest in what we were doing.

Reginald squinted at Leone before relenting, "My father sent us to check on the villages around here."

"Ah. That makes sense," she nodded.

"Though our final destination is Onforde," Reginald finished.

Leone gave a small smile, "So I did hear that earlier. When are you headed out?"

"In the morning."

"Well then, mind if I tag along?" Leone asked, looking at me and Myrril.

"Not at all," I replied.

"I-I don't have a problem..." Myrril said as timidly as usual.

"Then it's settled. I'll see you in the morning." Leone got up from her seat.

"Wait! Don't you want to know my opinion on this matter?" Reginald looked confused.

"Do you have a problem with it?" I asked.

Reginald shrank back a bit and stuttered, "W-well, not really... but..."

"Then there isn't a problem," Leone cheerfully stated.

"Yeah, I suppose..."

"Then I'll be off," Leone said before disappearing into the crowd.

I couldn't help but smile a bit. She seemed like a very energetic person. I had a feeling that our travel would get more interesting. I was especially interested in the dynamic between Leone and Reginald.

I finished off my drink and arose from my seat, "Well, I think I'll get some shut-eye."

"You sure?" Reginald asked.

"Yeah. I'm pretty tired, and we need to get back on the road in the morning. I'll see you guys then."

"Alright. See you in the morning."

Myrril nodded along with Reginald.

I headed upstairs to my room and removed my coat before lying on the bed. The day had been exhausting, both physically and mentally.

It wasn't long before I dozed off and entered the land of dreams.

Unfortunately, my dreams were less than pleasant.

In the morning, I made my way to the front of the inn. Outside was a groggy-looking Reginald standing next to the cart, the back of which held a sleeping Myrril wrapped in blankets.

"Morning," I called out to Reginald.

His eyes jolted open. "Morning."

"How late did you guys stay up last night?"

Reginald took a deep breath. "I have... no clue."

"Right..." I said slowly, "Are we ready to get those documents from Lord Martin?"

"Almost. We're just waiting for Leone," he replied.

"Okay."

I gave a short reply and leaned against the cart. I took in the cool morning air and the slight fog that had rolled in. It wouldn't be a problem, though; it would burn off in about an hour. Growing up on an island meant I was well acquainted with fog.

A few minutes later, Leone emerged from the inn. She was wearing a different outfit than we had seen the night before. She wore a set of durable boots meant for easy movement, gray pants, and a form-fitting light purple tunic over a long-sleeved white shirt and a set of chainmail.

She still had her belt carrying her silver bells and dagger, however, she also had a pack slung over one shoulder and a spear leaning against the other.

I also noted the glimmer of a necklace chain hidden under her collar.

"Good morning, everyone!" Leone cheerfully greeted us with a smile.

"Morning," Reginald and I responded.

"Ready to head off?" she asked.

"Yeah, we just have to swing by Lord Martin's and grab a few documents from him," Reginald said, mounting his horse.

"Alright." Leone dropped her bag into the cart and climbed aboard.

The sound of her pack hitting the wood woke Myrril from her sleep.

She jolted up in a slight panic, "I'm up!"

Leone smiled, "Well then, good morning, sleepy head."

Myrril wiped the sleep from her eyes and yawned, "Morning."

I climbed into the driver's seat and urged the horses forward, beginning to maneuver toward the lord's manor. Luckily, the inn we had chosen wasn't too far from the central fountain, so we made it to the manor gates relatively quickly.

Lord Martin was already out front, conversing with several individuals around a small table. Papers and diagrams were spread across the table, and they seemed to be in a heated discussion.

The guard at the gate let us in, saying that we had been expected.

"Lord Martin, your guests are here," the guard informed the lord.

"Ah, excellent," he said, excusing himself from the group.

"Good morning, my friends," Lord Martin said with a cheery smile. "I see that you have one extra today."

"Yes, this is Leone. We are headed in the same direction, so she hitched a ride with us," Reginald explained.

"Ah, very good. I have those documents you requested, however..." He had a look of apology on his face. "We had very little about a trio of mercenaries. We compiled what we have, but it isn't much."

Lord Martin handed over a small leather scroll case.

"Oh, and I took the liberty of adding something Lord Aulcrest may find interesting. A few months ago, someone had claimed to see a wanted man enter the town."

All four of us perked up at the sound of this.

"Who was it?" Reginald popped open the case and thumbed through the pages.

"A man known only by the name of Koberic. Apparently, he is wanted in the Faeron Kingdom for some sort of crime against the deceased. The only reason he was recognized was because the townsfolk who saw him had just returned from visiting family in Faeron." Lord Martin explained, "We looked into it of course, but we couldn't find the man."

I had a feeling that Reginald and Myrril were thinking the same thing as me. That Koberic moving through Riverbrook a few months before Lost Light wasn't a coincidence.

"Yes, I think that my father will be very interested in seeing this. Thank you, Reginald closed the case and bowed to Lord Martin, "however, we must be on our way now."

"Of course, of course. I have a meeting to get back to. Best of luck, and fair travels."

Lord Martin waved us goodbye before returning to his earlier discussion.

Not but half an hour later, Riverbrook had disappeared behind us. We had finally returned to the well-traveled road covered by a green canopy.

"Ah," Leone sighed in relief, "I always feel better in The Ashwood."

"You prefer nature to people?" I asked.

"No, I wouldn't say that. It's just..." Leone thought for a second, "The forest is so peaceful and quiet. There aren't any loud-mouthed dumbasses walking around like they own the place."

"I see..."

Myrril decided to join in, "U-um, Leone? D-do you enter the forest o-often?"

"Huh?" She looked at Myrril, "Oh, yeah. I don't really like traveling on the main roads, so I usually cut through the forest whenever I can."

"Really?" I looked back at Leone with a raised eyebrow, "What kind of things do you normally see in The Ashwood?"

She leaned back against the side of the cart. "Oh, just the usual animals that you typically find in a wooded area, an occasional Arache, and various kinds of Spiritual Beasts if you know where to look."

"W-what's an Arache?" Myrril asked.

Leone leaned toward me and whispered, "Am I doing something to make her nervous?"

"No," I assured her, "she's just a timid person."

"Ah." She leaned back and looked at Myrril, "Arache are large spider-like beasts."

The color drained from Myrril's face, "H-how b-big?"

"They vary in size, but the adults are anywhere from a medium to a large dog," Leone answered.

Reginald pulled up to the side of the cart. "Myrril, are you afraid of spiders?"

She shook her head, "N-no, but if they are that big..."

I couldn't help but chuckle, "I agree with you. A spider that big would give me the creeps."

"Well, you don't need to worry about them. I've never seen one this far north. They usually nest closer to Torrel and Mellgarde," Leone reassured Myrril.

Myrril took a deep breath, "Oh... g-good."

We kept going for another few minutes before a clearing came into view to our right. The canopy opened, and unobstructed sunlight hit my face, an increase in temperature along with it.

"Wow, that would have been a pretty good spot to camp if we had just passed through Riverbrook," I mused before catching something on the wind. "Though, maybe not for tonight. It smells like a storm is coming."

Having grown up on an island, my nose was attuned to how the air felt before a thunderstorm. It was second nature to me, a natural warning system.

Reginald looked up at the sky. "I don't see any clouds."

I took a peek at the sky and realized that he was right, the sky was blue as far as the eye could see.

"Huh..." I said, "I could have sworn there was going to be a thund–"

BTOOOM!

A loud crack was accompanied by a searing white flash that

forced my eyes shut. The hair on my arms was standing on end, and the horses were crying out in fear.

I blinked the white out of my eyes just in time to hear a crash. A tree to our left had fallen to the ground, the trunk was heavily charred.

"What the hell is that!?" Reginald yelled from the ground. His horse had thrown him off and disappeared farther down the road.

I was trying to rein in the panicking horses attached to the cart when I turned to look at where Reginald was pointing.

"Holy crap!" I shouted. "Reginald, get over here!"

Standing across the clearing was a swirling sphere of cloud and rock, with bolts of lightning periodically arcing across its surface.

Reginald scrambled to his feet and hopped into the cart next to me, and I handed him the reins.

"What are you doing!?" Myrril screamed as I tossed my armor and coat into the back of the cart. Leone, on the other hand, seemed intrigued as to my plan.

"We can't outrun it. I'm going to slow it down." I hopped out of the cart "Reginald, get going."

He nodded and whipped the reins, sending the horses into a dash, happy to get away from the creature.

"WAIT!" Myrril yelled as they sped off.

I had to admit, while we really couldn't have outrun this creature, I also had a selfish reason for fighting it. It was a rare sight even in my time, and the Aleurians who subjugated one were legends among my people.

I cracked my knuckles and stared down the ball of energy.

It waited as if studying me, then its shape began to warp. The clouds and rock pressed together forming a body, the lighting still arcing across its fur. Two eyes as bright as any blue stared at me from its new form.

"Wow, I wasn't expecting it to turn into an animal," I heard from next to me, "And it chose a bear, how interesting."

"Wha–?" I turned my head and saw Leone standing there, her spear resting on her shoulder.

"What are you doing here!?" I demanded.

"I wanted to see you fight." She shrugged, "Besides, you aren't the only one who knows what that is."

"Hm, fine," I grumbled, "but you don't want to be holding anything metal. The lightning is attracted to it."

"Good point," Leone nodded before sticking her spear headfirst into the ground. "So, how are you going to fight it?"

"Like this."

I bent my knees and pushed off the ground, launching myself toward the bear covered in blue fur and rocky armor.

The beast stood on its hind legs and let out a roar, but it didn't stop me. The lighting bolts it fired out, however, did.

I hit the ground, sliding beneath one of them, and jumping back to my feet on the other side, trying to maintain my momentum.

Another bolt fired, this time I put out my right hand and produced a shimmering shield of Megin. The lighting dissipated on the translucent barrier rippling out from my palm. However, I was unable to block all of it, and some of the energy carried through, forcing the muscles in my arm to tense momentarily.

The beast's clawed paw swept toward my head.

I used my forearm to stop the attack, contacting with its arm right before the wrist.

The force of its attack sent a sharp pain down my arm and into my neck, but I held firm and counter-attacked.

I curled my other hand into a fist and launched an uppercut into the bear's jaw with as much force as I could muster, sending it stumbling backward.

It quickly regained itself and lunged at me, wiping its claws once more. This time, however, they were laced with electrical energy.

With each swipe, I dodged backward, trying to gain a bit of distance, but it kept pushing forward.

Out of the corner of my eye, I saw Leone rushing forward. She grabbed the two silver bells hanging from her waist and threw them at the bear.

"Hati, Sköll! Sic!"

A set of howls echoed through the clearing as a pair of wolves seemed to form around the bells.

The first of the wolves had a coat that shone like the gentle white light of the moon. Its fangs and claws were made of silver, and its eyes were a piercing void.

The other was a roaring torrent of flame that took the form of a wolf. Its hide was reminiscent of the sun, and its eyes were the same dark void as the other.

They wasted no time in pouncing onto the back of the beast that had me on the defensive. Their claws dug into its back, and their jaws clamped onto its legs. The beast let out a loud roar and tried to swipe the wolves off of it, but they were too nimble.

I took the opportunity to attack again, putting as much force as I could into each strike. Stomach, chest, head; I threw punches into each one several times, but the beast was still up.

It roared once more, but this time the sound was deafening. The force of it was enough to push me backward as I struggled to stay on my feet.

"Damn! It has thunder for a roar!?" I yelled.

The roaring stopped after what felt like an eternity, but was only a moment. When I got my eyes back on the beast, its form was in the middle of shrinking.

It didn't become much smaller, but its overall form was

different. It was that of a wolf. A wolf the size of a lion, but a wolf nonetheless.

"How smart is this thing?" Leone shouted in surprise.

I had been thinking the same thing. Had the beast realized it was at a disadvantage with such a large form, or had changing it simply been instinct?

"I don't know, but we don't have much time to find out," I said just as another bolt of lightning arced across the ground toward me.

I moved out of the way just in time, but the proximity sent the hair on the back of my neck standing on end.

Leone's wolves took advantage of the moment and moved into the attack. The beast saw them coming and fired another bolt of electricity directly into the lunging moonlight wolf. It let out a whimper and rolled to the ground for a moment before getting back to its feet.

The one that looked like the sun, however, had made it to the beast. It dug its fangs into the beast's hide, sending the sound of searing flesh into the air. Then, lightning arced up into the sun wolf, and it jumped back in pain.

Apparently finished with the wolf-on-wolf combat, the beast cloaked itself in lightning and began to run. It made wide circles around me and Leone, its speed increasing dramatically until it was just a blur.

"What now?" Leone tried to keep her eyes on the lightning wolf as it passed but was having trouble.

"Uh... I don't know," I responded. "I guess we wait."

This was a move I had little idea of how to deal with. It was moving extremely fast, fast enough that even I was having trouble keeping up with it.

I racked my brain for anything I could do, formulating a series of plans on how to deal with the creature.

None of the plans I made covered what happened next.

The beast made a course correction that I barely saw in time. It was headed directly toward me at an unbelievable speed. If I had blinked, it would have hit me.

I had no time to put any of the plans I had in motion. I was caught completely off guard. Time seemed to slow as it approached.

Just before it hit me, my body acted on its own.

In a fit of pure instinct, Megin strengthened my leg, and it flew out with explosive force. My shin impacted with the beast's chest, and I could feel the cracking of ribs.

The beast let out a horrific cry of pain as it tumbled through the air, end over end, hitting its back into a tree with a sickening *Crack!*

It hit the ground with a whine just before the tree let out more cracks and creaks, leaning backward and collapsing into the woods.

"Holy crap..." Leone muttered.

The beast shakily got back to its feet. It was breathing heavily, and a thick blue liquid was dripping from its mouth. I could see the fear and submission in its eyes as they locked with mine.

It collapsed onto the ground and laid its head down, submitting its will.

I took the moment to take a deep breath and look over the clearing. What had once been a peaceful area was now pockmarked with craters and a few fallen trees.

I approached the beast and ran my hand through its fur, making my hand tingle slightly.

"You fought well. I would be happy to have you accompany me."

Leone approached, flanked by her wolves, "If that's what you want, then use one of these."

She dropped something into my hand. It looked like a silver flower on the end of a short cord.

"What is it?" I asked.

"That is how a Spiritualist contracts with their beasts. Drop it onto its back, the device will do the rest on its own."

I did as she said and dropped the silver flower onto the creature's back. It sank into its hide as if it were made of molasses.

The beast's form shimmered and shrank like being pulled through a drain until all that was left was a silver bell on the ground.

I picked it up and inspected it. The flower had closed around a small bluish stone, creating the appearance of a bell.

Leone sighed, "I can't believe you got a Storm Wolf to submit."

"Neither can I," I responded, pocketing the bell.

"So," I turned to Leone and her wolves, "you are a Spiritualist?"

She nodded, "I am."

"And a Spiritualist makes a spiritual creature submit to them so that they can be used in combat?" I asked.

"That's the basic premise, though the way you say it makes it sound like we're beast tamers," Leone smiled. "They are much more than tools, they are our partners."

She gave the flaming wolf a scratch behind the ear, which let out a happy yip.

"This one here is Sköll, he's a Solar Wolf." She moved over to scratch the other one, "And this is Hati, he's a Lunar Wolf."

"I thought so. Not many people encounter Solar and Lunar Wolves. How was it that you came by them?" I asked.

She smiled, "That's a story for another time. For now, we should probably catch up with the others. They must be worried."

"Oh, yeah. Good idea."

INTERLUDE

Holy Silas Kingdom – Gilded Hall of the Gods ~

A circular hall lined with pillars sat somewhere within the grand cathedral. In this chamber was a round table set beneath a dome depicting the thirteen gods in vibrant paint and excruciating detail.

Seated around this table were four elderly men deep in conversation, each wearing a blue pin on their collar depicting a three-pointed star. Three of the men wore a white cape lined with red and a somewhat pointed cap called a Mitre.

The fourth man sat somewhat isolated from the others. His cape was trimmed in gold embroidery, as was his cap, which was much more rounded and adorned with jewels in comparison to the Mitre of the others.

Behind the decorated man were two guards standing still enough to be mistaken for statues. Each was adorned in silver and gold armor from head to toe, with the same three-pointed star adorned in blue on their chest.

"We understand what you are saying, Oswyn." The man who spoke was one adorned in red, his face graced with a pointed white beard, "but we cannot allow anyone to shirk their duty to the gods."

The man he was arguing with, Oswyn, adjusted the spectacles resting on his nose and responded in a cold tone, "It was our duty to protect their village. Because we failed, they lost their crops and much of their manpower to those beasts. They are not able to pay their tithe."

"The gods care not for the–" the first man began to speak, but froze when he saw the adorned man signal for them to stop.

"Oswyn is right," the man adorned in gold spoke with a voice that had mediated many arguments. "We failed to protect many of the chosen people of the gods. However, Carpef is also correct. They cannot shirk their duty to the gods."

The two men who were arguing glanced at each other and back at the adorned man, who took a moment in silence before speaking once more.

We shall increase our patrols in the Verdant Fields and issue a tax relief for the town. However, they will be expected to pay back their debt over the next ten years.

"Yes, Cardinal." The two men bowed their heads slightly.

The adorned man, the cardinal, spoke to the third man in the room. "Gabele, what is the next issue?"

The third man, Gabele, had a round face and intelligent eyes. He held a series of documents that he updated whenever the cardinal made a ruling.

"The next issue we have is about the Valtion-Silma City-State Alliance, Cardinal." Gabele passed a small bundle of papers to each person at the table.

"I see." The cardinal accepted the papers. "What have they done this time?"

Carpef spoke up first, re-reading the paper multiple times.

"This cannot be right," he said, looking at Gabele. "What are the Inquisitors doing out there!?"

Gabele simply responded, "The information has been verified."

Oswyn finished reading through the report and adjusted his glasses. "It would appear that a necromancer appeared within the City-State of Edren and uncovered a tomb of heretics."

"Not only that!" Carpef spat, "it's said that they brought the heretics back to life! This blasphemy cannot be tolerated!"

"Oh?" the cardinal said, "and what is your opinion on the first part of the report?"

"What about it?" Carpef asked, confused.

"I believe that the idea is dangerous, Cardinal," Oswyn responded. "The necromancer was able to take the corpses of demons and create man-made Abnormals. If someone were able to create an army of them, it could threaten not only our dominance but the sanctity of our Holy Land."

"Elves," Carpef spat in disgust, "those Demons are more tenacious than anyone expected."

"The report also states that these Abnormals were destroyed along with their creator," Oswyn added.

The three men looked to the cardinal, who had closed his eyes in thought. After a few moments, he spoke.

"Send a missive to their lord. Our agents will retrieve the bodies of the Abnormals and cleanse the tomb. We cannot allow ourselves to degrade into heresy; the gods take such things very seriously."

"Yes, Cardinal," Gabele jotted down the cardinal's orders before moving to the next issue.

The fortified palace in Dorona – Capital of the Dolar Imperium ~

Seated upon a silver throne at the far end of a long audience hall lined with armor-clad knights was a man in his late twenties to mid-thirties. His body was covered in exquisite armor shining the same silver as the throne, with an opulent blue peaking from between the plates. Pinned beneath the pauldrons at his shoulders was a cape of the same fine blue.

A well-trimmed beard graced the noble features of his face,

and an intricately woven crown of platinum embedded with the purest sapphires sat upon his blonde head.

"Presenting Earl Cillian O'Donner, Lord of Southport and Karnel, arriving at the behest of Emperor Uriel Von Dorona," the palace steward announced, allowing several scribes off to the side of the chamber to properly document the audience.

The massive oaken doors at the far end of the chamber opened with an echo. A middle-aged man with dark brown hair and a distinguished stride approached from beyond the doorway.

He stopped and knelt a few feet away from the base of the raised podium upon which sat the silver throne, and the emperor upon it.

"Lord Cillian," the emperor spoke, "I wish to offer my condolences for the death of your son."

"Thank you, Your Majesty. Your kind words mean everything to my family," Cillian spoke with an accent that elongated the R's and seemed to make many of the vowels sound the same. Many people on the western coast spoke in such an accent, but not many were as easy to understand.

"However," he continued, "I feel it necessary to apologize for my son's behavior. He was always a wild one, but I never expected him to do something so heinous."

The emperor rose from his throne and approached Lord Cillian, placing his hand upon his shoulder, "You may rise. We have known each other for many years, and I do not blame you for this incident."

Cillian rose and looked the emperor in the eye. Where he had expected to see anger, he instead saw sorrow for his friend's loss.

"Thank you," he said.

"I wish to express my family's sorrow, as well as my own,"

Emperor Uriel continued. "If you must take some time to rest, I will provide temporary personnel to reduce your workload."

"Thank you, Your Majesty," Cillian bowed. "While I find solace in my work, my wife does not have such an escape. I had planned on taking her to our mountain villa. As such, I graciously accept your generous offer."

"Then I shall give you my blessing." The emperor turned on his heel, walked up the steps, and lowered himself back upon the throne. "I will arrange for the personnel to be transferred to Southport."

"I thank you for your generosity, Sire." Cillian bowed one last time before exiting the audience hall.

As the emperor watched his old friend leave, he couldn't help but think of the headache his son may have caused. Such an event may become the cause of a large diplomatic incident, and if that is the case, it would throw a wrench into the emperor's plans.

He rubbed his temple, already predicting the headache to come.

Vestri, the Western Continent – the Coast of the Faeron Kingdom ∼

On an uninhabited beach far from any town or village lay an elvish ship at anchor. Six figures disembarked from the ship and packed up supplies for the journey.

"Princess," an older elvish man with a decorated uniform said from the deck, "we cannot stay here any longer or we will draw undue attention."

The princess looked up at the man, her beautifully blue eyes locking with his.

"That is quite alright, Captain," the princess replied, "you have done more than enough for us already."

The captain bowed deeply, "Thank you for understanding, Princess. We wish you well on your journey, and good luck with your mission."

"Fair winds, Captain."

The Elven ship raised its sails once more and began to slowly make its way back out to sea.

The princess felt a tinge of sadness, but it was overwhelmed by elation at the prospect of finally escaping home after so many years that she couldn't help but smile.

"My Lady, we are ready," the lady-in-waiting approached.

The princess wiped the smile from her face and put on a serious expression before turning to her escorts. The four elvish soldiers stood ready at attention.

"I wish to thank all of you, as well; this will not be an easy journey," the princess said.

The elf who appeared to lead the soldiers saluted the princess. "We all volunteered for this, Your Highness. We will make sure you get to your destination!"

The princess let out a small sigh, releasing the tension in her shoulders before putting on a dazzling smile.

"Then shall we?"

CHAPTER 6

Onforde,
The City of Merchants

"Are you guys alright?!" Reginald yelled to us as we approached.

Both he and Myrril were standing next to the cart, and the missing horse, waving in our direction.

"A little singed, but yeah," I responded as we got a little closer.

Leone had already recalled her wolves and walked next to me with her spear against her shoulder.

On the walk back, she talked a little bit more about spiritualists, confirming many of my theories. Spiritualists form a type of pact or bond with a beast whose body is composed primarily of Megin. Normally, such creatures would be labeled as Abnormals, but they have been around longer than anyone can remember and are an intrinsic part of the world.

They are also very different from beast tamers. They tend to use force, magic, or selective breeding to tame beasts. Usually, they are used for transportation or for hunting down dangerous creatures, but Leone stated that many countries have been known to use them for war.

After taking a moment to reassure our companions that we were alright, we climbed back to our places on the cart and began to move forward once more.

"Hey, Elric. Can I ask you a question?" Reginald began.

"Go ahead," I said, tightening the straps on my armor.

"What was that thing?"

"It was a Storm Wolf. They are a pretty rare Vaettir, oh wait, I guess you call them Spirits. Anyway, they are a type of creature made up of Megin," I explained, "Storm Wolves are one of the Verndari, Vaettir who protect our world."

"So they are guardian spirits? That's pretty cool," Reginald mused. "But then why did it attack us? And why did you call it a Storm Wolf? It didn't look much like a wolf to me."

"They are made of pure Megin, meaning they can change their shape," I said. "We call them Storm Wolves because they most often take the shape of a wolf."

"This one seemed to like being a bear at first," Leone stated her observation.

"A-a bear?" Myrril gasped.

"Yeah, a pretty big one," I nodded, "As for why it attacked us, I'm not too certain, but I have a few theories."

"Such as?" Reginald asked.

"Well, for one, the Aleurian Empire used to revere them. They usually inhabited shrines made for them and often came and went as they pleased. Every year, we had a festival where people would make offerings to them, even when the shrines were empty," I explained. "Soldiers from around the country would approach the shrines on this day to be judged by the Vaettir. If the Vaettir liked them, they would initiate combat with the soldier, whose goal was to defeat the Vaettir. If they succeeded, the two would become partners for life."

"That's amazing," Reginald stated.

"I didn't know the Aleurians did that," Leone said.

"The Storm Wolf's shrine is probably nearby, deep in the forest," I continued. "Because nobody has ever seen it here, it was probably killed at some point in time. Perhaps even during the Aleurian civil war."

"Huh?"

"H-how could it be t-there if it was dead?" Myrril asked.

"Verndari, as with all Vaettir, are never truly killed. When they die, their body forms into a solid ball of Megin. Aleurian warriors who lost their partner would place the ball of Megin at a shrine for it to be reborn." I continued with the explanation, "The amount of time it takes for Vaettir to return to life varies, but it's usually predictable. Verndari, on the other hand, can't be predicted. They return at their own leisure."

"Could it have attacked us because it was no longer worshipped?" Leone wondered out loud.

"I doubt that. They aren't the vindictive type," I replied.

"Then why did it attack?" Reginald interjected.

"It could have been angry with the way Humans destroy and pervert nature," I said. "Don't get me wrong, the Aleurians did the same. However, they did it a little differently. There were a whole lot of ceremonies involved, and they usually got permission from the Vaettir."

"It saw us as a threat then?" Leone asked.

"Possibly, but I think it's more likely that it was searching for warriors. When it found someone it liked, it attacked them. It's something that would have been normal in my.... in the Aleurians' time, and if it went through a massive jump in time, then it wouldn't have known any better."

"Huh... so it was just confused..." Reginald mused.

After Reginald let that slip, everyone got quiet as we processed the sad reality of the situation. The Storm Wolf had awoken at the abandoned shrine, confused and alone. The people it killed had just been in the wrong place at the wrong time.

Just after midday, we officially crossed the border into the territory of Onforde. The border itself was a simple wooden watchtower housing a pair of bored guards, a few movable barricades off to the side of the road, and a flag hanging from the tower.

The flag was very detailed. It depicted a small fortification on the edge of a body of water; the sun was depicted shining upon the water, and a small mountain range was depicted in the background.

According to Reginald, this was the flag of Onforde.

"Hey, Reginald," I asked after we passed the watchtower, "are all of your borders this lightly guarded?"

He turned his head in my direction, "Mostly. Only the major roads have border forts. Though that's just because of the alliance."

"So the outer borders of the alliance are better fortified?"

"Yeah, of course. We've had enough problems with the Imperium's raids to dump some money into it, "Reginald replied.

"About half of the members of the alliance share a border with an outside country," Leone added. "Mellgarde, Edren, and Onforde are the only ones who don't."

"I see," I responded, "I haven't gotten a good look at any maps of the area, so I wasn't sure."

"Most maps are military secrets," Reginald informed me. "If you find any civilian ones, they most likely won't be very accurate."

"Ah, that makes sense," I nodded.

The Aleurians also kept their maps secret, though mostly just the ones of our homeland. We didn't really worry about the occupied territories. I suppose I was simply used to having one because of my father's position. I remember spending hours staring at the well-documented map hanging on the wall in his study.

We reached the final village on our journey not long after we crossed the border. There were only a few dozen buildings, mostly buttressed against the river, with small fishing docks wound between them.

The people were kind, and the village head was cooperative, if not confused as to why a neighboring lord was checking up on them.

We took a look around and asked a few questions, but the only thing of note was a small cluster of shrines dedicated to the gods. When I asked, a villager said that their settlement was too small for a church. In all, we spent about an hour there before getting back on the road.

By now, the forest had opened up to a golden plain of wild grain scarcely dotted with small trees. The only signs of life were a handful of homesteads to the north near a tall pillar of black smoke where charcoal burners were hard at work.

"Whoa..." Reginald and Myrril gasped.

"Yeah, this is quite a view," I expressed with a nod.

"Onforde is surrounded by this field on one side and The Porteloch on the other," Leone said.

"What's that?" I asked.

"The lake," she replied simply, "You'll be able to see it soon."

Sure enough, after about forty-five more minutes, we crested over a small hill and were greeted with quite the sight.

Off in the distance was a body of water one could easily mistake for the ocean. The water disappeared over the horizon, making the far end of it impossible to see. Only the top halves of the mountain range that circled the valley could be seen on the far side.

On the shore in front of us, still a ways out, was a large half-circle wall of gray stone bisected by the Tungsten River.

Small plumes of white smoke rose from beyond the wall, and an impressive amount of movement could be seen on the road in front of the gates.

Reginald and Myrril were speechless.

"Holy crap!" I exclaimed, "That lake is massive! I grew up on an island, so I'm used to large bodies of water, but we're so far inland. This is insane!"

Leone let out a small laugh, "Yep, that right there are the two reactions people normally have when they see it for the first time."

"B-but, Elric," Myrril stuttered, "I thought y-you've been here before."

I shook my head, "Not this far east. The farthest I'd ever been before was Edren."

"O-oh..."

"I bet it's even bigger up close," Reginald nervously guessed.

"It definitely is if it looks that big from this far away," I responded.

"Yep," Leone said, "but we'll never make it there if we sit around here all day."

"Oh, right," I hadn't even noticed that we had stopped the horses to take in the sights.

I nudged them into a trot and said, "We still have a job to do, guys. We can rest when we get there."

"Right," Reginald nodded and retook his spot in front of the cart.

As we came closer to the walls, the activity became more apparent. Mixed in with carts carrying farming goods and people traveling on foot were massive merchant caravans made up of dozens of wagons and tens of guards. There were so many that they drowned out the people visiting from the surrounding villages.

They were all in a pair of lines heading toward the massive wooden gate set into the wall. One line was filled with the previously mentioned merchant caravans as well as some smaller groups of people looking to sell their wares. The second line seemed to be for visitors, and it was moving much faster than the first.

"Hey, Leone," I turned my head to look at her, "do we have to wait in that line with the merchants since we have a cart?"

"No, thank the gods, we don't," she replied. "That line has to have all of its cargo inspected for contraband. Since we aren't selling anything, we wait in the other line."

"Got it, just checking," I maneuvered our cart to the back of the visitor's line and noticed that some of the others had carts as well, I just couldn't see them because they were blocked by the caravans.

While the line we were moving in was definitely faster, there were still a lot of people, so we ended up talking to pass the time.

"Is this gate usually like this?" I asked Leone.

"Yeah, but this one is the least busy," she responded nonchalantly.

"Huh?" Reginald and I simultaneously let out.

"The southern and northern gates see a lot more traffic because of how many goods the merchants still have," she explained. "This gate here, the western gate, doesn't take as long because the merchants have already been through at least two other major cities along the way."

"I see they call it the city of merchants for a reason," I muttered.

"An accurate nickname, by all accounts," Leone confirmed.

"How are you doing, Myrril?" I remembered how nervous Myrril could be around people and turned my head to check on her. She had shrunken to make herself as small as possible and covered her head with a blanket.

When I asked her how she was doing, she let out a little squeak in surprise.

"T-there are s-so many p-people here..." she said in a small voice.

"Just take a deep breath and try to calm yourself. Nobody is here to judge you; they are all as tired as we are from traveling," I tried to make her feel better.

"It's true," Leone jumped in, "and if anyone tries to mess with you, I'll knock their teeth in."

She let out an unnerving smile when she spoke about hitting someone, but Myrril seemed to respond well to it.

Then, Reginald came up to the side of the cart and ripped the blanket off of her head, "And take that blanket off, you'll get heatstroke."

"H-hey!" Myrril shouted at him.

"You didn't have to do it like that, Reginald," I scolded.

"Seriously?" Reginald raised an eyebrow. "Ever since we got out of the forest, it's felt like my armor is melting."

"Still, you should apologize."

Reginald sighed, "Yeah, you're right."

He turned to Myrril, "Sorry about that. I just didn't want you to get sick."

Myrril was pouting with her arms crossed.

"Well, there's a bright side to all of this," Leone smiled. "She isn't worrying about people seeing her anymore."

I looked at her as I felt a smile form across my face. Within a few moments, all of us were laughing. I don't know if it was because it was particularly funny, or if we were just releasing the tension, but the other people in line must have thought we were mad.

By the time we made it through the gate, the sun had begun to set, sending the horizon into a brilliant orange light. Luckily, we showed the guards our Association Medals, and after a quick glance in the back of our cart, they let us through without issue.

As soon as we made it into the city proper, I could tell the differences between Onforde and Edren.

All of the streets were paved with flagstone and laid out in an orderly fashion. There were several people on ladders lighting wrought iron lamp posts in preparation for the night.

The buildings lining either side of the main road were all several stories tall and made of red brick. The first floors were all storefronts, while the second and the occasional third floors were residences.

Even while the sun was setting, there were about as many people out as there were in Edren during midday.

"Do you guys already have somewhere to stay?" Leone asked.

"No," I turned my head so she could hear, "we were going to look for a place to stay once we got here."

"Of course you were," Leone sounded disappointed. "Well, you'll never find a place to stay this late. How about you crash at my place?"

"Are you sure?" I wasn't against accepting her offer, but I wanted to make sure she was okay with it.

"I wouldn't have offered if I weren't," she shrugged.

I looked at Reginald, and he nodded.

"Alright," I responded to Leone, "but first we need to board the horses and cart. Know anywhere nearby?"

"Yeah, it's not far," Leone hopped over the front of the cart and sat next to me on the bench.

She directed us down a road and to a large building with a horse carved above the door. The prices were acceptable, so we paid to have the horses put up for a few days.

Before we knew it, Leone was leading us down several side streets and through alleys, past the glamorous main street and into the more modest neighborhoods of somewhat less cramped buildings.

As the night drew closer, fewer and fewer people were seen out and about, but it seemed that Onforde had its own nightlife, and the streets were never deserted.

Leone stopped in front of a modest one-and-a-half-story house with a rooftop balcony and a small garden in front.

"Wait a moment," Reginald confronted Leone, "this is yours?"

"Does that really surprise you?" she asked. "I am five years older than you."

"W-what?" Myrril said in surprise, "Y-you're twenty-two?"

"That I am," Leone smiled amusingly, "but to answer your question, it's not mine. It's owned by a couple who retired to the countryside. They didn't want to sell this house, so they rented it out instead."

"Ah, yeah," Reginald nodded, "that makes more sense."

"What? You didn't think she could own a house?" I teased.

No, it's not.... That's not what I... I just mean, he stumbled on his words. It's just hard to imagine Leone buying a house.

"I feel the same way," Leone laughed. "Anyway, it's getting late. How about we continue talking inside?"

"Sounds good," I responded.

Leone approached the door and took a metal key from her pocket. She unlocked the door and walked right in, and the rest of us followed.

Before we could even close the door behind us, all four of us heard the pattering of footsteps rushing toward us from the back of the house.

Reginald, Myrril, and I braced for combat while Leone stood calmly, almost too calmly. I glanced at her only to see the biggest smile to have graced her face in our company.

Not but a moment later, we found out why.

"Leone!"

"Leone's back!"

A pair of voices preceded two small figures appearing from around a corner and latching onto Leone.

"Oh, I missed you guys, too." Leone knelt down and wrapped her arms around the two figures.

One of them was a lanky boy with scruffy hair around the age of twelve, while the other was a young girl with similarly disheveled hair who seemed to be around ten years old.

"K-kids!?!?" Reginald shouted in surprise while Myrril just stared with her jaw on the floor.

I gave a wry smile, "Okay, now this, I was not expecting."

As we stood there awkwardly, two pairs of brown eyes popped over the top of Leone.

"Who are they, Leone?" the boy asked quietly but quickly.

"Yeah, Leone. Who are they?" the girl mimicked, but much louder.

"These are my friends, and they needed a place to stay tonight," Leone explained, and she stood up.

The young boy gave me a wary look for a moment from behind Leone while the young girl dashed up to me.

"Hi," she looked up at me with a bright smile, "what's your name?"

"I'm Elric." I knelt down. "And who are you?"

"Oh, I'm Penny," she cheerfully said, "that's short for Penelope!"

"Well, hello, Penny. It's nice to meet you." I held out my hand and she took it in her own, wildly shaking it up and down.

Then, she dashed over to Reginald, completely ignoring Myrril between us.

"Hi. What's your name?" She went through the same process as she did with me.

"Come on, Jackson, introduce yourself," Leone pushed him.

The boy, Jackson, just stood behind Leone, staring at us.

His eyes darted between the three of us and Penny as if he couldn't decide on who to look at. He wiggled his feet around restlessly, and his arms and hands constantly twitched. His hyperactivity made him look like he was shaking, but it seemed to be that he was trying to hold himself back.

"Fine," Leone sighed and looked back at us. "This is Jackson. He's a little hyper, but he's a good kid."

I smiled and nodded at him, "Hello, Jackson."

His head snapped toward me as he looked me up and down.

"Penny," Leone called, and she broke off from talking to Reginald.

"Yes, Leone?" she said slightly louder than she should have.

"Have you and your brother already eaten dinner?" Leone asked.

"Mhm," Penny rocked back and forth.

"Awesome," Leone said, "then I think it's time for bed, isn't it?"

"Aww," Penny whined, "but you just got back."

Jackson nodded furiously.

Leone sighed again before smiling once more, "You can spend the night in my room if you want."

The kids cheered and ran up the staircase just to our left.

"I'll be up there soon!" Leone called after them.

She turned to us, "Alright, how about I whip something up for us?"

"Yeah, that sounds good," Reginald said.

"Do you need any help?" I offered.

"Nah, I think I got it," Leone said before heading into the kitchen.

The three of us dropped our bags by the door, then Reginald and I removed our armor while Myrril sat at the table. We followed shortly.

After a little bit, a wonderful smell wafted from the kitchen, and Leone brought us a hearty soup and a loaf of bread.

We were too enraptured by the food to speak during the meal, so we waited until afterward.

"Man, that was great!" Reginald patted his stomach.

"Y-yeah," Myrril agreed.

I leaned back in my chair. "I agree."

"Why, thank you," Leone smiled.

"By the way," I sat straight and looked Leone in the eyes, "I have a question about Penny and Jackson."

"Oh, they aren't mine," Leone said as if knowing what we were going to ask. "They're street urchins that I took in a couple of years ago."

"Ah," all three of us said in unison.

Leone sighed sadly as she recalled the past. "They had a rough childhood. Their mother died not long after Penny was born, and they never had a father. They had to do whatever they could to survive."

She looked through the open doorway and toward the stairs. "They were used by many unsavory folks, and it left an impression on them both. Jackson takes a long time to trust and has a habit of searching for escape routes in unfamiliar situations. That, along with his hyper nature, makes people judge him."

"What about Penny?" I asked.

"She never had any friends, and her only companion was her brother," Leone explained, "so whenever she sees a guy, she likes to latch onto them, even if they aren't always too friendly."

"Man, that..." Reginald couldn't seem to find the words he was looking for.

"Yeah, that sucks." I was unable to relate to their lives, but recent events made it easier for me to understand how they must have felt.

"Well, it's all in the past," Leone's face became cheery once more. "Right now, we should focus on the future! First order of business, sleeping arrangements."

"What do you mean?" Reginald asked.

"Well, we only have one guest room," Leone said.

"Oh, is that all?" I asked. "Myrril will take it. Reginald and I will crash in the living room."

"Huh?" Myrril looked surprised, "I-is that all right?"

Reginald nodded, "Yeah, I thought the same thing."

"We have bedrolls so we can sleep anywhere," I added.

"B-but..." Myrril started before being cut off by Leone.

"That sorts it then," she said. "I'll show Myrril to her room."

Leone grabbed Myrril's arm. "See you guys in the morning!"

"W-wait... I–" Myrril tried to say something but was dragged off by Leone.

"Poor Myrril," I said, "she's always getting dragged into things."

Reginald shook his head, "No, she's just too timid to express herself."

"I wish she had a bit more self-confidence," I mused.

"You and me both."

We turned to look at each other and let out a chuckle.

"All right, we should get some shut-eye as well," Reginald said, pulling a pair of bedrolls from our packs.

"Yeah, we have to meet with the Lord of Onforde tomorrow, right?"

"Merchant Elect," Reginald corrected, "but it's the equivalent of a lord."

"Ah, right. I remember someone calling him by that title." I laid my bedroll on the floor.

We talked a little bit longer as we got ready to sleep but eventually called it a night.

The air was heavy.

I opened my eyes in an unfamiliar place.

Trees. Expanding infinitely in all directions were blackened trees grasping for the sky like skeletal hands.

The ground was covered in long-dead leaves and twigs. There were no animals in sight, not even the chirping of birds one would usually find in a forest.

The only sound was the howling moan of the wind carrying the sorrow of the dead forest.

Snap!

I turned my head toward the noise, but it felt like I was moving through molasses.

Not far from me, running deeper into the woods, was a young girl with long blonde hair and pointed ears. The hem of her green dress was dirtied as she ran across the ground in a similarly slow motion as I.

"Wait!" I tried to call out to her, but she didn't react.

I willed my body to move through whatever was slowing me down and to chase after her.

No matter how hard I tried, I never seemed to get any closer.

Then, she curved around a tree.

I moved to intercept, but instead of a young girl running on the other side, it was a woman. She was slightly taller than I, but she had the same golden hair and elongated ears.

Something about her rang bells in my mind.

I knew her.

I knew who she was, but I couldn't find a name. No matter how hard I searched my memory, it felt just out of reach.

I reached out toward her and used all my might to push forward even faster.

"Who are you!?" I called out, my voice warping through the misty air.

She stopped, her head turning slowly.

A moment before my hand reached her, she seemed to slowly melt as she turned into a white mist that blew away in the wind.

Then, my eyes opened for real.

I was lying on the floor in Leone's house, breathing heavily. The sight of the woman turning to mist, just beyond my reach, had burned itself into my mind.

I never saw her face.

CHAPTER 7

Chasing Down Leads

I couldn't get back to sleep after the nightmare. I stayed up all night thinking about it and how different it was from the others. There had never been a familiar face before, nor had there ever been unfamiliar surroundings.

Eventually, I couldn't stand staring at the ceiling anymore and quietly snuck out the door, careful not to wake anybody.

Once outside, I took a deep breath of the cool night air. The sky was shining with countless stars dazzling like gems. It was somehow different, but the same as the sky I knew over Aleuria.

I sat on the ground on my knees and held my sheathed sword in front of me; The darkness of night making it difficult to see the plain scabbard in my hand. I set it down in front of me and closed my eyes.

I concentrated inward, focusing on the flow of Megin within my body. As I had become more and more attuned to myself since escaping from Kyrtvale, I began to feel a strange aura around my Megin. I did not know what it was, but I knew that I would eventually find out.

As I continued to focus inward, I also opened my senses to the outside world. I could hear the faint rustling of grass, the dripping of water, and the light breathing of my companions within the house.

I locked onto that feeling and reached my hand out to grasp my weapon.

As my hand my contact with the grip, I tensed every muscle in my body and flooded them with Megin.

I let out a deep breath as I opened my eyes and slowly got to my feet using only my legs.

I drew my sword, revealing the blade that grows thinner in the middle and thicker on either end. The light of the largest moon reflected off the decorated fuller as I brought it above my head.

The training technique I had started was called Motion. Its goal was to stress your muscles and Megin to the max while going through practice motions. This would not only build muscle memory and control but also increase your flow of Megin at the same time.

I went through the slow and methodical process of Motion until I could no longer hold my form and collapsed to my knees, drenched in sweat.

W-what was that? I asked myself while breathing heavily. *Is that the best you can do?*

I held Motion for less time than in Edren, probably because of my lack of focus. The dream was still flooding my head with images that I had hoped Motion would help me control.

No use, I said to myself before stumbling back to my feet.

I walked over to a nearby well and wiped myself off with a damp cloth, just as my stomach gave a loud request for food.

The sky had begun to lighten on the horizon.

"Guess I should make something to eat," I sighed and made my way back inside quietly.

We still had provisions from our travels, and I kept some ingredients in my pocket dimension to keep them fresh, so I was able to make a decent meal.

Not long after I started, Reginald walked into the kitchen, rubbing his eyes.

"You're up early," he said groggily.

"Yeah," I smiled, "I wanted to make something since we had a proper kitchen to work with."

I didn't want to worry him with my problems, so I left that part out.

"It will be done soon, so why don't you go sit at the table?" I suggested.

"Yeah, that sounds good."

Reginald left the kitchen and was soon replaced by Myrril, who had yet to put on her robe, so I was a little shocked to see her in normal clothes.

She wiped the sleep out of her eyes. "Morning."

"Good morning, Myrril," I said, ignoring the fact that she wasn't stuttering. I guessed that she probably just didn't care when she was tired.

"What 'cha making?" she mumbled.

"Some breakfast," I answered. "It will be done soon, so why don't you go sit at the table? Reginald's already there."

"Mhm," she gave a sound of affirmation and shifted off to the other room.

A few minutes later, I had finally finished everything and had begun moving it all to the table.

"Wha–" Leone was startled when she came down the stairs. "What's all this?"

Set out on the table was an array of dishes. There was a pot of porridge made from barley and oats, as well as a side of sliced apples and berries to be added. Next to that was a plate of chicken that I had grilled over a fire, and rye bread baked with honey for taste. It was a traditional Aleurian breakfast made with whatever ingredients I had.

"I made breakfast," I smiled.

"Yeah, and it smells really good," Reginald said as his stomach let out an audible growl.

Myrril groaned in agreement with her face resting on the table.

"Oh, you didn't need to–" Leone was interrupted by the pattering of feet racing down the stairs.

Pushing past Leone and into the dining room was Jackson, his eyes wide and darting restlessly between the dishes.

"Whoa..." he let out.

From behind him, coming down the stairs, was Penelope.

"Wait for me, Jackson!" she whined.

She took her place next to her brother, and her jaw dropped.

Leone looked down at them and smiled, "Well? Go on, take a seat."

The kids happily sped to the table and hopped into their seats. Both of them were excited, but Jackson took the cake. He was hopping up and down in his seat, his eyes darting from the food to Leone.

"Go on, you two. You don't have to wait for us," I glanced at Leone to give her permission.

The two kids also turned to her.

"You heard him," she smiled, "go ahead and eat."

They let out a cheer and began to dig into their breakfast.

"I'm sorry about their manners," Leone apologized as she sat down at the table.

"No worries," I waved it off. "Everyone else can eat as well."

We all began to eat our breakfast. The chicken was good and the bread was sweet, but the porridge was a little bland. Though that's why I set out the berries and apples, to add a bit of sweetness to it.

"I know I set out those berries, but does anyone want some of these?" I pulled out a small pouch full of bright blue berries and dropped some into my porridge.

"Whoa, wait!" Reginald jumped up from his seat and

slammed his hands on the table. "Don't eat those! Where did you get them?"

I was a little surprised by his accusatory tone and strange reaction, but I responded anyway.

"I got them from the forest, why?"

"Hold up," Leone jumped to her feet as well. "Are those what I think they are?"

"Yeah, they are Blunor Berries," he said to Leone before turning back to me. "They are extremely poisonous!"

"What do you mean?" I was unable to hide my confusion. "I've been eating these for weeks."

"WHAT!?" Leone and Reginald both shouted and ran over to me.

"Are you feeling anything strange?"

"Does your stomach hurt?"

"Is your hair falling out?"

"Are you coughing up blood?"

Along with the barrage of questions came poking and prodding and tugging on my hair.

I grabbed both of their hands and lightly pushed them away, standing from my seat.

"Enough!" I shouted with annoyance. "What is this all about?"

"I-I don't get it," Leone said. "Anyone who eats a Blunor Berry dies within the hour. How could you have been eating them for weeks?"

Reginald smiled wryly, "Is this another one of your crazy abilities?"

"I have no idea what you are talking about. See?"

I grabbed a handful of the berries and tossed them into my mouth while the three of them stared at me wide-eyed.

"See," I said, "I'm fine."

Leone slumped back into her chair with a bewildered expression, "I just don't get it..."

"Leone," Penny piped up, "can I have one of those berries?"

Jackson lightly hit her shoulder, "No, stupid. They'll kill you."

"Hey," Leone snapped, "don't call your sister that."

"S-sorry, Leone," Jackson shrank back.

Leone turned to Penny, "But he is right, those berries are extremely deadly."

Penny crossed her arms and pouted, "But how come he's fine?"

Leone glanced at me from the corner of her eye, "He's.... a unique case, I guess."

After breakfast, Leone gave us directions to the Merchant Elect's home and told us she would be heading to the Association branch after she spent some time with the kids. We also talked for a little bit about the city and the best way to get around.

Just as Leone had said, the streets of Onforde were packed with people despite the morning hours. We were shoulder to shoulder with all manner of races, mostly human, as we moved through the streets. The crowd often had to push even closer together to make way for a train of wagons to pass through.

There were points where we could only navigate using tall landmarks such as church steeples.

The voices of individuals melted together into a cacophony of unintelligible gibberish that only resembled words.

"Leone was right," Reginald raised his voice to speak over the crowd, "there was no way we would have gotten the cart through here."

"Yeah," I shouted back before looking toward Myrril. "How are you doing, Myrril?"

She had her head down as she held onto the back of Reginald's armor, allowing him to lead her forward as I took up the rear. It's possible that she responded, but I was unable to hear so if she did.

"I think she's okay," said Reginald, "but how about you, Elric?"

"Me?" I asked.

"How are your ears?" he clarified. "You have sensitive hearing, right?"

My people had much more sensitive hearing compared to humans. Our relatively impressive senses, once seen as a blessing, were revealed to be more of a curse in the human world.

"I'm okay," I replied. "It was pretty loud in Tors, so I should be able to get used to this."

Despite saying this, I could already feel a headache developing.

After wading through the crowds for a little bit longer, we arrived at one of the four well-built stone bridges within the city that allow for easy crossing of the Tungsten River.

As we crossed over the bridge, we stopped for a moment to observe barges laden with trade goods pass beneath us.

The opposite side was surprisingly less crowded, allowing us to take a bit of a breather. Not only were the people on this side mostly dressed better, but the shops seemed to be more expensive, as well.

As we made our way down the street, we passed by many of these shops selling a wide variety of high-quality goods. We saw furniture stores, smiths, jewelers, and much more.

Past that, we soon came upon private residences and an increased guard presence. They were dressed much like the guards of Edren but carried symbols of Onforde on their armor.

Not long after, the well-made brick houses turned into manors and full-on estates complete with high fences and personal guards.

"Wow," Reginald stared at the buildings with wonder in his eyes, "there are some big homes in Edren, but nothing like this."

"T-they are really n-nice," Myrril agreed.

Now that Reginald had pointed it out, I realized the lack of manors in Edren. Even in the Inner District, all of the homes were modestly sized and of the same design.

The architecture of these manors caught my eye. Despite being unfamiliar to me, as was the usual around here, I could spot many design features that seemed to be taken from Aleurian architecture. I suppose you could call it a Neo-Aleurian style of construction.

The buildings used plentiful arches and pillars, as was the standard of my people, but I also noticed that many of the carved decorations were blended in a way I had only seen in Elven architecture before. It wasn't nearly as good as the elves did it, but it was still very impressive.

"I like them," I said. "They remind me of home, just a little."

I reminisced as we walked, and soon we made it to an oblong fork in the road. According to Leone, it was the result of a land dispute between merchants. Neither side wanted to have less land than the other, so the road couldn't be moved to better fit the area.

Anyways, we took a left at the fork and headed up a slight incline, passing a few more structures before arriving in front of a grand estate.

A tall fence surrounded the multiple buildings that encompassed the estate. The main structure was by far the most impressive. The white stone building was made in a similar, if not more grandiose, style as the other manors.

It wasn't on the level of ostentatious, but the building spoke with a glance. It was all but obvious that someone important lived here.

We could already see several heavily armed guards stationed around the grounds, as well as a few patrolling with dogs. One of the two guards stationed at the front of the wrought-iron gate spotted us and whispered something to the other.

When we changed our direction toward the gate, the first guard called out to us.

"That's close enough!" His voice was deep and clear. "This is not some tourist destination, you had best turn yourselves around."

All three of us stopped in our tracks. I let the shock show on my face as I turned to Reginald, who was equally surprised.

"I mean, I know we don't look like official envoys, but..." I whispered.

"Yeah," he whispered back, "I get the feeling they are a little on edge."

I couldn't help but wonder if it had anything to do with the attempted assassination of their lord, the Merchant Elect, before realizing that it was a stupid question.

"My apologies, good sirs, but we are not tourists. We are–" I started to explain to the guards before I was cut off.

"It matters not!" The two guards lowered their halberds toward us. "Clear off before we arrest you!"

"What?" I blurted out in surprise. I genuinely didn't think they would simply ignore my attempts at an explanation.

The two guards began to march forward, using their halberds to try and force us back.

Reginald thought quicker than I in this situation and pulled out the letter we had received from his father.

"I am Reginald Lee Aulcrest, Son of Samuel Aulcrest, Lord

of Edren," he shouted at them with a commanding tone that was very unlike him. "We were sent as an envoy of Edren to address the Merchant Elect. This letter explains our mission, personally given to us by the Lord of Edren and current chairman of the Valtion-Silma City State Alliance."

After Reginald made such a statement, the two guards stopped in their tracks and gave each other a sidelong glance.

"Approach," the guard who hadn't yet spoken ordered, "but only you."

With his hands still in the air, Reginald gently approached the two men and held out the letter. The guard grabbed it and gestured for Reginald to step back.

Once he had returned to our side, the guard glanced over the letter and carefully opened it in such a way as to not break the seal. His eyes widened as he read over it, and then he showed it to his fellow guard, the one who had first addressed us, and whispered something to him.

The first guard sighed and headed into the gate with the letter.

"Apologies, Envoys of Edren." The remaining guard lowered his head slightly. "As you can imagine, we have been on edge since the attempted assassination."

"That is quite alright," Reginald held up his hand. "We understand your circumstances and hope to help."

The guard lowered his head once more and returned to his post.

"Hey, Reginald," I started to ask as we waited, "I didn't know your father was the leader of the Alliance."

"Really?" he asked, surprised, "I thought you'd have looked into all of that by now."

"Yeah, well," I shrugged, "I've been a little busy lately."

"I can briefly explain it then," Reginald said. "Every year, the Alliance chairman changes from one member to the next. This year, my father is the chairman. He is in charge of directing how the Alliance does business as well as settling disputes between members."

"I'm impressed," I said. "He didn't look like he was juggling so much work."

"Yeah," Reginald agreed, "even I'm not sure how he does it."

Myrril tapped on Reginald and pointed, "H-he's back."

We looked where she was pointing and saw the guard returning from the main structure.

"That was fast," I remarked.

Reginald nodded in agreement.

The guard opened the gate, "Please, follow me. The Merchant Elect will see you."

We followed the guard down an impressively decorated hallway. The walls had beautiful paintings and silver sconces over the top of a pleasing blue wallpaper. The wall to our left was broken up by windows as clear as crystal, peering out into a well-kept garden of countless flowers. From the ceiling were many awe-inspiring chandeliers hanging at a set interval, and the carpet beneath our boots was seemingly made of only the finest material.

The guard stopped at a gilded door and gestured for us to enter.

"Please, wait here. The Merchant Elect will be with you shortly."

We thanked the guard and entered a gaudy waiting room reserved for only the most distinguished of guests. A crystal chandelier hung above the most comfortable-looking couches arranged around a table set with hot tea. There was a large bookshelf in the back of the room filled with old tomes, many of which were not written in the common tongue. Set upon the mantle of a cold fireplace were delicate vases of immeasurable value, and a massive painting depicting the settlement of a city on the edge of a lake hung on the wall above them.

The door closed behind us.

Each of us stood in place, taking in the room of priceless décor.

"W-what is this?" Reginald asked nobody in particular.

I couldn't help but let out an uncertain smile. "This seems to be the room used to meet foreign dignitaries."

"B-but why us?" He was clearly frazzled.

"I mean, we ARE foreign dignitaries... in a sense," I said.

Despite being part of the same alliance, both Onforde and Edren are independent states. Since we announced ourselves as Envoys of Edren, we are being treated the same as they would an envoy of a nation outside the alliance.

"It's okay," I gave Reginald a teasing pat on the back, "just don't break anything."

"What?" he froze as I walked past him.

"Come on," I said, lowering myself onto one of the couches, we don't know how long we have to wait, so we might as well get comfortable.

Myrril was the first to give in, surprisingly, and sat next to me on the couch. As soon as she hit the seat, she let out a gasp.

I smiled, "I know, feels like clouds, doesn't it?"

She nodded, "T-this is amazing."

I picked up one of the teacups and gave it a waft. It had a bit of a sweet smell to it, coupled with another scent that I couldn't quite discern. Though it was of no surprise, I wasn't much of a tea person.

The tea was bitter, as I had expected, but the aftertaste had some sweetness to it. Still, it wasn't to my taste, so I set it back down.

Myrril, however, seemed to enjoy it.

From near the door, Reginald let out a sigh and drooped his head.

"Alright," he said, "scoot over."

We made room for him on the couch. With him on my right and Myrril on my left, I was now firmly in the middle of our group.

Reginald also partook of the refreshments and commented on their sweetness, to which Myrril agreed. I couldn't quite understand what they thought about it was sweet, but I wasn't going to criticize their personal preferences simply because they differed from mine.

After a surprisingly short period, the door to the room opened once more.

Entering were two men, both dressed in the finest of attire. The man in front had on an earth-tone coat over a red vest. His brown hair was combed to the side, and a pair of spectacles sat upon his nose.

The second man was a little bit taller, wearing a long blue coat with ruffled white cuffs. He had short black hair parted on the side, and a small, curled mustache graced his upper lip.

Behind the two men were a pair of guards carrying short swords for close combat engagements, and a tired-looking scribe. The guards moved into position on either side of the room, while the scribe set up on a small writing desk in the corner.

The man with the glasses sat on the couch across from us while the one with the mustache stood behind him.

"Greetings, Envoys of Edren," the man with the glasses

spoke with slightly guttural R's and a lack of stress in each word, something I had come to learn was indicative of the people of Faeron.

"I am Jean-Luc Pierre, Merchant Elect of Onforde," he continued, "and this is Hans Zerrick, the Head Administrator."

The Head Administrator respectfully nodded his head.

"I have read the letter from Lord Samuel, however, I believe it best to introduce yourselves regardless," Jean-Luc gestured toward us.

Reginald responded, "Of course, Merchant Elect. I am Reginald Lee Aulcrest. The man to my right is Elric Wolfram Tors, and next to him sits Myrril Delahaye."

"Welcome, Reginald, Elric, and Myrril. Let us get down to business." Jean-Luc put his hands together, "You wish to know about the assassination attempt a few weeks ago, yes?"

"We do," Reginald responded.

"Then I shall explain what occurred," he started.

"About nineteen days ago, during the dead of night, three masked figures broke into the manor we were in. After meeting no resistance outside, they made their way into the manor, where they killed three of the guards and gravely wounded a fourth. Then, they entered one of the studies and killed my body double. They somehow got in and out of the grounds without raising the alarm." Jean-Luc grimaced. "It took over ten minutes to discover any of the bodies. If it wasn't for the surviving guard, I doubt we would have figured out what had happened."

"Do you think there is a traitor in your midst?" Reginald leaned forward.

"We looked into it but were unable to find any proof," the Head Administrator spoke up with sharpened vowels.

"It is as Hans says. To be frank, the investigation has come to a standstill," Jean-Luc confirmed.

I was satisfied with his explanation of the events, but there was one more thing on my mind.

"Merchant Elect, if I may," I waited for him to gesture for me to continue. "May I ask, why was it that these assassins killed your body double? Where were you at that time?"

"Ah, yes, well," Jean-Luc smiled in slight embarrassment, "I was out taking an evening stroll at the time."

"Against my advisement," the Head Administrator added.

"Yes, well, I am grateful that I ignored your advice that night," Jean-Luc teased.

The Head Administrator did not seem amused at this.

"Thank you for the explanation," I respectfully lowered my head.

"It is no trouble," Jean-Luc waved it off. "However, I have a question of my own. Lord Samuel seems to believe a group of mercenaries was involved. Do you feel the same?"

"We do" Reginald stated. "They are called Lost Light. We worked with them for not but a few hours before they took their chance to ambush us. It is a long story, but the similarities are striking."

Jean-Luc leaned back in his seat and looked to be thinking, "Lost Light... Lost Light. Where have I heard that before?"

He turned his head to look up at the Head Administrator, who shook his head.

Then, the scribe spoke up.

"Merchant Elect, sir, Lost Light was the group that defeated the Gorodian Crab a few weeks ago."

A light went off in Jean-Luc's head, "That's right!"

"Ah, yes, now I remember the group you speak of," the Head Administrator said. "It was a group of three, if I remember correctly."

"And they were here during the correct time frame," Jean-

Luc added. "Yes, I can see how this could be connected. We should investigate at once."

"Please, allow us to follow this lead." Reginald stood and bowed to the Merchant Elect.

"Are you certain?" Jean-Luc asked.

"We are," Reginald affirmed. "It is our task to investigate Lost Light and to mitigate any damages they may have caused. I believe this falls under our purview."

"Hm, what do you think, Hans?" Jean-Luc asked.

"I see no issue with this. If the lead turns out to be tangible, then they will have helped us greatly. If it proves to be a dead end, we won't have wasted our own resources to discover it," the Head Administrator gave his thoughts.

"Yes, I suppose we can look at it that way." Jean-Luc turned back to us, "You have our permission to operate within the city. I suggest stopping by the Association branch, they are the ones who posted the extermination request at our behest."

"I see," Reginald nodded, "then, I believe we best be off."

Reginald stood from his seat, and Myrril and I followed.

"Thank you for your assistance, Merchant Elect." Reginald slightly bowed his head before turning to leave.

"Ah, one more thing," Jean-Luc said, stopping us. "If you wish, we would be happy to provide accommodations on the manor grounds."

Reginald turned his head toward me, his face plastered in question.

I shook my head slightly. While I couldn't communicate my reasoning now, I'm sure Reginald knew we would have less autonomy if we stayed here.

He turned back to the Merchant Elect. We thank you for your invitation but respectfully have to decline.

"Are you certain?" Jean-Luc asked. "We have a lovely guest house."

"We are," Reginald gave a polite smile.

Jean-Luc sighed, "Very well then. I look forward to an update on your progress."

Reginald once again gave a polite nod and turned to leave, with Myrril and myself in tow. As we left, out of the corner of my eye, I saw the Head Administrator's shoulders drop slightly as the tension in the room eased.

CHAPTER 8

Gorodian Crab

The Association building in Onforde was similar in size to the one in Edren, but its material was vastly different. The walls were made of an almost tan stone, and the roof was quite odd. The aged copper slanted at a steep angle before leveling off almost completely, with rounded windows set in the slope, making the attic a usable third-floor space.

Above the set of heavy oaken doors at the front of the building were the words The Wensworth Association for Wayward Souls in a beautifully carved motif.

"Is it just me," Reginald started, "or does this place look a lot nicer than the one back home?"

"I-I was thinking the same," Myrril stuttered.

"Yeah," I said, still staring at the building, "it's a very interesting style, to say the least."

The architecture wasn't bad in my opinion, but it was so odd I couldn't help but feel that something was off. Though when I looked back at our trip through the city, I realized that several other buildings were of the same style.

Pushing that thought away for the moment, I turned to my companions.

"Shall we go inside then?"

We probably looked a little strange standing in the middle of the road, staring at the building.

"Oh, uh. Yeah," Reginald replied, "but first, what exactly should our plan be?"

Myrril tilted her head to the side, "A-aren't we just going in and a-asking about Lost Light?"

"I mean, I suppose we can be straightforward about it," Reginald responded.

"You were thinking of another way?" I asked.

"No," he shook his head. "I just didn't know if we needed to be particularly careful about what we ask."

"Hm, good point." I thought for a moment, asking myself about the possible repercussions of not being delicate with the matter. The news was already out about Lost Light, and they were dead, so we couldn't incur their wrath. I supposed that the only thing would be tying members of the Association to the attempted assassination of the Merchant Elect, but the Association had already denounced them, so it was a tough one.

"No, I don't think we will have much of an issue," I said. "Let's just not make any accusations out in the foyer. We don't want to make a scene."

"Sounds good," Reginald responded, with Myrril nodding in affirmation.

"Alright then, let's go."

Reginald and Myrril followed behind me as I grasped the handle to the Association building and opened the surprisingly heavy doors. The sight that greeted me was similar to the Association building in Edren.

The floors were made of gray marble and polished to a shine. Instead of wood rafters, the vaulted ceiling was supported by stone columns that ran up the walls and into beautiful arches. Brass chandeliers hung from the ceiling at set points in order to efficiently light the room, and a long reception area that resembled a tellers desk sat at the opposite end of the room from the front doors.

And one other detail. The interior was packed.

Massive lines ran from the reception area almost to the doors we had just opened. Every chair and bench was taken by waiting mercenaries, while many people simply stood and chatted. It was at least as loud as a tavern during an evening festival.

"Gods, why does this whole city have to be so damned loud," I muttered to myself.

"What was that?" Reginald asked.

I turned to him, "Oh, I was just saying that we should get in line."

"Good idea, we don't want it to get any busier," Reginald said, "Come on, Myrril."

He gently took Myrril by the arm and guided her forward as she went into her turtle mode. I called it that because she hid in her robes and looked at the floor, relying on one of us to guide her.

When we got into line, I had hoped that it looked worse than it was, but then I got a glance at the receptionists frantically running back and forth behind the desk and realized that it would probably be a while.

"Tsk. They've never taken this long before," the man in front of us grumbled.

He was fitted in light combat gear, carrying a round wooden shield called a Targe in one hand and a polished but well-used spear in the other.

"This does seem particularly bad, even for such a crowded city," I mused.

The man in front turned around to face me. He seemed to be in his early thirties and had a scar running down the side of his chin and neck.

"You don't know the half of it, bud," he said in his gruff tone. "Apparently, some team came through a few weeks ago and said they'd take out a beast in the lake, but I guess they never did it. Just took the payment and left."

"Whoa, really?"

"That's what I heard, but the Association hasn't said

anything about it." The man squinted his eyes and took another look at the three of us.

Come to think about it, I don't think I've seen you folks here before. Just got into town? he asked.

"Yeah, yesterday," I replied.

"How've you been liking our fair city?" He gave a wide grin.

"It's very pretty," I said, "but also really loud."

The man let out a hearty chuckle, "It's true. Our city is quite a noisy place, but you get used to it after a while. Name's Zade. "He stuck out his hand.

I grasped it with my own, "Elric. This here is Reginald, and the shy one is Myrril."

"Welcome to Onforde." He gave my hand one firm shake before releasing his grasp. "Where're you hailing from?"

"We work out of Edren."

"Ah, the center of the valley," Zade smiled, "but I've never heard an accent like yours, Elric. Were you born in another part of the continent?"

"Ah yeah," I had forgotten my accent was strange. "I come from much farther west."

Zade looked as though he was taking in the information, "Hm, I haven't been too far west yet. What's it like?"

"The buildings and people are different, but life moves forward all the same."

"I feel that, bud," Zade snorted, "I feel that."

While we were talking, the line had started to slowly creep forward, and new people had appeared behind us. After a few more minutes, Zade eventually turned back around when we ran out of things to chat about.

The wait was terribly boring and left me alone with my thoughts. Lucky for me, I wasn't alone with them for long.

"Hey, you guys got in line already. Smart," a familiar voice said from near the entrance.

I turned to see Leone, in her combat gear, smiling as she approached. She quickly joined us in line, eliciting glares from the people behind us.

"Hey, Leone," Reginald greeted her.

"Hope I didn't keep you waiting too long," she said with a smile.

"Not at all," I said. "This line is just taking forever."

"Really?" she asked. "How long have you been here?"

I shrugged, "Not sure. Maybe half an hour."

Her eyes widened, "That's not right."

She peeked past the crowd and saw how the receptionists were acting.

"Um. What exactly is going on?" she asked, perturbed.

"Not sure," I said. "Sounds like they are dealing with some sort of beast issue, but nobody is certain."

"They haven't said anything even after this long?" Leone gasped.

"Nope. The line has been moving forward at a slo–" I started before being cut off.

"Excuse me, can I get everyone's attention, please?"

The room came to a calm as everyone looked toward a door on the wall next to the counter. One of the receptionists had stepped out and began to speak.

"I-I wanted to apologize for the long wait. We are in the middle of something that requires our full attention. We are going to have to ask everyone to wait a little bi–"

The room erupted into a roar of protest that caused the receptionist to shrink back in fear.

"U-um, we are really sorry..."

The receptionist tried to continue speaking but was being assaulted by shouting from all sides.

"EVERYONE SHUT THE HELL UP!"

A voice boomed out into the room, eliciting silence from the crowd. The source of the voice was none other than Leone. As everyone turned to look at her, very few started talking again, but were quickly silenced by their friends. I couldn't help but be surprised at how much people seemed to respect her.

The receptionist looked toward Leone with gratitude. That's when I saw the opportunity to get some information.

"I'm sorry, but could I ask a quick question?" I said, breaking the silence.

All eyes in the room were on me, making me slightly uncomfortable.

"Could you explain the reason for the wait?" I asked.

"W-well," the receptionist took a deep breath and regained her posture, "like I had said, we are in the middle of something and–"

"I'm sorry," I cut her off, "I don't mean to be rude. But that's not much of an explanation. I'm sure everyone would feel much better about the wait if they knew the reason they were waiting."

A few people in the crowd nodded their heads in agreement.

"Well... I mean..." The lady started to stutter before another receptionist came up from behind her and whispered in her ear.

"Ah, well. It seems that everything is ready anyway," she sighed. "There have been rumors that a group of mercenaries pretended to defeat a beast and took the reward for it. This is true."

Whispers began to ripple through the crowd.

"We only just found out about it a few hours ago and have been scrambling to gather the funds for a new reward. I was just told that we have finished the paperwork for it and are announcing an emergency job."

Cheers erupted from the people as they forgot about the long wait they had endured. The reason was simple. Emergency jobs issued by the Association paid much better than normal ones. Now, everyone was hyped for a payday.

"Hey! What exactly is the job for?" someone from the crowd shouted.

"A Gorodian Crab."

When she uttered those words, the room fell silent once again.

The cheering had been replaced by petty excuses. Some complained that they were too tired to hunt it down, while others suddenly had an appointment they couldn't miss.

"Tsk. Bunch of cowards," Zade sneered.

"Does that mean you'll take on the job?" I asked.

"What? Of course not. There is no way I would survive that," he quickly stated.

I couldn't help but feel like he was being a little hypo-critical.

He seemed to notice my expression, "Oh, come on now. At least I have the balls to admit I'm not strong enough instead of making up lame excuses."

I sighed, "That's fair."

"Oh! Hey, Zade, didn't see you there." Leone grasped his hand.

"Leone! Buddy! It's been a while."

"That is has, Z. You still leaning to the right when you attack?"

"Ah, you caught me," Zade looked embarrassed. "It's not as bad as it used to be, but it's still there."

"Well, at least you've improved. Still running solo?"

"Yeah," he replied. "I did team up with someone for a bit, but it didn't work out."

Leone placed her hand on his shoulder, "Someday you'll find a partner."

"Yeah, someday," Zade said. "I just have to keep trying until then."

"Hey, um... I didn't want to interrupt, but I had been a little caught off guard, You two know each other?"

"Oh, yeah," Leone said. "We used to train together back when we were rookies."

"There weren't many spear users who would teach us, so we trained each other," Zade reminisced.

"Ahem," Reginald cleared his throat. "Elric, the receptionist said something important, right?"

"Huh?"

"She said it was for a Gorodian Crab," Reginald started. "Isn't that what Lost Light was supposed to have killed?"

My eyes went wide, "Oh shit. That's right."

"This means we are going to have to kill it, right?" Reginald asked.

After he said it, I realized that this fell under our contract to clean up the mess they caused.

"Yeah..." I replied, "Yeah, it does."

I turned to Leone, "Hey, the three of us are going to take the job."

"Really? Sounds like fun. Can I come?"

"Oh, uh. Yeah. Of course." I was taken off guard by her enthusiasm.

Leone turned back to Zade, "Well, I have to be off now. We should catch up later."

"I agree," Zade said. "Leave a message for me at the desk when you are free, and good luck with that Crab. If you're there, I'm sure it will be a walk in the park."

The receptionist was very happy that we came forward to accept the emergency job. Apparently, if nobody accepts one, the reward is raised a considerable amount until it is.

We were given some information on the Gorodian Crab, including where it's been seen and places around the lake that are desirable for its species.

The information we were given says that the crab is fifteen feet tall when it is standing and is covered in a hardened shell, Leone read the papers aloud as we rolled along in the carriage outside of town.

I put a hand to the side of my head and winced. "That doesn't sound like it will be too much of an issue."

Leone put the papers down and looked at me. "Still got that headache?"

"Yeah," I said while rubbing my temple.

After we had secured our cart and left the city, a throbbing pain built up in my head. I could almost hear the blood pumping to my brain. The worst part is that it was the type of headache that only happens when it's quiet, as a result of being in a loud place for too long.

"I'll be okay, though. It's not an issue," I smiled through the pain.

"U-um, I was wondering," Myrril started speaking, "w-where do Gorodian Crabs c-come from?"

"Huh?" Leone was shocked for a moment but soon shook it off. "They come from the Gorodian Lowlands, near the southern end of the continent."

"Then why is one here?" Reginald asked.

Leone shrugged, "I have no clue. It could have been a baby someone released several years ago, I suppose."

We spoke a bit more about the topic before arriving at our destination. We all hopped out of the cart and made our way down to the lakeshore. Unlike that of the beach, the shore of the lake had no sand but was grass right up until the water.

Well, it was like that in most places. However, in some spots, such as the one we were approaching, the ground sloped into a muddy strip of land caused by variations in the water level.

As I stepped onto the mud, I nearly slipped but managed to catch myself.

"You good, Elric?" Reginald asked, his hands moving back to their side. I guessed that he had instinctively moved to catch me.

"Yeah," I responded. "Luckily, it's just a little slippery. If the mud was deep then we wouldn't be able to fight in it."

The others gingerly stepped onto the mud as well, getting used to it as we trudged farther along the shore.

After a few moments, we spotted a jetty jutting out into the water over the mud. Nearby was what looked like the remains of a small boat. Or, well, half of a small boat.

As we drew closer, I spotted a splattering of slightly darker mud near the ruined boat.

"Wait," I held my arm out and whispered, "it could be nearby. Stay alert."

The others nodded at me and readied their weapons. Reginald held his new broadsword opposite to his shield, Myrril gripped her staff tightly, and Leone grasped her silver bells with her offhand.

We slowly moved closer, keeping an eye on the surroundings.

Once we made it to the boat, I gestured to the others to look around. Myrril stayed close behind me while the other two split up and searched the area.

I crouched low to the ground and picked up a clump of the darker mud.

"Blood..." I muttered.

Taking another look at the boat, I noticed the broken fragments of wood hadn't been weathered and still smelled of fresh oak. That's when Myrril tapped my shoulder and pointed to the mud.

What I hadn't seen before was a smattering of partially buried supplies sticking out of the mud.

Alerted that something was amiss, I closed my eyes and focused on my Megin, willing it to fortify my senses. My hearing became sharper, my nose more sensitive, and my sense of special awareness drastically increased. Even without my sight, I could see the outlines of objects around me.

The boat to my right, Myrril behind me, and Reginald next to the boulder.

Wait... boulder?

I flew open my eyes and spun to look at Reginald. Next to him was a smooth boulder seemingly shaped by the movement of water after thousands of years. But no, this lake didn't move enough water to do that.

A tingle went up my spine as even my instincts knew something was wrong.

"Reginald! Get back!" I shouted, but it was too late.

Reginald shifted backward, twisting his body to turn to me, but he wasn't fast enough.

What we had thought was a boulder launched from the ground at incredible speed and wrapped around Reginald faster than a human could blink.

"Reggie!"

"N-NO!"

Leone and Myrril screamed in surprise.

"GAAH!" Reginald yelled as he was lifted into the air, the air in his lungs struggling to escape.

Looking at what had grabbed him, there was now a thinner

boulder connecting the bigger one to the ground. No, it wasn't a boulder. We all knew what it was.

Our fears were soon confirmed as a great patch of mud arose from the ground, sloughing off around the massive creature that was hidden underneath.

KKKSSHHHHHHHH

The creature hissed as it arose. Its eyes rose out of stalks from within its gray shell. A pair of long antennae hung to either side of its insectoid mouth, and within its massive claw, capable of grasping a full-grown bear, was Reginald, screaming in pain.

It rose even taller out of the ground on its six armored legs, with another set of flat, paddle-like legs tucked behind it.

We froze.

Imagining the size of something with units of measurement is difficult. When Leone had said it was fifteen feet tall, I knew it was big, but I hadn't understood just how big. Now that I was seeing it in person, however, I knew for certain its size. The creature in front of us, the Gorodian Crab, was big enough to crush a single-story house.

"GRAH!" The sound of one of our own crying out in pain snapped us out of our shock.

"A little help here!" Reginald called out.

He had managed to twist his body in such a way that the pincers were bearing down on the side of his shield. However, it wasn't quite large enough to fully protect him, and his sides and back were still being crushed.

"Right!" I said, drawing my sword. "First priority is getting Reginald out of that claw."

"Got it," Leone gave a firm nod and locked her eyes on the claw.

"Myrril, blast its shell to distract it. And watch out for the other claw."

"R-right."

After giving out orders, I gripped my own weapon and led the charge forward. Leone made a beeline toward the crab's right claw on my left while Myrril moved around to the right to get a better firing spot.

"*Firestorm!*" shouted Myrril as a spinning tornado of flame erupted from the Bloodstone at the top of her staff and slammed into the side of the Gorodian Crab.

KKKSSSSSSS!

The crab let out another hiss and wildly swung his left claw toward the source of the fire. Though it had little effect, it was enough to distract the beast.

Leone and I took advantage of the opening. Leone swung her spear at the beast's right claw with a loud *CLANG* as the tip of her spear bounced off of its hardened shell.

"Damn!" she cursed.

One of the Crab's eye stalks turned toward her, and its left claw swung around toward her.

Being in between the claw and Leone, I had no choice but to hit the ground and slide underneath it as it swung above me. The sight of it so close made my heart skip a beat, but as soon as it was past me, I jumped back up to my feet and made it to my destination. The legs.

Myrril unleashed another burst of fire from her staff, hitting the side of the crab once again. Luckily, it was a big target. Unluckily, I was now underneath it.

As flame passed by me, I swung my blade into one of the tree trunk-sized legs holding the crab above the ground.

Like Leone, my blade also deflected off the shell, but I was able to get a closer look at the beast's leg.

"The joints!" I shouted, "hit the joints!"

As I shouted this, the crab realized where I was and lifted

one of its giant legs into the air, bringing it down swiftly atop me.

I pulled back right in time as the leg landed in front of me, but another one had lifted to make another attempt.

I dodged around the first leg as the second slammed into the ground where I was just standing, sending mud flying into the air. Then, I saw one of the massive, paddle-like legs swinging toward me. It was too late to dodge, so out of sheer panic, I instinctively swung my fist toward the massive leg as it tried to swat me like a fly.

CRACK!

A jolt of pain shot up my arm as a resounding crack echoed through the air. Where my fist had landed was now a spiderweb crack on the leg's carapace. My fist didn't come out unscathed, but it didn't feel broken.

I dodged and rolled out of the way of another leg, covering myself in mud, as I heard another shriek from the creature.

KSKSKSSHHHHH!

Leone had jammed her spear into the crab's claw joint and had hopped on top of its claw. In response, the crab gripped its claw even harder and began to wildly swing it around.

"AHH!" Reginald screamed, "Any time now would be nice!"

"I know!" Leone shouted back, "I'm trying!"

"Fire Bird!" A wide arrow of fire, vaguely shaped like an eagle, slammed into the crab's fleshy shoulder joint.

KSHHHHHHHHHHHHHHHHHHHHHHHHK-SKSKSKS!

The crab screeched and flailed its arm wildly. Its eyes, full of hatred, turned toward Myrril.

"Oh no, you don't!" I yelled as I made another pass for the crab's legs in order to slow it down.

Unfortunately, I never got the chance. The crab began to

skitter toward Myrril with immense speed. It raised its free fist high into the air, attempting to squash the bug that had just burned it.

"Damn it!" I yelled, grabbing the silver bell I kept in a pouch at my side, Tempest! Sic!

I threw the bell as hard as I could and watched as a blue energy formed around it.

AROOO!

A howl sounded as a bolt of flashing blue energy burst forth from the massive blue wolf that had appeared, hitting the Gorodian Crab in the back of the shell. The lighting curled up and around the shell, sending the beast into a frenzy.

KSSHSHSHSSHSHSH!

The blue wolf bolted to the beast and jumped onto the hardened carapace covering its back. In one swipe, the wolf dug its claws into the armor, breaking through to the soft flesh beneath.

"*Flameburst!*" Myrril shouted. It was the same spell she had used to beat Carla, but I hadn't been able to see exactly how it worked until now.

Three balls of quick-moving flame flew forth from her staff in rapid succession, all three impacting the same location.

The crab let out another scream of pain as the flames had scorched its shell, probably even making it into the beast's internals.

"Got it!" Leone shouted as her spear finally hit muscle, releasing Reginald from the creature's grasp, eliciting a groan from him as he hit the ground with a loud *thump*.

Leone jumped from the crab's claw as it looked toward us with hatred in its eyes.

"Hati! Sköll!" She threw out her own silver bells and summoned the Solar and Lunar wolf she had contracted with.

The two spirit wolves bared their teeth at the crab and growled intensely.

The crab now realized the situation it was in. Being a creature more suited to ambushing its prey, it was wildly outmatched. Perhaps having some semblance of intelligence, or maybe just in an act of self-preservation, the crab scurried toward the water as fast as it could.

CHAPTER 9

The Cavern at the Edge of the Lake

"Don't let it get away!" Leone sprinted toward the crab, her wolves in tow.

"Stop!" I yelled after her with as much of a commanding tone as I could muster.

"Tsk," Leone expressed her disapproval, but ground to a halt, just as the crab submerged itself in the water.

"Half our people are down," I said to her as she faced the lake, "not to mention that it has an advantage in the water."

"Half?" Leone turned around.

Behind us, Reginald lay on the ground groaning, his armor partially crushed. Farther back, Myrril was on her knees, drenched in sweat and trying to take control of her heavy breathing.

"We'll come up with a plan after we take care of them."

"Right..." she replied, her tone held a hint of anger.

She was probably pissed that the Gorodian Crab almost killed Reginald, and I couldn't really blame her.

I patted her shoulder, "You did your job, and you did it well. Reginald is alive because of you."

"I... I know." She sighed, releasing the tension built up within her.

"Good," I smiled. "Then if you're done feeling sorry for yourself, come help me with him."

Her glaring eyes locked with mine.

"See, feeling better already."

"Hmph," she snorted with annoyance but followed me back to the others nonetheless.

"Shit man," Reginald groaned. "I thought I was going to be juiced by that thing."

We were all resting not far from where the muddy lakeside began, underneath the shade of a pair of small beech trees.

Reginald had removed his heavily bent armor and had bandages wrapped around his torso. They were less so for the various small cuts that had occurred from when his armor started crushing in on him and more to keep his cracked ribs from moving too much.

Next to him was Myrril, blissfully bandaging his shield arm, which took a lot of force from the Gorodian Crab's claws as well.

"I'm glad you weren't crushed..." I heard Myrril whisper to herself.

"Huh? Did you say something?" Reginald looked at her.

Myrril shook her head quickly, "N-No. N-Nothing."

Her face was slightly red as she redoubled her focus on bandaging him. Before today, I didn't even know Myrril knew how to do first aid, but when we got Reginald's armor off, she immediately volunteered.

I supposed it made sense; she probably helped him all the time when it was just the two of them.

Leone had a slight grin as she watched them.

"Hey, Leone, thanks for getting me out of there."

Reginald turned his head to her.

"Don't worry about it," Leone waved him off.

"Either way..." Reginald looked like he wanted to press further, but changed the subject, "By the way, Elric. Something's been bothering me."

"Hm?" I looked up from what I was doing, a small hammer in one hand and Reginald's dented chest plate in the other. The stump anvil I had purchased from Fergus was being put to good use.

"When did you get a Spirit Wolf?" he asked earnestly.

I looked over at the blue wolf, a streak of white shooting down its back, as it rolled around and played with Hati and Sköll.

"Oh, that's the Storm Wolf that Leone and I fought."

"Huh?"

"He submitted to me, so I brought him with us." I continued, "I gave him the name Tempest."

The Storm Wolf's ears perked up when I said his name, and he looked this way for a moment before returning to whatever game the three of them were playing.

When I looked back, even Myrril had stopped to look at me with shock.

Reginald gave an uncomfortable smile.

"You really are a strange one, aren't you?" he said in disbelief and a tired acceptance, prompting the other two to nod in agreement.

But I didn't let myself be bothered by it. The cultures of Humans and Aleurians were completely different in some respects. Back home, I would be celebrated for not only defeating a Storm Wolf but for taming it as well.

That was just one of the many differences I would have to get used to. However, the fact that human culture modeled itself off of my people made the situation easier to adapt to.

After I did some field repairs to Reginald's armor and we rested up a bit more, we started making our way back toward town.

On the way, we discussed our next move.

"Should we go camp out at another spot?" Reginald asked.

"No," I answered, "I think we should head back and rest up. Start fresh tomorrow."

"What? Why?" Reginald's tone was full of bemusement.

"You're still hurt," I tried to explain.

"No, I'm not. I'm right as rain!" Reginald held up his arm and flexed, prompting a slight wince from him.

"Well, maybe you can tough it out, big guy, but what about Myrril," huh?

Leone laid on the guilt.

"W-Well, I..." Reginald tripped over his words, having forgotten how exhausted Myrril was at the end of the battle. Even while she was taking care of him, she had very clearly been out of energy.

Myrril uncharacteristically interrupted, "N-No, I'm fine as well."

"Are you sure?" Leone asked her with a motherly concern. "You used a lot of magic during that battle. Are you sure you aren't too tired?"

Myrril shook her head, "I'm good to go."

Leone didn't look entirely convinced, but she relented.

"Alright," she let out a sigh, "then what's the plan?"

All three of them looked toward me for an answer.

I couldn't help but let out a little smile at the interaction.

"If I remember correctly, the information we had mentioned a cave."

"Yes," Leone answered my question. "There is quite a large one on the other side of the lake at the base of the mountains."

"I don't think this type of crab will go above ground to enter a cave," Reginald argued. "It seemed similar to a mud crab, in my opinion."

Leone shook her head, "I agree with you on that one, but the cave is still an option. It connects directly with the lake."

"So the water flows into it?" I asked.

"Seems to be the case," she nodded.

"Huh, interesting," I took a moment to think.

The idea that a mud crab would use a cave wasn't out of the

question. It's not like I knew much about crabs, but just as their names suggest, mud crabs prefer to hide in the mud. The likelihood was low that it would hide in a rocky cave, but if it felt threatened on the beach...

"Alright, let's do it."

I voiced the conclusion I came to.

"Normally, I wouldn't consider it, but since it ran from us, it could try to hide away from where we can get to it."

"Ah," Reginald looked as though he realized something, "so if it thinks we can't get to it, the cave may be its best option to hide."

"That's my conclusion," I confirmed.

"O-or it could have retreated there because it felt like it had an advantage..." Myrril shyly interjected.

"True," I agreed, "but the only thing we can do is prepare as much as we can. After that, it's up to our own abilities."

Preparation is key in unfamiliar territory. It allows you to somewhat balance out the advantage your enemy has. Though it could only go so far.

"Well, this is all well and good," Leone began, "but how exactly are we going to get there?"

"Hmm," I began to think as the city came into view. From our approach, we could see past the walls, revealing the countless sails docked at the wharf.

I let out a smile and snorted in amusement before turning to the others.

"I would have thought it was pretty obvious."

"Hm?"

"Well, I have to admit. This was pretty obvious," Leone admitted as she leaned against the side of the small boat we had rented through the Association.

It was a little thing, barely able to fit the four of us and the singular, triangle-rigged mast in the center. On Aleuria, these kinds of boats were used for simple shoreline traversal or recreational sailing. I, myself, was quite experienced with them.

"Are you sure it's big enough? It's practically just a rowboat with a sail strapped onto it." Reginald voiced his concern with obvious discomfort. He had his reasons, I'm sure. One of which was most likely the fact that he wore a lot of heavy armor, and falling out of the boat would cause him to sink like a rock.

"Don't worry," I reassured him, "I'm a skilled hand at this thing. Why do you think I had you sit at the bow?"

"To offset the weight better?"

"Right," I replied, "and with me in the back moving the sail, we will have less chance of capsizing."

Reginald seemed to relax a bit at my explanation.

"But if anyone is still worried about falling out, you can use the rope down there to tie a lifeline around the mast."

After making my suggestion, Reginald reached for the rope before shaking his head and sitting back down.

Myrril, on the other hand, took the suggestion to heart and tied off a lifeline.

"Alright, everyone ready?"

My companions responded affirmatively, so I loosed the sail and began maneuvering us out of the wharf.

It didn't take me long to get back into the swing of things and deftly steer the small boat out and onto the open water. I felt some of the tension release from my body, and a smile grew on my face. While it wasn't the same as smelling the salty sea air, the feeling of being on the water helped to calm my nerves.

"You look like you're enjoying this," Leone pointed out.

I couldn't help but smile, "Yeah. It reminds me of home. Though it doesn't have quite the same feeling as the ocean."

"Oh?" Leone seemed a bit surprised. "you grew up near the ocean?"

"Yep," I confirmed, "it wasn't far from my hometown."

"Hmph," Leone snorted. "I find it kind of hard to believe that such a vast amount of water exists."

I was taken aback by her statement for a moment but realized that she had probably never left the landlocked valley.

"It does exist," I looked off to the horizon, trying to picture the sight from my memories. "It's a vast plain of blue waves going far beyond the horizon."

I looked back at her. "I'll have to take you guys there someday. It's a beautiful place, my homeland."

"Pft."

Reginald burst into laughter.

"I'm sorry, I'm sorry," he said as he attempted to regain his composure. "It's just that we are so close despite knowing each other for only two months, and you've known Leone for even less!"

"Heh. That is quite funny," I let out a chuckle of my own, "but it doesn't matter. Whether we have known each other for a week, or a year, for a warrior, the bonds of friendship are forged through combat."

It was an undeniable truth of my people. We formed friendships quickly with the ones we have fought side by side with. For my companions here, we had been through many trials in the little time we had known each other, yet I felt comfortable around them.

We spoke of various subjects as we traveled and ate a quick lunch on the boat.

As we approached our destination, the base of the mountains slowly came into view, showing that the lake was just big enough to make the far shore impossible to see.

When we drew closer, the cave we were looking for became clear. However...

"Th-that's the cave!?" Reginald shouted in surprise.

"You can't even call that a cave anymore..." I let out as a bit of anxiety welled within me.

"It's more of a cavern," Leone whispered in awe.

Indeed, the cavernous opening into the side of the mountain was a monolithic hole. I surmised that at least three warships could pass through it side by side with some coordination.

If such an opening had feelings, to call it a cave would be a grave insult.

I started pulling the boat off toward the shoreline next to the cavern when Leone posed a question.

"Are we not sailing right in?" she asked.

"No. Definitely not." I gave a sure answer, causing the others to look at me questioningly, as if urging me to explain.

"We have no idea what's inside there," I continued. "There could be rocks, cliffs, and other dangers. Not to mention the fact that we know the Gorodian Crab can snap a boat in half."

The others looked as if they had forgotten that last part. However, nobody questioned the decision to leave the boat on the shore.

We all hopped out of the boat, and I tied it off to a large stone I deemed capable of keeping the boat in place; then we began to march for the cavern.

We remained on guard as we approached, Reginald and I in the lead, with Myrril and Leone behind us. The size of the gaping mountain maw was not to be understated. It was taller than it was wide, and more impressive up close. Such a feat of nature was astonishing, not only to me but to the others as well.

Luckily for us, I spotted a narrow rocky path next to the cavern wall that looked big enough for us to use.

"Over there," I pointed at the path. "I think we can use that."

Reginald squinted toward where I was pointing. "Oh, I see it now. Are you sure we can fit on that?"

I shrugged, "We won't know until we get a bit closer."

The others agreed that it was probably our best course of action, and we began moving in that direction.

The area around the so-called cave was a rocky mess with very little in the way of vegetation. It was akin to the top of a mountain or the bottom of a waterfall. There was a fine layer of gravel covered in countless stones of various sizes, ranging from being able to fit in the palm of my hand, to boulders taller than a person.

As we drew closer, the narrow path widened a bit, making it a much more comfortable size to walk through.

"Oh, hey," I put my hand on the entrance to the narrow path, "this was carved."

I could see a chisel pattern along the wall, long faded with time, but still barely visible. It didn't seem that the entire path was carved. From what I could tell, the chiseling was broken off as the cavern wall began to arch overhead, meaning there was probably a path here originally and that it was simply widened by some intrepid explorer.

"Who would spend the time to carve out a path?" Reginald asked.

"Probably someone who likes caves?" Leone proposed.

"O-or bandits..." Myrril added.

Myrril made a good point. The cavern was far from any settlements, and surprisingly little was known about it.

"Let's be on high alert," I suggested as we crept forward.

With the water immediately to our left, and the wall to our

right, the path was only wide enough for one person to go at a time; so Reginald took the lead with his shield, followed by myself, then Myrril, and Leone taking up the rear.

Not far in, it became harder for my companions to see as the sunlight found trouble making it further into the space. I was still okay, my people were blessed with better eyesight, which included the ability to see in low-light areas. However, I wasn't immune to darkness. Soon, even I would need a light source to see.

That time, however, never came. As soon as it had gotten too dark to see effectively, we spotted a small lamp hanging from a sea-weathered post of old wood. The candle inside was topped with a dancing flame, the wax no more than half melted. It couldn't have been more than a few hours since it was lit.

The sight of this confirmed that there were indeed people within the cavern. And by the look of the post, I could only come to one conclusion.

"I think Myrril is right," I whispered to the others, "be ready for a fight."

The others nodded, and we slowly and carefully made our way farther down the path, our weapons fully drawn and ready for anything that may come.

We passed one, two, three more lanterns before Reginald raised his hand and signaled for us to halt.

"There's an archway ahead. It looks like it opens into a large room. There's a lot of light coming from it," Reginald whispered through the side of his mouth back to us, never letting the opening leave his sight.

"How big is the opening?" I whispered back.

"Same size as the walkway, Reginald replied, We'll have to spread out the moment we're through.

Same size as the walkway," Reginald replied, "We'll have to spread out the moment we're through."

"Sounds good." I looked back at Leone and Myrril, who both gestured that they were ready, and turned back to Reginald.

"Just a moment." I closed my eyes and focused on my hearing. The slow movement of water, the slight rustling of fabric, and the breath of my companions filled my senses. Feeling out toward the opening in the rock, the faintest breath of sound came to me.

Unable to make it out, I grasped onto the subtle rushing of Megin within me and gently nudged it to concentrate around my ears. My hearing sharpened, and I had to block out all unnecessary information entering my head.

From the stone arch came a variety of sounds. The light movement of parchment, a rustle and light scrape, the sound of liquid sloshing in a container, and a small yawn.

I opened my eyes.

"Elric?" Reginald glanced questioningly toward me.

"There are five," I reported. "Two are asleep, and one just woke up or perhaps has been awake for too long. There is another with a drink and one going through pages of some kind."

"What in the Vale? How would you know all of that?" Leone sounded exasperated and surprised.

"I enhanced my hearing," I nonchalantly replied, "but we can talk about it later. For now, we need to focus."

Myrril also looked like she wanted to ask questions, but it was neither the time nor the place for such things.

"Right."

Leone returned to her combat mentality, and I addressed Reginald once more.

"I cannot tell exactly where they are, but the one that

yawned and the one with a drink are closer to us than the others."

A small smile crept onto his face.

"I'll have to ask you for the details later. For now, let's roll with it."

I nodded in response and shifted the bag I carried on my back.

This wasn't our main goal, but if they were bandits, then we needed to subdue them. It was the policy of the Alliance to attempt to capture any bandits or brigands alive so they may stand trial for their crimes, but it was not looked down upon if they were killed in the process of capture. I was happily surprised that they understood how difficult it was to capture someone capable of inflicting serious harm upon you.

For the record, Aleurian law had a dead or alive clause. Those who turn to banditry forfeit their right to live in a civilized society, and their lives are in the hands of whoever catches them. It's a brutal, but very effective way of doing things.

Reginald signaled for us to follow and silently approached the opening. Once we were there, he looked back at us to double-check our readiness and turned back to the rocky arch. With a deep breath, he pushed in, shield up.

I followed directly behind, then Myrril and Leone. We moved to either side of the archway to allow the person behind us to make it in.

"What the...!" A man yelped.

The room was lightly furnished. About fifteen feet to our right was a small table set against the wall with three rickety stools. A gruff-looking man holding a tankard stared at us in surprise. Close to that was a small writing desk where another man, this one of smaller stature, was flipping through what seemed to be a ledger. His eyes widened as he saw us.

On the ground behind the desk was a small chest and a crate full of objects, probably pilfered by the bunch.

The far wall was about twenty feet away from the arch, and the base of it was lined with a row of bedrolls. Two of which were occupied.

To our left, after a few feet, was a drop off into the water, about half a foot down, and in front of us was the very surprised young man who seemed to be half asleep.

After that quick glance, the men jumped to their feet and drew weapons. The ones who had been asleep a moment ago were also part of that.

"Hank!" the one who had been drinking shouted at the young man in front of us, "you're supposed to alert us if someone is approaching!"

"I-I'm, sorry, Uncle! I just dozed off for a second, promise!" The young man, Hank, backed away from us and fumbled for his weapon.

"Why you–" Hank's uncle started again but was interrupted by the man who had been going through the ledger.

He was a tall man covered in scar-ridden muscles, a shaved head, a full brown beard, and a pair of spectacles upon his nose.

"Now, now. We have guests."

As he spoke, he folded up his glasses and set them on the table. I deduced that this was their leader.

The bandit leader turned to look at us.

"You four, you are mercenaries, are you not?"

He eyed each of us up and down as he spoke. His attitude and body language were both full of grating confidence.

"We are," Reginald answered him, "and I'd advise you surrender before anybody gets hurt."

The bandit leader smiled, "The only ones getting hurt here are you."

He reached his toughened hand out and grasped a hulk of a mace that had been leaning against the wall.

I heard a *Tsk* from Reginald at the bandit leader's response, and soon we were being assaulted from all sides.

The bandit leader beelined for Reginald, swinging the massive mace above his head, bringing it down upon Reginald, who just narrowly managed to dodge it. The mace dug into the rock wall, sending shards of rock flying. The young man, Hank, came up from behind Reginald and tried to strike him, but he was too inexperienced and fumbled the attack.

The pair that had just woken up made for the girls. Leone jumped in front and fended off both of the men with her spear while Myrril took action of her own.

"Fire Arrow!" she shouted as a bolt of red light shot forth from the bloodstone atop her staff and impacted the chest of one of the men with a mighty force. The man was sent flying but managed to recover enough to redouble his attack.

As for me, I was being assaulted by Hank's uncle. He was obviously heavily intoxicated, yet his footwork hadn't suffered. I guessed he was an avid alcoholic.

He brought his chipped short sword toward me in fast jabs, all of which I quickly parried. I brought a swing of my own, but the man's movements were a little erratic.

Despite my initial praise, he wasn't that good of a fighter. Against a new trainee or an inexperienced human, he would be a threat. But I had gone through the harsh training of the Aleurian Empire; fought, briefly, in a civil war; and spent two years in Kyrtvale. This drunken bandit was no match for me.

To my left, Reginald was still managing to fend off the bandit leader's attacks. He moved to the side as the mace came from above once more and used his shield to push Hank off balance.

Hank stumbled backward toward the water.

A cacophonous sound akin to a wave breaking upon a rocky shore echoed through the chamber as a wall of water appeared without warning. A blood-curdling scream rang out as a massive, grey claw emerged from the wall of water and snatched Hank off his feet.

"GGGHHHAAAAAA!"

The water fell back into the lake, revealing the hardened carapace of our quarry: The Gorodian Crab.

None of us had expected it to appear, least of all the bandits.

As we froze in surprise, Hank reached his arm out and spoke his last breath.

"U-Uncle.... H-Help..."

KKSSSKSSS!

A sickening crunch resounded as the life was crushed from the young man.

Hank's uncle was the first one to recover from the shock.

"HANK!" he yelled, turning away from me. The grip on his weapon tightened, his teeth clenched, and his face red with rage.

"I'LL KILL YOU!" he screamed at the crab as he ran forward with all his drunken might.

The bandit leader tried to stop him, "Frank, no!" but it was too late. Hank's uncle had been driven into a grief-stricken, alcohol-induced rage.

As he reached the shoreline and was preparing to jump onto the back of the crab, the second claw emerged from his right side. Faster than he could react, the armored appendage connected with his body. The whole room shook as the claw impacted the wall next to the stone arch, and a bloody flower painted the grey stone.

The rest of us had managed to pull back and regroup, the remaining bandits did the same.

"Hey, Bandit Boss," I called out to the massive man, "let's finish our fight later."

"Agreed!" He smiled, but there was no joy in his face. "I'm in the mood for some seafood right about now."

I didn't have it in me to point out that this was a freshwater crab after he made such a perfect one-liner.

"Hey, Boss, I'm going to have to sit this one out." The man who got hit with a fire arrow winced and grasped his chest.

"No worries. In fact, both of you sit this one out. You don't have the right weapons for this," the bandit leader replied.

"I've got that covered."

I dropped the bag I had been carrying onto the ground and opened it up, revealing a small warhammer, a pair of maces, and a warpick.

These were some extra tools we picked up in town for our fight against the Gorodian Crab.

The bandit leader looked at me in shock, "You were hunting this thing, weren't you?"

I smiled at him, "Guilty as charged."

"Ha, I like you." He let out a chuckle. "Alright, grab a weapon then."

The bandit who was in better shape grabbed a mace and got ready.

"Alright, Reginald and Myrril stay back," I started doling out orders, "Leone and I will take care of this."

"Why me?" Reginald sounded a little hurt.

"Because you still have broken ribs," I explained. "Originally, we would have needed all of us, but now we have some good backup. Just protect Myrril."

Reginald gave in without further argument, "Alright, I can do that."

"Good." I handed the warhammer to Leone and grabbed the warpick for myself, "Let's kill a crab."

Killing a crab is easy. Killing a Gorodian Crab isn't.

The four of us rushed forward as the crab dropped Hank's limp form from its claw and let out another hiss.

KSSSHHHHKSKSKS!

The sound it made was much louder in this enclosed space. With the crab's form taking up the entire open side of the chamber, and with the small passage as the only exit, we had steeled our resolve to kill the beast. Well, we were going to kill it anyway, but now we had no means of escape. In essence, the situation wasn't looking too good.

The crab swung its bloody claw in a wide arc before us. I chose to hit the deck and slide beneath it, while the bandit boss faced it head-on. He swung his massive mace forward, knocking the claw away. The crab pulled its arm back and let out another cry in pain as cracks spread from the point of impact.

Leone didn't let the opening go to waste and swung her warhammer firmly into the crab's shoulder armor, sending more cracks, albeit small ones, snaking up the carapace.

She didn't bring her wolves out this time. We had agreed ahead of time that there wasn't enough space for all of us and the spirits as well. It was already cramped enough trying to fight shoulder to shoulder.

The other bandit seemed to be having a little more trouble than Leone. One of the crab's legs had appeared from the water and was harassing him.

"Whoops!" I shouted as an arm-sized mandible came toward me. I lost focus on my own battle to keep an eye on the others. I pulled my sword into my offhand and used it to fend off the incoming attacks in sequence with the warpick.

These things are basically its jaw. How is it so adept at using them in combat?

Thoughts began to race through my head, but I had to force them out. Distraction during a battle is one sure way to lose your life. I shook them from my mind and focused ahead of me, taking in the situation.

First things first, the crab. It was keeping one of its eyestalks focused on me, while the other kept watch on the others, meaning it was at least able to multitask efficiently.

Another thing was the weapons it had at its disposal. As we have seen, its claws can be used for crushing objects within them or for smashing stuff outside of them. Then it has its legs. They are as dangerous as spears if you are caught underneath one of them. Luckily, the crab was mostly in the water and wouldn't be able to use all of them. In that same sense, it also wouldn't be able to sit on us. I shuddered at the thought of how much it weighed.

The one that really surprised me was its mandibles; the small arm-like appendages that help it consume its prey.

As for its reach, we were in luck. The creature was too large for both of its massive arms to fit into the opening at the same time, so even though it had been switching between them, we only had to deal with one at a time.

Where I stood was a different story. Its mandibles had decent reach, and if I moved outside of them, then I would be back in range of its claws. The more I analyzed things, the harder it was to say whether the beast had some level of intelligence or was fighting off pure instinct. It was a blurred line, for sure.

"Gah!"

The bandit that had been wounded yelped as he was tossed

backward by the force of the crab's leg and hit the ground like a sack of potatoes. He wasn't getting back up anytime soon.

I made the split decision to pull back and rejoin the line with the others.

"How's it going?"

My question was directed toward Leone, who seemed to be struggling with the warhammer.

"I'm... I'm good. This thing is just really heavy." She sounded out of breath.

I told her to fall back if she needed to, and she nodded. It was exhausting work to use a weapon you weren't familiar with, especially one so top heavy as a warhammer.

KSKSKSKSKSHHHHH!

The crab threw another swing, which was aptly parried by the bandit boss.

"Tsk," he said, "this thing's getting on my nerves."

"Just hold on a moment, we'll make an opening," I responded to the man, remembering our first fight earlier in the day.

"Myrril!" I called back to our timid mage.

The crab raised its arm again to prepare for a swing. Then, a bolt of red light screeched past us as it displaced the air around it and smacked into one of the crab's eyes.

KSHHHHHHH!

The crab cried out in pain, and its swing went wide, smashing apart a natural stone pillar sticking out of the water.

The three of us still in the fight rushed forward as the crab swung his other arm wildly toward us.

The bandit boss steadied his stance, and with a mighty blow, shattered the shell surrounding the creature's arm and dug his mace deeply into the soft flesh beneath.

Leone made a follow-up attack, smashing the arm joint with a sickening *Crack!*

KKKKKKSHHH!

Foam flew from the crab's mouth as it screamed, its arm gone limp.

I had been making my way toward its charred face but took a different route once I saw it open.

Crouching slightly, I sprang to the top of the crab's limp claw in one moment, and in the next, I was dashing up its limp arm and onto its slippery shell.

From the top, I could see exactly what I had been looking for, the long scratch across his back that Tempest had inflicted.

The crab shuddered, and I let myself slip onto my side and slide down its back. I slammed my hand against the shell and felt my fingers catch on the wound. A jolt of pain shot through my hand as it suddenly had to support my entire body weight.

From the strange angle on its back, I pulled back the warpick and dug it into the exposed flesh with as much force as I could muster. Then I tore it out, ripping flesh along with it, and dug it back into the wound again and again. With each motion, the crab screamed a sickening cry.

Whoosh!

The sound reached my ears too late before the wind was knocked out of me, and I was sent tumbling off the side of the crab. It had brought up one of its paddle legs and slapped me off its back.

I hit the water with a splash, but before I could regain my bearings, the other paddle leg appeared from the darkness and slammed into my body, launching me out of the water. I heard someone calling my name right before I slammed into a stone pillar, sending stones flying to either side.

My body ached all over, my joints were stiff, and it hurt to breathe, but I was alive. I pulled my head up and took in my surroundings.

The crab had launched me a little way away. I was now

seated in a person-sized space carved from the natural stone pillar by my impact. The base of the pillar disappeared into the water but was surrounded by scraps of wood, cloth, and other remnants of ships.

"And that's why we didn't sail in," I pointed out to nobody in particular as I got to my feet. A throbbing pain came from my right calf.

Some of the stone pieces had become embedded in my leg. It wasn't something I could take care of at the moment, so I paid it no mind.

My only goal at that time was to make it back to the fight. But I no longer had the war pick, so unless I made it back to the soft spot without getting hit off, I would have a tough time.

KSHKSHSSSHHH!

The crab's hissing echoed through the cavern, which was much bigger from where I stood. The darkness kept going far beyond where my eyes could reach, occasionally broken up by naturally formed pillars like the one I was standing on.

My first thought was to swim back, but then the Gorodian Crab would just smack me away again. I could have made it back to the narrow pass, but it wasn't a good place to get caught.

Then it hit me.

I tested my range of movement, and despite the damage to my leg, I could still move it enough for what I had planned.

I crouched down and locked my eyes on my target. I gently altered the flow of my Megin to gather in my legs and offer me explosive power.

My legs trembled, but I didn't care. With a flash, my legs were like springs, launching me across the open space and to a thin stalactite. I wrapped my arms around it and swung my body to the opposite side, where I launched myself once more, the stone cracking beneath my feet.

From one foothold to the next, then the next, I flew across

the cavern like an acrobat. In the end, I felt one of the stalactites give way and wasn't able to put my full force into the jump.

"Shit!" I said in panic as I began to fall toward the waters below.

My body moved on its own and reached out to grab something, anything. That's when my fingers found purchase.

I grasped as hard as I could and felt a jolt in my shoulder, but I pushed through the pain and let the momentum swing me.

My eyes were blurry with the pain, but I saw my saving grace: a ledge in front of me.

With as much timing as I could afford, I swung my legs out in front of me and released my grip, hoping that the gained momentum from my legs would be enough to carry me forward.

I whipped my body forward and pulled my legs back to try and bring an extra boost. My efforts weren't in vain, as I was barely able to grab onto the ledge with my fingers.

Looking down, I could see the battle raging on just below me. My fumble had somehow gotten me closer to my goal. But I was still at least a hundred feet up and losing grip. My fingers began to slip as I spotted a heaven-send below me.

There, stuck in the back of the crab, was the warpick. I had thought it was knocked from my hand and sank into the waters, but it looked like the warpick had managed to stay dug in.

A plan quickly formulated in my mind, and I let go.

When that kid ran up that massive arm, Emmerson thought

he was crazy. He seemed to have a plan, but what he had done seemed stupid and insanely dangerous.

What the hell is that kid thinking!? Emmerson couldn't help but ponder as he wrenched his great mace from the creature's arm.

He had managed to finally get through the beast's armor, and then the lady with the warhammer knocked the whole arm out of commission. That's when the kid hopped up there with a look on his face, almost like he was searching for something. Whatever he was looking for, it sounded like he found it with all the screaming coming from the thing.

Well, none of that mattered after the crab raised a leg that looked almost like an oar and slapped the kid into the darkness as if swatting a fly.

"Elric!?" the woman with the warhammer called out in surprise, but the other two of his companions were less vocal. In fact, at a glance, they didn't seem phased.

The kid with the shield grabbed the last mace from the bag and ran to join us.

"He's fine, this happens."

The confidence in his voice was astonishing.

Emmerson had started to like these kids early in their fight. The one with the shield had fended him off personally, all while having broken ribs, according to the kid who got sent flying. The mage girl was a little timid, but she packed a lot of punch. Emmerson also enjoyed the tenacity of the lady with the warhammer. Though he felt that she was familiar somehow.

The one that truly surprised him was the last kid. He didn't seem more than twenty years old, but he had a certain air about him. Emmerson had clocked him as the leader almost immediately. However, he lost points for being so stupid against the crab.

Speaking of the crab, it was still a fighter. Even after losing the use of an arm, it never let up its attacks. Its creepy face and loud noises were a bit distracting, but that didn't stop Emmerson.

He sent swing after swing into the crab's hardened shell, sending light cracks snaking through.

Even though it was rough going, Emmerson was enjoying himself.

Then, the unthinkable happened.

"HYAAA!"

The voice of the kid that had been sent flying reappeared above the beast. Emmerson's eyes went wide as he saw the kid flying, no, falling, above the creature. His fist reared back at the ready, a crazed look in his eye.

What happened next seemed to occur in slow motion.

My original idea had been to drop onto the warpick and drive it into the back of the Gorodian Crab with my body weight, but I quickly realized the fault in that plan.

The warpick was only so big, and jamming it into the crab's back would have been like stabbing someone with a toothpick. While it would hurt, it wouldn't be very effective.

Instead, I went with plan B.

As I fell toward the grey mass of armor below me, I performed a great taboo within Aleurian Martial Arts.

Instead of gently nudging or redirecting the natural flow of Megin to increase the speed or power of my strikes, I forced it to gather within my hand.

I could feel the Megin moving unnaturally through my body and gathering in my clenched fist. It carried with it a great pressure beneath my skin and the feeling of all my veins being dried out. Sharp jabs dug into me as the Megin was forcibly dried from the channels that carried it.

But I had to endure.

The memory of what my fist had done to the crab's leg flashed through my mind as I made the decision, only reinforcing what had to be done.

As my mind moved faster and faster, time seemed to slow down. I pulled my arm back and let out the air in my lungs to give me just that split second of extra explosive energy.

Then, like releasing the torsion of a great siege engine, my arm shot forward just as I reached the unaware crab.

My fist impacted the carapace with the force of an Onager. The moment my knuckles touched the shell, it cracked and warped with the pressure, and that pressure only spread.

Great cracks spread across the beast's back like a web. Great chunks of shell began to break off and fly into the air, unable to handle the expanding shock wave.

KKKKKKKK-!

The Gorodian Crab tried to scream, but its internals were liquified by the force of the impact. Its brain, completely destroyed.

I stumbled forward, rolling off its back and onto dry land just as it began to sink into the water. Soon, the only evidence of its remains was its massive claw, acting as an anchor.

"Grh!"

I let out a pained groan as my muscles began to seize, and I dropped to my knees. My lungs wouldn't obey me, and my arms felt like they had been cut to ribbons and filled with lead.

Energy was still gathered in my closed fist. I quickly dissipated it, allowing the Megin to return to its natural flow.

Within a moment, I could feel the river-like stream of Megin return to my body in a diminished form.

"Elric!" My companions rushed up to me, "Are you okay?"

I got back to my feet and shook the spots from my vision. "Yeah, I'm good."

I whipped around to face the bandit boss and drew my weapon. But we aren't done just yet.

CHAPTER 10

Gathering Evidence

"All right, bud, how about we just put that weapon down?" the bandit boss said in an attempt to de-escalate the situation, which was funny since he escalated it in the first place.

"And why should I?" I responded, still reeling from the pain. My companions had also joined me with weapons drawn. The bandit boss in front of us was outnumbered five to one.

"Well, we need to clear up this misunderstanding."

I was surprised by his response. I wasn't sure what misunderstanding he was thinking about, but I wasn't going to let my guard down.

"See, I thought you were the competition. I didn't realize you were hunting a Beast like that," he continued, "I'm real sorry about attacking you."

"Huh?"

My weapon dropped a little bit. I had heard of a bandit apologizing to try and save his skin, but this didn't feel like that. He seemed genuine in his words.

"Why would a bandit apologize?" Reginald asked, his eyes narrowing on the man in front of us.

"Oh yeah." The bandit boss snapped his finger as if remembering something. "That's the other thing I wanted to clear up. We aren't bandits."

"Oh yeah?" I said sarcastically. "As if I would ever take a bandit at their word."

"Yeah. The name's Emmerson."

The name seemed to make something click in my companions' heads.

"Wait, THE Emmerson?" Reginald asked.

"A-as in The Emmerson G-Group?" Myrril jumped in.

Leone turned to the others, "The independent mercenary group?"

"The one and only," Emmerson smiled with pride. "We specialize in ambush tactics and guerrilla warfare, so we're often mistaken for bandits."

Emmerson pulled a folded document from his pocket and held it out for us to see. It appeared to be an official document sanctioning them to operate within the Valtion-Silma City-State Alliance and even had an official stamp.

I turned to my companions for confirmation before sheathing my weapon.

"Then I suppose it was a misunderstanding," I said, "but even if you are a mercenary group, why are you operating out of this cave?"

That detail had been bothering me since he said they were mercs. This place was obviously more than a stash, but also less than an HQ.

"Oh, well. The person who hired us wanted us to be ready at any time. This was the best location," he explained, "but we can talk more about that in a minute. I gave you my name, how about you tell me yours?"

"Elric," I said without hesitation. The more I spoke with him, the less I felt that he was a bad guy.

I turned to introduce the others when my knee gave out, almost throwing me to the floor.

"Whoa!" Reginald caught me and helped me stand.

"Hey, bud," Emmerson started, "I don't know what you did to that crab, but it obviously took a lot out of you. Here, take a seat."

He brought over a stool, and I graciously accepted. As soon as I got into the seat, my legs gave way. The adrenaline had finally worn off.

I had the thought of why he wasn't helping his wounded men, but I noticed that they were already taking care of themselves.

"Thank you," I said to Emmerson. "As I was saying. This is Reginald, Myrril, and Leone."

I pointed to each as I said their name, prompting them to nod toward Emmerson. Well, Myrril didn't, but that's not unusual.

"Leone, eh?" Emmerson stared at Leone, scratching his chin. Then, he snapped his fingers.

"OH! That Leone. I knew you were familiar. I've seen you around the Association Hall."

"Oh? You go to the Association Building?" I was a little shocked that an independent merc would go there.

"Well, yeah. Even if I'm not a member, they still have a ton of information."

I honestly didn't know that non-members could access their information network, so this was surprising to hear.

"But anyway, you wanted to know what we were doing here, right?" Emmerson asked.

"Well, yeah. But we don't expect you to actually tell us," Reginald replied.

"Oh, normally I wouldn't. But, well, I don't think we'll be able to continue the job in our current state..."

He had just lost half of his troupe, and the two surviving members were in bad shape. If he valued their lives, the smart thing would be to pull out.

Emmerson pulled up another stool and sat in front of me. As he did this, I realized that my hand was still shaking. Moving it in any way sent a sharp pain down my arm, ending at my elbow. I figured it was broken.

I pulled a small pack of medical supplies from my pocket

dimension and began to pull out the things I would need. However, wrapping your own hand proved to be more difficult than I thought.

"Need some help there?" Reginald saw as I struggled.

"No," I waved him off, "I think I've got it."

I used my fingers to twist part of the bandages together and quickly pulled them around my hand once. The bandage stopped moving and allowed me to properly wrap my hand. I did this while listening to Emmerson speak.

"It all started a few months back when we were approached by a well-dressed man," Emmerson began. "He said he represented a powerful individual and had a job for us. 'Course I was skeptical at first, but he had the money and the clothes of someone in that position, so I heard him out. At first, he just wanted us to make sure nobody bothered a group of travelers coming in from Roswin, that was simple enough, but then he asked us to do it without them knowing!"

Now, why would that be? My mind started racing.

Probably seeing the look on my face, Emmerson said, "I was thinking the same thing, bud. It was a strange request to protect someone without them knowing, but it paid well. The problems started just after that."

As Emmerson put it, the man who came to them wanted them to start terrorizing folks. Scaring travelers and putting off merchants from certain routes is a pretty standard hire around here.

Then, the Merchant Elect was almost killed.

"We didn't think much of it at first," he explained, "but then the whole thing with the Merchant Elect happened, and we got a little suspicious. I may not be the sharpest, but this was something I could see."

"Why not go to the guard?" Reginald asked a sensible question. "It would have been the rational thing to do."

"I told him to," one of the guys from Emmerson's group interrupted, "but he said he'd take care of it himself."

Emmerson scratched his neck, looking embarrassed.

"Yeah.... So I went to confront our contact," Emmerson continued. "When I showed up, the guy was accompanied by a city guard."

"Really?" I asked. "How did that go?"

"Well, when I started asking questions, the representative waved more cash in my face, and well..."

"He got greedy," the guy from Emmerson's group jumped in again.

"Y-yeah, but he just wanted us to keep scaring off merchants for double our original pay. How could anyone refuse!" Emmerson frantically tried to justify his blatant greed.

"By saying no..." I heard Leone mutter behind me.

Emmerson turned back to me with a pained smile, "Well, anyway, yeah. That's what's been going on."

"I see..." Thoughts poured through my head like the spillway of an overflowing dam.

Then, something clicked.

"Hey, Emmerson."

"Huh?" He moved his body back a bit, not expecting my tone.

"You didn't take the job without a contract, right?"

Emmerson looked offended, "Of course not! That's the only proof an independent merc has that they were promised pay."

"Could I see it?" I asked politely.

"Huh? Uh... sure, I guess?"

Emmerson's face was plastered with confusion, but he retrieved the contract nonetheless.

"Here you go. Not that it has any names on it."

Emmerson handed me the contract, and I opened it, scanning through the contents. As he had said, the amount paid was quite high, not that I had any basis for the going rate to scare off merchants.

What interested me the most, however, was the seal stamped at the bottom.

A bird wreathed in flame.

I held the document up for Reginald and Myrril to see, eliciting a gasp.

"Wait a minute, that's the same one on the documents found in Koberic's lab!" Reginald said in surprise.

"Yeah," I confirmed.

But if these two incidents are connected, does that mean those travelers...

I quickly turned back to Emmerson.

"Those travelers that you protected. Were they a group of three? Two men, one really big, and a single woman?"

"Wha–" Emmerson's eyes widened, giving me all the confirmation I needed.

"How did–" he started, but I cut him off.

"We've encountered them," I explained. "They are the ones responsible for the attempted assassination of the Merchant Elect."

All the blood drained from his face, "N-no... that means... I..."

The guilt on his face quickly turned to anger. With teeth clenched, he said, "I swear I'll find them and make this right."

"I'm sorry to say that you'll have to make amends another way," I interrupted once more. "They are already dead. We killed them."

"What?" Emmerson's face turned to shock, "But then how... how am I supposed to..."

I shook my head, "I don't know. I can't tell you how you can make up for it. Only you can do that."

Emmerson wasn't a bad guy. He was just caught in a bad situation, and he would have to atone for that in his own way.

"How will I know?" he asked. His eyes were filled with sorrow.

"Hm," I put my hand on my chin and looked off to the side in thought, before bringing my eyes to his once more.

"I think you'll just know when the time is right."

"I see..." Emmerson looked down. "I have a lot to think about."

He stood from his seat and walked over to the small writing desk where we had first seen him. He plopped down in the chair there and stared off into space.

I really didn't want to interrupt his existential crisis, but I had one more thing to ask.

"By the way, can we take this with us?" I held up the contract.

"Huh?" He looked over to me, his eyes devoid of life. "Yeah. I don't ever want to see it again."

I was a little taken aback by how hard he was taking it, and I wasn't the only one.

"Do you think he'll be okay?" Reginald asked in a hushed tone.

"Yeah, I think so... But we should probably not stay any longer than we need to," I responded, getting up from my seat.

Oh shit!

I had just remembered something important and grabbed at my calf. It had stopped bleeding, and I couldn't find a trace of the wound besides a small number of faint scars.

"Is something wrong?" Reginald asked.

"No... No, it's fine..." I replied, knowing full well that it was not fine.

My wound had healed too quickly, and now there were a bunch of errant shards of stone stuck in the muscle. I'd have to take care of it eventually, but it was going to be a painful process.

"Let's just grab some proof of the kill and go," I drew my sword and walked toward the remains of the crab.

We made it back to Onforde by the time the sky showed off the final displays of sunset. People were already out lighting the various lanterns meant to illuminate the streets as people went about their business, even in the darkness of night.

I was utterly exhausted, but it wasn't just my muscles and hand that ached. There was a clear line that could be traced within me by following the pain. While Megin didn't have a physical form within the body, it acted much like an artery. What I was experiencing was a side effect of forcing all of my Megin out of its natural pathway. Now that it was restored to its normal flow, the pain had subsided, but not completely. It left a lingering ache like the day after a heavy workout. Still, I was the only one who could steer the boat, so I pushed through.

Small waves lightly moved around us as I gently pulled the boat up to the pier we had cast off from.

My companions let out a sigh of relief as we exited the craft.

"Ah, man," Reginald mused, "I'm glad to be back. The boat was nice, but the water was disconcerting."

"I've been on a boat a few times before, but I can never get used to the isolated feeling of being out there," Leone agreed.

"I-I actually liked it..." Surprisingly, Myrril had been the one who enjoyed it the most, besides me.

"Yeah, that was nice," I tiredly said with a pause. "Let's get this thing to the Association so we can sleep."

"Whoa, um, is something wrong?" Reginald looked surprised.

His question confused me. "No?" I responded.

Looking around, I noticed that the other two looked taken aback as if I had said something strange.

"What is it?" I asked.

"Oh, well, you just sound really um... irritated," Reginald hesitated in his reply.

"Well, I'm not. I'm just really tired," I replied.

"Oh... okay."

With that settled, I reached my hand into the cold lake water and grabbed hold of the object we had strapped to the side of the boat. With a mighty heft and a grunt, I pulled the object from the water, revealing the massive, severed claw of the Gorodian Crab.

"Let's get going." I grabbed hold of either side of the claw, my muscles screaming in pain, and lifted it onto my shoulder. All I could say was, it was heavy.

"Man... even though this is the second time seeing it, I still can't believe it," Leone mused.

I had picked it up earlier to bring it to the boat, so for my companions, it wasn't a new sight.

The bystanders, however, looked as if their eyes would burst from their heads. As we walked down the street, countless gawkers stopped what they were doing to stare. It's not every day that they see someone carrying something twice the size of a carriage, after all.

Luckily, we had used thick fabric to wrap the part we cut, so no fluids were spilling out all over the streets.

It seemed that word had spread, as by the time we reached the Association, there was already a crowd of mercenaries gathered around the small square in front of the building.

At the front were several receptionists and a large man I had never seen before. He had a thick beard, short hair, and arms like battering rams, which were folded as we approached. He appeared to be the one in charge.

We stopped in the middle of the square, and I dropped the claw at the foot of the man in front.

"Is this good enough proof?" I asked, trying my best not to sound tired.

The mercs who had gathered shrank back a little as I spoke, their eyes widened.

"Oh, man, that really sounds like he's mad..." I heard Reginald whisper behind me.

"Hmmm..." The man I was addressing looked me up and down; then, each member of our group before responding, "Well, you folks do look pretty banged up."

He noted our bandages and dented armor.

"Not to mention that this is a lot more proof than those others gave," he continued, circling the claw before stopping at the fabric and taking a peek beneath. "And looking at this wound, it was cut methodically. No way the Gorodian Crab would have just let you do this."

The man smiled, "I would say it's a job well done."

The crowd of mercenaries, now joined by countless bystanders, started to whisper among themselves.

The man stopped in front of me and held out his hand, "The name's Hank Doring. I'm the director of this Association branch."

Hank? What are the chances of meeting two Hanks in three hours? I thought to myself as I grasped his hand and shook.

"Elric."

"Elric, eh? You the one from Edren?"

I nodded.

Hank's eyes brightened like he had connected dots in his head, "Ah, well, that makes some sense now."

He pointed a thumb over his shoulder at the claw, "Have any plans for this?"

I shook my head, "No. You can have it."

"How generous!" Hank replied.

"Anyway, have fun with that. It's a little heavy," I waved my hand and started walking away, my companions close behind me. The crowd made a hole to allow us to exit.

"If you lifted it, then it shouldn't be a problem." Hank seemed lost in his thoughts for a moment before realizing we had started to leave.

"Oh, wait!" he called after us. "Don't forget to collect your reward!"

I looked back and waved him off, "Keep it."

We had discussed the matter of the reward on our way back and came to a consensus. It felt wrong to take the money as it was already part of our contract to clean up after Lost Light. Leone, while not part of the job we had taken, agreed with us.

As I responded to Hank, the crowd really went wild. The reward for killing a beast of that size was quite large, and when you included that it was an emergency request, the pot became even larger.

We quietly walked back to Leone's place as the sounds of the crowd grew distant behind us.

The director gave a wide grin as he watched Elric and his companions walk away. They had killed a Gorodian Crab, carried a piece of it back, and then refused a reward.

They're really something, Hank thought, smiling at the group of youngsters who walked away into the night.

Not long ago, he had received a letter from Louis Renard,

the director of the Edren Association branch, that explained their situation. While not even having made it past their second decade yet, those three had already accomplished quite a feat and garnered the attention of a lord.

Even with Leone accompanying them, this victory was quite a tantalizing feat. Hank imagined it would open up many future opportunities for them.

Moving on from that train of thought, Hank turned his attention back to the massive claw blocking the square.

"Could you make sure Storehouse Three is open, please?" he politely asked one of the receptionists.

"Yes, of course, Director," she politely answered before making haste around the back of the Association building.

Hank turned back to the crowd and pointed out a pair of individuals.

"You two, help me carry this around the back. It'll be a bit awkward to move it through the alley."

All three men together crouched down and lifted the great Gorodian Crab claw from the ground, each one straining under the weight.

Seeing this, a few more men rushed over to help.

For the bystanders, it had been quite a confusing spectacle to watch. First, a somewhat skinny young man had carried the entire claw on his shoulder and set it in the square. Then, it took six hardened mercenaries to not only lift the thing but to move it at any sort of pace.

"How the hell did that kid carry this!?" one of the mercenaries complained as they maneuvered the claw into the alley.

"This... this thing weighs a ton!" another managed to squeeze out.

"I'd say about half, maybe a little more," a third retorted.

"Quiet down, you guys, only a little farther to go."

Hank shut them up and got them to put all their effort into shuffling through the now-open storehouse doors.

Still, he couldn't help but think, *How is this only 'a little heavy'?!*

That night, I was too tired to dream. A surprise, but a welcome one, to say the least. Reginald awoke while I was eating a basic breakfast of bread and dried meat and ended up joining me.

"Morning."

"Huh?" Reginald replied with a groggy tone, "Oh, yeah, uh, good morning."

He sat at the table and grabbed a loaf of bread, breaking off pieces and slowly eating them as he stared off into space.

"How are you feeling?" I asked.

"My ribs are still killing me, but I'm doing well otherwise," he replied between bites, "How about you?"

"I feel a lot better." I smiled.

In reality, I wasn't doing too well. My body still ached from overextending my Megin, and my right hand wouldn't stop its light shakes. My superficial wounds had already healed, but my broken bones would take another day or two. As for whatever damage I caused to my Megin channels.... I had no clue. There was a reason why what I did was forbidden.

"Well, if that's the case," Reginald started, "after breakfast, I could use a sparring partner."

"Hm, sounds good."

I had actually been feeling a little off lately. I wasn't sure if it was because I had been mainly fighting beasts and Abnormals while being trained to fight people, or if there was some other reason. Either way, doing some training would help me get back into a healthy mindset.

Reginald had gotten better with the blade. His stance was improved, and his strikes were more precise. On the other hand, I found myself struggling during the first half. My sore body, along with an unsteady hand, really gave me trouble. With every move, it felt like my veins were on fire. However, the pain slowly subsided as we went, and I regained better control of my weapon.

By the time we were finished, everyone else was already ready for the day. Leone and Myrril were seated on the couch and chatting away while Jackson and his sister chased each other around the house.

After getting cleaned up, we started to form a game plan.

I placed the contract we had gotten from Emmerson on the dining room table as the four of us gathered around, as well as producing some of the other materials we had received from the lord; just copies, but they were accurate.

"This is everything we have on Lost Light and the mad scientist Koberic," I started. "As Reginald pointed out yesterday, the firebird symbol on the contract is the same as the one on the orders both groups received."

"What about the other guy? Kane Ovid, was it?" Reginald promptly asked.

"They didn't find any physical evidence linking the groups besides Lost Light's actions and the words of his cronies," I replied.

"From what you all told me on the boat, this necromancer guy seemed to be behind it," Leone jumped in. She was knowledgeable about our exploits thanks to a discussion we had after meeting Emmerson. We had felt that she should be in the loop.

"That's the conclusion the lord of Edren came to," I agreed, "and it makes the most sense. Nearly all of the pieces fit, but a few things come to mind."

"Like what?"

"Well, for starters. Who is Kane Ovid? How has nobody ever heard of him before?" This was the biggest missing piece in my mind. Kane Ovid was an unknown, and therefore, a danger. He may not have seemed very dangerous when we faced him before, but the fact that he was able to hide from the public eye with such skills was a cause for concern.

"Then there is the fact that each part of the operation seemed to be meticulously planned so as not to draw attention to themselves. But if that was the case, why try to kill the Merchant Elect?"

"Hm. That would only complicate things..." Leone thought aloud.

The more we thought of it, the more it seemed strange. For such a careful planner to make such clumsy mistakes... I couldn't make sense of it.

"Wait..." Reginald snapped his fingers. "What if he had planned to come here next?"

"Well, killing the Merchant Elect would certainly destabilize the area for a while," Leone mumbled.

"Making it easier to do whatever he wanted," I followed her train of thought. Was killing the Merchant Elect part of another plan, or perhaps an even greater one? Killing the Merchant Elect, destabilizing the region, taking over Edren. What do all of those have in common? Other than a grudge or personal gain, I couldn't help wondering if it was the prelude to a full-scale invasion. If that were the case, then it would be imperative that—

"D-does that mean he's here?" Myrril asked in a voice only slightly higher than a mumble and laced with fear. Her question pulled me from the unsubstantiated rabbit hole my mind had begun to dive into. I shook off the complex thoughts and answered her question.

"I... I don't know. I wouldn't think so..."

I was at a loss. It had never occurred to me that Kane Ovid could be in Onforde. I mean, it didn't make much sense for a necromancer to be here. There were no tombs I was aware of, no sites of large battles, or really much that a necromancer could work with.

Unless....

"What if he's not thinking like a necromancer..." I mused.

"What was that, Elric?" Leone asked.

"Oh, sorry. I was just wondering if perhaps we should stop thinking of him like a necromancer," I proposed. "I mean, it wouldn't make much sense for him to be here in that context, but if we look at it another way..."

"Maybe he is here for something else?" Reginald jumped in.

"Exactly!" I felt pieces fitting together in my head. "If we just make a slight change to that thought, it makes sense. What would someone come to Onforde for?"

"Th-the lake?" Myrril guessed.

"Money."

"Yes!" I jumped at Leone's answer, "it's the city of merchants. What other place would someone go for some capital?"

"That would also explain why he wants to stop certain merchants from arriving," Leone added.

I could see the gears turning in all of their heads as they began to piece everything together. I had done the same thing a moment ago and was waiting for them to come to the same conclusion I had.

"So," Reginald started, leaning back in his chair, "Kane Ovid is in the city and planning something big."

The look on the other two indicated that they agreed with this statement.

I smiled, "It would seem so."

"And?" Leone leaned forward intently. "What's the plan?"

"First things first. We need to confirm our theory."

Myrril tilted her head to the side.

"We have a description of the guard Emmerson saw, and we know he had the night shift, I started, so, where does a guard go after their shift?"

The three of them looked at each other, and then back at me with a synchronized response.

"The tavern."

Taverns. When one thinks of a tavern, one usually imagines a dingy room filled with round tables, loud conversation and laughter, and beautiful bar wenches. This is not incorrect.

However, there are many types of establishments that one may consider a tavern. There are bars that only serve drinks, dining halls usually strapped onto an inn, and the most common one, an establishment that serves both food and drink but with an emphasis on the drink.

Of course, fine dining places usually served alcohol as well, but these were unaffordable on a guard's salary.

Even taking all of those businesses off the list, there were over a hundred places to check in the city. Given that we had no clue where the guard was stationed, we had no way of narrowing the search.

We had already checked well over ten taverns by the time we approached one named The Headless Huntsman. It was a rickety old building located in a less fortunate area of town, and it looked like the perfect place for bandits and thieves to gather.

"Look," Reginald spoke up as we approached the shady-looking building, "we've been at this for a while. How do we know the guard even drinks?"

He made a fine point. There was no guarantee that the man we were looking for had a taste for drink, and given that it was already past noon, we had no indication that he would even be out at this time. However, Reginald forgot one crucial thing.

"Have you known any guard who doesn't drink?" I asked him.

Reginald pondered the question for a moment before he responded.

"Fair enough. Let's go inside."

The inside of the tavern was just as run-down as the exterior. A fair number of shady-looking individuals filled the seats within. At the bar was a tired-looking middle-aged man lazily washing a mug.

Leone took the lead, as she had with all the other taverns.

"What can I get for you?" the man behind the counter asked as she approached.

"Ale. With a side of information." Leone quieted her voice for the second part.

She put some money on the counter, which the bartender slid into his hand, and began pouring a drink.

Now, some may think that a bartender wouldn't know much about what's going on, but in reality, they hear more gossip than an information broker. People went to bars to drink, and drink loosens the tongue, so to speak. As long as you show them you can pay for the information, they won't mind telling you if they have what you're looking for.

"Hm. Depends on what you're looking for." The bartender placed the drink in front of Leone.

"A guard with the night shift who may have come into some extra money in the last few weeks," Leone deftly responded.

The man scratched his chin for a moment, "I may have heard a thing or two."

Leone slid a silver coin across the bar, which the bartender deftly swept up with a rag as if cleaning the counter.

I didn't know what all the secrecy was about. I mean, this place looked like one that wouldn't care about something like this, but maybe I was just naïve.

The bartender nodded toward a table in the back.

"That one's been in here a lot recently. Drinks himself half to death nearly every day."

The table that was pointed out was occupied by a single man, passed out and cradling a drink.

"Much obliged," Leone grabbed the ale she had ordered and beckoned for us to follow.

Leone didn't like alcohol, but I had an idea as to what she was doing with it.

As soon as she got to the table, she slammed it down, jolting the man awake.

"Here, friend. Looks like you could use another."

Leone invited herself to sit at the table, a familiar sight to the three of us as we stood back a bit and let her work.

The man, groggy and with a red face, merrily grabbed the ale Leone had set down before him.

"Thant... than... thansh," he slurred words of thanks and took a hearty swig from the mug. He slammed the mug onto the table and squinted his eyes toward Leone. His body was swaying heavily from left to right, and his words were incomprehensible. I was just lucky that I understood enough to translate.

"H-Hey... you're... you're kinda pretty," he stumbled over his words, poorly whispering the next part. "Are you an angel?"

Leone simply smiled at him, "Something like that."

The drunken grin left the man's face and was replaced with one of confliction. "Are you here... here to punish me, angel lady?"

"Why would I need to punish you?" Leone asked gently and with an almost motherly tone.

The man looked down at his drink.

"C-cause... cause I did something bad..."

"Oh? You did?"

"No." The man pulled back a bit, almost like a child denying his wrongdoing.

"Are you sure?" Leone nudged.

The man let out a sigh and relented, "N-no..."

"So, what was the bad thing you did?"

"I... I probably shouldn't talk about it... But you're pretty, so I guess it's okay."

The almost childlike innocence this man projected was off-putting, to say the least. Reginald and Myrril felt the same way, as anyone would when a thirty-something-year-old man started acting as though he were five.

Anyway, the man began to regale us with his bad deed. I'll save you the pain of his exact words and summarize.

In essence, a bureaucrat from the Head Administrator's office offered him a lot of money to make a slight change to the guard schedule at the Merchant Elect's estate. It was right at the end of his shift, and he figured that it was important, so he did as he was asked. The next day, he was shocked to find that someone had killed the Merchant Elect's body double and figured it out right away. Then, the same bureaucrat showed up again and blackmailed the guard into helping him do some other things, including protection against a mercenary the bureaucrat was supposed to meet.

After that whole thing, Leone spoke to the man again.

"I see. That must have been tough. I'll be right back, okay?"

"Okay..." The man's voice was full of melancholy.

Leone approached us.

"So, what do you guys think?" she asked in a hushed tone.

"It sounds to me like this bureaucrat might be Kane," Reginald spoke first.

"O-or they are working together..." Myrril added.

"True," I agreed. "Either way, there seems to be a mole in the Head Administrator's office.

"We needed to inform the Head Administrator right away. If they are still planning to carry out the assassination, then it could come from within."

"I agree," Leone nodded, then looked back at the drunken man, "But what should we do with him?"

I gave my thoughts on the matter.

"I kind of feel bad for him, getting roped up in it, but he's an accomplice to murder."

"I wholeheartedly agreed. If justice worked here as it did back in my day, then the lord, or Merchant Elect in this case, would give the punishment directly. Perhaps he will see to spare the man... Or perhaps not."

CHAPTER 11

The Head Administrator

The drunken guard put up no resistance and allowed his fellow officers to take him away. I was a little concerned that they would just release him, but seeing the look on their faces when we told them what he had said changed my mind.

After watching them drag him away, we made haste toward the manor of the Head Administrator. We crossed the bridge to the more posh side of town and followed a different road than the one for the Merchant Elect's estate.

The sun was getting steadily lower on the horizon by the time we made it to the Head Administrator's manor.

The building in front of us was a three-tiered structure that looked to be a cross between a townhouse and a castle. Many pillars decorated the sides of the massive brick structure, and even more windows graced its walls. Its roof was the same peculiar kind we had seen around the city, with the roof pitching at a drastic angle before becoming nearly flat at the top. A small perimeter fence cordoned off the area, and a pair of guards stood by the gate.

"Halt! State your business," a guard called out to us as we approached.

"We've come to see the Head Administrator. We bring urgent news about the investigation."

The men looked at each other for a moment after hearing my statement before the second one spoke up.

"Ah, yes. Now I recognize you. You are the ones who spoke with the Merchant Elect."

"We are, and it is imperative that we speak with the Head Administrator."

"Hmm, I see. Well, Head Administrator Zerrick is quite busy at the moment..." one of the guards started.

"The information we have cannot wait."

I was starting to get annoyed with the guards and began pushing even more.

"If you will not let us in, then we will go straight to the Merchant Elect," I threatened.

At that, the guards had a look of panic in their eyes.

"W-wait now. No need to be hasty."

"Yes, we can tell the Head Administrator that you've arrived. Please, come with me to the parlor."

The two men were all but happy to accommodate us after I threatened to go over their heads. They were the type of person I disliked the most, but nonetheless, we followed them into the manor.

While the manors I had visited since my escape from Kyrtvale had been fairly modest, or well-decorated yet not overly lavish, this manor was nothing less than gaudy.

The floors were coated in carpets of the finest silks, the walls were plastered in expensive artwork, gold and silver fittings, and jewel-embedded vases. Even the chandeliers and sconces were made of rare metals and affixed with magical lighting, which, based on my own experiences in the human world, were not easy to obtain.

We were led down a hallway and into the parlor, which was also an ostentatious display of wealth. Even to someone untrained as I, the paintings and even the furniture were of remarkable quality. I shuddered at the thought of how much it all must have cost. To put it in simple terms, even the room in the Merchant Elect's manor that we had waited in was put to shame even by a parlor.

"Please, be seated. I will go and inform Head Administrator Zerrick."

One of the guards gestured toward the lavish couch before exiting the room, soon replaced by another guard seemingly from nowhere. Now, there were two of them posted in front of the only exit, making it feel as though we were being kept there.

Reluctantly, the four of us sat on the couch, but we didn't have time to enjoy the cloud-like feeling.

"Something's not right here..." Reginald was the first to speak up, keeping to a hushed tone.

Leone shifted her eyes toward the guards, "Normally, I'd agree, but this place must have cost as much as an army to furnish. I wouldn't trust random mercs either."

Myrril nodded along.

"Sure, but did you guys also notice how few maids there were on the way here?" I pointed out.

While walking through the manor, we encountered no less than ten separate guards and yet only saw a single servant. I was unsure if the house was kept with magic or if there was some other reason for it.

"And the way the guards reacted was suspicious," I continued, "I mean, I was trying to push them, but they were way too accommodating after I mentioned the Merchant Elect."

The others glanced at each other before Reginald responded with a question.

"Do you think Kane has people here as well?"

"It's possible," I answered.

If Kane had gotten to the people in this manor, not only the Merchant Elect but the Head Administrator could be in danger.

Honestly, I was impressed. It may seem like an obvious

thing to infiltrate someone's organization and take them out from the inside, but very few people actually think like that. It takes a cunning mind to not only realize the obvious but to pull it off without a hitch. Though we figured it out' so it wasn't entirely without a hitch.

"What should we do?" Leone asked earnestly.

"I'm not sure. Guess I'll just wing it," I casually whispered as I left my seat, proceeding to approach the double doors. I could feel my companion's eyes focused on my back as I moved.

"Is there something I can help you with?" one of the guards asked as I approached. His stance dropped slightly, barely noticeable, but it was clear he was experienced.

"Yeah, um, I was wondering if you could direct me to the restroom?"

The two men glanced at each other with a look of annoyance.

"Well, we can't really have you wandering about..." one of them replied.

"Ah, yes. I understand that, but... nature calls... heh," I awkwardly smiled at the two of them.

The one who seemed to be older had a look of understanding and turned his head toward his younger compatriot, who shook his head. With a little more pushing stare, the younger guard relented with a sigh.

"All right. I'll take you there," he said, reaching for the handle. That's when the older guard leaned in and quickly whispered something in his ear before letting him go.

I followed the younger guard out of the room and down the sickeningly gaudy hallways once more.

"I appreciate this," I said to him. "We learned of the information and ran straight here, so I didn't have time before now."

The young guard smiled a bit, "Yeah, I understand that. Been in a similar situation a few times myself."

"Even still, I wanted you to know how thankful I am," I decided to lay on the praise a bit.

"There's no need," the guard insisted, "the young will be swallowed by the old if we do not assist each other."

I felt surprised at the odd words of wisdom coming from such a young man but managed to hide it and continued to converse.

"Oh, yes, that is very true indeed. The world is unkind to those who have yet to fully experience it."

The young guard gave a brief chuckle, "I'm glad you understand."

After making a bit of a connection, I decided to fish for information.

"I was wondering," I started, "how is it working for the Head Administrator?"

The guard took a moment to ponder the question.

"Well, the hours are terrible, but the pay is pretty good."

"I see. I suppose he pays you well to prevent theft," I mused. "A well-paid man is less likely to steal the valuables he is meant to guard, or something like that."

"Huh. I never thought of it like that."

The young man seemed somewhat surprised at the notion of preventing theft by increasing pay. People who are charged with guarding a great deal of wealth will often feel that they are paid unfairly. There are two ways to combat this. The first is to hire only the most outstandingly moral people, which is a lot harder than it seems. The second is to pay them more. It was something I learned from my father, and I was glad to see it was still relevant.

"And, another thing," I began to ask another question. "Is it always normal for guests to wait to deliver urgent information?"

"What do you mean?"

"Well, wouldn't it be better to just go directly to the Head Administrator?"

The guard let out a bit of a chuckle, "The Head Administrator wouldn't make his guests go up all those stairs."

I couldn't help but smile internally.

Soon after, we stopped some ways down a hall.

"This is it," he said to me, gesturing toward a singular door.

I faced the young man and said my thanks once more, eliciting a pained smile from him. I turned and reached for the handle when I heard a small scraping sound from behind me.

As I reached forward, I curled my hand into a tight fist, dropped my stance, and pulled back my arm. I twisted my waist and used the momentum, as well as the explosive force of my arm, to launch a single right hook behind me. The young man's face began to change expression, but by then, my fist had made contact with the side of his jaw. His hand released the partially drawn blade at his side as he stumbled, his eyes rolling into the back of his head.

I quickly moved to catch the now-unconscious guard before he hit the floor.

"Being so friendly when you plan to try and kill me..." I grumbled under my breath.

Indeed, the young guard had been told to take me out when we had reached our destination. It may have worked, too, if I hadn't overheard their whisper at the parlor door. Never have I been more grateful to have better hearing than a human. Though I did get some valuable information from him, so it wasn't all bad.

I opened the door to the restroom and pulled the unconscious guard inside. It was surprisingly simple, compared to the rest of the manor. There was a single toilet, a large bowl for washing your hands, a small shelf holding a number of books, and a cubby holding incense.

Still, I had no time to admire it. I set the guard down and bound his arms and legs with a bit of rope I kept for emergencies. While he was knocked out now, he wouldn't remain that way for long, so I stuffed some cloth in his mouth and took his weapons, just to be sure. I felt a little bad about it, but he had tried to kill me, so at the very least, I felt justified to do this much.

Once I finished with all of that, my plan had come to an end. I wasn't lying when I said I would just wing it.

I carefully listened to my surroundings, much like I had done inside the cavern. A small tinge of sharp pain hit my head as I nudged Megin to coalesce within my ears, heightening my hearing.

I blocked out all unnecessary sounds and concluded that there were around three people within a hundred or so feet of me at all times. Though I was also trying to hear through multiple walls and floors, so my accuracy wasn't great. Then, I picked up a set of heavy footfalls approaching from down the hall.

I crouched down and peered through the gap in the door as I followed slightly metallic footfalls in my mind. Soon after, a figure passed by. It was a guard doing his rounds.

Once he had gained sufficient distance, I took a deep breath and slowly opened the door, careful not to make a sound. Glancing down the hallways, nobody was in sight. I slowly shut the door behind me and quietly made my way down the hall.

I wasn't sure exactly where I was going, but from what the guard had said, it sounded like the Head Administrator was upstairs. Not that I knew where he was or even the general layout of the building. I was practically fumbling around in the dark, and I couldn't just check every room.

Or could I?

No, of course not. That's silly. It would be much more efficient to ask someone where it was. Though it's not like they would just tell me. Hm, what a pickle.

I shook my head. It was no time for indecision. Thinking logically, this manor was decorated in a way that shows off its owner's greed, achievements, or ego. I didn't know much about Head Administrator Hanz Zerrick, but I did know that anyone who would decorate to this degree couldn't help but make this easier for someone like me.

So I asked myself. If I were greedy, egotistical, or a showoff, where would I put my office? Well, I would probably put it high up, somewhere I could look over my domain. Since Hanz Zerrick is the Head Administrator of Onforde, his office was probably on the third floor. Probably.

With my lack of confidence in my assessment, I slowly crept my way along the hallways, heading away from the main stairwell. This may seem like a dumb idea since I wanted to go up, but in reality, it was a very good one.

See, whenever a manor is being built, the builder always keeps two things in mind. Where are the guests and inhabitants going to travel through, and where are the servants going to travel through? Normally, you want to minimize the contact between lords and servants. This allows a more efficient way of getting work done. Servants don't have to stop and pay their respects, and the lord doesn't have to get distracted by them.

As such, many of these manors are built with staircases meant for the servants to use. Even bigger places, such as castles and palaces, often come with even more servant-related infrastructure, such as hallways that nobles and the like never pass through.

I grew up in the house of a count, yet I thought this practice was strange. We all lived together under the same roof, and I considered many of the house servants to be like family. Though maybe that was just me.

Either way, I was slightly worried that this place wouldn't have any of these staircases after seeing the lack of servants, but I was happy to spot one after very little searching.

Some would say I was lucky not to have run into anyone yet, but that wasn't quite true. I used my hearing to help me avoid patrols, though there were a few close calls that required me to duck into a room to avoid detection.

This technique, along with my general knowledge of the basic layout of noblemen's residences, is what allowed me to plant that letter on Lord Aulcrest's desk in Edren without getting caught. However, that time was a little easier since I was able to scout the building's exterior first. I suppose I also owed that to my time exploring manors as a child. Yet another example of something that hadn't changed much in the last thousand years.

I waited a moment to make sure the way was clear before tiptoeing up the surprisingly plain spiral staircase that ended on the second floor.

"No luck going all the way up, huh..." I muttered to myself.

I peeked out of the open archway and took in my surroundings. My heart dropped when I realized that the second floor looked the same as the first. Normally, there was at least some variation between the different areas of manors, be they a change in decoration, layout, room sizes, and whatnot. This place, however, was almost built like an exorbitantly decorated maze.

Just then, I heard hurried footsteps coming from my right. I must admit, I panicked a bit. I was standing in a wide open archway in clear view of anyone coming down the halls, and my options were limited.

In that moment of panic, I bolted across the way and entered the first door I could find.

The room was decently spacious, about a twenty-foot

square, and it seemed to be a guest room of sorts. There was a large bed against the far wall opposite a tall armoire. Luckily for me, it didn't seem like it was occupied at the moment. Various pieces of furniture were covered in white sheets, and there was a fine layer of dust across the room.

I cracked open the door just enough to peek down the hall and was somewhat surprised by what I saw. A maid was running down the hall as fast as she could in her heels.

She was young, in her early twenties or late teens. She had wavy brown hair and a pretty face, which was currently plastered with a look of terror. Her eyes darted from door to door as she ran, looking for something.

I pulled back a bit so as to not be seen when I heard something that gave me pause.

"Oh, come on, Tessa. I'm not going to hurt you. I just want to talk!" An unfamiliar male voice filled with calm rage echoed from the direction she came.

My head was telling me not to get involved, but my heart just couldn't let that happen. The young maid ran up to the door opposite the one I was behind and pulled on the handle, only to discover it was locked. She hurriedly glanced down either side of the hall for another option, spotting the stairwell I had come up.

She couldn't tell, but if she made for it, she would be seen. I could hear the man's footfalls about to round the corner.

Right as she turned to run back up the hall, I popped out of the room and grabbed her from behind, putting my hand around her mouth and quickly dragging her backward to the room I had hidden in. I swiftly closed the door behind us and stayed very still.

The woman, on the other hand, wouldn't stop struggling. She seemed to be trying to scream, but it was being muffled by my hand.

"Calm down for a moment. I'm not going to hurt you, but if you keep making noise, you'll alert the guy who's chasing you," I quickly whispered into her ear.

Realizing the situation, she calmed herself down somewhat, though she was still visibly shaking.

"Come on, Tessa. Don't make me angry," the voice called out once more.

Each moment that passed felt like hours as I could hear not only the sound of my own heart but the rapid beating of the maid's as well.

Eventually, the footsteps passed by the door, and we waited another few painful moments until we were sure he had left.

"Alright. I'm going to take my hand off of your mouth, okay?" I told the maid, "Just don't scream."

She nodded, so I slowly removed my hand from her mouth and released her from my grip. She took a few steps forward and whipped around to look at me.

"Who... who are you? How did you get in here?"

She was obviously still wary about me.

"My name is Elric," I answered, "I'm here to speak with the Head Administrator."

As I finished, she jolted her head like she had remembered something.

"The Head Administrator! I have to warn him!"

"Warn him about what?"

"He... He's in danger!"

I clicked my tongue, "Damn, I knew it."

"Wh-what?" The maid was shocked.

"I came to warn him about a possible assassination plot."

She held her head, "This is really bad. I mean, I knew it was bad, but if someone else found out, then it's even worse than I had thought..."

"Alright, hold on a moment. Tell me what happened."

She began to tell me about what had occurred earlier that day. She had been doing her rounds as usual when she over-heard some of the guards talking as she went down a set of stairs. To her surprise, they were talking about an assassination plot that was going to take place tonight. In her shock, she dropped her feather duster and was found out.

"So that's why you are being chased?" I asked.

"Yes," she replied, "but they've kept me from getting to the third floor so I can't warn the Head Administrator."

I internally jumped with joy that I had guessed correctly as the maid became distraught.

"What if it's too late?" she asked with tears in her eyes.

"I don't think it is," I reassured her. "The sun hasn't set yet, so it's still day."

My reasoning was flimsy and full of holes, but she seemed to take well to it.

Creeeaaaak...

The sound of the wooden floor squeaking outside caught my attention. The door handle jiggled slightly as I cursed myself. I had been so caught up with the story that I had forgotten to keep an ear out.

The maid's eyes widened, and she looked to me. I put a finger to my lips and jumped backward to stay out of view of the door.

It slowly crept open, and a shadow grew in the light coming from the hall.

"There you are, Tessa. I thought I had heard something."

I didn't have to see the man to know the look on his face.

The maid, Tessa, grew white as the color drained from her face. She slowly backed up farther into the room as the man followed after her.

Now with a clear view, I could see that it was indeed one of the household guards. He began to draw the shortsword at his waist.

"Now it's time you get what's coming to you."

The malice in the man's voice permeated the room.

I gripped the dagger that I had affixed to the back of my belt and drew the antler-gripped blade as I approached him.

"I don't think you want to do that," I pressed the blade against the front of his neck from behind.

"Oh? You had a friend." The man's tone didn't change, "And what do you think you can do with an edgeless blade?"

I smiled a bit, "Oh? It's edgeless, is it?"

I pressed the blade harder against his skin as I nudged a bit of Megin to flow into the dagger. The antler shimmered for but a moment, and a red line began dripping from the man's neck.

The man winced, "What in the–?"

"I don't take kindly to your tone," I whispered into his ear before sliding the blade across his throat.

The man grabbed at his neck and made a horrific gurgling sound as he drowned in his own blood. Within a moment, he dropped to the floor, a pool of crimson growing around his still corpse.

I wiped my dagger clean and stopped the flow of Megin, allowing the incredibly sharp blade to return to its normal form before sheathing it once more.

"It's this way."

Tessa was giving directions as I led the way, keeping us hidden when need be.

I was very grateful for her cooperation. Without it, I may have become lost in the manor for some time.

She had already led us to another servant's staircase, which brought us to the top floor. Now, our destination was in sight.

At the end of another overly decorated hallway was the tackiest sight I had ever had the displeasure of laying eyes on. A pair of double doors made of polished ebony and inlaid with scrawling figures made of thread-thin gold and platinum. The door handle, which was encrusted with glittering gems, was attached to the door in such a way that it seemed to be coming from the mouth of a lion. At least, I think it was a lion. It could have been a dog, I guess.

Any level of impressiveness I felt was vastly overwhelmed by how sick the sheer amount of wealth put into this door made me feel. Tessa's face twitched a bit as it came into view, making me realize I wasn't the only one who felt this way.

Tessa ran up to the door and gave it a light knock.

"Head Administrator?" she softly called out.

After a moment without reply, she tried once more, with similar results.

One moment, I placed my ear against the door and focused on listening. The inside of the room was completely silent.

"I don't think anyone's here," I informed Tessa.

"What?" Tessa put a hand to her mouth. "But this is where he always is at this time."

From some conversation earlier, it seemed that the Head Administrator was a very punctual person. He had never been late to a meeting during his tenure and followed a precise schedule to the letter. In fact, this was one of the things that his staff struggled to keep up with.

If what Tessa said was true, then this was very unusual indeed.

"I think we need to get in there and make sure he is all right," I suggested.

"But how?" Tessa asked, "I don't have a key and there isn't another way in."

Her tone was becoming more and more distressed.

"It's okay," I tried to reassure her, "We'll figure something out."

I went over our options in my head. The first one would be to find a key, but neither of us knew where to even start. Second, would be to pick the lock. Yeah, not happening. I neither had the knowledge nor the tools to do so. Finally, we could break the lock or kick down the door. Neither of which would be easy and would cause a degree of noise.

Then it hit me: the fourth option.

"Okay, give me a moment. I'll be right back." I grasped the handle of a room next to the office and was relieved when it opened without issue. There, I made my way straight for the window.

"W-wait. Where are you going?" Tessa shuffled after me.

I pulled the window open and stuck my head outside. As expected, we were in the roof area of the building, something akin to an attic space. The way that the roof sloped so sharply gave this upper floor plenty of space.

"Wait by the door. I'll go around and unlock it from the inside," I informed her as I clambered out of the window. My feet met a ledge just barely wide enough for me to stand before a thirty-foot drop. The sun was halfway gone beyond the horizon, and the sky was lit up in a beautiful array of oranges and reds.

Tessa stuck her head out the window to look at me with exasperation.

"Are you crazy! You'll fall and die!" she chastised in a loud whisper.

"This isn't the craziest thing I've done," I assured her with a smile before shimmying across the rooftop.

Tessa pulled her head inside with a huff and let me get on with my plan.

She was right, though; this was a dumb idea. A fall from the third floor was enough to kill a human, and while it probably wouldn't be as bad for an Aleurian, we weren't immune to breaking our necks.

Either way, I was confident in my abilities and smoothly made my way to the next window without issue.

Peering into the room, I was unable to see anything amiss. There was a finely carved mahogany desk set up so the user would have their back to the window for natural light, a series of bookshelves lined another wall, and a beautifully painted portrait of Head Administrator Hanz Zerrick himself was hanging on the wall.

Slightly perturbed that there was no sign of him, I put my fingers under the windowsill and gently pulled the window open without resistance.

I pulled myself inside and closed the window behind me. I quickly made my way to the door and turned the lock, opening it slightly to peek out. Once I made sure there was nobody nearby, I called out for Tessa.

"Tessa," I loudly whispered, "I've got it."

The door we had entered to the side of the office opened slightly, revealing Tessa glancing through. When she saw me, she hurried to join me in the Head Administrator's office.

"Did you find him?" she nervously asked.

I shook my head as I closed the door behind us. "No, I didn't."

Tessa surveyed the room. "Well then, I don't know where he could be. Maybe he had to leave urgently?"

She began searching the papers on his desk for any information as to where he had gone, while I looked just about everywhere else.

One thing I could say about Hanz Zerrick is that he kept his office clean. The floors were freshly polished, everything was neatly organized, and there wasn't a speck of dust to be found.

"Oops!" Tessa yelped as she accidentally knocked over a stack of papers, and several fell underneath the desk.

"Here, I'll get them." I reached my arm under the section of the desk with housed drawers and grasped around for the papers. I eventually found them, but not before my arm hit something curious.

I got down onto the floor and peered underneath the desk.

"What is it?" Tessa asked.

"Some kind of lever?" I thought aloud as I grasped an out-of-place block of wood. I tugged at it and heard a click from above as Tessa gasped.

"I see," I said as I stood, "it's some kind of hidden compartment."

Indeed, the block I had grabbed was a lever or button of some sort, and pulling it had caused a part of the flat surface of the desk to lift slightly. While I had been somewhat hopeful that one of the bookcases would have swung open to reveal a secret staircase, this was still exciting.

I grabbed the panel and pulled it up, much to the reluctance of Tessa.

"Wait! What if those are secret documents?!" she chastised.

"Really? You're going to say that now?" I rolled my eyes and let them rest on the opening, "It will be fine, they can't be... that..... bad..."

My gaze landed on a small pile of papers within the hidden space, letters, it would seem. Each one had a different correspondent, and for various reasons. However, they all had one thing in common. They each had a seal upon them, one of a flaming bird.

I snatched the pages from the hidden space and skimmed through them. Some were setting up meetings, others were transferring funds, and some had more implicit dealings. They seemed to be replies to other letters as well as some records of previously sent ones. As if to prove me right, I found a letter addressed to one Kane Ovid for arrangements to travel into Alliance territory.

"No..." I muttered as I spotted the final nail in the coffin.

"What's wrong?" Even Tessa could feel the tension I was exuding.

I reached into the space and pulled out a single rod of wood about four inches long. It tapered at one end to a flat plane, upon which was carved the image of a bird wreathed in fire.

As I stood there, something clicked in my head. What the drunken guard said, Emmerson's contract, the attempted assassination of the Merchant Elect; we had assumed it was Kane Ovid because he is blamed for perpetrating the Incident in Edren. However, when we tried to line it up with events here, they didn't fit. Only when we changed our thought pattern to that of a merchant did the pieces start to come together.

Who profits from terrorizing certain merchants? Who has something to gain from killing the Merchant Elect? And who benefits from destroying Edren?

Wait... destroying Edren? We assumed that it was for some necromantic plot, but what if that wasn't the case?

A vague memory popped into my mind. When we had confronted Kane underneath Edren, he had said something. He had said that he was tasked to purge Edren so that "They" could use it. We had glanced over it, but now that I was remembering, he spoke of someone else. Someone above him.

This person would have to benefit from the destruction and subsequent takeover of Edren, a central diplomatic powerhouse in the region. Whoever controlled Edren had great power over the flow of goods across the continent.

Then, this person would also have to benefit from the death of the Merchant Elect. In the case of the Merchant Elect's death, his second in command takes his place until the next election.

Now that I was seeing it all together, everything made sense. The final piece of which was what I held in my hands. A seal, a seal of a firebird that I had seen many times before. I could only find one conclusion.

Hanz Zerrick, Head Administrator of Onforde and accomplished merchant, in all his grand machinations, was the mastermind behind it all.

CHAPTER 12

... And the Merchant Elect

"Shit... oh shit!" I exclaimed as the pieces fell into place.

"What!?" Tessa jumped at my sudden outburst.

I grabbed her shoulders, "Listen. I was sent to Onforde to investigate the assassination attempt on the Merchant Elect. These papers," I held them up, "they prove that the Head Administrator was behind it!"

"What? N-no..." She could hardly process what I was saying.

"The plot you had overheard," I continued, "it's probably another attempt to kill the Merchant Elect."

Tessa's eyes darted back and forth as she took in everything I was saying.

"But wait, they said it was tonight!" she cried.

My eyes widened, and I flew to the window. The sun was nearly gone.

"We need to move fast. The–" I started before being cut off by a large explosion that shook the building.

Glancing back outside, I saw a small plume of smoke coming from underneath us as three familiar figures were locked in combat with several manor guards.

I let out a groan of exasperation, "By the Goddess, why now!"

"What was that!?" Tessa shouted.

"Just my friends," I answered. "Sorry, but we have to get down there fast."

"What do you mean, sorry?"

The look on her face made me feel a little bit guilty about what I was about to do.

Several minutes earlier, just after Elric left the parlor ∼

"Why is Elric always going off on his own?" Reginald silently grumbled as he sat on the very comfortable couch within the parlor.

This wasn't a completely uncommon occurrence within their group. At times, Elric would either go off on his own or attempt to take care of things by himself. This left the others somewhat frustrated, unbeknownst to him.

"D-does he not trust us?" Myrril asked rhetorically.

Leone, being the newest addition to the group, had less experience with this tendency and wanted to stay out of it. However, with the growing discontent, she decided to voice her opinion.

I haven't been with you for the other times he has done this, she began, but, in this case, at the very least, his decision was a sound one. If we are to figure out what is happening, then we must first exit this chamber.

"But we all could have gone," Reginald argued in a hushed tone.

Leone shook her head, "No. Not if we wanted to be sneaky about it. One, maybe two people could probably wander the halls unnoticed, but not all of us."

One or two people can quickly hide in a little space or can be written off after catching just a glimpse of them. It's surprising how much the human mind can convince you that everything is alright when something isn't too abnormal.

With a large group, you will end up making more noise and requiring even more space to hide should you need to. Not to mention, it's slower to inform every member of a group about the need to hide than it is for a single person. The more people, the slower the reaction time, and the harder it is to stay quiet and unnoticed.

"I see..." Reginald mumbled in thought.

Myrril, on the other hand, responded almost instantly.

"H-he could have at least t-told us the plan..." she trailed off.

Leone nodded in agreement, "Yeah. Even though we're on a time crunch, it would be best if we were all on the same page."

After a few minutes of waiting, the door to the parlor creaked open slightly, and another manor guard stuck his head in. He immediately went and whispered to one of the guards in the room, who nodded and turned to address the group.

"The Head Administrator is on his way here. We are going to have to ask you to relinquish your weapons," the guard said with a forced smile.

Reginald instantly felt suspicious and got to his feet.

"For what reason do we need to do that?" he asked. "We weren't even required to disarm when we met with the Merchant Elect."

As soon as he pointed that out, the guard's face twitched in irritation.

"That is because the Merchant Elect did not ask for it. However, the Head Administrator has different views on this matter," the guard answered with a smile unbefitting of his eyes. The glare with which he looked at Reginald was full of malice.

Reginald glanced at his friends, who joined him in standing.

"I do not think we will disarm," Reginald said with confidence.

"This is not a request."

Reginald's face grew serious as something in the back of his mind snapped.

He had been trained with the utmost respect and dignity as befitting a member of a ruler's family. He knew how to speak with members of the high classes, he could deal with commoners, and he could even defuse situations before they reached their boiling point. However, there had always been something in the back of his mind that rebelled against the rest. Something beyond logic. At this moment, it was that something that reared its head.

A wicked grin grew across Reginald's face, unsettling the now three manor guards.

"Then why don't you come and take them?"

Within a single moment, the parlor was painted red. The first guard had gone to draw his weapon when Reginald brought his own blade down, cutting through the soft tissue at the base of the neck and shattering the man's clavicle.

Before he could even make a sound, the first man was dead. His blood splattered across the wall and fine décor behind him.

The second guard froze as his face lost all color, while the third one let out a scream of terror. Even Myrril and Leone were caught off guard by this vicious attack, but not for long.

Leone ran forward and skewered the guard who had frozen, just barely having enough room to use her spear.

Myrril pulled back into the room and fired off a beam of crackling red energy.

"*Fire Arrow!*"

It flew through the air and impacted the third guard's

helmet with a loud Ping! sending him tumbling to the side and out the open door.

Reginald rushed after him, the man screaming as he approached, before mercilessly ending his life.

Then, just as quickly as that something had come, it was gone, and Reginald's mind returned to clarity. Though it wasn't as if it had clouded over. It was as though he had another desire that took precedence in those few moments.

Then, the group heard the sound of many footsteps rushing down the hall toward them.

"We need to get outside!" Leone called out. "It will be difficult to fight in here."

She was right. In such a confined space, both Reginald and Leone would have a hard time moving their weapons while the manor guard, with their shortswords, would have the advantage.

"The entrance was this way!" Reginald signaled for the others to follow and went into a full sprint down the hallway.

"OVER THERE!"

A shout came from behind them as a dozen or so armored guards chased after them. Now, they had no choice but to move forward.

"Don't look behind!" Reginald shouted. "Just keep moving."

The group ran past many side halls and splits, sometimes seeing even more guards who would also take up the chase. When they reached a certain point, they bolted around a split to the right and could finally see the entryway before them.

Unfortunately, it was blocked by about a half dozen guards, all with swords and shields at the ready.

Reginald knew they didn't have time to fight them. If they did, they would be quickly surrounded and killed, but he didn't have any other ideas on how to get by them.

Then, Myrril pointed her staff toward the guards in front. "*Flame Storm!*"

Megin gathered at the tip of her staff, and flames flickered to life. They began to move on their own, swirling forth from the Bloodstone like a tornado of fire, growing bigger and bigger with each passing moment until the flames engulfed the entire hall.

The six men in front of the entranceway had no time to move out of the way as the flames pushed past and through them, searing their flesh. They dropped to the ground in agony, some dying from shock.

But the flames didn't stop there. They rammed into the front doors with such force that they were blown from their hinges with a mighty crash.

Guards from outside ran toward the doorway while Reginald, Myrril, and Leone ran from it. The ones who had been following them gave pause for a moment, but it didn't buy them much time.

Myrril fired one spell after another, Leone swatted away guards with her spear, and Reginald cut down anyone who came close, but it was a losing battle. Even if they made it several yards to the gate and into the streets, the pursuit wouldn't end. To make it worse, it may even get civilians caught up in it.

It was at that time, as men started filing through the smoking doorway behind them, that another sound caught the ears of everyone nearby.

The sound of shattering glass was followed by the screams of a young woman.

Reginald couldn't help but let out a nervous chuckle as he glanced behind him at the sight that had begun to unfold.

I had decided to commit the stupidest thing I had ever done in my life. I started by pushing the Head Administrator's desk out of the way with a loud screech.

"What are you doing? Why won't you answer me?" Tessa asked in frustration.

"No time to explain!" I ran over and picked her up into my arms.

"EEK!" she screamed, kicking and hitting me. "Put me down!"

"No can do," I replied, "you might want to hold on tight!"

Her eyes grew wide, and I pushed off the ground and into a sprint. Tessa's arms locked around my neck as the room flashed past in an instant. With my shoulder forward, I ran directly into the window at full speed. The window frame bent and splintered as each pane of glass shattered outward.

Time seemed to slow, giving the illusion of flight. But I knew better. My senses had heightened from the adrenaline, but I was by no means flying. In fact, I could very clearly see the ground beneath me steadily growing closer as Tessa screamed into my ear.

With a glance, I noticed a pair of ornate doors lying in the grass, heavily charred. The doorway from which they came had small flecks of embers still embedded in the wood. From it also came another smattering of armored men, flanking my companions as they valiantly fought through the smattering of exterior guards.

I couldn't help but smile at how well they were doing.

As I approached the ground, I tucked my legs to the side. Dirt and grass flew as I hit the ground, but I leaned into the roll and planted my boots firmly on the ground at the end of it, pushing myself back to my feet.

Tessa was shaking in my arms, her eyes glassy, but she would probably be fine.

"Nice of you to join the party!" Reginald called out to me with a smile.

I gently set Tessa onto the ground and drew my sword, returning the smile.

"Had to take a bit of a detour." I launched myself forward and caught a blade coming down toward Leone, deflecting it sideways and using the opening to cut across my opponent's belly.

"I can see that," Reginald parried a blade and caught another one with his shield before kicking its owner away. "Who's the maid?"

My fist impacted with the metal armor of one of the guards, crumpling the chest plate inward and sending him to the ground.

"An eyewitness," I answered, and brought my weapon down upon another guard. This one managed to block the blow but took a flaming bolt into his side.

"Good," Leone was the one who spoke this time. "What did you find out? Where's the Head Administrator?"

I watched as she swung the haft of her spear around and knocked the final guard upside his head, sending him tumbling to the ground.

"A lot," I said as the others caught their breath. "We need to get to the Merchant Elect, now."

Noting my tone of urgency, the others nodded.

"Can you explain it on the way?" Reginald asked.

I pulled out the documents I found, as well as the seal, and handed them to him before picking Tessa back up. "Take a look at those."

We quickly began to run away from the Head Administrator's manor and toward the Merchant Elect's estate. It wasn't too far away, but far enough for Reginald and the others to become completely filled in about the situation.

"I can't believe we didn't see this!" Reginald shouted in exasperation.

Leone gritted her teeth, "It was so obvious."

"Don't beat yourselves up. We were working with the information we had," I tried to comfort the others as Myrril nodded along.

We rushed through street after street, past civilians and guards alike as the last light of day slowly disappeared. Not long after, we could see the Merchant Elect's estate at the far end of the road, but something was off. Even from a distance, it was easy to see that far too many windows were dark. In an estate that size, the hall lights would be lit by now.

The second thing that was off had to do with the front gate. Instead of the normal uniformed guards on duty, there was a handful of figures dressed in somewhat pieced-together gear.

When they saw us running toward them, they dropped into a defensive stance.

A familiar voice rang out.

"Hey! Slow yourselves down!"

It came with an unprofessional tone, much like someone who isn't trained to deal with visitors, only leading to the voice we all recognized.

"Zade!?" Leone called out in confusion.

"Leone!?" Zade returned.

Our group slowed down as we approached the mercenaries guarding the entrance to the estate. The one that seemed to be in charge was none other than Zade, the man we met in the Association Branch.

"Leone. What are you doing here?"

The others in Zade's troupe relaxed their guards.

"I should be asking you the same thing, Zade," Leone answered.

"Well, we were hired to guard the gate," Zade pointed his thumb behind them.

Leone's eyes widened, and I could see her thought process as clear as day. The Merchant Elect wouldn't have hired them to protect the gate when he had his own personal guards.

"What do you mean? Who hired you!?" Leone pressed.

Zade backed up a bit with his hands up, "Whoa, Whoa. What's gotten into you? It was the Head Administrator. He wanted extra protection for the Merchant Elect."

"Oh fuck," Reginald said under his breath.

Leone looked exasperated, "Shit, I can't believe this."

Zade looked over to me, confused.

"What's going on?" he asked.

"The Head Administrator is the one plotting the murder of the Merchant Elect."

Zade and his companions looked on in shock.

"What in Kyrtvale do you mean by that?"

Reginald handed me the documents, which I passed to Zade.

"We found this in his home."

Zade skimmed through the pages and came to the same conclusion as us.

"Whoa, whoa, whoa. Hold up a minute." He handed the documents back so his troupe could read them. "What the hell would they hire us for then?"

"Don't you see?!" Leone shouted in frustration. "You're going to be the scapegoats!"

Zade looked off to the side in thought, "Shit."

"So, what do we do?" one of his companions asked. "The Head Administrator is already inside."

I grimaced, "Then we need to get in there. Send someone to alert the city guard and... wait..."

That's when I realized something else was off. The last time we were there, several manor guards patrolled the grounds. At that moment, however, it was completely deserted.

"Where are the guards?" I asked with fear in my chest.

The mercenaries looked behind them and noticed the same thing. One of them cursed and pulled out a set of keys, quickly fumbling with them to unlock the gate. Another ran up to Zade and said a few things before bolting down the street to gather the city guards.

Zade turned back to us.

"Okay. What do you need us to do?"

I set Tessa down next to the iron fence that surrounded the estate. She had fallen asleep at some point on the way over.

"Someone needs to stay outside to relay what's happening to the guards when they get here. Everyone else comes in with us."

Despite having little leadership experience, a feeling washed over me as I took command. It was a feeling of nostalgia from when I watched my father at work. His ability to lead had always been alien to me, but the realization that I was mirroring him at that moment only boosted my confidence.

"We don't know how many of the manor guard are still loyal to the Merchant Elect, so use your own judgment when the time comes." I continued, "If you do find some who are loyal, have them wrap a white cloth around their arm so we can identify them, and watch out for the manor staff. In the worst case, they may be used as shields."

There were no objections to the plan, and as we each looked toward the manor, past the now-open gate, we readied ourselves for battle.

One of Zade's companions made it to the door first and gave a tug.

"It's bolted," she yelled back as she slung a bag off her shoulder. "Give me a moment to try and unlock it."

"There's no time, get back!" I barreled forward, "Reginald! Shield!"

Reginald took no time to toss his shield toward me with a simple "Yep."

I grabbed the shield out of the air while running and braced it in front of my shoulder. As I drew nearer to the door, the woman jumped out of the way as I ducked my head behind the shield and slammed it shield-first into the door. With a loud bang and a crunch, followed by the rending of metal and shattering of wood, the doors flew open. The metal pins affixed to the frame that had kept the door locked had either bent or ripped out of the wood altogether. I said a silent apology to the Merchant Elect for destroying his very nice door.

"That's one way to do it," Zade mused with a slightly impressed tone.

The others followed behind me into the darkened foyer.

"Reginald," I handed the shield back, "thanks."

He smiled, "No problem. I've gotten used to your crazy ideas by now."

Zade spoke up, "Hey, uh. Shouldn't the guards have swarmed us by now?"

Reginald's face darkened, "Yeah. And the lights here should be lit."

The mood in the foyer was tense. None of us knew where to start, and our entrance had made a lot of noise. We could be attacked at any time, from any direction.

I heard a slight rustling of cloth from somewhere and moved my eyes around the room. I followed the curving stairs upward to the second level, where I heard the movement again.

"LOOSE!"

A command from the top of the staircase was followed by the dull *thwang* of many crossbows. Bolts fell upon us from above.

Reginald moved his shield up, a bolt bouncing off of it, as he covered Myrril and pulled her into the hallway to our left. Another bolt had grazed my arm, but I managed to bat another one away with my blade as I ran to meet up with my companions.

Zade's group wasn't so lucky. One of the bolts pierced the clavicle of one of his group, dropping him in a pool of blood.

"Gah! George!" Zade leapt and rolled to his right along with the woman who had tried to pick the door earlier. A bolt was sticking out of his breastplate, but it didn't seem to have done any real damage to him.

"Zade! We'll take this side. You two take the other," I called out to him before turning to Leone, who had been in the doorway when the attack began and was forced to duck back outside. "Leone, can I ask you to take care of this?"

"Of course. No problem!" she called back. "I'll catch up with you when I'm finished here."

"You sure?" Zade asked from the other end of the foyer as he pulled the bolt from his armor.

"Yeah, it's for the best considering the current situation," I responded, "But be careful! If they set up an ambush here, then they knew we were coming. Who knows what else they have in store?"

Another barrage of bolts, this time split between the two sides of the foyer, came close to hitting us.

"Right," Zade nodded. "See you on the other side!"

I returned his nod before turning back to Reginald and Myrril.

"Let's move."

We ran down the labyrinthine halls of the Merchant Elect's estate. It was much bigger than Hanz Zerrick's and, thankfully, was tastefully decorated. As we ran, I sheathed my longsword and willed Megin to gather forth and project in front of me. Soon, a small whirlwind of air appeared. My hand disappeared into the vortex as I grasped what I was looking for.

Emerging was a beautifully carved hilt, followed by a polished blade about half the width of my longsword. This was the rapier my father gave me as part of a matching set with my longsword and spear. I usually kept it in my pocket dimension unless it was needed, and such a time had come.

Longswords were very effective weapons with good reach. However, in an enclosed space, their reach becomes a liability.

From my pocket dimension, I also grabbed the shortsword we had taken from Connor O'Donner and tossed it to Reginald.

He grabbed it and quickly latched it to his belt.

"You read my mind, I was just about to ask."

Reginald's broadsword had the same issue as the longsword, but to a slightly greater degree.

"No pro–"

WAUGH!

I was rounding a corner at the head of our group when an arrow passed right in front of my nose. I pulled back behind the corner as quickly as I could, thankfully faster than they were able to launch another missile. Hugging the wall, I slowly peeked around the corner with just the side of my eye. Down the hall was a makeshift barricade formed with a bunch of different furniture all piled up. Behind it, I could make out a pair of armored folk with short bows.

"It's a barricade," I informed the others.

"Shit," Reginald growled after taking a peek himself, "We'll get shot before we reach it."

"W-what do we d-do now?" Myrril asked, her hands shaking as she grasped her staff.

We were in quite a predicament. The people behind the barricade had bows, meaning they could reload quite quickly. That in itself was an issue, but the distance we had to travel to even get to the barricade could be deadly, not to mention getting past the barricade itself.

"I think I have an idea," I thought aloud and drew my dagger with my offhand, holding it in a reverse grip.

"Whoa there. You're going to tell us your plan first this time," Reginald grabbed my shoulder before I could initiate my idea.

"Oh? Okay," I said, "I'm just going to rush the barricade."

Reginald looked at me like I was crazy.

"Look. I know you are extremely capable, but that's crazy!" he said. "And what are you going to do with a blade like that?"

He pointed at the edgeless dagger in my hand.

"This is meant for parrying. It's a really good mix for my rapier."

I pulled my shoulder away from him.

"Don't worry. I've been trained for this kind of thing."

I thought back to the training my father had put me through. It included all kinds of subjects from basic combat to indoor and even lightless fighting. He was not only a great general but a genius when it came to practical combat. While many wanted to teach more traditional approaches, my father decided that it was better to learn skills we would use rather than die because all we were taught was fancy moves.

A memory surfaced as I thought about the past. It was my brother and I being lectured by our father during a training session. He had instructed us to bring some of the old furniture into the house and make makeshift barricades. As we stood behind it, he approached from the front.

"Very good, boys," he praised. "Building it in such a tight space prevents me from moving around it, and the funnel means you can throw magic and missiles at me with impunity."

Then he paused, and a mischievous smile grew on his face.

"If I cannot go around it and I cannot go through it, what then is the solution to this conundrum?"

My brother and I glanced at each other, wondering if the other knew the answer.

I couldn't help but smile at the fond memory as I gripped my weapon.

"You go over it, of course."

I repeated my father's words under my breath and launched myself around the corner as quickly as I could.

As expected, a pair of arrows flew toward me. With my Megin nudged toward my senses, I easily parried both arrows with my dagger as I bolted down the hall. Each arrow that was fired at me was ruthlessly cut down before it reached me.

As I drew near, I saw one of the men start to panic a bit, but the show hadn't even started yet. Not a moment later, I used the technique my father had at that time; the one that had sent fear through our hearts.

I leaped to the side and planted my foot firmly on the wall, kicking off of it, then kicking off the opposite wall. In a split second, I had gone from low to the ground to bouncing from wall to wall overtop the barricade.

The two men looked up with wide eyes as I dropped between them. Before they had time to react, my rapier was jammed upward through the solar plexus of the man on my right. I let Megin flow through my offhand and into my dagger just before I dug it into the neck of the man on my left.

Just as fast, I pulled my weapons toward each other to try and deal as much damage as possible. Blood splattered across my face and body as the two men fell lifelessly to the ground. I quickly pulled my dagger in front of me and dropped into a defensive stance, not knowing if there were more enemies. Thankfully, there didn't seem to be any more in sight.

Footsteps came from behind as Reginald and Myrril caught up with me.

"I... I don't know why I said I wasn't surprised anymore, "Reginald shook his head in exasperation.

"Th-that was cool..." Myrril mumbled.

Then, a loud howl came from the direction of the foyer.

"Looks like Leone's pulled out the big guns," Reginald mused.

I nodded, "Probably a good idea. Her spear would be fairly unwieldy in here."

"Should we keep going or wait for her?"

"We should keep going," I answered. "We don't even know if the Merchant Elect is still alive."

"Good point."

The two of them clambered over and around the barricade before the three of us ran farther down the hall.

As I had said before, the decorations were a million times better than in Hans's manor, but this place was also much larger. While we could search every room, it would take an immense amount of time. It would be better to go straight to the Merchant Elect's office and start there.

While I was having this thought, I spotted something out of the corner of my eye and slowed my pace.

"What is it?" Reginald asked.

"That room," I pointed at a set of double doors. "That was the reception room we were in before, right?"

He turned his head toward it.

"Yeah, I think so," he answered. "Why?"

Before I could say another word, Myrril pointed to the base of the door.

"B-blood."

What I had seen out of the corner of my eye was a streak of blood that looked like something, or someone, had been dragged across the floor and into that room. With only moonlight to illuminate the hall, it would have been difficult for anyone to spot.

I reached for the handle and looked to my compatriots, who nodded in understanding and got into a defensive position.

My heart pounded at the thought of what we could find behind those doors. If it were the Merchant Elect, for example, then we would have already failed.

My hand grasped the handle, and I slowly pushed it open. Moonlight filtered in through the open door, slowly revealing the interior.

As I took a step inside, my vision was soon filled with that of an object rapidly approaching.

"Leone, can I ask you to take care of this?" Elric's voice called from within.

"Of course. No problem!" Leone called back from her position, slumped against the wall just outside the door. A wooden crossbow bolt had struck her left bicep, and another had lodged in her stomach.

She tried to hide her pain as she finished her sentence.

"I'll catch up with you when I'm finished here."

Elric shouted commands at Zade for a moment before both of their groups disappeared down the halls on either side of the Foyer.

Leone moved her head slightly to peek around the corner. There, she could see the body of one of Zade's companions splayed across the floor. Leone had known him in passing, but she never caught his name. Something she now wished she had done.

She moved her gaze to the top of the stairs, where about eight men dressed as manor guards with crossbows were nearly finished reloading. Leone also noticed a ninth man standing behind the line dressed in slightly more impressive armor. He must have been the one giving orders, she thought.

"Heh," she let out a small laugh that made her wince. Her hand grew wet as she grabbed her stomach. Looking down, a red spot had appeared around the bolt sticking from her midsection and was continuing to grow.

Looks like I'll have to make this quick, she said to herself.

Leone reached down and pulled a single silver bell from her belt. She tossed it in front of her, and for a moment it hovered in the air. Then it seemed as though all the moonlight was being pulled toward the bell and condensing. Within the blink of an eye, a wolf with a coat of pure moonlight stood before Leone.

"Hati," Leone said, her voice weakening, "I need you to take care of those guys for me, okay?"

The wolf looked toward her with concern.

"I'll be fine. Don't worry about me," Leone reassured Hati. "I just need to rest for a moment."

Hati didn't seem convinced, Leone knew this. She had learned their facial expressions through her time with them. Nonetheless, Hati did as he was told.

He let out a resounding howl and bounded through the open doorway.

"What is that!?" the commanding manor guard yelped in surprise. "Kill it! Kill it!"

Before the men were able to aim their crossbows, Hati let

out another howl, and his fur stood on end. Then, a brilliant white light flashed forth and blinded anyone looking.

The crossbowmen screamed and held their eyes as Hati ran up the staircase and began to tear into them. One of the men stumbled over the banister and fell to the floor with a loud thump, while others began fighting for their lives while half-blinded.

"Retreat!" the commander shrieked. "Retreat to the ballroom!"

The remaining men scrambled to their feet and ran as fast as their legs could carry them. Hati would have pursued if it weren't for Leone's next command.

"Hati, Heel."

The obedient wolf returned to his master and let out a whimper when he saw the state of her. She had begun to sweat profusely and had a massive red streak going down her clothes.

"Hati, I need you to make sure none of those bad guys try and come through here, okay?" Leone directed.

Hati turned his head as if asking why.

"We don't want anyone to flank our friends or to escape. Just make sure you subdue anyone not wearing a white band on their arm, okay?" she explained.

Just then, she heard many metallic footfalls approaching. From the front gate came two squads of city guards led by Onforde's Captain of the Guard. They each had a piece of white cloth wrapped around their arms and were being led by the two members of Zade's group who hadn't gone inside.

"Leone!" one of them called out and rushed toward her.

The Captain of the Guard, seeing the state of the foyer, commanded his squads to secure the room before jogging over to Leone as well.

"Hold on, lass. You did well," he said with a kind tone

before turning his head around. "Get the medics over here, now!"

Leone grabbed the guard captain's arm and swallowed heavily. Her vision was already blurry.

"The.... they retreated... to the ballroom..." she managed to say as the pain began to overwhelm her.

"The ballroom?" the captain asked to confirm.

Leone managed to nod.

"Thank you, that's a big help," the guard captain said before noticing exactly how poorly Leone was doing. "Hold on, lass. Hold on for a few more moments..."

He continued to speak to her, but she no longer heard what he was saying. A moment later, everything went dark.

Crash!

A thousand fragments of glazed porcelain went flying as a vase shattered against my face.

"Gah!" I screamed out and grabbed my face. "Ow, fuck!"

"Oh my gods, I'm so sorry!" a feminine voice called out. "I thought you were one of them!"

A hand grasped my shoulder and pulled me back as I wiped the dust and sharp fragments out of my eyes. Blinking a few times, my vision returned to see Reginald in front of me with his shield in a defensive position.

Beyond him was a middle-aged maid with her hands over her mouth. She must have been hiding behind the second door, ready to swing at whatever entered.

"Who else is in here?" Reginald demanded, pushing the door as far as it could go whilst also maintaining a defensive position.

The new sight we gained from the moonlight showed a stark difference from the first time we had been in this room.

Furniture was overturned, several items had fallen off of the walls, and it was just in a general state of disarray. Over to the left side of the room were another two manor servants huddled up in a corner, and close by were a pair of unconscious guards tightly tied at their wrists and ankles. There were also signs that their bonds had started being worked on as if someone was trying to help them escape.

The right side of the room was in worse shape. There, on the floor, was the still body of another manor guard with blood pooled around him. Next to him were two more bodies, a butler, and a maid. They seemed to have been slashed across the chest, their blood sprayed up the walls.

"I-it's just the five of us..." the maid replied with fear and anxiety. They locked us in here and showed what would happen if we tried to escape.

Her eyes wandered over to the corpses on the other side of the room before locking back onto us, a thought seeming to appear in her mind.

"Y-you aren't with them... are you?"

She took a step back as she spoke, her voice shaky.

Reginald was about to speak, but I put my hand on his shoulder to signal that I would answer.

"We are here to save the Merchant Elect if that's what you mean."

The maid relaxed her shoulders at my response.

"Oh, thank the heavens." She dropped to her knees as the tension left her body. "We.... we've been so worried that nobody would come."

Seemingly on the verge of tears, the maid valiantly tried to hold them back.

I motioned for Reginald to push into the room. He moved forward with me behind him and Myrril taking up the rear.

Indeed, it was as she had said. The five of them were the only ones in the room.

"Why are they tied up?" I pointed toward the two guards, although I had a good idea as to the answer.

The maid we had been talking to turned her head and began to explain.

"They were trying to help us when the traitors tried to lock us in here, but..."

Her eyes shifted to the deceased guard on the floor.

"They didn't think the other would attack them..."

"I see."

I could imagine what happened fairly easily. The three of them were walking down the hall when they saw the servants being corralled into this chamber. They tried to figure out what was happening when another traitorous guard showed up and stabbed one of them from behind. They forced the other two to surrender or die.

"We can hear you, you know," one of the guards, who I had assumed was unconscious, called out.

"Myrril, help me untie them," Reginald motioned for her to follow him.

Soon, the two men were back on their feet and eager to help.

"You're here to help the Merchant Elect? Let us come with you. "One of them approached, "We were caught off guard last time, and even though you may not have that high of an assessment of us, we're actually fairly well-trained."

"That won't be an issue," I said. "We need all the help we can get. Our only issue is finding the Merchant Elect."

As I finished my sentence, I could have sworn I saw movement on the other side of the room. Turning my head over, I saw the other two servants who were huddled up in some kind of conversation. One of them seemed to be trying to push the other one to speak.

"Do you know where we can find him?" I called over to them.

The one who seemed reluctant froze and shook her head. The second one sighed at their friend before responding to me.

"She says she heard them talking about the ballroom."

"The ballroom is a pretty defensible position," one of the guards chimed in. "Anyone trying to attack from outside would be funneled into one of two doorways, and the room itself is fairly large. If someone wanted to choose a spot for final defense... well, that would be my pick at least."

I couldn't help but agree. Depending on where it was positioned, it could be a very effective spot for a last stand or hardened defense. If your enemy isn't smart about it, they could lose a substantial number of troops trying to take it.

"Ballroom sounds good then," I nodded. "At the very least, it's a good place to start."

The guard loosened his shoulder, "Then shall we get going?"

"Wait a moment," Reginald called from across the room. He was pulling open drawers and cupboards in search of something.

"Aha, got some."

He pulled out a large piece of white cloth, possibly a curtain. Unfortunately, we will never know what it was as he started tearing it into strips.

One of the maids gasped.

"Don't worry," Reginald reassured, "I'm sure the Merchant Elect will forgive us."

I couldn't help but admire his confidence and quick

thinking at times like this. He would have fit right in with the Aleurian Imperial Army.

"Everyone take a piece," I said. "Tie it around your arm. This is how we are differentiating friend from foe."

Reginald handed out a strip of cloth to each person in the room before approaching me.

"We should wear it as well. When the city guard arrives, they will be identifying us with these, as well."

"Good thinking," I took hold of a strip and wrapped it around my arm. The white cloth was much more vibrant than my worn coat. It was a little strange to think that they had once been the same color.

"Alright, let's get going then."

"W-wait a moment!" The maid stopped us somewhat frantically. "What about us?"

"You should stay here. Last we saw, the way out wasn't secured yet."

Even as I answered, I focused my hearing toward the way we came but could no longer hear the sounds of battle. It had probably ended by now, but it was better to play it safe.

"Oh... okay," the maid seemed a little worried.

"It'll be fine," one of the guards said with a grin.

I wasn't sure if he was trying to reassure her or make her more worried, but she seemed to take it well.

"Okay. We'll stay here." The maid seemed more at ease.

"You should also barricade the door, just in case," I suggested.

She nodded, "Yes. We'll do that."

"The ballroom is just over here," the guard said as he led us down the halls.

My mind was a little tired from mentally mapping the

Head Administrator's manor earlier, so I was grateful that we had a navigator.

As we approached, I began to hear a large number of footfalls coming from a hall that crossed our own just ahead of us.

"There are people," I whispered in urgency.

The five of us moved to the wall and made ourselves as flat as possible in an attempt not to be seen.

Passing through the hallway running perpendicular to us was about two squads of armed soldiers led by a large man with decorated armor. Each one had a white band of cloth around their arms.

I tapped Reginald's arm and pointed, "Friendlies. They must be the city guard."

He nodded, "I noticed that, too."

"Then let's go introduce ourselves before we almost kill each other," one of the guards we had rescued suggested.

We moved forward in a jog to catch up with the soldiers, who had stopped at the end of the hallway just before a corner.

I waved toward them and called out in a loud whisper.

"Hey!"

The men turned toward us with weapons drawn, dropping into a defensive stance.

"Friendlies! Friendlies!" I quickly shouted, making our white bands known.

The well-decorated one, most likely the commander, ordered his men to stand down and approached us.

"Stand down, men, we were looking for them," he said as he approached and stuck his hand forward.

"I'm the captain of Onforde's City Guard, Dane Ursun."

As he got close, I finally got a good look at him. He wasn't a tall human as I had thought, but instead a massive Bear Beastfolk. He was around seven feet tall and covered in a dark gray fur. Across one side of his face was a heavy scar that went from above his eye and down the side of his jaw. His armor covered the majority of his body, and he wore a large steel helm with small cutouts for his round ears to peek through.

I firmly grasped his gauntleted hand and gave it a shake. "I am Elric. These are my companions, Reginald and Myrril from Edren. Those two are men loyal to the Merchant Elect."

The way the guard captain spoke was nostalgic to me. You see, during the height of the Aleurian Empire, my people decided to send colonies to the Northern Wastes to attempt to tame them. The Northern Wastes were sparsely inhabited, but those who did inhabit it were mostly hearty Beastfolk well suited to the harsh winter environment.

My people were surprised to find that they had a similar warrior culture as we did and managed to live relatively peacefully with them. Out of respect for their similar way of life, we cooperated with them. They ended up adopting our language and many of our architectural styles. It was one of the few instances where the Aleurians peacefully coexisted with others without trying to conquer them.

Since Captain Dane was a Bear Beastfolk and had very little accent, it was safe to assume he, or his parents, were from the Northern Wastes.

"Did you already meet up with Zade?" I asked.

"Yes. He is just ahead, checking on the situation in the ballroom," Captain Dane answered. "Do you have any information you can give us?"

"Yes, quite a bit."

I began to fill the captain in on everything that had transpired, from our mission to what happened at the head administrator's manor, and everything we learned after breaching the Merchant Elect's estate. I made sure to hand him the documents we recovered as proof.

The Captain of the Guard seemed to take it in for a moment before responding.

"Damn. To think all of this was happening under my watch," he started. "Tsk. Who would have thought Hans Zerrick would go this far in his thirst for wealth?"

After hearing that, I supposed that the Head Administrator's greed was well known in Onforde.

"Anyway, this is good information," he continued. "We can do much with this."

"By the way," Reginald spoke up, "have you seen the fourth member of our group?"

"Ah, if you mean the lady out front, she took quite a hit from those crossbowmen."

Reginald and I gasped at this information, but what really surprised us was Myrril.

"Is Leone alright!?" she nearly shouted in panic.

Captain Dane smiled, "She's alive. Our medics managed to stop the bleeding, but she'll need some time to rest."

We let out a collective sigh of relief. We had no idea she was injured, and my mind wandered through when it must have happened. If it was during that first barrage, I couldn't help but feel guilty about asking her to take care of the crossbowmen.

Still, I couldn't let those thoughts cloud my judgment. I would just have to find her afterward and apologize.

"Captain," one of the soldiers called out, "they're back."

"Perfect timing." He turned to us, "Come with me."

We followed him to the first squad of soldiers and saw Zade and his group talking amongst themselves.

"Glad to see you're still alive," Zade said as he saw us.

I smiled. "It wasn't much of an issue after the foyer."

"It was the same with us," he replied before turning to

Captain Dane. "We finished scouting the ballroom as you asked."

"Good," the captain responded. "What did you find?"

"We confirmed the Merchant Elect and the Head Administrator are inside the ballroom," Zade quickly explained. "There are also around twenty or so armed men, all dressed as manor or city guards. We could see three with crossbows while the rest had shields and either shortswords or longswords."

"I see," Captain Dane scratched his furred chin.

"They are all positioned to intercept anyone coming through the door, keeping the hostage and the Head Administrator behind them," Zade continued, apparently not finished. "However, they appear to have neglected the far entrance. We may be able to sneak some troops into a flanking position."

"Hmph," Captain Dane snorted, "seems we've found their weakness then."

A few thoughts ran through my head. *Why would they neglect their rear? How long did they have to prepare this defense? From the sound of it, the Merchant Elect was still alive. Why?*

"I wonder if they weren't expecting resistance," I mused.

"What was that?" Dane looked at me.

I shook my head a little, "Oh, sorry, I was just wondering why they would leave their flank exposed. If they had ample time to plan this, I mean."

"Hm, I see what you mean," Captain Dane responded, "but we do not have the time to ponder this too deeply. Whoever goes to the rear will just have to be careful."

I nodded in agreement.

"Who will you send?" Zade asked the captain.

Captain Dane thought for a moment before giving his answer.

"Squad Two," he called out, prompting about half his soldiers to stand at attention, "Zade and his group will bring you around the rear. You are to flank and engage the enemy, however, your number one priority is saving the Merchant Elect."

The men of the second squad saluted their captain and looked toward Zade for guidance.

Zade sighed and looked at Captain Dane, nodding at him with a single word, "Sir," before heading off to bring the second squad to the other door.

"What about us?" I asked the captain.

"You'll be with me and Squad One," he said. "We'll need the extra strength for the frontal assault."

"Got it."

The captain gave us a toothy smile. "Take a break while you can. We'll give the others a few minutes to get into place before we move."

"How are you guys holding up?" I asked my companions.

We were leaning against a wall while we waited for the signal from Captain Dane, and we had a few minutes to kill.

"I'm okay," Reginald replied. "This has been less intense than my fight with Edd, so I've still got a good amount of energy."

Despite running all the way here right after a furious battle at the Head Administrator's manor, I was inclined to believe him.

Myrril nodded as well, "I-I'm happy that Leone is alright."

"Oh yeah, that too," Reginald added.

I voiced my feelings on it as well.

"I was relieved to hear it," I said, "but I'm still worried about her."

"Oh, don't get me wrong, I am, too," Reginald responded. "I'm just glad she's alive."

"Mhm!" Myrril agreed.

I smiled a bit at their responses. It was heartwarming whenever people had a genuine concern for others. Even though I had come to expect it from them, it was still something I felt like smiling for.

"Hey," a soldier approached us, "Captain says it's go time. He wants you with him."

I looked to the others, "Guess it's time."

We all took a deep breath and readied ourselves before heading up front to join the captain.

The Ballroom – Manor of the Merchant Elect ~

Everything had been going so smoothly. Merchants had begun to turn away from certain routes, allowing an unbothered monopoly on certain shipments, public opinion was slowly turning against mercenaries, and the seat of the Merchant Elect was almost up for grabs.

Hans Zerrick had been planning this coup for a very long time. Ever since the people elected Jean-Luc over him as the Merchant Elect, Hans had been plotting and scheming his downfall.

It would have all been over by now if those damned mercs didn't mess up the first time, he thought. It would be the last time he uses a referral for this kind of thing.

It did not matter, he could adapt his plans. Then the head of Edren sent people to investigate, another roadblock, but one they solved by investigating in the wrong direction.

What luck! Hans thought. He could nearly jump for joy when they were sent away on a wild goose chase.

So, he put his plan into motion.

What he wasn't expecting was for those people sent from Edren to stumble upon Hans's operation. Their luck must have been extraordinary! But it was too late to stop the plan, it was already in motion.

Oh, the look on Jean-Luc's face when Hans appeared before him and revealed his intentions elated Hans at the time.

Now, however, he was in a bind.

Those investigators sent from Edren figured it out and made their way to the Merchant Elect's manor. Hans had to act quickly to prevent his coup from failing again. He decided to hole up in the ballroom and take advantage of the situation. He could blame multiple groups of mercenaries for this and further push his agenda.

He never expected Captain Dane Ursun to appear.

That damned man, Hans thought, *of course he had to appear.*

The Beastfolk Captain was as straight-shooting as anyone could be. Hans knew he could never get him on his side, and he especially didn't want to have to face him. That's why he devised a plan to frame the captain for conspiring to murder Jean-Luc.

Now, everything was falling apart.

"Not going as you planned?" a voice said sarcastically.

Hans looked down and sneered at the man who had spoken, Jean-Luc Pierre, whom he had tied up at his feet.

"Nothing is certain in this world," Hans said as small beads of sweat formed on his forehead. "No plans survive first contact with the enemy. That's why it's so important to be able to improvise."

The Merchant Elect snorted, "I've known you for a long time, Hans. You were never one to improvise."

Hans tried his best to ignore the man he had once served and focus on quickly forming a plan, knowing all too well that his enemies were closing in.

"You ready?" Captain Dane asked as we approached.

I secured my vambraces, the bracer-like armor on my forearms, and nodded, Ready as we can be.

Standing to either side of the large set of double doors that led to the ballroom were the first squad of soldiers the captain had brought, as well as the men we had rescued, and the captain himself.

In preparation for this assault, I stowed my rapier and returned to using my longsword. While the rapier was very effective in the somewhat cramped halls, the ballroom would be a much different story. Not to mention the enemy was equipped with shields, rendering my rapier a somewhat disadvantageous position.

A grin momentarily graced the edge of the captain's mouth before he motioned for one of his soldiers to move up to the door. The man who moved carried slightly more gear than the others, with a larger belt accompanied by more bags. I suspected that he was carrying just enough as to not become an issue in combat, something that could only be discovered through vigorous trial and error.

The soldier approached the door and gave the handle a

light shake to confirm it was locked. Then, he grabbed a heavy-looking rod of metal from his belt, around two or so feet in length with either end hammered flat, and inserted it between the pair of doors. The man looked to the captain for confirmation; then, once he got it, he pulled a hammer out from a side pouch and hit the end of the metal piece with great force.

With a loud crunch, the metal rod was jammed farther into the door, breaking the locking mechanism. A second man moved in front of the door within a single moment and gave a resounding kick.

The pair of doors flew open, the metal rod clattered to the floor, and the squad of soldiers rushed into the room with their captain in the lead, followed by the three of us.

Once inside, I could get a better view of things.

Forming a semicircle around the main entrance to the ballroom was a line of shielded guards. Three men with crossbows stood behind the line and readied their shots. Further back into the wide ballroom was none other than Hans Zerrick. At his feet was the Merchant Elect, Jean-Luc Pierre, bound and with a blade at his throat.

Captain Dane stopped short of the shield wall, his soldiers moving quickly to match the enemy formation, indicative of their training.

Myrril, Reginald, and I stood behind the captain with weapons at the ready. We did not know what he was planning, but we had decided to follow his lead.

"Captain," Hans started, "I've been expecting you."

"I wish I could say the same," Captain Dane growled.

"Oh, don't be uncouth. This was bound to happen eventually," the Head Administrator continued. "For two hundred years, this city has been wasting its potential. It only needed someone with a firm hand to come along and guide it."

"That is why you are doing this? To become the Merchant Elect?"

"Of course," Hans Zerrick scoffed, "the position of Merchant Elect has the potential to become the most powerful position in the continent!"

"From here, you can control nearly all trade going through Vestri," he began. "If you go south then you have to compete with the Holy Silas Kingdom and its heavy taxation; North is the Dolar Imperium, which has a historically closed border with Elderoth; and of course, the Dwarven Kingdom of Guldar doesn't allow trade to pass through its mountains."

"These lands we are in, the Eye of the Continent, are the perfect trade route in the entire western continent, and we've squandered it for generations!"

The ranks of soldiers that came with the captain grew noticeably more tense as the Head Administrator spoke. I supposed that his slandering of their city was more than a little perturbing.

"You had your chance, Hans," Captain Dane retorted, "and you could have had it again."

"Hmph," Hans Zerrick sneered, "you think some little election is the way to create true leaders?"

I felt a twitch as he spoke. His words reached the core of my being.

"Leaders are not created by status and power," I retorted, "they are forged through their actions, and the actions of those around them."

Hans moved his eyes to meet mine as a grin spread across his lips.

"That is a naïve approach to the world! Do you think the greatest kingdom of this world, the Aleurian Empire, managed to become so strong with such a mindset!? Nay. They grabbed power and forged it to work for them!"

I could feel rage begin to build within my chest as I heard this man lecture me about my people.

"The Aleurians are dead and gone, Hans. Their downfall should have taught us a valuable lesson about having too much power." Dane unlatched the greatsword hanging from his back, *a lesson you've clearly ignored.*

Captain Dane dropped into his fighting stance, the men around him hardening their resolve to fight alongside him.

"Let him go. Now." Dane's voice lowered into a growl.

That's when I realized the unnatural body language of Hans Zerrick. His demeanor and tone were that of a man filled with confidence. Even though he had been caught, his plans ruined, and his forces outnumbered and outmatched, Hans Zerrick was still maintaining his normal front. It was only natural, for he still held the greatest card in the deck.

Hans pulled the Merchant Elect to his feet and repositioned the blade at his throat.

"You are in no position to be making demands," he spat. "One more move and his blood will soil this lovely chamber."

The captain and his forces hesitated for but a moment before Captain Dane locked eyes with Jean-Luc. Despite the threatening situation, the Merchant Elect wasn't panicking. Instead, he simply nodded.

A toothy grin grew on Captain Dane's Beastfolk face. He whispered out the side of his mouth, directing his words toward us.

"Be ready."

I knew what he was getting at and shifted my focus back to the enemy at hand.

The lack of fear in the Merchant Elect's eyes was enough to dissuade the men's fears. Reassured, they were ready to save their beloved leader.

A throaty growl began to build up within Captain Dane's

throat. The sound resounded from his chest, he threw back his head, and released a mighty roar. The chandeliers shook from the force of his voice, and the line of traitors in front of us instinctively took a step back.

"Wait... no. Don't you know what you are doing!?" Hans shouted out, his voice now lacking the confidence it had earlier. "Do you care at all for the life of your leader?!?!?"

The three crossbowmen didn't hesitate to fire upon the captain. The captain knocked one bolt out of the air with his back hand, the second just grazed his helm, and the third bounced off of his resilient hide, much to my surprise.

Captain Dane let out another roar and charged forward, his men following his lead. The sound of running boots and furious war cries echoing in the chamber was enough to strike fear into the average man.

However, my companions and I were unfazed and quickly followed the captain's lead.

I sprinted forward, knocking the blade out of a shocked guard's hand before following it up with a fist to the face. With him down, I moved forward to the next.

The battle quickly became a confused cluster. There were no more lines, just a large number of people fighting for their lives. Those who got in the way of the captain were the most unlucky of the bunch.

He brought his great sword down on top of one man who had raised his shield to block. The greatsword crumpled the shield and slammed down upon the man with enough force to flatten him against the floor.

A second and third man attacked the captain from behind, only for one to have his chestplate caved in with a kick and the other to be shredded to ribbons by a set of massive claws.

The crossbowmen had reloaded by now and decided to target the captain's units. They fired, their bolts hitting their marks. Two soldiers' armor were pierced while the third got lucky; the bolt got caught in an enemy shield that happened to move into place at just the right moment.

Another blade came down upon me, but I managed to deflect with my vambrace and struck back instead. I managed to wound the man, but my blade mostly caught armor.

He came back at me, a wild look in his eyes.

"Just lie down and surrender," I said to him with little effect.

The man continued to swing his blade at me in a wild manner, allowing me ample time to deflect each and every one. Eventually, I found a good opening and planted my foot in his chest to send him off balance before giving him another good strike. This time, he fell to the floor.

Not far away, Reginald taking on two men at once as he defended Myrril, who was firing her spells to try and support the soldiers. They didn't seem to be in much trouble, so I focused myself forward, locking my eyes on the Head Administrator.

Captain Dane had the same idea. He left his men to handle things and made a break for Hans Zerrick.

It was about this time that I began to wonder where our flanking group was when the doors at the other end of the chamber burst open. Armored men covered in blood were led by another with a staff and a robe. None of them wore a white band.

It was easy for us to realize that reinforcements had arrived, but they weren't ours.

The enemy troops ran forward to intercept the captain and me while Hans Zerrick slowly backed up with the Merchant Elect, heading toward the rear doors.

"Halt. You will not be going anywhere," the man in front

pointed his staff toward us. It was a large, gnarled branch with a single red gem affixed to the top, a bloodstone.

"You want the mage or the men?" I glanced at the captain beside me.

Captain Dane cracked his neck. "I'll take the men."

With that, he sprinted forward, letting out another resounding roar as he went to face off against a nearly full squad worth of men.

Windbolt!

A swirling spire of compressed air sped forth from the mage's staff, heading for the captain. I quickly pushed forward and brought my hand out in front of it, willing the Megin within me to project forth from the palm of my hand. The bolt of wind slammed into the rippling shield of magical energy hovering just in front of my hand.

"You'll be fighting me," I said as the mage looked on in horror.

"WHAT THE KYRTVALE WAS THAT!?" he screamed out before firing off a barrage of Windbolts at me. Apparently, he wasn't too happy that I had a counter for his magic.

I dodged as many as I could as I made my approach, however, the mage managed to calm himself down in time to pull out a new trick.

Airwhip!

A massive cord of air sprang forth from the top of the man's staff and began moving on its own. It lashed toward me with a loud crack as it bounced off the magical barrier I pulled up to protect myself with.

Then, at the same time as maintaining this cord of air, he fired off more windbolts, putting me in a defensive position. I could hardly move anywhere and had to spend all of my time focusing on defense. Although I wasn't sure exactly how powerful these spells were, they marked up the polished ball-room floor whenever they hit and left gashes in the stone.

Just when I was being forced backward, a streaming red bolt of light flew from behind me on a collision course with the mage. Seeing it, the mage set off another spell, and a swirling whirlwind akin to clouds during a hurricane appeared before him and dissipated the bolt.

Out of my periphery, the whip the mage had conjured flew out from behind the shield and flicked toward me at great speed, too great for me to block.

Just before contact, a figure jumped in front of me and took the whip against his shield.

"Need some help?" Reginald asked with a wide grin.

"Just in time," I returned his smile and pulled out around him.

Myrril stood behind us, already focusing on her next attack as Reginald and I stood shoulder to shoulder, facing the mage.

Without the need to communicate, we knew the plan.

The two of us split off to either side of the mage and ran forward with all of our might. The mage, now having to focus on attacking two approaching foes and defending from another mage, was beginning to sweat. He conjured a second whip and continued to fire off windbolts whenever he could.

Reginald and I fended off his attacks as we slowly drew nearer. Then, Myrril fired off another round of magic.

Flameburst!

Three orbs of burning fire sped forward, causing the mage to put up his shield of cloud once more.

This was the opening we were looking for.

Reginald and I darted in, knocking away the whips as they became more aggressive. The mage's shield was forcefully dissipated by the impact of the flameburst, allowing one of the orbs to make it through and shatter the mage's staff.

Like that, Reginald and I struck the mage from opposite sides and sent him to the afterlife.

"Phew," Reginald was breathing heavily, "that was a rush."

"It's not over yet." I turned my head over to see an enemy flying through the air after being battered away from the captain.

Then, we heard more footfall coming from the rear door.

"Not more," Reginald groaned.

Out from the doorway appeared about half a squad of soldiers with white bands, led by Zade.

I couldn't help but smile. The Head Administrator was now trapped. But soon, my smile fell.

Hans Zerrick, seeing the situation for what it was, saw no way out.

"FINE!" he screamed. "If I can't win, then neither can you!"

He raised his blade above the Merchant Elect's head and brought it down.

Thoughts raced through my head. *Could Myrril hit him? No, it would take too much time to aim her staff and cast the spell. What about Captain Dane?* I looked to him, but he was being held back by a few stragglers and could only watch in horror.

A last-ditch effort appeared in my mind, and I acted on it. I reached my arm back and grasped the dagger at my waist, quickly drawing and throwing it in one motion as I prayed to the Goddess Aleura that my aim was true.

The dagger flew with incredible speed as I had put all of my strength into the throw.

It seemed like all eyes were watching as the dagger spun through the air, our collective breaths held.

"GAH!"

The Head Administrator yelled out as my dagger pierced his arm, knocking away the blade he held.

He grasped his bleeding arm and tried to run, but Zade didn't let that happen. He sprinted toward the fleeing man and leaped, tackling him to the floor. Within a moment, no less than five armored men had dogpiled onto the traitor.

Within a few minutes, those who were alive surrendered, and those who were incapacitated were captured; thus marking the end of the short-lived coup d'état of Hans Zerrick, Head Administrator of Onforde.

INTERLUDE

The Faeron Kingdom – Royal Palace ∽

Captain Hugo of the Faeron Royal Guard walked briskly down the garish halls of the Royal Palace. Sunlight shone through the stained windows and reflected off of his polished armor, adorned with a sparrow holding a thorny vine in its beak; the symbol of the kingdom.

He single-mindedly made his way through the winding corridors. His destination, the chamber of the king.

As he stopped at the gold-leafed door, he hesitated. Every time he was forced to bring news to the king, it left a bad taste in his mouth. However, he steeled himself and knocked on the door.

"Your Majesty," Hugo's voice was deep and unwavering. "We have received some information you may find interesting."

He had a slight accent, which made the R sound more guttural and instituted a rhythm to how he spoke, similar to reciting music.

"Hmpf," a man with a similar accent spoke from within the room. His tone gave the air of annoyance. "Come in then."

Hugo braced himself and opened the door.

The royal bed chamber was massive, almost as big as the audience hall, and it was needed to hold the man within.

Seated on a bed big enough to fit ten men was an ogre of a man. His belly was so huge that his royal raiment stretched to its limit to contain it all, despite being custom-tailored.

He stuffed his layered face with roasted meats and fruits, drinking enough wine to drown a village.

As if that wasn't all, the smell was overwhelming. It was a mixture of greasy body odor and overused perfume.

To either side of him were women clothed in rags, their wrists and ankles chained, and their pointed ears on full display. Their entire purpose was to feed, bathe, and massage the massive king without him ever having to leave his bed.

The king plucked a sausage from a platter held by one of the slaves, his fingers pinched by golden rings, becoming indistinguishable from the contents of the platter.

"Speak," the king said before inhaling his sausage and reaching for another.

"Your Majesty," Captain Hugo bowed, "we have received word that an elven ship was spotted on the coast earlier this morning."

The king looked uninterestedly at the captain, motioning for him to continue.

"The ship is already long gone, however, it was reported that they dropped off a group of elves," Captain Hugo hesitated for a moment. "One of them appears to be a High Elf. They are heading in the direction of the Great Forest and—"

At the mention of a high elf, the king paused his consumption and his face contorted into one of desire.

"Send the Rangers at once!" the king yelled, interrupting Captain Hugo, "I must have this High Elf!"

"But Your Majesty, the Rangers are busy holding off Elderoth in the north," Hugo explained.

"Did you not hear me?!" Food flew across the room as the king shouted, his immense stomach jiggling back and forth. "I do not care about the North! I would give Elderoth all the land they wanted if it meant I could get my hands on a High Elf!"

"Y-yes... Your Majesty," Hugo relented, "I will send them at once."

"Good," the king settled down, "now begone!"

"But, Your Majesty, there is still the matter of the prince..."

"Bah! Let him run. He's just a dirty sympathizer. The only place elves deserve to be is dead or enslaved!" The king let out a rambunctious laugh, causing the elven slaves to wince away from him.

Leaving him to his laughter, Captain Hugo bowed and exited the chamber of King Alphonse Aubert of Faeron.

An Unknown Place – Somewhere in the World ∼

A man was hunched over in the corner of a rocky room. His black hair disheveled, his robes a mess, and his glasses smudged. In one hand was a knife that he was using to carve symbols and equations into the stone.

His mumbling echoed in the dark, cave-like chamber as he scratched on and on. The occasional drip of water falling from a stalactite interrupted his crazed mumbling

"If I just put this here and this here... no, NO! That won't do." He let out a crazed chuckle, "I need more.... MORE!"

His voice echoed as he scratched out an incomplete equation, and his mumbling continued.

Then, the scratching stopped. The silence that filled the air was almost sickening as the man was on his hands and knees, staring at what he had just made.

"YES!"

The man jumped to his feet and screamed, his voice echoing an unknown distance.

He ran his hands through his hair, slicking it back as best he could. He readjusted his robes and wiped the grime from his glasses. Turning around, his wild eyes were filled with confidence, and the image of a lunatic he had projected just moments before was gone.

A smile spread across the face of Kane Ovid as he finalized his newest plan.

CHAPTER 13

Rest and Relaxation

And then what happened? The young girl Penelope jumped as she gripped the side of the bed.

It was the day after the failed coup d'état. We were back at Leone's house, all gathered around her bed as she rested. Well, at least tried to get some rest. Ever since she awoke a few hours earlier, Penelope and Jackson had been begging for details.

"How can she have so much energy in this heat?" Reginald sluggishly mused as he melted in his seat. He was wearing normal clothes, as were we all.

Summer had fully reared its head, giving us an intense heat wave. While we had experienced some hot days in recent times, as well as a few in Edren, those days were nothing compared to the weather that came after the Coup.

I shook my head in response to Reginald's question as I focused on my work. I had in front of me a very primitive fan. It was basically a piece of parchment tied onto a pair of sticks in a V shape.

Once satisfied, I moved over to the side of the bed.

"Well, the guard captain showed up just in time," Leone explained somewhat energetically despite her blood loss, "though I'm not sure about the rest. You'll have to ask the others."

When the captain of the guard was mentioned, Jackson's eyes lit up. In fact, I hadn't seen Jackson fidget or get distracted once during the whole story.

"We joined up with the captain and beat up the bad guys, it was as simple as that," I joined in. "Here, Leone, try this."

I began to fan Leone with the small fan I had pieced together. Almost instantly, her face relaxed.

"Oh, that's nice."

"I'm glad it works well. I've never made one before, but it's just so hot that I decided to give it a go," I explained.

Despite having a higher temperature tolerance than humans, I was still feeling the heat. It was definitely uncomfortable, meaning it must have been scorching to my companions.

"C-can I have one?" Myrril shyly requested from the corner of the room where she had been nose-deep in a large book.

"Sure, I can make one for everyone. Just give me a—"

As I was replying, there was a loud knock at the front door.

"I'll get it," I said.

Penelope reached her arms out toward me, "I want to help Leone!"

"Hey!" Leone snapped, "where are your manners?"

Penelope shrank back a bit with a look of guilt on her face.

"C-can I please use the fan?" she asked more timidly this time.

"Yes, of course," I handed her the fan, eliciting an excited bout of hops from her. "I'll be right back."

I left the room and headed down the stairs. As I approached, I could hear a bit of shuffling from outside the door. I guessed maybe three people in metallic armor. Considering what happened the day before, I could easily guess as to what it was about.

I opened the door and was greeted by none other than the Beastfolk captain himself and two of his soldiers. Unlike the day before, they each wore a lightweight cloak over their armor despite the heat. It was actually an ingenious decision as it prevented their metallic armor from becoming superheated and dangerous to wear. I had heard of my people doing something similar on the southern continent.

"Captain Dane! This is unexpected. What can I do for you?" I asked with a bit of real surprise.

"Ah, Elric was it? I have something for you and your group." The captain held out a thick letter toward me. As I accepted it, he continued, "The Merchant Elect wished to thank each of you again for your help, but with the current state of the governing body, he was unable to do so in person."

"That's really not necessary. We were just doing the job we were hired for," I tried to explain.

"Bah," Captain Dane waved me off. "You went above and beyond what Lord Aulcrest had hired you for. And even if you hadn't, your actions are still worthy of thanks. That is why I am here, as well, to once again thank you for your assistance."

The captain and his two men bowed their heads, which I was extremely uncomfortable with.

"No, No. Please, do not lower your head to me. If you wish to show your gratitude," I stuck out my hand, "then a simple handshake will do."

The captain raised his head and looked me in the eye for a moment before grasping my hand in his own.

"A handshake it is then," his lips curled back in a massive beastial smile, "and if you ever need anything from me, don't hesitate to ask."

I returned his smile, "I'll do that."

Then, a pair of feet came bolting down the stairs as quick as a flash. Standing next to me, his mouth agape, was Jackson. His eyes, filled with stars, were locked on Captain Dane.

"Oh? Who is this one?" Captain Dane said playfully.

"This is–"

"I'm Jackson. I wanna be just like you!"

Before I could answer, Jackson jumped right in. That's when I realized what the look on his face was. Admiration. Captain Dane must have been like a legend to Jackson, someone he looked up to. It was familiar because I was once like that. Whenever my grandfather visited us, I felt the same thing as Jackson did at that moment.

"Oh? You want to be like me, do you?" Dane chuckled a bit, knelt down, and placed his massive paw on top of Jackson's head, "Well, if you decide to be a soldier when you grow up, I'll take good care of you."

Jackson nodded furiously as the captain got back to his feet and turned to me once again.

"I must be going now. Be sure to tell your friends they can come to me for help should they ever need it."

"I'll be sure to pass that along."

"Do you ever miss it? Your people, I mean."

Reginald and I were sitting at the end of a pier, fishing rods in hand. A few days had passed since Captain Dane visited us, and the weather had cooled off a bit. Leone was also doing much better; she was no longer confined to bed but was still a little unsteady. We had all wanted to get out of the house, so Myrril suggested that we split up and make a day out of it. That's how Reginald and I ended up fishing at the pier while the two of them went off somewhere else.

"Ah... sorry. I shouldn't have asked," Reginald quickly said, mistaking my silence for distaste.

"No, it's quite alright," I waved him off. "Of course I miss my people, our culture, the life I had before..."

Thinking of the fact that I may be the only Aleurian left was almost unbearable, but I couldn't help but remember what that beast had said in Kyrtvale, that others like me had made it out. Whenever the thought crossed my mind, hope replaced the sorrow in my heart.

"The human world is so strange," I continued, "yet so familiar. Wherever I go, I see echoes of my people. In the language, the architecture, the culture. Everything has a strong root with my people."

"I think I understand," Reginald nodded. "Well, maybe not understand," he added as an afterthought, "but I believe I can imagine what you are feeling. I like to look back at previous rulers, my ancestors, and realize that while the world was different for them, it was also the same."

"I suppose it would be a similar feeling, yeah."

Thinking back on the history of my people also elicited awe at how far away they felt, yet how similarly they lived their lives.

However, the main difference is time. For me, my people were destroyed around two and a half years earlier, but for the world, it had been over eleven hundred.

But I didn't wish to delve into those thoughts on such a beautiful day. Fishing was a way to relax and listen to nature, or talk about joyous things.

"Hey, Reginald."

"Yeah?"

"I was wondering something. How long have you known Myrril?"

I had asked the question in order to change the subject, but I was also curious as to the answer.

"Phew, that's a tough one," he replied. "Well, she wasn't born here. In Edren, I mean. She came here when she was very young."

"Wait a second," I interrupted, "didn't you say before that both of you have lived in Edren all your lives?"

"Yeah, well. She has her own circumstances," Reginald

explained. "It's not my place to get into them, though. Saying that she's always been here is easier on her."

"I see..."

I suppose I understand. When I told Reginald and Myrril who I was, I ended up with a flood of questions.

"Well, anyway," Reginald moved to continue, "she lives with some family members in Edren, a very nice older couple who used to be merchants. That's actually how we met. We were around five years old at the time."

"So what's that? Twelve years?"

"Yeah, we met twelve years ago," Reginald took a moment to soak in that information, his face reading amusement, perhaps at how time seemed to fly. "But she ended up leaving for about two years after she turned twelve, so I suppose we've only known each other for ten years."

"She left?" I asked curiously.

"Not my place to explain," Reginald shook his head before continuing, "both of us joined the Association when we turned fifteen, and we've been working together ever since."

"Hm," I nodded and looked out at the water while soaking in the information. When another question came to me, I moved to ask it.

"Was she always this timid?"

"Ha!" Reginald chuckled. "She's always had a timid personality, but it got worse when she came back. When we were younger, we got into all sorts of trouble."

I smiled and let out a snort-like chuckle. "I know that feeling."

"Oh?" My words seemed to catch Reginald's attention: "What were your childhood friends like?"

I grimaced for a moment before softening my expression. It was my own impulsive words that caused this.

"When I was younger, I didn't have very many friends. My

grandfather was a legendary figure, and my father was famous in his own right. For a long time, my only real friends were my siblings, Kadyn and Reina. But I was lucky enough that it wasn't the case forever. My first real friend was a girl named Layla Alders. She was the daughter of Duke Alders and my fiancé."

Reginald, who had been quiet while I explained, nearly jumped up in surprise.

"F-fiancé!?"

"It was an arranged betrothal," I waved him off. "In my case, I was just lucky we became good friends."

"I-I see..."

"Layla was the epitome of a proper lady... at least, when she needed to be. In reality, she was a bit of a tomboy. We fought and played and got into mischief, as any of the children at that age would. However, it never got really bold until we met Faye," I felt a fond smile subconsciously come over my face. "She was an elvish child who stayed in Aleuria for several years. Layla and I made fast friends with her and introduced her to all types of mischief she had never experienced."

"Ah, those were the days..." I reminisced. "I smile fondly at those memories, but I've realized over the years how dumb and childish we were. We used to fight using sticks, pretending we were knights or seeing how far we could launch a cherry pit out of our mouths like most kids, but some things we did were really dumb."

"We used to sneak into manors and try and see how long we could sneak around without being caught, pretending we were exploring ancient ruins. Though at the time we didn't realize that the manor servants liked to pretend they didn't see us." I laughed. "Other times we just ran around disrupting the markets because we thought it was funny."

"Ha!" Reginald chuckled, "That reminds me of my childhood. I guess kids will be kids, no matter the era."

I smiled, "I'll have to tell you about the time we thought it was funny to sneak into the woods and throw rocks at the animals. It's a long story, but it's also my first encounter with a Direwolf."

"Your friends sound like a lot of fun," Reginald commented.

"They were," I responded. "Layla was always good with words and had her own air around her, but Faye was different. Thinking back, I can't quite put words to it, but she just had this presence about her that drew you in."

"Oh?" Reginald raised an eyebrow.

"Actually, now that I think about it, I'm having trouble putting together an image of her in my mind." I furrowed my brow as I wracked my head. "All I can remember is her smile. And those eyes that sparkled like starlight."

I grew frustrated trying to piece together a full image, but it felt as though something was blocking it from happening.

Out of the corner of my eye, I saw a knowing smile stretch across Reginald's face.

"Hey, what's that smile for?" I said almost defensively.

"Oh, nothing," he responded.

"Hmm. I don't know what you think you know, but–" I began before Reginald interrupted, nearly jumping from his seat.

"HEY! You've got something!"

In that moment, I remembered we were fishing. I moved my attention to the fishing rod in my hand; the heavily bent rod was fighting as if trying to pull free from my grasp.

I stood to my feet and pulled the rod backward to begin to reel it in.

"This is a tough one," I muttered.

The fish was pulling hard against the line, almost throwing me off balance. I moved my legs and planted myself in a former position to continue to pull the fish toward the pier.

By then, Reginald had run over and began pulling in the line as I held it steady.

A fin appeared above the water as the fish pulled as hard as it could.

Hand me the line and grab the net!" I yelled.

Reginald passed the rope to me and grabbed the small net set on the pier. He lay down on his stomach and held the net out as far as he could. With a heavy tug, one that threatened to snap the line, the fish was pulled out of the water. Reginald swiped the net underneath it with amazing dexterity and successfully grabbed the fish before it landed back in the water.

"Woo!" Reginald got to his feet and we exchanged a high-five, "this is a big one."

The fish was about three feet in length with beautifully glistening scales and a pair of long whiskers above its mouth, as well as an assortment of smaller ones around them.

"You can say that again. I've never seen a freshwater catfish this big," I said with a big smile. "It's got to weigh what, fifteen pounds?"

"Yeah, that sounds about right," Reginald confirmed as he held the massive fish in his net.

"Do you want to stay longer?"

"Naw," Reginald shook his head, "this is more than enough. Anything more and we would be a burden to Leone."

"That's fair, I don't think she has somewhere to store fish."

So we packed up early and started to make our way back to Leone's house with our massive catch. Most people ignored us as we walked through the crowded streets, but every so often we would get an approving nod or a smile from a man in the crowd.

The people thinned slightly as we began to walk down a few less busy streets, but the city was still as bustling as ever.

"Hey, can I ask you something about what you were saying earlier?" Reginald suddenly asked.

"Hm? Sure."

"Layla... did you two get married?"

"No," I shook my head, "it kept getting postponed. We were originally going to be wed after we both turned fifteen, but then I joined the army. We were going to hold it after I got back from boot camp, but one thing or another kept cropping up. Then, of course, the civil war happened."

"Gods, what horrible luck," Reginald commented.

"Maybe it was," I said. "Maybe the universe was saving all of my luck for when I needed to escape from Kyrtvale."

We walked on for another few moments in silence.

"Perhaps it's better this way," Reginald suggested. "I mean, arranged marriages don't often end in happiness."

I couldn't tell if that's how he truly felt, or if he was just trying to cheer me up. Either way, the sentiment was touching.

"We'll never know," I replied with a shrug. "I mean, it wasn't going to be a loveless marriage. She was my best friend, and I loved her as such, but... not even the gods know what could have been."

My mind once again shot to Faye, our conversation reminding me that I couldn't remember what she looked like. No matter how I wracked my brain, I couldn't form a coherent image.

"How odd..." I began to mumble before a tingling feeling shot up my spine.

I stopped in my tracks and focused on the feeling,

completely switching mental gears as I gazed upon the nonde-script warehouse across the street.

"Is something wrong?" Reginald turned and asked.

The warehouse was a large brick building with a few windows up high and a semi-circular roof, about as normal as you can get. But something about it was bothering me.

"Is there anything strange about that warehouse to you?" I asked Reginald as I scanned the area.

"Hm?"

Reginald turned back and looked at the building with me.

"It looks like there's someone inside." He nodded toward a shadow moving in one of the windows near the roof. "Probably just a worker."

I shook my head, "It's some sort of lookout."

While the figure was shadowy and hard to see, I was able to make out a few details. The person wore a dark cloak and sported at least one weapon on their back. They didn't look like a thief, they looked like they were scanning the street, possibly for people who were getting too curious, like us.

"Huh. You want to head around the front and get a better look?"

I couldn't help but smile a bit. I guessed that we had spent enough time together that he was used to my curiosity, or he was also curious.

"Yeah. I mean, it's our day to relax, so just a quick look."

Reginald didn't seem completely reassured, but we made a wide berth around the street. At the front of the building was a set of massive wooden doors with a pair of smaller ones built into them. In front of them was a decently sized yard filled with crates, carts, and neatly stacked piles of assorted lumber.

There was a small building placed next to the closed iron gate where we could see a bored man lazily keeping watch.

"Anything look off?" Reginald asked me even as he scanned the area.

"I'm still not sure. I just have a sense of foreboding as I look at this place," I explained. "It's almost like I'm missing something that I shouldn't be missing."

"Like something's missing?"

I shook my head a bit, "No. It's more like something is here that shouldn't be."

The feeling was difficult to describe, but I felt that was an apt description. I tried to wrack my brain for what I could be missing, for a similar feeling I've felt in the past. It felt like it was on the tip of my tongue.

"Do you need to get closer?" Reginald asked with a side smile and a raised eyebrow.

"I don't know what that look is for, but getting closer couldn't hurt."

Despite the knowing look I got from Reginald, he was right. I wanted to get closer to the building to figure out what I was feeling.

Reginald handed me the net, fish and all, which I quickly put away in my pocket dimension, and we started to cross the street.

As we got closer, the feeling got stronger before I finally realized something. I was sensing an energy from within the building, Megin. Several sources of Megin were emanating from within the structure, and they were quite strong. The feeling of purity mixed with immense fear was what caused my sense of foreboding.

"You look angry," Reginald whispered to me. "What's wrong?"

"Reginald," my tone was dead serious, "slavery is illegal here, right?"

"Huh?" He looked taken aback, "Of course it is. Why? Does it have something to do with this building?"

"I can feel them. They are scared."

"You can feel who?"

"Elves."

We didn't need to say another word to understand the situation. Without missing a beat, I once again summoned the swirling vortex that acted as the opening to my pocket dimension and pulled out weapons from within.

Both of us were in casual clothing, but we didn't feel like going home and changing. If anything was alike between the two of us, we both desired to help those in front of us.

We strapped our blades to our sides and approached the sleepy guard.

As he saw us, his head snapped to attention in surprise, like he didn't think anyone would have the audacity to approach him. He wiped the sleep from his eyes and addressed us with an unwelcoming tone of annoyance.

"Can I help you?"

"Yeah, actually. Can you tell us who owns this building?" Reginald promptly asked, ignoring the man's disrespectful attitude.

"This is the property of Mr. Bryher, so scram."

The man had somehow been extremely helpful and not very helpful at the same time. I had no clue who this Mr. Bryher was.

Then I remembered something Mattias had said. When he spoke of his logging permit not being renewed, he had mentioned a Viden Bryher, owner of the Onforde Logging Company.

This was too much of a coincidence for me. If the same man who bribed officials in Edren to put his competitor out of business was also trafficking elves, we would have a much bigger issue on our hands.

"Yeah... we can't do that." My anger had begun to bleed into my words.

"I wasn't asking."

The man pulled a massive crossbow from below him and rested it on the table, pointed at me, the bolt loaded and ready to fire.

"Neither was I," I gritted my teeth and grasped the cast iron bars of the gate in front of me.

"What do you think you're going to do, huh? I'm the only one with the key. You'll never be able to– WHAT?!"

The man's eyes seemed to burst from his skull as the sound of creaking metal filled the air. I had funneled Megin into my arms and pulled the metal bars apart like they were made of parchment, opening a large enough hole for Reginald and me to walk through.

I calmly stepped through the new opening and approached the stunned guard.

"Y-you clearly aren't from around here!" he stuttered in a panic. "Anyone who messes with Mr. Bryher is in for a world of hurt. He is one of the most powerful men in the city!"

I got close and whispered in his ear, "Bring it on," before I threw my fist into his ugly mug and sent him into the back wall of his small guard post without him ever firing his crossbow.

"Man, you are a little scary sometimes," Reginald mused behind me.

I turned to the main entrance of the warehouse and stared at it for a moment.

"Let's not kill anyone. While we may be on good terms with the captain, we don't want to ruin that relationship."

"Got it," Reginald gave a nod.

I tossed him a length of cord to tie his blade to its scabbard, making an improvised club that he could use without worry.

We approached the front of the warehouse, passing through the still yard unimpeded, only for the smaller set of double doors at the base of the large gate to open.

A group of four armed men came from within the building. Each and every one of them looked like crooks. Their patchwork armor soaked with mystery stains, and the wild look in their eyes made me feel even less remorse for what I was about to do, if it was even possible to feel less than nothing.

"Well, well, well. If it isn't a bunch of troublemakers," a grungy-looking man in the front spoke first, the men behind him snickering.

"Take a look in a mirror lately?" I spat.

The man squinted his eyes toward me with irritation.

"You–"

"I'm going to make this simple," I interrupted him. "You're going to hand over the elves, and we'll leave you relatively unharmed."

The man let out a laugh that sounded as if he actually found our conversation amusing.

"Last time I checked," he said after calming down, "you were outnumbered."

One of the men behind him drew a rusty, single-edge shortsword and stared at me with a look that made me a little uncomfortable.

I sighed, "I've grown tired of your faces. Move aside, now."

The man with the shortsword let out a war cry and sprinted toward me, his blade in the air.

Anyone caught in the situation wouldn't have had time to draw their weapon and block the attack. For a swordsman, it was a horrible position to be in. Luckily, my father was extremely thorough with his training.

I dropped my weight back as the man approached, his blade in the air. As he swung it down upon my head, I moved my left arm to completely block his attack at the wrist. My right hand shot forward like a serpent and grasped the front of his armor, my right leg moved forward and swept his feet out from under him, and I pulled with all my might. Within the blink of an eye, the man went from on the attack to being thrown over my shoulder and hitting his back hard on the ground. But I wasn't done. I twisted his sword arm with a sickening CRACK! And left him screaming in the dirt.

The remaining men seemed to lose their nerve for a moment before charging forward, their main focus was on me. However, I wasn't alone.

Reginald intercepted one of the men coming toward me and knocked him upside the head with his sheathed blade. The man lost his momentum and fell backward, hitting his head on the ground.

The remaining two came toward me with weapons drawn. One of them had a pair of strange weapons. They seemed to fit around the knuckles, with large dagger-like spines protruding from them. The other pulled out a wicked-looking curved blade, almost like a large sickle.

The first man jabbed at me with his strange weapons, forcing me to dodge back for a moment before knocking his fist to the side and delivering my fist to his stomach. As I wound back for another strike, his friend intervened with his curved sword, forcing me to abandon the counterattack in order to dodge.

Now, the two men were on the attack together. With jabs to my right and swings to my left, I fell back slightly before using an opening caused by their inexperience fighting like this to strike back.

I swung a wide kick into the side of the first man, his bones creaking as I made contact, before swinging around and delivering a strike into the second man. With both of them reeling, I sent a left hook into the second man's face before landing an elbow in the first man's stomach.

Reginald came up from behind, and together, we quickly finished them off.

"I didn't know you were good in hand-to-hand combat," Reginald mused.

I shrugged, "I'm really not. It's just that Aleurian martial arts don't have a counter in this age."

"Hm," Reginald snorted, "very true."

"Let's get inside, I don't want them to harm the elves."

We walked to the now-sunlit entrance and stared inside. Not far back were three more crooks looking scared as they stared at us. These men were younger, around my age, I had guessed.

"D-don't come any closer!" the one in the front trembled, "I-I'm warning you."

With a single look between us, Reginald and I rushed forward at the same time and struck down the two behind the trembling boy before turning to him.

He screamed and ran toward the entrance.

"We should probably stop him," I said as I started to run after him.

Then, another silhouette appeared in the doorway. The kid stopped in his tracks in front of the man, and I slowed down out of caution.

A moment later, a small white flame appeared from the silhouette, and the kid was sent flying back into the warehouse without even being able to scream.

Reginald and I dropped into a combat stance as the figure approached.

"Hm. I came here to investigate some illegal activity, and yet it appears I was beaten to it."

The man spoke melodically, with guttural R's and rounded U's. The words flowed together in a strangely beautiful manner. All of this was indicative of the language of the Kingdom of Faeron.

As the bright background faded, we could finally make him out. He was dressed in a well-tailored tailcoat with white gloves, gray hair, and a clean-shaven face. I could only describe his appearance as that of a butler.

"I assume that you two are the ones responsible, Oui?"

"We are," I answered, still in a defensive posture despite the man's calm demeanor. "Is that going to be an issue?"

"Ah, non. Not at all," the man replied. "In fact, it is quite a relief to know that this matter would have been resolved even without my investigation."

"Who are you?" Reginald finally spoke up.

"Ah, my apologies," the man gave an elegant bow. "My name is Pierre du Blanc. I am currently under the employ of Monsieur Viden Bryher."

"I am Elric, this is Reginald," I answered in kind before asking another question. "If you are investigating on behalf of Viden Bryher, does that mean he doesn't know what's going on here?"

I had been starting to feel more suspicious about Viden Bryher, but perhaps it was misplaced.

"Oui, that is correct," Pierre responded. "He saw some discrepancies in his records and sent me to investigate. He believed that his warehouses were being used for illegal activities, and it would appear to be true."

"Yes, it is," I said. "They have elves here..."

As I spoke, I glanced around to find where that feeling was the strongest.

"Over here," I jogged up to a large crate with Reginald and Pierre behind me. "Help me open this."

Reginald grabbed the opposite side of the crate, and the two of us pulled the entire piece off. It was a false wall made to look like a shipping container.

"Impressive, it would have taken me some time to find that," Pierre mused.

Behind the false wall was a small room with a large set of bars on the opposite side to section off a cell-like chamber.

Inside were several people, men and women, all dressed in lightweight cloth and leather with recognizable Elven designs. Each of them had elongated ears and a fearful look in their eyes.

As the light entered the chamber, the men quickly moved to huddle up around the women as a protective wall.

A man around his eighties, fairly young by elvish standards, ran up and grabbed the bars.

"You Curs! When we get out of here, I'll rip you apart myself!" he yelled in the Elvish tongue.

"What is he saying? I can't understand it," Reginald said to nobody in particular.

"My apologies. I, too, do not know what language he speaks," Pierre answered, "but he appears to be quite angry."

The Elvish language was a beautiful one. Its words flowed in such a wonderful way, and it even managed to soften many of the harsher sounds that naturally developed. Even when being spouted as insults, it was like an expertly crafted musical number that carried emotion with its every word.

"He is," I informed them. "It sounds like he thinks we are with the guys we took down."

Both of them looked shocked, though Pierre only for a moment.

"You can understand them?" Reginald asked in disbelief.

I nodded, "Yes, I speak several languages, including those of the Elves, Dwarves, and a bit of the Giants."

Pierre's expression changed in very minute ways as I spoke, which to me looked as though he wasn't entirely convinced.

"That's not important, though. One of those guys will have the key to their cell," I pointed out. "I'll try and calm them down if you guys could take a look."

"Can do," Reginald responded while Pierre simply gave a polite nod.

I turned back to the elvish man, who was still yelling at me.

"...*the things I'll do to you, your funeral will have to be closed casket!*"

The man's knuckles were white as he gripped the steel bars, and his eyes were full of hatred.

"*That's enough, Liem'Tel. You should not waste your energy,*" one of the other elvish men snapped.

"*He is right, you know,*" I said in the Elvish tongue, eliciting a series of shocked faces and wide eyes. The man who was gripping the bars and shouting, Liem'Tel, was so shocked that he stumbled backward.

"*This... this can't be!*" he shouted in denial. "*Our people would never teach our language to a human!*"

"*I cannot believe they have brought someone who cannot only understand our every word but speak it as well. Is this truly the end for us?*" an elvish woman fearfully mumbled.

"*I would like to correct your misconception,*" I stepped closer to the bars, "*I am not with the men who have kept you here.*"

"*Like we would believe you!*" Liem'Tel spat.

I pointed my thumb behind me, "*Don't take my word for it.*"

One of the elvish men peered behind me with a bit of a squint at the bright light and gasped, "*I recognize those men!*

They are the ones who guard us, but they seem to be unconscious."

Liem'Tel was painfully stubborn and had to see for himself. Once he did, his eyes widened once more as he fumbled for his words.

"Enough, Liem. It is obvious he is here to help us."

A third man smacked Liem on the back of the head before turning to me, *"We are grateful for your help, and we apologize for this one's attitude."*

"No need," I waved him off, *"I would be just as on edge if I were in your situation. We will be getting you all out of here in just a moment, but... how many of you are there?"*

It was still very dark, and I couldn't see much, so I focused my Megin into the palm of my hand and imagined it springing forward. I summoned the image of morning light and the feeling of the sun on my skin.

The next moment, a miniature ball of stable flame, like a tiny star, appeared floating above my palm. The space was immediately filled with a soft light. By my count, there were about fifteen elves of various ages, though none that I could call elderly. I was also able to see that each elf had a pair of tight metal bands across their wrists with unfamiliar magical symbols carved into them.

The elves winced as their eyes adjusted to the light.

"By Lorhas'Mir! What is that light?" An elf shouted in surprise.

"I-I've never seen such a creation of magic!" another stammered. *"It's beautiful."*

One of the older elves, maybe around middle-aged for his people, narrowed his eyes toward me in an inquisitive manner.

"The way you are creating that light is closer to our magic than that of a human," he observed. *"You must be a sorcerer."*

"I believe that's what I've been called, yes."

Just then, Reginald shouted from behind, "Found the keys!"

"Good," I responded in the common tongue, "toss them here."

Reginald ran up to the opening and did as I asked. I caught the many keys affixed to the large key ring and began to rummage through until I found the one that opened the door.

With a click and a creak, the door was opened, and the elves were free.

As they piled out one at a time, some weaker than others and requiring help, the oldest man stopped and grasped my hand. No words were exchanged, only gratitude.

CHAPTER 14

The Second Request

"Dammit. Another horrible crime that's happened under my nose."

We were standing in the warehouse yard, and I had just finished explaining what had happened to Captain Dane, who had shown up not long after we reported the incident.

Several members of the city guard were watching the tied-up kidnappers while many others were searching the warehouse with Pierre in tow to open any locks.

"It's not your fault, I tried to comfort him. You can't be everywhere at once. Speaking of, why–"

"Why am I here?" he finished for me. "Kidnapping and Trafficking, especially of elves, is a serious crime. And ever since the whole thing with the Head Administrator, I've needed to crack down a lot more and make sure things are done right."

With the public eye on the coup attempt and the corruption within the city guard, Captain Dane needed to not only ensure there were none left but also to regain the trust of the people.

"I wish you well in your endeavors."

"And I to you," the captain replied.

"But," I continued, "I was wondering what's going to happen to them?"

I looked over at the group of elves we had rescued, huddled up and keeping their distance from the guards.

"Yes, I was thinking the same," the captain sighed. "This isn't the first instance of elvish kidnapping we've had. Even going back the last two centuries."

As Captain Dane explained, the entire valley encircled by the Serpents Crest Mountains was once part of the Dolar Imperium. However, when they broke off and split into the various city-states, the group did away with the discrimination against non-humans. This caused plenty of issues at first but made the Valtion-Silma City-State Alliance a haven for escaped slaves. However, many parts of the world couldn't stand it at the time and attempted to steal back what they considered their property.

When most of the world abolished slavery around the fiftieth year of the third era, the kidnapping attempts calmed down. However, that didn't stop everyone.

"We've had a massive problem with kidnapping attempts, not only historically, but even just during my time here," Captain Dane continued. "The Faeron Kingdom has been behind many of them, as I suspect they are responsible here as well. However, we've rarely had any cases of kidnapping make it this far."

"What does that mean?"

"Well, by itself, it would mean a profuse apology by the Merchant Elect and the Captain of the Guard. However, these elves are not citizens of our city nor any member of the Alliance."

As he put it, only a handful of them could understand a minute amount of the common tongue, and none of them could speak it beyond a few broken words.

"So where did they come from then? Are there still free elf tribes?" I asked with anticipation and hope.

"Of course," Dane answered, sending relief through my body, "I'm betting these elves are from the Hollowood to the north of The Porteloch. They sometimes send people if they are in need of supplies, like during droughts or tough winters, as well as for simple things that they can't get their hands on, such as metals."

"Are they part of the Alliance?" I asked inquisitively.

"Not officially, no. However, they are considered an honorary member and have been invited to many of the Alliance meetings. Though, as far as I've heard, they've never shown up."

"So, is there a different way you have to deal with this?" I was trying to get an idea of how Onforde dealt with possible political ramifications such as these.

"Probably," Dane shrugged, "we'll have to take them to the Merchant Elect. I'm sure there is some policy or guideline on what to do, but I wouldn't know it. This situation is above my pay grade."

I chuckled a bit, "I feel you there."

I've had several times in my life when I had to try and deal with situations that were beyond me. During my time stationed in Tors, I had to deal with an uppity noble. He was complaining about various things, but I had been told not to talk back to him and to just follow along with his antics.

I begrudgingly did as I was told and later discovered that he was being used as bait to attract a criminal ring. The man later found me and apologized for his conduct, but if I had given in to what I wanted to do, then it could have blown the whole thing.

The point of the story is that we are told to do something for a reason, and while we may not know exactly why, there is a purpose. Besides, you can always find out why you did it later.

I offered to come with the captain so I could translate, but he respectfully declined.

"We have a few elvish members of the guard who can help us with that," he explained. "Besides, we can't ask any more of you. You're starting to make us look bad!"

We had a good laugh at his joke before parting ways. I waved goodbye to the elves as they were led down the street.

"I'm glad we stopped," Reginald said as he stopped beside me.

"Yeah, so am I."

"This is really good," Leone said between bites.

"Mhm!" Myrril nodded along.

"But really, guys? Today was supposed to be relaxing."

We were back at Leone's place, seated around the table enjoying an evening meal of freshly caught catfish, warm bread, and fresh fruit.

Leone had already told us about their day. They had gone on a walk through nature, then checked out a few stores on the main road, and we were finishing up talking about our little fiasco.

"I mean, it was relaxing," Reginald nodded toward the fish we were all eating.

"I also had a great time saving those elves," I pointed out before taking another bite of my food.

The catfish was good, if not a little disappointing. Its taste was milder than I had expected, even though the meat was of good quality. I suppose that was the difference between freshwater and saltwater fish.

However, I was finding it a little hard to fully enjoy the meal with all the thoughts crowding my head. I couldn't help but ask myself why these attempted kidnappings were occurring. I knew that the Faeron Kingdom had a long history of enslaving the elves, but we weren't in the Faeron Kingdom.

"Elric," Leone spoke up, noticing my mood, "is something wrong?"

I sighed, "Look. I'm not from around here, but even I can see something is wrong in this Alliance."

"H-how so?" Myrril asked a little defensively.

"These kidnappings, they've been happening for hundreds of years, and yet there has been no real solution," I explained. "The Faeron Kingdom just does what it wants, and it appears to me that the Alliance doesn't have the balls to stand up to them."

"You have to understand, they are a much larger kingdom," Reginald said, a little annoyed, "and we *have* been doing what we can."

"You've done everything besides stopping the problem at the source," I pointed out. "Even if you cannot fight your neighbor, these occurrences are too frequent in Onforde for them to be simply crossing the mountains. And if they are, then that's another problem entirely."

"What are you suggesting?" Reginald asked.

"To the south is a place called Torrel; I'm sure you know of it. They are the city on the border between the Alliance and the Faeron Kingdom," I started. "From what research I did on the city-states, I know for a fact that Torrel is the most docile of the seven. I wouldn't be surprised if they refused to confront people at the border."

Reginald looked angry for a moment before calming down as he processed what I was saying, "My father knows of how non-confrontational Torrel is, but we've never thought anything of it." He continued, "What you say makes complete sense. I-I should talk to my father about this."

"Will he have the power to do something about it?" I asked.

"N-no..." Reginald looked dejected.

"I'm sorry for getting political," I turned to Leone, "it's just really bothering me.

"No, you aren't wrong," she said. "We in Onforde have had

the same suspicion for a long time, but we cannot do anything about it."

"I-I wish you could..." Myrril muttered.

"Speaking of Torrel, we heard something interesting today, didn't we?" Leone turned to Myrril.

Myrril nodded, "Th-the border is closed."

"Really?" I nearly jumped up in surprise. If this were true, then my whole hypothesis about them not doing anything could fall apart.

"Mhm," Myrril answered, "b-but it wasn't Torrel that closed it..."

"Yeah, get this. Apparently, the border was closed off by Faeron," Leone jumped in. "It probably has something to do with the border skirmishes on their northern border."

I recalled a basic map of the area I once saw, "That's with... Elderoth, yeah?"

She nodded, "Yeah, but I don't think they are telling the truth about it. I'm not sure what the real reason is, but closing it because of Elderoth just doesn't make sense."

"Not just because of how far it is," I pointed out, "but also because they are stopping a massive amount of trade from entering their country."

"Man... What is going on over there?" Reginald mused.

"I don't know, but whatever it is, I hope it means a massive change is coming."

The rest of the group agreed with my statement.

I was there again, standing in the forest of gnarled trees.

A low fog covered the forest floor, enough to just barely be able to see the ground.

The laugh of a little girl echoed nearby.

I quickly spun in the direction of the sound and spotted the girl once more. She dashed between two trees, her green dress dirtied at the bottom and her flowing golden hair whipping behind her.

"Wake up, sleepy head."

The girl's voice echoed once more, this time with words; words I had heard before, in a voice so familiar yet distant, a fleeting memory.

She dashed to another tree, her form slowed like she was running in molasses. I tried to move after her, but my legs were rooted to the spot.

Another childish laugh rang out like she was enjoying a game of hide and seek.

"Catch me if you can!"

The playful taunting was once again directionless as I spotted the girl moving in the corner of my vision.

Whenever I saw her, her face was hidden from view. The only features I ever managed to catch were her long, slender ears.

Then, the laughter and sounds of children playing stopped. All was eerily silent.

I tried to move, to look around, but my body was locked in place. The next moment, I felt a presence hovering above my shoulder, a gentle whisper caressing my ear.

"Come find me..."

Thump Thump Thump!

I was awoken by the sound of somebody knocking on the door. I jolted up in surprise and wiped the sleep from my eyes.

The early morning sunlight was creeping through the curtains, and I could faintly detect the sound of the city in full swing.

The person at the door knocked once more.

Thump Thump Thump!

"I'm coming!" I called out as I approached the door.

Peeking through the small, curtained window next to the front door, I could make out that our visitor was some kind of runner, a person who ran messages for city officials.

I unlatched the lock and opened the door.

"Can I help you?" I asked.

"Apologies for waking you," the young man said as he presented a letter, "I have an urgent message for a Leone Scarlette and her friends."

"Oh, well, Leone isn't awake yet–"

"That's alright, I was told you could also accept it, Mr. Elric," the runner cut me off. "They said that the original recipient may still be injured and described you as the alternate recipient."

"Oh," I was a little taken aback, "well, that works then."

I took the letter from the runner's hand, prompting a salute from him.

"The parcel has been delivered!" he declared. "I will now take my leave."

Before another word could leave my mouth, the young man was already halfway down the street. I couldn't help but admire his dedication, but I wished that he had at least let me thank him.

I dropped the letter onto the table and slumped into a chair, my hand on my head. The dreams were getting worse, more forceful, but I was no closer to figuring out what it meant than I was before.

In the Aleurian culture, there were tales that dreams were a window into your subconscious. We believe that vivid dreams, such as the ones I was experiencing, were a way for your mind to tell you something. However, not even our most prophetic seers could tell you what they mean; that was up to you to decipher.

If my dreams were a warning, I believe as though it would have a more sinister feel to it. What I was experiencing wasn't sinister but perhaps foreboding. The girl's actions had evolved since I last saw her, this time speaking to me. It was off-putting, to say the least.

Plus, there was the forest. I had never seen a forest such as that, and yet my mind had constructed it. What if...

"Hey," a voice cut off my train of thought, "who was at the door?"

"A runner," I replied to Reginald, who had just woken up. "He dropped off a letter for Leone."

Reginald walked over to the table and sat opposite me.

"Is something wrong?" he asked. "You seem distracted."

"No, I shook my head. Nothing's wrong. I was just... thinking."

"Do you want to talk about it?"

I shook my head in response.

"Well, if you change your mind, I'm here for you."

"Thanks, I appreciate that."

Once everyone had awoken, I handed the letter to Leone.

"What's this?" she asked

"A runner came by earlier and left this for you," I informed her.

"Hm."

She pulled a letter opener from a drawer and cleanly cut open the envelope. Inside was a single page.

Leone skimmed through the contents and furrowed her brow.

"What's wrong?" Reginald asked first.

Leone shook her head, "It's nothing. The Merchant Elect wants to meet with us today."

This statement sent the room into confusion.

"B-but didn't he just..." Myrril began.

"Yeah," I answered before she finished, knowing what she was going to say, "he said he was too busy to speak with us personally."

When Captain Dane showed up at Leone's house a few days earlier, he gave us a large letter, which ended up being multiple letters in a single package. We received thank-you letters from several maids, including Tessa, as well as from guards we helped, various ministers, and, of course, the Merchant Elect Jean-Luc Pierre. In his letter, he profusely apologized for being unable to thank us in person due to the mass of work left behind from the coup attempt. He also included several monetary bonds that we could exchange at the treasury for a sum of cash as a token of thanks for our work. We couldn't really refuse them since they were already in our possession, but we had yet to use them.

"What could have changed?" Reginald mused before turning to Leone, "Does the letter say what it's about?"

"Yeah, it does," she responded, "here."

Leone handed the letter to Reginald, who also furrowed his brow as he read it.

"Well, this is... interesting," Reginald stated with a slightly nervous tone.

Myrril, who read the letter over his shoulder, nodded in agreement.

I held out my hand, "Can I have a read?"

"Yeah, knock yourself out."

I took a look at the letter and realized what they were talking about.

I am aware that you will be leaving the city soon on your return to Edren, and I wish you safe travels. However, there is a slight disruption with my work, and I would like to invite you to my home this afternoon to discuss a possible solution for the elf problem, which seems to have cropped up out of where only the gods know. I understand if you are unable to assist in this case, as you are ultimately under the purview of Lord Aulcrest. If this is the case, then I bid you farewell as I deal with the political issues that have been so graciously left for me by a mysterious benefactor.

~ Merchant Elect Jean-Luc Pierre

"Oh..." was my only reaction to the passive-aggressive letter I had just read as I finally understood Reginald's nervousness.

"So, what are we going to do?" Reginald asked.

I looked up from the letter and chuckled nervously, "Well, we don't really have a choice, now do we?"

"I... I suppose not."

"Well, it looks like you've gotten yourselves into a bit of a pickle," Leone said with her arms crossed and a wide grin across her face. "While you deal with that, how about I take Myrril to visit a Mage friend of mine?"

Myrril's eyes lit up, "R-really!?"

"Mhm," Leone nodded, "really."

"I hate to burst your bubble, ladies," Reginald interrupted, "but I don't think you'll have the time."

"What do you mean?" Leone asked.

"Well, the letter was addressed to all of us, right?"

Leone let out a "Tsk" in response.

"S-so no Mage?" Myrril asked with a twinge of hope in her voice, though I believed she already knew the answer.

"Sorry, Myrril. Another time," I apologized.

Myrril clutched her staff closer and looked off to the side in thought.

Reginald approached her and patted her shoulder. "And don't worry about us having to meet with the Merchant Elect," he reassured her. "You've met my father and came out just fine. You can handle this."

"Mhm," Myrril nodded absentmindedly.

Leone appeared beside her and locked arms with Myrril. "Come now, Myrril. We need to be getting ready. I think I have a few outfits that would look good on you."

"Wait, what?" Myrril snapped out of her thoughts.

Reginald and I just stood there, unable to decide if we were supposed to help as Leone dragged Myrril up the stairs, her eyes pleading for us to do something.

After they disappeared from view, neither of us spoke for a moment.

"So... did you bring anything formal to wear?" he asked me.

"Well... kind of..."

We weren't kept waiting at the gate this time. As soon as we arrived, the guard showed us in.

The front doors of the manor had been replaced, but the evidence of the coup attempt was still present all around us. They had done a good job of cleaning things up, but the mental toll on the people of the manor would take much longer to fix.

As we were being led down the long and familiar hallways, I once more looked over our group.

Leone wore a similar outfit to the one we had first seen her wear in Riverbrook. She had high boots with light brown pants and a white blouse with a complimentary corset of a darker color. Around her neck, she wore a necklace I hadn't seen before; the image of a crescent moon curled around the right half of the sun. As usual, she also had her Association Medal hanging from her belt.

Myrril was a bit of a shocking sight at first. She wore a long, light green skirt with a white, short-sleeved top nicely put together with a high-waisted leather belt and her Association Medal hanging around her neck. She looked wonderful, yet she was very obviously uncomfortable with all the looks she was getting. Except for the glances from Reginald, which she didn't seem to mind.

"You look really good in green," Reginald leaned over and whispered to Myrril.

Myrril shyly turned her head away from him at the unexpected compliment, her cheeks had begun to turn a shade of pink.

I turned my eyes to Reginald, who was wearing an outfit that was well-suited for his frame. He wore dark trousers and boots that complemented his dark green surcoat with an intricately patterned border of golden thread. Around his waist was a fashionable brown leather belt and a polished silver buckle elegantly engraved with a wolf carrying a shattered blade within its maw, his family crest.

It was the first time I had seen him wear an outfit befitting the son of a lord, and he wore it well.

As for me, what I was wearing wasn't too different from my usual wear. I wore the pair of black boots and trousers I kept in my pocket dimension as well as my white longcoat buckled at the waist overtop a starch-white cotton blouse and maroon waistcoat. My belt was double-wrapped, styled as though to hang a sword from the lower loop.

I had modeled my outfit off of some popular designs from the Aleurian Empire, but it was just thrown together with whatever clothing I had stored away. When I died, my pocket dimension had been full of backup supplies to deal with unexpected situations like this. Ironically, death was the only situation I hadn't considered while packing.

When I had first thrown the outfit together, I had been a little worried that it didn't look good, but the others said it suited me well, so I stuck with it.

Of course, none of us were armed when we arrived at the manor. At first, Myrril refused to go without her staff, but she eventually acquiesced when I offered to store it in my pocket dimension.

"Ah, good. You are all here," Jean-Luc Pierre greeted us as we were shown to a sitting room within the manor.

Since the last time we saw him, he had gained heavy bags under his eyes from the increased workload. However, the look in his eyes defied the exhaustion apparent in his body.

Seated across from the Merchant Elect were a pair of middle-aged elves from the group we had rescued the day before. These were the two that had seemed to be in charge when we had spoken with them. Behind the couch that they sat upon was a soldier with his helm tucked under his arm. A pair of pointed ears graced the sides of his head.

"Please, take a seat," the Merchant Elect gestured to an empty couch.

As we sat upon the comfortable furniture, I thanked the Merchant Elect for his invitation.

"Thank you, My Lord, for the invitation. I must admit that

we weren't expecting anything because of how busy you have become as of late."

A wry smile appeared on Jean-Luc's face. "Yes, well. This matter is of the utmost importance. Depending on how it's handled, it could become a much bigger issue."

"Indeed," I grimaced. "We heard a bit about it from Captain Dane, and I have a few words of my own I would like to say."

"Elric..." Reginald whispered with a tone of caution. His look suggested that there was a time and place for such things, and right now wasn't either.

I knew he was right.

"However, I will refrain from such untoward comments," I added. "Now, may we get onto why we have been asked here?"

The Merchant Elect nodded in agreement.

I believe you have already met our guests, he gestured to the elves, This is Yure'il and Gyramir'hel of the Hollowood Forest.

The two elves respectfully nodded at their names, looking toward us with smiles on their faces.

"They do not speak much of the common tongue, so this young man in the back is here to translate for us."

The elvish guard gave a quick and precise nod.

"Though," Jean-Luc snorted, "I heard that you don't need a translator, Elric."

I nodded, "I know the elvish tongue."

"Good. Your ability to communicate with them is exactly why you are here."

He gestured toward the two elvish men.

The one on the right, Yure'il, spoke.

"*Sir Elric,*" he began in his native tongue, "*we are in need of an escort back to the Hollowood. We fear that we may be set upon once more should we try and return unprepared.*"

"*I understand,*" I responded in Elvish. "*It would be wise to have an escort. We do not know if those were the only kidnappers, and I am beginning to doubt the security of the borders with Faeron.*"

The young guard was translating our words as we spoke, eliciting a wince from Reginald at my comment.

"*We would kindly ask that you and your group be the ones to escort us back,*" The second elf, Gyramir'hel, said. "*We trust you and the man next to you. Being able to speak with us is also a great boon.*"

"Hmm," I turned back to the Merchant Elect, "so that is the reason we are here."

He nodded, "It is. I know that you are under the employ of Lord Aulcrest, but I would ask this small favor of you anyway. You being the ones who saved these people."

That last part sounded a bit forced, like he wanted to say something else but restrained himself.

I let out a sigh as I thought.

"*We didn't necessarily have to return to Edren right away. I mean, I really did want to get on with finding my fellow countrymen, and the reward would enable me to do that... But it wasn't going anywhere. These people were right in front of me, and I had the power to help them.*"

"I'll do it," I said, "but you'll have to ask the others individually."

"Of course," Jean-Luc said, looking at the others. "Will you join your friend in this small task before you return home?"

"Yeah, of course," Reginald said without hesitation.

Myrril nodded along, "Y-yeah."

Leone folded her arms and leaned back, letting out a sigh.

"I mean, I'm kind of already home... But, oh what the vale, why not."

As the guard translated our words, the elvish men let out a sigh of relief and thanked us for our help.

"But we'll need another cart or two," I said to the Merchant Elect. "Our current one won't be enough."

He let out a small chuckle, "That can be arranged. When will you leave?"

I looked at the others with the same question on my face.

"Tomorrow?" Reginald shrugged.

"Yeah, I can do that," Leone said while Myrril just nodded.

I turned back around and affirmed our decision.

"Tomorrow."

CHAPTER 15

Hollowood Forest

"But Leone! Why do you have to leave again?" Penelope whined.

"Because the Merchant Elect asked me to do this," Leone explained. "When I get back, how about we do something fun together, okay?"

Leone was saying goodbye to the kids as we packed up the cart in front of her home. It was a sweet sight, if not a little sad. I had also spent some time with those two, and while they were a little rowdy, they were good kids. I saw a lot of potential in both of them, but Jackson just had that spark in his eyes that made me feel he would be a great warrior someday.

"Can we go swimming?" Jackson asked as he bounced up and down.

Leone smiled, "Sure, we can go swimming. What about you, Penelope? What do you want to do?"

"Um..." she said as she thought about her decision. "How about you read me a book?"

"Deal."

Leone put her hand forward, and the two kids shook it with enthusiasm.

"Now, be good, you two. I should only be gone for a few days. There is food in the pantry and some extra money in case you need anything."

"Okay!" Penelope nodded happily.

Leone began to make her way to the cart before pausing and turning back around.

"Oh, and try not to set the house on fire again."

After she spoke, Penelope looked a little embarrassed, and her brother began to tease her.

Leone climbed into the back of the cart, and we all waved goodbye as I guided us through the small back streets of Onforde.

"Gods! That took forever," Reginald complained as we finally arrived in front of the Merchant Elect's manor.

He was right. The streets were as crowded as always with people and carts, so we ended up taking longer than expected. However, it didn't seem to matter.

As we arrived, we saw a little more than a dozen elves talking as they packed up the cart in the manor yard.

We approached, eliciting waves from some of the elves.

"*Ah, Sir Elric,*" Yure'il called out as he spotted me, "*I apologize for our tardiness. Many of my people haven't been here before and were excited to see the differences between how our people live.*"

We had spoken a bit more after the meeting the day before, and I learned that Yure'il and his partner, Gyramir'hel, are the ones who lead the expeditions to Onforde to trade for what they are unable to get in the forest. They've made this trip numerous times over the last hundred or so years and like to bring different people along with them each time if they can. This way, their culture doesn't completely stagnate in their isolation.

"*Not to worry, Yure'il. We were running a little late as well,*" I responded.

Just then, the front door to the manor opened, and the Merchant Elect stepped out onto the lawn, flanked by guards. A third younger man, possibly a squire, was close behind with a pile of swords cradled in his arms.

Yure'il bowed to the Merchant Elect.

"My lord," he said, *"I wanted to thank you again for your generosity."*

"It is my pleasure to help the people of the Hollowood," Jean-Luc replied, "however, I have one more gift."

He gestured for the squire to move forward, who presented the swords he was carrying to Yure'il.

"You will need to be able to protect yourselves. Even if you have these fine mercenaries with you, they won't be there forever."

"Thank you, Lord of Onforde. We will use these well."

Yure'il motioned for some of the older men of the group to take a weapon while the Merchant Elect turned to me.

"Thank you, Elric," he started, "not only for translating but for taking them back home. We are in your debt."

I couldn't help but think that a lot of lords were starting to owe me. It was unintentional, but maybe it would become a great boon in the future.

"It's not a problem, my lord," I replied. "These folks need someone they can trust to help them back to the Hollowood. I fear that if they do not, then they will keep a grudge against humans for hurting them."

He nodded, "Yes, I too am afraid of this outcome. But I have faith. Something about this situation feels... it feels like it's supposed to happen. That probably doesn't make any sense."

I shook my head, "It makes perfect sense."

I had been having the same feeling since I awoke that morning. It was a feeling of completeness, like this was what I was meant to do. I didn't fully understand it, but my gut was telling me to help these elves, and that is what I intended to do.

Getting out of the city was a job in and of itself, and all the while, we got stares from the crowd. I'm sure it was their first time seeing this many full-blooded elves in a group, but it was still uncomfortable for our passengers.

Once we finally made it past the gate, our tension eased. The open fields of wild grain were once again in front of us as we made our way through the gentle hills.

The road going north was a little way down the one heading west toward Edren, but it didn't take too long for us to finally be headed toward the Hollowood.

Unfortunately, because of how hard it was to get out of Onforde, we didn't quite make it to the forest before nightfall. However, Yure'il told me that it was better this way, and the Hollowood wasn't a place to camp unless absolutely necessary, so it worked out in the end.

It didn't take long to set up camp near the Tungsten River, and the elvish women started working on dinner.

"Hey, Elric," Reginald approached me as I was finishing with my tasks, "it's been a while since we last sparred. You up for a few rounds?"

"Yeah," I responded, "just give me a minute to finish up here."

"No problem, I've still got to check my gear."

"*Pft, you guys still have to train?*" A voice approached full of false superiority, "*That means you're still amateurs. What a load of crap this is.*"

I turned to see that Liem'Tel had approached and over-heard our conversation, which struck me as odd because I was under the impression that nobody here knew the common tongue.

Reginald gave me a look asking if he should do anything. He didn't understand what the young man was saying, but he could hear the hostility in his voice. I gave him a look back to tell him I would handle it, so Reginald nodded and went to check his gear.

"*I can't believe you're the ones that are supposed to protect us,*" Liem scoffed.

"*Everyone trains, no matter how good they are. Training keeps us in top fighting form,*" I responded to the young man, nodding toward the sword at his waist, "*If you know how to use that, then you should already know this.*"

"*Of course I know how to use this!*" he practically yelled, "*I'm a great swordsman! That's why I don't need to train anymore.*"

He made his flawed logic sound so matter-of-fact that it threw me off guard.

"*Oh, I didn't know you were such a great swordsman.*" A massive hand grabbed onto Liem's head and turned him around. There, Gyramir'hel was standing with a wide grin. "*I could have sworn you wet yourself when we were ambushed, oh great swordsman.*"

"*WHAT!? N-N-No I didn't!*" he whined.

The way that Liem reacted was telling of what had happened, and Gyramir seemed to be having fun with his teasing.

"*Alright, now get going, Liem,*" Gyramir slapped his back. "*Stop bothering our friends.*"

Liem'Tel begrudgingly stomped off, grumbling under his breath.

"*Sorry about him,*" Gyramir turned to me. "*He's a good kid, a bit full of himself, but a good kid.*"

I took a deep breath and sighed. "*It's fine. I used to deal with people like him all the time in the army.*"

Gyramir raised an eyebrow, "*Army? You look far too young to have served in an army.*"

"*Hm,*" I snorted, "*I'm actually over a thousand years old if you would believe it.*"

Gyramir looked at me with a confused face for a moment before we both burst out into laughter.

"*Oh, that was a good one!*" He wiped a tear from his eye, "*But I'll let you get back to work now. Wouldn't want to keep your friend waiting.*"

He walked away, chuckling to himself.

"You're still dropping your elbow," I said to Reginald after our training session. "It's better, but your reaction speed is still too low."

"Man. This is more difficult than I thought," he mused as he took a drink of water.

"That's why it's important to train right the first time. Breaking muscle memory is neither a simple nor easy process," I explained, "but we'll get it down eventually. Once you're able to accelerate your attack speed, your Air Cutter will be able to perform at its best."

Reginald nodded along and looked down at his blade.

"I still can't believe this weapon is so old. It's in such amazing condition."

"Trust me, I'm just as surprised."

"*Sir Elric!*" One of the elves called from the center of camp, "*Dinner's ready.*"

I waved back to let her know I understood and let Reginald know.

"She said that dinner's done."

"Oh good, I'm starving."

The next day, we were up and on the road at first light. Yure'il told me that the Hollowood was a dangerous place to wander and especially dangerous when it gets dark, so we decided to head out early so we could hopefully make it to their village before nightfall.

It didn't even take another hour before the Hollowood came into sight as we crested a small hill.

Spread out before us, spanning all the way to the base of the mountains, was an incredibly large forest, but the sight of it brought me no joy.

As far as the eye could see were thousands upon thousands of darkened trunks, millions of gnarled branches, and not a speck of green in sight. A forest of petrified trees.

"What in Kyrtvale happened here?" I mumbled in shock.

"I... I've always heard stories about the Hollowood," Reginald said in disbelief, "but it's so much different actually seeing it."

"*Sir Elric,*" Yure'il called out to me, "*I see you are shocked by the look of our home, but fear not. This is how it has always been.*"

The Hollowood was an ancient forest that had been around long before the Aleurians set foot on the continent. Its history, however, was as mysterious as the reason for its state. All evidence says that it was once a lush forest, but nobody knew how long ago it was.

As we approached the edge of the woods, I couldn't help but feel a sense of anxiety creeping over us, like we were being watched. The feeling didn't go away as we entered the stone forest.

"*There are no roads here. We will have to take it easy so as not to break the carts,*" Gyramir explained. "*Allow me to help navigate us through.*"

He hopped into the driver's seat next to me and began to assist in our journey. It was rough going, bumpy, and overall quiet... too quiet.

There was not a single sound of a bird or insect, simply... nothing.

"*Is it supposed to be this quiet?*" I asked.

"*Yes. Living creatures like to avoid the Hollowood... well, most of them anyway.*"

As we went onward, traveling over roots and between rocky outcroppings, we eventually found a small clearing where we decided to take a break. The horses did not like the Hollowood, they had been overly skittish since we had entered, and they needed rest.

We pulled the carts into a small U shape around where we were going to rest before coming down from the carts. Reginald and I hopped off the side facing the forest to keep an eye out while Leone and Myrril helped unpack the cart. Some of the elves began to set up a small cooking station for lunch while others patrolled the perimeter.

But... I couldn't help but get a sense of déjà vu as I checked out the space. The layout of the trees, the stones, the long dried leaves and sticks that layered the ground... it was all familiar.

"Wait..." I thought aloud.

"What is it?" Reginald asked.

My eyes began to dart back and forth as the image appeared before me.

"I know this place.... This... this is from my dream."

Reginald placed a hand on my shoulder. "Which one?"

"There was a little girl... she wanted me to find her. She was here, running between the trees."

I began to retrace the steps I took in the nightmare, following each footfall carefully as I pieced it back together in my mind.

Myrril and Leone saw what I was doing and curiously made their way over to us.

"What's going on?" Leone asked.

"He's been here before, in one of his dreams," Reginald responded.

Leone crossed her arms with a look of doubt on her face and in her tone, "Really?"

"Hey, I believe him. Don't you, too, Myrril?"

"Y-yes, I do."

After a moment, I recognized the tree in front of me. It was the one that the little girl kept disappearing behind. But before I could reach it, I heard the sound of foliage rustling in the woods.

I stopped in my tracks, halting the rest of us as well. Normally, I wouldn't be so concerned about the sound of leaves in the forest, but this wasn't a normal forest. Ever since we got here, the only sounds were the slight howl of the wind and whatever we made, but what I had heard hadn't come from our camp.

The horses suddenly got up from where they were resting and began to whine. They had also sensed something.

"There's something out there," I said to my companions before switching to Elvish, "*There's something in the woods!*"

The elves immediately got from their seats and readied themselves for battle. Those who had weapons in the center of camp made a circle around those who didn't, while the elves patrolling froze in their place and dropped into their stances.

I saw Liem'Tel out of the corner of my eye, sweat was dripping down his face, and his hands were shaking as he held his weapon in front of him.

Then, I heard the sound again, almost like a skittering.

"AHHH!"

A scream resounded out along with a loud hiss as a creature with a black carapace pounced on Liem.

We turned toward the beast, and Myrril lowered her staff toward it. I could feel the faint flow of Megin around her.

"Myrril no!" I pushed her staff down, much to her surprise. "We're surrounded by flammable material. It will only take a single shot to set this entire place ablaze!"

I rushed forward toward the creature as it bit down upon Liem.

"He's right, just... sit tight," Reginald told Myrril before following me in.

I took aim for the small spaces between its chitinous plates and stabbed my blade into it. The beast let out a horrendous cry as it slumped down, unmoving.

Up close, I finally got a good look at it.

It was about the size of a large dog. Its body was covered in black, insectoid armor and sharp spines. It had a pair of long antennae atop its head, massive black eyes, and a set of horrific-looking mandibles. The body looked like it was meant to run around on all six of its legs, but it could also stand somewhat upright and allow its front legs to be used as weapons. Both its front and middle legs ended up in sharp, sword-like natural blades, while its back legs were devoid of weapons. Its tail was short, but it was flexible and was mounted with dual spines akin to pincers.

I glanced at Liem as a pair of elves dragged him from under the creature. He had large lacerations across his chest and some good cuts on his face, but he was alive and very much in shock.

"*Don't let your guard down,*" one of the elves said to me. "*This is an Ohrwurm, and there's never only one.*"

I relayed the information to the humans in the group and kept an eye and ear out for more of these beasts.

They dragged Liem back behind the cart and to the rest of the group, where one of the non-combatants began to hurriedly patch him up.

At that moment, we were down to five armed elves and the four of us. We pulled back to the carts and set our sights ahead as the elves continued their circle in the center of camp.

"I've never seen or even heard about an Ohrwurm before," Reginald said aloud as a bead of sweat rolled down his face.

"I have," Leone spoke up. "They are vicious creatures that are a serious threat by themselves, let alone as a pack."

"H-have you fought them before?" Myrril asked.

Leone took a moment before speaking, "No... No, I haven't."

We heard more rustling in the woods and a horrific clicking sound, but we couldn't lay eyes on the creatures as they moved.

"Myrril," Reginald started as the skittering got closer, "I've known you a long time, and I hope to the gods you've been hiding a non-fire spell from me."

"U-Uh.... Um..." Myrril shook her head.

"Alright, then get up in the cart and grab a mace from the bag," Reginald responded. "If they get to you... start swinging."

Leone scurried atop our cart and started to rummage through the bags in search of the weapons we had bought to fight the Gorodian Crab.

The rest of us closed in around the base of the cart to protect both her and the horses. My ears also picked up skittering from across the clearing, but I didn't have time to worry about that. The elves would be able to handle it.

I focused on the situation in front of us. Taking a deep breath, I willed the Megin within me to flow stronger through my ears, strengthening my perception, and what I picked up concerned me.

"There are at least five of them out there," I told the others before glancing at Leone.

"Hey, um, Leone? Is your Solar Wolf able to uh... not set stuff on fire?"

"I... Maybe," she responded.

I grimaced and looked back in front of me. There, I finally caught a glimpse of movement.

"They're close, get ready!" I called out.

"Tsk," Leone clicked her tongue before grabbing the silver bells at her waist and throwing them in front of her.

As they flew through the air, one began to let off a white mist while the other released a red mist. Before you could even blink, the radiant bodies of the Sun and Moon wolves appeared with a howl.

I also grabbed my own bell and released Tempest with a cloud of sparks.

He looked up at me with puppy eyes.

"Tempest, we've got trouble."

His face locked in, and he turned toward the sounds in the forest, baring his teeth in a growl.

Finally, all hell broke loose.

The creatures rushed forward as fast as lightning, three of them converging on our position. Their mandibles clicked as they approached.

Two of them assaulted Leone, getting intercepted by her Beasts and locked into a heavy battle. She swung her spear at them as the wolves attempted to lock their jaws, but the Ohrwurms' heavy carapace stopped that from happening.

The third was quickly run backward by Tempest, who fired a bolt of lightning that removed one of the creature's legs and let out a horrible smell like someone had decided to light rotting fish on fire.

It retreated with Tempest in pursuit as another Ohrwurm appeared from our side. One of them impacted with Reginald's shield while the other went around the side to try and attack where he couldn't block.

I quickly bolted in and kicked the oversized bug to the side, but it quickly recovered.

Through the gap between the carts, I caught a horrific sight. A half dozen Ohrwurm skittered from between the trees, one crawling over a fallen truck, as they rushed toward the camp. The elves were about to have a lot harder time than we did if we couldn't clean this up quickly.

I brought my weapon down in a decisive slash, but the Ohrwurm snapped its mandibles shut around my blade. A horrific scraping sound resounded as I pulled the weapon free, new scrapes embedded in the blade.

To my side, Reginald managed to push his creature off himself and went on the attack. It flailed its scythe-like appendages wildly at him as they fought.

Focusing back on my opponent, I deflected its blade arm just in time to prevent a hit and lopped its appendage off at the joint. It let out a horrific screech and redoubled its efforts to attack me.

By this point, I had gotten sick of fighting that disgusting creature and decided to end it. I launched my leg into its side and followed up with a heavy punch against its head, cracking the shell. It pulled back in a daze, allowing me to quickly slice through the gaps in its armor and through its gooey interior.

With one down, I assessed the situation.

I could no longer see Tempest, who had chased one of the beasts into the woods. Behind me, Leone had managed to dispatch one of the creatures with her spear, as was evident by the green gunk on her weapon, and her wolves were in the middle of frying the second one.

Reginald had also just about finished up, with him landing a series of clean strikes against the Ohrwurm, cleaving off piece after piece until it fell.

"Leone!" I called out, "the elves need help!"

She turned to me and nodded, leaving the wolves to finish off the last Ohrwurm as she ran around the cart.

It only took one glance between Reginald and me to know what we were doing.

We ran and clambered over the cart before jumping down the other side, slamming into one of the creatures and crushing its thorax. We had arrived just in time to save one of the armed elves, who had been flanked and wasn't looking too good.

"Pull back! We have this," I tapped him out and swapped places while Reginald took its side. Together, we made short work of the beast before moving on to the next.

In quick succession, we dropped the creatures one by one as they were no longer able to fight together. It only took a few more moments before the rest of them were dead.

"How are our wounded?" I asked Yure'il.

"Mostly medium wounds with a few light scrapes here and there, but Fol'or is in pretty bad shape," he responded. *"One of the beasts managed to grab him with its tail and messed his arm up pretty badly. He may lose his hand."*

"Dammit."

I had hoped for better news, though I also supposed that nobody being dead was considered better news for many.

Just then, Myrril screamed.

"REGINALD! HELP!"

All eyes focused on her as an Ohrwurm crawled into the cart and began to attack her. She flailed the mace wildly at the creature to no effect.

"MYRRIL!"

Reginald screamed and bolted toward the cart with me right behind him.

She was doing what she could to protect herself, but the creature was too much. Her arms soon became covered in cuts and dyed crimson. She screamed out once more before

Reginald jumped clear over the side of the cart and slammed his entire body into the creature, sending himself and the beast over the side.

I climbed over the cart and grabbed Myrril, assessing the damage to her arms, but she was entirely focused on Reginald. She grabbed the side of the cart and screamed for him once more. That's when I realized something was wrong.

Lying in the middle of the cart were Reginald's sword and shield. He must have dropped them when he tackled the beast.

I quickly looked over the side to see Reginald wrestling with the monstrous bug, his legs locked around its thorax and his hands grasping its mandibles. He yelled as the creature's sharp arms began to cut across his back, but it wasn't in pain. The blades were mostly scraping off armor. His yelling was in anger.

He pulled his arms farther and farther apart, his body straining as he did so, but the anger in his tone was apparent. Blood was leaking from his palms as the sharp mandibles dug into his skin.

The creature was letting out a horrific sound, one of pain perhaps, as its jaw was being forced open farther than they were made to. Not but a moment later, there was a sickening snap as the creature's face was ripped open, its mandibles torn from its skull.

Reginald was breathing heavily as the creature sputtered up green blood beneath him, its final moments in agony.

"Reginald!" Myrril jumped over the side of the cart and ran at him.

"Hey!" I tried to stop her but was too stunned at that moment to react in time.

Myrril threw her arms around Reginald as tears began to stream down her face. She was speaking, but her words were completely incoherent.

Reginald looked around awkwardly with his hands out, not knowing what to do.

I looked him in the eye and gestured for him to comfort her.

He nodded and nervously wrapped his arms around her.

"It's okay," he whispered, "I'm alright."

He continued to whisper comforting words for the next several minutes as she cried her heart out.

As this was happening, Tempest returned from the woods. He dropped the charred corpse of an Ohrwurm next to me and happily wagged his tail.

I rubbed his head as I watched over my friends, ensuring there were no more surprises in store for us.

CHAPTER 16

A Call for Help

We didn't spend long in the clearing, just enough time to tend to our wounds and unpack our travel rations. I spoke with Yure'il and Gyramir'hel after the attack, and we decided it was best to move on, so we were back in our carts in less than an hour.

This time, Leone took the lone horse as Reginald was in the cart with Myrril, who had exhausted herself and fallen asleep in Reginald's arms. And since we didn't want to wake her, Reginald had to hang out in the back of the cart.

However, we did manage to bandage her arms before she fell asleep. They had been pretty torn up and would have caused a nasty infection if left any longer.

The other injuries in the group were relatively minor, except for Liem, who was definitely going to scar, and Fol'or, whose wrist wasn't looking too good. If we had any chance of saving his hand, we needed to get to the elvish settlement as quickly as possible.

After another handful of hours, I spotted something in the distance. It was greenery. The forest of dead trees suddenly gave way to a beautiful arrangement of healthy woods.

The sounds of birds and other forest critters returned as we drew closer.

"What is this?" Reginald asked in disbelief.

I relayed his question to Yure'il, though I was thinking the same.

"*This is the area of the Hollowood surrounding our home,*" he responded. "*It is not much farther now.*"

With our question only partially answered, we entered the inviting green haven and felt a wave of relief from all of us.

Around this time, Myrril woke.

"Where... ow, ow, ow." She clenched her hands and winced.

"Hey," Reginald held her hands still. "Clenching will only make it hurt more. Relax your muscles."

She did as he said and relaxed as the pain partially dissipated.

"It's still going to hurt for a while," I explained. "The Ohrwurm did a number on you."

Myrril's face dropped, "B-but..."

"Don't worry," Reginald interrupted, "your arms will be fine. They just need time to heal."

"Yeah. If Reginald had been a moment later, that creature would have cut through your arteries."

Myrril looked between me and Reginald as if she was remembering the entire thing all over again.

"You saved me!" She wrapped her arms around Reginald again, wincing as she forgot how hurt she was.

"You would have done the same for me," he replied.

She pulled back and looked him in the eye, "B-but still."

This is when she got another look around. "Um... w-where are we? A-are we still in the Hollowood?"

"Yep," Leone rode up to the side of the cart. "We are close to the village. Also, good to see you're okay, Myrril."

"Thanks," she responded.

"*Elric!*" Yure'il called from the cart behind us, "*We're here.*"

I looked back in front of us and took in the impressive sight.

The forest seemed to continue forever until I realized that

it had turned into a continuous wall of bark almost perfectly fused together. Several well-made structures were cradled on the wall, forming a defensive position against threats. I couldn't see much past the wall, but what I could see was that the forest continued inside without an indicator of being trimmed back and no clear-cut area.

"Wow..." Myrril whispered while the others held in their shock, though their faces betrayed them.

We approached an alcove in the wall where Yure'il directed us. It appeared to be a gate of some kind, covered in bark like the rest of the wall, but much easier to identify.

We stopped just outside the gate, and Yure'il hopped out of his cart. I looked around as we waited, but I couldn't see any signs of people. Either they weren't there, or they were really good at hiding themselves. Knowing the elves, I was inclined to believe the latter.

My heart began to race as the familiar creaking sound of many bows being drawn sounded subtly from the wall.

"*Yure'il,*" a female voice called from somewhere in front of us, "*you know you cannot bring outsiders here.*"

Yure'il, now close to the gate, called back.

"*They saved our lives, Cyria, many times over.*"

"*It matters not!*" the voice, Cyria, snapped. "*The rules are clear. They cannot be allowed to live.*"

Yure'il took a single step back in surprise, "*W-wait, Cyria. This is a much bigger deal than you realize. These people are—*"

"*Move our people away from the humans,*" Cyria interrupted. "*Now!*"

I leaned back and whispered to my companions, "Reginald, get your shield ready."

"Why? What's happening?"

"Nothing good."

I jumped down from my place on the cart.

"*We are not people you should be making an enemy out of,*" I advised the person behind the wall, eliciting whispers as I spoke in the elvish tongue. "*We were sent here by the Merchant Elect of Onforde as well as Lord Aulcrest of Edren.*"

"*I do not know how you speak the tongue of my people, but it matters not.*" The lady regained her composure. "*You will not live long enough.*"

An arrow flew toward me from a seemingly solid spot on the wall, but I had already expected violence. I dropped my stance and nimbly dodged to the side as I swung my forearm and deflected the arrow.

"*How!?*" Cyria yelped.

I looked up at where the arrow came from. "*This is your last chance. We have severe wounds in our group that need immediate attention, and if you refuse to open the gates, then I'll just have to knock them down.*"

I couldn't help but feel anger and annoyance at the woman on the wall. We had risked much to save her people, and yet her first instinct was to kill us.

I could feel Cyria pause, thinking for a moment before her orders came.

"*Loose!*" she yelled, and a dozen arrows flew toward me without hesitation, each one fired by an experienced hand. However, experience only helps if it allows you to predict your opponent's moves, and these people had never seen the likes of me.

I rolled forward as each arrow dug itself into the ground where I was once standing. I sprang to my feet and dashed for the large oaken gate in front of me.

More arrows flew as I ran. What few I didn't dodge, I deflected.

Then, I felt a horrible tearing pain as an arrow sank itself into my back, right next to my shoulder blade, with a loud

Thunk. The force of it almost threw me off balance, but I managed to keep my feet on the ground.

I kicked off the ground as hard as I could and threw myself at the gate. With not but a moment's hesitation, I once again willed the Megin within me to gather in my fist. The sharp tingling pain that shot through my body was sickening as the channels upon which my Megin flowed were forcibly dried. I felt an uncomfortable pressure building in my fist as I pulled my arm back. The moment had come.

Despite never wanting to use this technique again, I had little choice if we wanted to get Fol'or treated. I launched my arm forward with as much force as I could muster and unleashed the full force of my Onager Strike against the solid wooden gate. With loud creaks and cracks as the Megin forced its way through the wood grain, the gate buckled. With a loud crash, the wooden bar locking the gate was snapped in half; a sizable chunk of wood shattered and splintered around where my fist made contact, and the gates swung open. They slammed into the side of the gateway as they opened at an uncontrollable speed.

I landed back on the ground and released the buildup of Megin with my hand. Relief from the pain that wracked my body soon appeared, but my hand was shaking uncontrollably. I could feel that something was wrong, a fractured or broken bone... again. The pain was unbearable as I tried to move my fingers, but I had bigger problems in front of me.

Standing with spears down were three dozen elves forming a half-circle around the inside of the gateway. They wore many different greens and browns underneath their metallic armor that seemed to have the texture of bark and very few visual imperfections.

Behind them, posted along several higher points, were another two dozen elves with longbows drawn to full breadth.

Several others were above and to either side of the gateway, aiming down toward me. I could feel the nerves emanating from them. It was a similar feeling to the new recruits in the Aleurian Imperial Army, giving me the impression that not many of them had ever seen real combat.

We were in a standoff. Nearly seventy elves against one Aleurian with a broken hand. The odds were ever so slightly not in my favor.

Though the situation also gave me my first look at the elven village.

Behind the wall of spears was an amazing sight. A forest fully enclosed by a natural-looking wall of bark. Woven between the trees were many modest homes with beautiful exteriors. Each corner of the homes was a living tree that had been grown, or perhaps coerced, to conform its body for what the elves needed. The main staple was having the trees bend themselves overtop the constructed walls of the elvish homes, turning their canopies into living roofs.

Several other homes looked to be formed by nothing but curved trees spiraling around the interior, while others seemed to be grown in the higher boughs of the taller trees. I had never personally seen an elvish town, but I had read much about them and seen many images in various books.

But I had no time to properly take it all in.

A woman with pointed ears jumped down from the wall and stood behind the line of spears.

"I do not know how you did that," the look in Cyria's eyes was palpable, *"but you will go no farther. Men, advan—"*

"That's enough!" Another voice cut her off.

Several elves turned to look at the owner of the voice as he made his way down the small slope before the gate.

He didn't look too old, maybe in his late forties, but for an elf, that meant he was around three centuries old. He wore no armor and held no weapons, but his clothing set him apart. He wore lighter colors along with the same green as everyone else, along with a sash of imprinted leather across his chest.

"*My lord, this human is a danger! We must take care of him before he causes more damage,*" Cyria said with a sense of urgency.

The man kept walking, the wall parting for him as we approached. He stopped not but ten feet in front of me.

He looked me up and down, squinting as he did before his eyes widened.

"*You... something about you is not right,*" he said. "*You cannot be human...*"

"*That's because I am not,*" I responded, eliciting a curious look from the man.

"*You also speak our tongue, interesting,*" the man mused. "*If you are not Human, then who, and what, are you?*"

"*I am Elric Wolfram Tors, son of General Bertram Wolfram Tors of the Second Imperial Army of Aleuria.*"

Many of the elves began to whisper.

"*Impossible!*" Cyria yelled in disgust.

"*I would normally be inclined to believe the same,*" the elvish lord said, "*but what I'm seeing here is not the Megin of a Human.*"

Megin? I thought to myself. *What was he talking about?*

Then, I realized my mistake.

The Elder Races are able to see the aura of creatures, the Megin that leaks from them, and each aura is unique to what it comes from. However, there are certain markers you can feel that tell you the race of the individual if you already know what it feels like. It had completely slipped my mind that my own aura could be detected. Thoughts ran through my head as I wondered how many others knew that I wasn't Human.

"*That doesn't mean anything!*" Cyria said. "*Even if he isn't a Human, he could just be a descendant of the Aleurians. That would explain his strength."*

I turned to Cyria and looked her in the eye before speaking in my native tongue.

"You would be best to shut your mouth before it is shut for you."

"Wha... What did he say?" Cyria took a step back, *"What language was that!?"*

The lord smiled, *"That was the Aleurian tongue. I have no clue what he said, mind you, but I believe he is telling the truth."*

He stretched his hand, *"I am Illith'ir, lord of the Hollowood. It is a pleasure to meet you, Elric of the Aleurians."*

That evening, a massive bonfire lit up the night sky from within the elvish settlement. An impromptu festival of sorts had been thrown together as a thanks for saving their people. Laughter echoed across the village as the people drank and made merry. Reginald and Leone were having fun with the elves, talking and drinking and telling stories of their adventures, though, of course, Leone's drink was non-alcoholic.

Myrril was having a tougher time but seemed to be warming up to the situation when a gaggle of elvish children started playing with her. A smile grew on her face as she played with them. I did note that all of the kids she was playing with were probably older than her, because of how elves develop, but she seemed happy, so I didn't want to spoil it.

"I must apologize for Cyria's actions," Illith'ir said after taking a drink. "She is a little overprotective."

"It's understandable, given the history of Human and Elf relations."

We were seated at a table, watching over the merriment as we drank and spoke. Right after the fiasco at the gate, our carts were pulled in, and those who needed treatment were taken to a healer. Around that time, we discovered that many of the villagers spoke the common tongue, including Illith'ir.

"How's the hand?" he asked.

I looked down at my heavily wrapped sword hand. When I saw the village healer, they told me that it had broken along a recent fracture line that hadn't yet healed. I was shocked when I heard this, as my people normally didn't need very long to heal a fracture, maybe two weeks. I also had an amazing recovery speed, even among my people, so the fact that it wasn't completely healed was a cause for concern.

"It's going to be okay," I replied. "They had to realign the bone, but it isn't too bad. I'll keep stimulating my healing abilities with Megin to speed up the process."

"Mmm," he hummed while mid-drink, "you should be careful when doing that."

"Why?" I asked, confused.

"It can exhaust you really quickly," Illith'ir informed me, "and it can cause more problems in the future. Your body won't naturally set your bones, after all."

He made a good point. If I healed my wounds too quickly without proper treatment, I would start to run into issues. Actually, I already had. I shuddered as I remembered the shards of stone stuck in my calf.

"Thanks for the advice."

I took another deep swig of my drink and looked out over the crowd. It had been some time since I had been with this many elves, all of them carefree and happy. Even in Edren, where they don't discriminate, the elves still had a cloud hanging over them. But here, the skies were clear.

I saw Yure'il and Gyramir'hel enjoying the feast that had been brought out, laughing as they spoke. The others we had traveled with were also there, out and about, talking and drinking and making merry. It was a wonderful sight.

About halfway into the night, one of the men assigned to the wall came to report to the lord. He leaned down and whispered in his ear.

"*Bring him here,*" Illith'ir responded in elvish.

The guard nodded and ran off into the darkness of night.

"What's that about?" I asked.

"You'll see."

A moment later, the guard returned with another exhausted-looking elf. He had a scar above his left eye, and his ear on that side had been damaged at some point in his life, the point no longer there as if it had been cut off.

He was dressed for travel, with dirty boots and a large pack on his back. He dropped to his knees and breathed erratically as though he had just ended a long run.

Illith'ir knelt down. "What's your name?"

The elf took a deep breath and swallowed before speaking in common.

"My... my name is Minyr'al. I come from the Great Forest of Aryl'lin."

"So you are a runner?"

"Yes, Milord."

"Get this man a drink," Illith'ir ordered.

Not but a moment later, a wooden tankard was brought for the elvish runner, who drank the whole thing without hesitation. Reginald and Leone had seen the runner arrive and approached us at this time. Myrril soon followed.

"Do you have a message for us?" Lord Illith'ir asked.

"Yes," Minyr'al said after finishing his drink, "the people of Aryl'lin are requesting aid. The princess has arrived in the Great Forest, and plans have been made to free our people."

"Our princess!?" Illith'ir asked in shock.

The runner nodded, "Yes. She has taken charge of our people in Faeron and plans to free those still enslaved."

My head was spinning. The princess of the elves had arrived in Faeron in order to free her people, and she was sending for help from the other elvish groups still around.

"Hmm," Illith'ir thought for a moment, "This is a fortuitous day... but I do not know if we can help."

The runner's face dropped.

"You must understand," Illith'ir explained, "we are not in a position to help at this time. The Hollowood is a very perilous place and to send our defenders away..."

"I-I see," Minyr'al said with dejection.

"I wish there was another way..." the lord started.

As he said, The Hollowood was a perilous place to live in, even within the lush area around its center. We experienced it firsthand on the way there, but these people have lived here all their lives and were intimately aware of the dangers.

I could see the pain in their eyes; the conflicting feelings they all had as they tried to justify leaving to assist their brethren in Faeron. However, they could not make that choice. I, on the other hand, knew what must be done.

"I'll go," I interrupted.

The elves looked at me with confusion.

"What?"

"I said I'll go."

"Are you sure?" Illith'ir had a deep look of conflict on his face as he asked. However, seeing how serious I was, he instead leaned into a whisper and offered his warning, "You may not be able to hide who you are if you go."

I nodded with conviction.

"I'm sure."

Illith'ir pulled back and closed his eyes in thought. His face relaxed as he came to terms with my decision. "Then I will support you."

The runner had a strange look on his face, and he looked back and forth between Illith'ir and me.

"I do not mean to be rude, but how will you be able to help?" His confusion seemed to be based on his view of me. From his perspective, I would have been an ordinary Human, though I'm also sure he was confused about why Humans were here in the first place.

"Any way I can," I replied curtly.

Minyr'al seemed taken aback but accepted my determination.

However, I didn't have the leeway to relax just yet. I turned around to look at my companions. They each had a troubled look on their faces.

"So..." Reginald started, "Faeron Kingdom, eh?"

I nodded. There wasn't much else for me to say at this moment, even though I wanted to.

"But why?" he asked. "I mean, I know you want to help people, but this is on an entirely different scale."

Myrril nodded along, "H-he's right. W-we're talking about a rebellion, n-not just helping a few people."

"It is a big jump," Leone said offhandedly.

"I know it is," I responded with confidence, "but I have to do this. I want to make a change, a real change, and it will never happen if the source of the rot is left to fester."

"And honestly..." I scratched the back of my head with an uncomfortable smile, taking a deep breath as I did. "I just want to do it. I guess... maybe saving the elves of Faeron would make me feel closer to some of my old friends..."

I knew that this was where we would have to part ways. There was no reason for them to follow me into such a dangerous situation and for such a selfish goal. I had to mentally prepare myself for such an outcome.

Reginald nodded as he listened and smiled, "That's a good enough reason for me. I'm in."

"What?" I blurted out, "I can't ask you to do that."

"I-I'm coming too."

"No, we've already been through so much together, I can't ask you to come with me."

"That's precisely why we can't just leave you," Reginald stated.

Myrril nodded, "Y-you're our friend."

"And besides, what kind of people would we be if we just ignored a call for help?"

I couldn't help but smile at them. A pure, genuine smile that showed my emotions for what they were, not a dulled shell that I had to force through. They were such amazing people, and they understood my reasons more than anyone. I vowed that I would cherish our friendship for as long as I lived.

Friends? I thought, *When did I start considering them as friends?*

I couldn't help but ponder as to when my view of them changed, but it no longer mattered. They were my friends, and there was nothing that would change my mind.

"Ahem," Leone interrupted my thoughts, "I would love to join you as well, it sounds like a lot of fun to smash the heads of some stuck-up bastards, but..."

"The kids?" I finished for her with a nod.

"Yeah. I promised them I would be back, and I can't just leave them unattended for however long this will take."

Leone looked really torn as she spoke. It was clear that she wanted to come with us to Faeron, but she also couldn't abandon Jackson and Penelope. She was a good person, and I already knew she wouldn't leave those kids for her own desires. If anything, doing so would have made me leave her behind.

I smiled at her response, "I understand, Leone."

"Thanks," she replied with a look of relief adding to her conflicted look.

"So it's settled then?" Illith'ir spoke up with a hopeful tone, "You three will answer the call?"

I turned back to him and spoke with great pride.

"Yes. Yes, we will."

EPILOGUE

In the morning, we said our goodbyes to the elves and packed up the carriage for our long journey ahead. Leone was going to travel with us until we were out of the Hollowood, where we would have to go our separate ways. With the border to Faeron closed, we would have to go through Elderoth to the north and then cross into Faeron from there.

The trek through the forest was uneventful, unlike the day before. The greenery turned gray, and the petrified trees reached out into the sky like skeletal hands, but even that seemed not to last as long as before.

Soon, we were out of the forest and on the road that ran north to south.

Leone hopped out of the cart with her bag in her hand and her spear resting upon her shoulder.

"You sure you don't want to take the horse?" I asked.

"Yeah," she responded, "The walk back will give me time to think."

"Fair travels, Leone," Reginald shook her hand and smiled.

"And you too, Reggie."

Myrril ran up and gave Leone a hug.

"I-I'm going to miss you."

"I'll miss you too, Myrril," Leone said. "Don't forget to rely on those two for help if you need it."

"Mhm!"

They stayed like that for a moment before Myrril somberly climbed back into the cart. I could still see how conflicted Leone still was about not being able to join us; she had a pained look on her face.

I walked up to Leone to say my own goodbyes.

"It's been a pleasure, Elric," she said.

"The pleasure was all mine," I replied.

We shook hands, and she pulled her bag onto her back.

"Wait just a moment" I stopped her. "Could I ask you to deliver something for me?"

"Hm? Sure."

I handed her a bundle of letters.

"There should be a barge arriving in Onforde from the Hidden Grove Logging Company. If you could hand these to them, that would be great."

"No problem." She took the bundle with care.

"Also," I started, "if you change your mind about joining us, one of those letters will explain the situation and you'll get a ride with the barge."

She smiled a bit, "Thanks, but I don't think–"

"I know, I know," I cut her off, "but a second letter there is for Erwyn Lux in Edren. She manages the Ouroboros Initiative, the company I own. They help reintegrate people into society and take care of their kids while they work. That letter is for her, asking her to look after Jackson and Penelope."

Leone's eyes widened.

"I know how conflicted you were," I explained, "so if you still want to go to Faeron, take the kids to Edren, where they will be looked after, then come find us."

Leone looked down at the bundle of letters and then back at me, her uncertain face changed to one of a joyous smile.

"You really are something, aren't you?"

I shrugged, "What can I say?"

Leone laughed a bit and tucked the letters into her bag.

"I guess I'll be seeing you soon," she said.

"We'll be waiting."

With that, she shouldered her gear and began to make the

long walk back to Onforde. We watched her go for a while before she disappeared, along with the road, behind a hill.

I hopped back onto the cart and turned the horses north. Our destination: The Faeron Kingdom.

Edren – Office of Lord Aulcrest ～

On the night that Elric and his friends received the message from Faeron, the Lord of Edren was working late in his office when he was visited by one of his most trusted advisors.

"Well, this is quite odd," Lord Aulcrest stated. "You do not normally approach me in such a... normal way, Zed."

Standing in front of the lord's desk was a tall man cloaked in all black; their face was covered by a polished obsidian mask devoid of expression that covered all of his features, not even leaving holes to see from.

"I felt that this was an appropriate way to inform you."

The man named Zed spoke in a cold, calculating tone nearly devoid of emotion.

Lord Aulcrest furrowed his brow. "What information?"

Zed had been an advisor to the Aulcrest family for nearly five generations and was a trusted advisor, despite the lack of information on who he was. He usually showed up at times of importance or when a hard decision had to be made.

"It is time for me to take my leave," he stated bluntly.

"What?" Lord Aulcrest blurted out in shock.

The black mask focused on Lord Aulcrest's face.

"I came to guide your family during their greatest crisis over a century ago," Zed explained in his usual monotone voice. "Now, however, you face a new crisis."

Lord Aulcrest calmed himself and listened intently to Zed's words.

"We managed to solve the crisis, didn't we?"

"No," Zed stated curtly.

"What do you mean?"

Lord Aulcrest began to feel a sense of dread.

"The incident with the necromancer was not the event I spoke to you about. A crisis still descends upon you and the Alliance."

A chill ran down Lord Aulcrest's spine as he remembered Zed's words.

"In the near future, this country will be destroyed."

Lord Aulcrest believed that the necromancer had been what Zed was referring to, but now Zed had made it clear that this wasn't the case.

His mind began to work harder as Lord Aulcrest attempted to analyze the facts that he knew in an attempt to discover exactly what the crisis was.

However, Zed interrupted his thinking.

"That is why it is time for me to step away. The only way for you to continue to grow as a people is to do it on your own terms."

Lord Aulcrest felt his heart drop at Zed's words. He wasn't sure if they were up to the task of surviving an unknown crisis without Zed's help. Though that feeling was exactly what Zed spoke of. The people of Edren had become too dependent on Zed's council.

"I... I understand," Lord Aulcrest said reluctantly.

"Good. Then I shall leave you with one last piece of advice." Zed turned around and made his way toward the exit before turning his head to glance back at Lord Aulcrest once more. "There will come a time when you will be given a choice between your people and your position. Do not hesitate to cast off your lordship at that time, or you will come to regret it."

With those ominous words, Zed melded into the shadows and was gone. Lord Aulcrest slumped in his chair and let out a long breath as the tension left his body and fatigue took over.

The future of Edren was uncertain.

Notable Characters:

Elric Wolfram Tors – A young man in his late teens who was killed over a thousand years ago only to bust his way out of the underworld. A relic of a time long past and possibly the last living Aleurian. The story is written from his point of view.

Reginald Lee Aulcrest – Son of Samuel J. Aulcrest, Lord of Edren. Reginald is a mercenary and close friend of Myrril Delahaye. After working together with Elric in the Tomb of the Fallen, Reginald journeys with him to the City of Merchants.

Myrril Delahaye – A timid, but very talented young woman. She is close friends with Reginald and has spent the last two years working with him as a mercenary. She is very shy around new people and cannot handle crowds, but she opens up once she gets used to you, especially if you start talking about magic. She worked with Elric in the Tomb of the Fallen and now journeys with him to the City of Merchants.

Leone Scarlette – An old friend of Reginald and an avid spear user. The group met her on the way to Onforde, where she joined them on the way. Afterward, she got caught up in their mission because she "thought it would be fun".

Samuel J. Aulcrest – Lord of Edren and current head of the Valtion-Silma City State Alliance. He, along with Louis Renard, is the one who sent Elric and the group to Onforde to investigate the attempted assassination of the city's leader.

Louis Renard – Head of the Edren Association Branch. He is very interested in Elric's abilities and wishes that he would join the Association. He, along with Samuel Aulcrest, sent the group to Onforde.

Jean-Luc Pierre – The Merchant Elect of Onforde. He comes from the Faeron Kingdom where he started as a merchant before moving his base of operations to Onforde. He won the last election to lead the City-State.

Hanz Zerrick – The Head Administrator of Onforde. He comes from the Kollund Kingdom and made a name for himself as a merchant. He was the runner-up in the most recent Onforde election.

Dane Ursun – A bear Beastfolk and the head of the Onforde city guard. He is kind and courteous to his friends, and deadly to his enemies.

Yure'il – One of the Elves of the Hollowood. He leads the expeditions to Onforde to gather supplies the Elves cannot produce themselves.

Illith'ir – Lord of the Hollowood. He believed Elric was an Aleurian and de-escalated the situation at the gate.

General Information:

Abnormal/Ondvaettr – An Unnatural Creature not of this world, occasionally twisted and mutated Beasts. Often times the line between Beast and Abnormal blurs, as such the Abnormal is defined as a creature that cannot naturally reproduce. The Aleurians used to refer to these creatures as Ondvaettr, translating directly to "Evil Spirit".

Aleuria – An Island off the coast of Vestri. It was once home to the Aleurian People, during which time it got its name. After their downfall, it was renamed to Alurland over time.

Aleurian – The People of the Island of Aleuria. One of the Elder Races, the first races to appear. They Aleurians were often said to have "The cunning of the Dwarves, the magic of the Elves, and the strength of the Giants". They died out over eleven hundred years prior to the story. Elric is seemingly the last of his kind. They have an average lifespan of 120 years.

Aleurian Empire – The nation of the Aleurian People whose history spans over eight thousand years. It once controlled all of Vestri, as well as some of Nordri and Sudri.

Arache – Large spider beasts found in many places around Talmara, including the Ashwood Forest. They are not as varied as normal spiders, but they do come in many types. The most common type is about the size of a German Shepard (legs not included) and look like a Brown Recluse.

Ashwood Forest – The second of the three forests within the Eye of the Continent. It is much safer to travel the roads than the Silverfang Timberland due to the lack of Direwolves, however, that doesn't mean it's safe. Deep in the forest are the Arache, who subsist off the abundant Grell population, and any poor souls who wander too close to their territory.

Association/The Wensworth Association for Wayward Souls – A mercenary organization that covers all of Vestri, the Western Continent. They are not a mercenary company but are instead closer to information brokers and job screeners.

Association Medal – The Association Medal is a form of Identification and a way for employers to know that you are reliable. The image on the front of the Medal shows how highly the Association ranks your skills based on the historical abilities of all of its members over the past several centuries. The back contains information about who you are, and the completion rate of the jobs you have accepted through the Association.

Beast – A natural-born creature who cannot be labeled as a normal animal. Many times Beasts are mixed up with Abnormals, in such a case a Beast is defined as a creature that can naturally reproduce.

Beastfolk – Beastfolk are, for lack of a better term, Humanoid Animals; Humanoid Land Mammals to be exact. They often have abilities that surpass those of a Human, and as such they were persecuted for a very long period of time. However, if one were to close their eyes and have a conversation with a Beastfolk, they would be indistinguishable from a human.

Bloodstone – A natural stone of condensed Megin found deep within the earth. They can hold a tremendous amount of magical energy, like a magic battery, and are often used as a spellcasting focus to aid mages. In the past, the Aleurians knew that Bloodstones were notoriously difficult to manage, and only the most talented, or the craziest, ever used one to amplify their Megin. It is named Bloodstone after its deep crimson color.

Blunor Berries – A bright-blue berry indigenous to the Eye of the Continent. They are considered extremely deadly causing a mess of side effects such as nausea, bloody vomit, hair loss, random bleeding, and acute skin damage. For some reason, they don't seem to affect Elric.

Continents – The Western Continent is named Vestri, the Northern is Nordri, the Eastern is Austri, and the southern is Sudri.

Direwolf – A Beast that is much larger than a normal Wolf and sports bone-like armor on its arms, shoulders, and back. They are known to lead packs of normal wolves and other direwolves. They come in an equal number of variants as there are regular wolves.

Draugr – Sentinels who guard ancient tombs even in death. They have shrunken, mummified skin and carry the arms and armor they were buried with. Often seen as a myth to scare away grave robbers.

Dwarf – They have a shorter and broader stature than a human, with round faces and large eyes. They are known for their massive underground fortresses and unmatched techno-logical innovation. They have an average lifespan of 300 years. One of the Elder Races.

Edren – A city in the center of the Eye of the Continent. It was once a human village that was taken by the Aleurian Empire and transformed into a central powerhouse of the region. In current times, it serves as the central hub for trade between several large kingdoms and as the current seat of power for the Valtion-Silma City State Alliance.

Elder Race – The oldest and most powerful races on Talmara. They were the first to inhabit the planet. They consist of the Aleurians, the Elves, the Dwarves, and the Giants.

Elf – Normally indistinguishable from humans beyond the pointed ears and long lifespan. Elves are experts in Megin manipulation and Magecraft. They originally had three types, the Common Elf, the High Elf, and the Wood Elf. When people say "Elf" they most often refer to the Common Elf. High Elves are the Elvish royalty and have unconfirmed life spans, however it is said that the current elvish king has been around for more than five millennia. Wood Elves were a group of elves that lived as one with nature, creating massive living cities and fortresses. For unknown reasons, they went extinct many millennia ago. The average lifespan of a Common Elf is 400 years. One of the Elder Races.

Elfbane – A slur used by Elves to describe the Humans of the Faeron Kingdom who overthrew their ancestors and enslaved their people even to this day.

Etterkommer – Meaning descendant. Used to refer to people descended from Aleurian blood. These people are more powerful than the average human, but fall far short from the power of the Aleurians.

Eye of the Continent – The valley situated between

the Serpents Crest Mountains. When viewed on a map, the area resembles an eye.

Gorodian Crab – A type of beast from the Gorodian Lowlands in the Kollund Kingdom. The Gorodian Crab is about the size of a single-story home and closely resembles mud crabs.

Grell – Small nuisance creatures with a high rate of population, similar to Coyote's in that aspect. They are about the size of a dog with six legs and a face that looks as though someone mixed a bat and a hog, then curb-stomped it and gave it rabies.

Half Elf – A mixed race individual crossed between an Elf and a Human. They have an increased lifespan of close to 200 years.

Half Orc – A mixed-race individual crossed between an Orc and a Human. They often take more traits from their Orc parent than their Human parent but tend to have a more human-like appearance.

The Hollowood – The third forest within the Eye of the Continent. It consists mostly of dead, petrified trees except for the center, which is a lush forest landscape home to a tribe of Elves. Nobody knows why the Hollowood looks how it does; it has looked that way for as long as history has been recorded. It is exceptionally dangerous and home to many disgusting creatures such as the Ohrwurm.

Husk – The corpse of a Human, devoid of its soul, who wanders mindlessly on pure instinct. Until recently, they were only naturally created by pooling Megin and the result was a fairly weak individual. However, a new type of Husk has emerged as the result of Koberic's unnatural experiments.

Kyrtvale – The Afterlife; the Underworld. The place where the soul goes after death. For some it is paradise, for others; a punishment. Often referred to as "The Vale" and used as substitution for the world "Hell" in several expressions. For example, "What the hell?" would be "What the Kyrtvale?" or simply "What the Vale?"

Lich – An undead mage.

Lizardfolk – Lizardfolk are sometimes described as "Human Sized Lizards that walk on their hind legs", and nothing is more accurate. Like Beastfolk, they often have abilities that differ, or are superior, to human abilities. However, also like Beastfolk, their mental facilities are indistinguishable from humans.

Lunar Wolf/Moon Wolf – The Lunar Wolf (or Moon Wolf as some refer to it) is one of the Vaettr, or Spirits, who protect the natural balance of nature. It has a coat that shines like moonlight and uses abilities that look like the power of the moon itself.

Mage – The ancient term meant "A person who uses magic". However, the modern meaning is "A person who uses spells".

Magic – The manipulation of Megin to create or modify natural and unnatural phenomena.

Megin – The lifeblood of the universe, a type of energy that flows through all living and non-living things.

The Midnight Massacre – A historical event that marked the end of the Hundred Year Wars, a long era where the Humans fought against the Elder Races. The Midnight Massacre refers to the time when the Humans broke through into the Elvish Kingdom of Faer'on, slaughtering and enslaving as they went. Despite the name, the Midnight Massacre took place over several years.

Ohrwurm – A disgusting creature the size of a large dog. Its body is covered in black, insectoid armor and sharp spines. It has a pair of long antennae atop its head, massive black eyes, and a set of horrific-looking mandibles. It has six legs, with the ability to run on all of them as well as the ability to stand some-what upright and use its front legs as sharp, sword-like weapons. It has a short but flexible tail mounted with two spines at the end akin to pincers. Nobody knows if they are Beast or Abnormals as nobody has been able to confirm, or disprove, their reproductive abilities.

Onager Strike – A great taboo within Aleurian Martial Arts for its recklessness, destructive power, disregard for the standards of magic, and the harm it does to the user. The Onager Strike forces your Megin into your fist and, at the moment of impact, forces it forward and into the target with the force of a siege engine.

Orc – A nomadic race of people. They have greenish-grey skin, tusks, and natural chitinous armor around their arms, legs, and vitals. Their intelligence is indistinguishable from a human.

The Ouroboros Initiative – A company that Elric founded with the sole purpose of helping Elvish refugees successfully integrate into human society.

Serpents Crest Mountains – A tall range of mountains that encircles a valley nearly five hundred miles in diameter.

Silverfang Timberlands – The forest that takes up most of the Eye of the Continent. Home to a vast variety of dangerous Beasts, the most abundant being wolves and dire-wolves. Named after a famous silver Direwolf, Silverfang, nearly 800 years prior to the story.

Spell – A magical equation used to create the exact same effect each time. Uses Megin gathered from the surroundings as its energy source.

Solar Wolf/ Sun Wolf – The Solar Wolf (or Sun Wolf as some refer to it) is one of the Vaettr, or Spirits, who protects the natural balance of nature. It has a coat that shines like the sun and uses abilities much like the fiery rays of the sun.

Sorcerer – A magic user who uses the Megin within their own body to cast magic. Very rare to see a human Sorcerer due to their low amount of internal Megin.

Solaire – The currency of the Aleurian Empire. Came in three types of coin; Gold, Silver, and Bronze.

Sovereign – The official currency of the western continent, it was introduced by the Dolar Imperium and eventually spread to all the other nations on Vestri, even those who dislike the Imperium. They come in three kinds of coin; Gold, Silver, and Copper.

Storm Wolf – The Storm Wolf is one of the Vaettr, or Spirits, who protects the natural balance of nature. It has a coat of deep blue with a white stripe down its back and uses abilities that make it seem like a living thunderstorm.

Talmara – The name of the World in which the story takes place.

Tomb of the Fallen – A tomb found in every Aleurian city used to house the bodies of fallen warriors.

Vaettr/Spirit – Vaettr (more commonly known as Spirits) are the protectors of the balance of nature in the world. They have been around longer than written history and are extremely rare. As such, it is difficult to pin down how many there are. There may be multiple of the same types of Vaettr, but also just as possible that there is only one per type. Vaettr are neither Beast nor Abnormal, but the very will of nature itself.

Valtion-Silma City State Alliance – An alliance of city-states that spans the Eye of the Continent. The members consist of Leindale, Roswin, Dancastle, Edren, Onforde, Torrel, and Mellgarde. The current chairman of the Alliance is Edren.

The Gods

The Elder Gods:

Aleura – Goddess of Creation and Order. She was heavily worshipped by the Aleurian people, whom they named themselves after. The Opposite of Njordurn; Order cannot exist without chaos.

Njordurn – God of Destruction and Chaos. The opposite of Aleura, but acknowledged as a required force. Chaos cannot exist without Order.

The Patron Gods; The Thirteen:

Murmanus – God of earth and stone and the patron of miners and Dwarves; all that happens within the dirt is his domain.

Oceanis – Goddess of the sea and patron of sailors. She is both kind and fair, yet her temper is the fear of all men.

Polimus – God of life, protector of the forests, and Patron of healers.

Ormr – God of Beasts, Patron of huntsmen and herders. He is seen as the progenitor of all beasts.

Duruna – God of Time, Keeper of the Sands, Lord of the Hourglass. The Unbiased God.

Tors – God of Craftsmen and Storms, Patron of all those who work with their hands.

Jurian – God of Wisdom and Knowledge, Patron to scholars.

Verona – Goddess of Hearth and Home, Patron God of families.

Famir – God of Agriculture, Patron of farmers.

Elena – Goddess of Love and Emotion, Patron of young men and women. She is known to toy with the emotions of the young. Married to the God of War.

Khrom – God of War. Armies pray to him before battle, and rulers consult with his priests before war.

Emmerich – God of Travelers and Tradesmen, Patron of Merchants, and those who travel along the roads.

Aegar – God of Megin and Magic, Patron of Magic-Users and worshipped by the Elves.

The Cardinal Gods:

Noth – God of the Northern Winds, a white bear in the deep north

Sao – God of the Southern Winds, a tri-tailed scorpion of the scorching deserts

Erst – God of the Eastern Winds, a majestic stag of the old forests.

Wern – God of the Western Winds, an eagle soaring in the far skies.

Association Ranks

Væng – The first and lowest rank. It's given to everyone who signs up with the association and is represented by the symbol of a single folded wing. Also called Rookies, these people make up around thirteen percent of members.

Fella Væng – The second rank. Represented by two folded wings, these Novices make up nearly twenty-four percent of members.

Svífa Væng – The third rank makes up close to thirty-nine percent of members and is represented by two open wings.

Örn – The fourth rank. If you manage to make it to this point, you are considered an expert by the Association. This is represented by a flying eagle and makes up about nineteen percent of members.

Stjarna Örn – The fifth rank. Most people cannot

achieve this rank because of their own physical limitations. Hiring someone of this rank costs an extraordinary amount of wealth and they are highly sought after by kingdoms wishing to keep them on retainer in case of invasion. They are represented by a soaring eagle with one star underneath and they make up about three percent of members.

Skínandi Örn – The sixth and final rank. These people are few and far between, with only three appearing in the last few centuries. These living legends are represented by a soaring eagle with two stars underneath. If you ever meet one, you would either be the luckiest or the unluckiest person in the world.

Drew R. Stowell was born and raised in southern California where he is the second of three children. He maintains a close relationship with his family and enjoys assisting his grandparents and spending quality time with them.

From a young age, Drew exhibited an imagination that surpassed that of his peers, which he channeled into his writing. *City of Merchants* follows his debut novel, *Necromancer's Folly*, and both showcase his creative prowess as an author.